PRAISE FOR

RED HOT FURY

"Urban fantasy readers looking for something new will thrill to this exhilarating debut, populated with creatures from Greek myth . . . Riss is the perfect urban fantasy heroine—fresh, sassy, smart, and determined—and a cavalcade of fully developed side characters keeps this twisty tale moving quickly." —*Publishers Weekly* (starred review)

"I loved it. Kasey Mackenzie is a brilliant new talent, and *Red Hot Fury* is fun, inventive, and has an awesome heroine. Easily the best book I've read this year."
—Karen Chance, *New York Times* bestselling author of the Cassie Palmer series

"A fantastic, wild ride of a debut. I couldn't put it down!"
—Nalini Singh, *New York Times* bestselling author of the Guild Hunter series

"Pulls you in from page one, and the action doesn't stop there. Marissa is a Fury with sass, skills, and leather . . . not to mention a sexy Irish Warhound by her side. If you're ready for a unique spin on all things paranormal—and you're ready to stay up a little too late reading—grab *Red Hot Fury* and prepare to dive in. Kasey Mackenzie's first Shades of Fury novel sets a new standard for urban fantasy."
—Chloe Neill, author of the Chicagoland Vampires series

"Warning to readers: You may become hooked and gain little sleep while reading *Red Hot Fury*. Debut author Kasey Mackenzie really knows how to weave an action scene to pull on readers' emotions. Fans of Laurell K. Hamilton, Charlaine Harris, and Karen Chance will keep on the lookout for Ms. Mackenzie and the Shades of Fury novels!"
—*Romance Reviews Today*

"The bright start to a new series, *Red Hot Fury* is a constant maze of excellently realized twists and turns combined with a sharp sense of humor." —*Fresh Fiction*

Ace Books by Kasey Mackenzie

RED HOT FURY
GREEN-EYED ENVY

GREEN-EYED ENVY

A SHADES OF FURY NOVEL

KASEY MACKENZIE

ACE BOOKS, NEW YORK

THE BERKLEY PUBLISHING GROUP
Published by the Penguin Group
Penguin Group (USA) Inc.
375 Hudson Street, New York, New York 10014, USA
Penguin Group (Canada), 90 Eglinton Avenue East, Suite 700, Toronto, Ontario M4P 2Y3, Canada
(a division of Pearson Penguin Canada Inc.)
Penguin Books Ltd., 80 Strand, London WC2R 0RL, England
Penguin Group Ireland, 25 St. Stephen's Green, Dublin 2, Ireland (a division of Penguin Books Ltd.)
Penguin Group (Australia), 250 Camberwell Road, Camberwell, Victoria 3124, Australia
(a division of Pearson Australia Group Pty. Ltd.)
Penguin Books India Pvt. Ltd., 11 Community Centre, Panchsheel Park, New Delhi—110 017, India
Penguin Group (NZ), 67 Apollo Drive, Rosedale, Auckland 0632, New Zealand
(a division of Pearson New Zealand Ltd.)
Penguin Books (South Africa) (Pty.) Ltd., 24 Sturdee Avenue, Rosebank, Johannesburg 2196,
South Africa

Penguin Books Ltd., Registered Offices: 80 Strand, London WC2R 0RL, England

This is a work of fiction. Names, characters, places, and incidents either are the product of the author's
imagination or are used fictitiously, and any resemblance to actual persons, living or dead, business
establishments, events, or locales is entirely coincidental. The publisher does not have any control
over and does not assume any responsibility for author or third-party websites or their content.

GREEN-EYED ENVY

An Ace Book / published by arrangement with the author

PRINTING HISTORY
Ace mass-market edition / July 2011

Copyright © 2011 by Heather Faucher.
Cover art by Judy York.
Cover design by Judith Lagerman.
Interior text design by Kristin del Rosario.

ISBN: 978-0-441-02049-2

ACE
Ace Books are published by The Berkley Publishing Group,
a division of Penguin Group (USA) Inc.,
375 Hudson Street, New York, New York 10014.
ACE and the "A" design are trademarks of Penguin Group (USA) Inc.

PRINTED IN THE UNITED STATES OF AMERICA

10 9 8 7 6 5 4 3 2 1

This one's for you, baby.
Thank you for being my best friend
and my soul mate;
not to mention putting up with me.
I love you, Shawn.

ACKNOWLEDGMENTS

I'm keeping it brief this time—promise!

I have to thank my fabulous husband, Shawn, and my beautiful baby boy, Zack, first and foremost once more. You both mean the world to me, and I am so blessed to have you in my life. I thank God every day that I get to be your wife and mother.

Thanks again to my family and friends, both real-life and online, for always being supportive and understanding when I'm going through a deadline crunch. Julie: I know I can call you up any time of day or night and you will be there for me, and that means so much to me!

Of course, I have to thank my agent, Ginger Clark; my editor, Jessica Wade; my publicist, Rosanne Romanello; my cover artist, Judy York; and the art department at Ace. You all truly rock!

To the readers, booksellers, and librarians: Without you, I wouldn't get to live out my dreams of writing for a living, and I owe you more than words can adequately express. So I'll just keep it simple: Thank you.

CHAPTER ONE

EVERYONE KNEW THAT CATS GOT *WAY* MORE
than their fair share of lives, but the poor guy spread-eagle
on the alley floor would have called BS on that. Well, if his
life hadn't been permanently snuffed out—not an easy thing
to do to one of the shape-shifting children of the Egyptian
goddess Bast. I had to give his killer an A for effort. He (or
she) had gone to extreme measures to put an early end to this
Cat's ninety-nine lives.

Yeah, ninety-nine. The Bastai, also known as Cats, weren't
confined to a measly nine lives like Garfield; unless, of course,
someone hastened them to an early grave—as with the
dark-haired man on the ground. Usually, the only way to
keep a Cat six feet under involved decapitation or incineration. But while the corpse sprawled on the ugly concrete
had taken a beating, his head and skin were still present
and accounted for. Mostly.

Which left little ole me, Fury and Chief Magical Investigator, puzzling over why tall, dark, and deceased wasn't pulling the usual feline resurrection routine.

The heavenly aroma of my personal nectar—Starbucks coffee—had me spinning from the corpse and catching sight of my mortal partner on the Boston Police Department. Trinity LaRue, five feet ten inches of Southern charm and grace packed into a gorgeous body that caused all too many men to underestimate her. Criminals who made that mistake only got to make it once. When Trinity got done disabusing them of their sexist notions, they wound up either incarcerated—or dead.

I accepted the jumbo green and white paper cup—just my size—she held out, and flashed a smile. "I *knew* there was a reason I let you be my new best friend."

She took a sip of her low-fat, no-sugar, caffeine-free cup of blandness (gods save me from mortal health kicks) and rolled her eyes. "You *let* me be your new best friend because nobody else wants to put up with your moody ass."

I smirked. "Yeah, there's that. Plus, you drive a bitchin' car."

Her eyes lit up her dark-skinned complexion at the mention of the electric-blue classic sports car her big brothers had rebuilt for her recent birthday. (Turning the big 3-0 *definitely* does a number on mortals, as Trin's new obsession with blah food and copious amounts of exercise showed.) The *bitchin' car* made the hot pink fuzzy dice I'd gotten her as a gag gift look much snazzier than expected. Then again, just about *anything* looked good in a Porsche Spyder.

Trinity nodded toward the vic. "So?"

My breath huffed out as I finally admitted what I'd been trying to deny. "Same MO."

This time, she drew the same word out in her signature Southern drawl. "Soooo?"

"Soooo, same killer as the other two."

Proving that she was indeed my new best friend, she took the opportunity for a little gloating. "And?"

I shot her an annoyed look but gave her what she was digging for. "You were right and I was wrong. Boston has its first arcane serial killer."

SHE DID HER BEST TO LOOK SOLEMN, BUT THE lips-twitching-upward thing was a dead giveaway to how she *really* felt. Not that she took pleasure in the Cat's death—Trinity was, quite simply, *very* good people—but at the challenge we faced. I could count on one hand the number of arcane serial killers to hit the headlines over the past couple of decades. Nationwide. It wasn't that we supernatural types were less violent than mortalkind—*far* to the contrary—we just tended to be much more in-your-face when it came to killing. We were also less prone to going batshit insane, not counting the magic-fueled Rage that gave Furies our super strength and speed and, all too often, drove the weaker-willed of us quite literally crazy.

Add that to the fact most arcanes did everything they could to avoid drawing the attention of Furies, who embodied the magical equivalent of mortal law enforcement, and it explained Trinity's current excitement.

In the months since we'd taken out the traitorous Fury who tried to break the Peace Accord between mortals and arcanes, our caseload had been relatively mundane. Several tragic but easily solved murder cases. A few incidents of domestic violence in Boston's magical Underbelly. A straightforward robbery of the Belly's biggest—okay only—arcane bank. Not surprisingly, a goblin-on-goblin affair. They put the *greed* in *greedy*. All open-and-shut cases for the most part. Things had finally heated up again a couple weeks ago, when the first of two—make that three—male Cats had been discovered tortured and disemboweled in downtown alleyways.

Trinity tilted her head and looked down at the corpse. "What's that smell?"

I raised my paper cup toward her in a mocking gesture. "*Real* coffee, not that no-taste soy crap. You probably forgot what it smells like."

"No, seriously." She knelt next to the corpse, slapped a latex glove on her left hand, and started prodding the odds and ends littering the patch of concrete around the Cat.

I got down to business myself and handed my coffee cup to a hovering newbie before opening myself to the stores of magical energy beneath the ground. I shifted to Fury form, blond-haired and blue-eyed mortal body morphing into charcoal-haired, emerald-eyed badass, complete with the red leather uniform that served as the immortal world's equivalent to a police badge. My eyes were drawn to the brilliant red serpents tattooed on each arm as magic changed them from ink-on-skin portraits to living, breathing Amphisbaena: the pair of magical creatures bonded to a Fury. Part companions and part magic-boosting familiars, Nemesis and Nike were the two accessories I *never* left home without.

They hissed at me in greeting, twining themselves around my arms much as they did in tattoo form. I gave each one a caress before kneeling next to Trinity. My nostrils flared as I took in a breath. This time, armed with the enhanced senses that came with the whole Fury schtick, I smelled what she had right away: a heavy, pungent odor that reminded me of a cross between freshly mown grass and skunk. Yum.

Then again, with the scents of refuse and rot around us, no big surprise I hadn't smelled it in mortal form. Autumn in New England meant that allergies could be hell. Yeah, even immortal badasses have to deal with high mold and pollen counts.

I took another, larger sniff and made a face. "What *is* that?"

"Copycat," Trin said. "I already asked that question."

"Funny you mention felines." The detective who held my empty coffee cup sidled closer, pitching the cardboard container in a Dumpster as he passed. Since he didn't seem petrified of my serpentine ladies—and they weren't spitting venom his way—I let him.

Suddenly, he said, "Catnip."

Trinity snapped her fingers and nodded, while I just blinked. "Huh?"

"You know, kitty crack? *Some*body has a really warped sense of humor." The newly promoted detective—the badge hanging from his leather belt identified him as Cass—squatted beside me and nodded toward the corpse. "May I?"

I arched a brow at Trinity, who just shrugged. Oh, what could it hurt? Maybe he'd pick up on something we hadn't. "Go ahead." He slipped on a latex glove, then leaned forward and took in a deep breath. His eyes seemed to flash with some inner light as he sniffed the air. My nostrils flared in sympathy. Better him than me, seeing as how my sense of smell was now enhanced.

Cass's gloved hand whipped toward the Cat's mouth and pried it open before I could stop him. The mown-grass-and-skunk smell tripled in intensity. The rookie grimaced but didn't back down from the grisly sight revealed: The Cat's tongue had been ripped out and replaced with a thick wad of jagged-edged triangular leaves. Catnip.

I stared down at the Cat with morbid fascination. "Warped sense of humor, my ass. This killer gives a whole new meaning to the phrase *Cat got your tongue.*"

Trinity made a disgusted noise, then frowned at the

catnip. "Wait, the other two vics didn't have that shoved in their mouths. Did they?"

Good point. "Nope. No way Sahana would have missed that. Neither had his tongue cut out, either."

"Okay. So . . . Killer decides to start taking the tongues as a souvenir. But why the catnip?"

Cass looked up at her. "Calling card."

"Huh?"

"Killer doesn't think the police connected the first two murders together, so he decides to leave a calling card. Ripping the tongue out could show personal rage at this vic. The catnip . . ." His voice trailed off, and he shot me a distinctly uneasy look.

Aw, c'mon, Cass. Don't go chickenshit on me when I was just starting to warm up to you. "Go ahead, you're doing okay so far. What about the catnip?"

He cleared his throat as if needing the time to choose his words. "I studied arcanes a lot before I managed to land the assignment to this unit, Chief." Chief? Oh hell, I might actually have to make this guy a full-fledged member of our newly formed Magical Crimes Unit. "Especially on the interracial relations of the arcanes with the largest populations in the Boston area. I know I don't need to tell you about the race known as Cat Public Enemy Number One."

Now *I* was starting to feel distinctly uneasy. Not hard to figure out why, since I was sleeping with Scott Murphy, a member of the race known as Cat Public Enemy Number One. "Let me get this straight. You're hypothesizing that our perp is a Hound based on, what, the fact that Cats and Hounds are archenemies? Cass, have you ever heard of a little thing called a racial-profiling lawsuit?"

Trinity let out a snicker at that.

Cass tightened his lips at the derision in my voice, but again, he didn't back down. "No, Chief. I may be new to

detective work, but I served as a patrolman for five years.
I'm not a *complete* schmuck, you know."

Damn, either I was getting bad at guessing mortal ages,
or he had a real baby face. I wouldn't have put him much past
twenty-two or so—the same age as Scott's baby brother.
And *there* was someone I didn't want to think about at that
particular moment.

He pointed to the Cat's partially open mouth. "In ancient
times, Cats used to rip the tongues out of their enemies.
Sorta like certain Native Americans collecting enemy
scalps." Trin and I both winced in sympathy. "The practice
is called *counting coup* in honor of another Native American practice that allowed warriors to gain honor for striking
enemies without getting injured. Since the race Cats warred
with the most, especially in ancient Egypt, were the Hounds,
they started reciprocating in kind except, of course, they
took it one better."

I screwed up my nose. "Let me guess. They shoved catnip in their mouths to replace the tongues."

"Exactly. And historically, that was the gravest insult
you could give a Cat. It was like saying they were lower
than domesticated animals. And Cats who survived having
that done to them in ancient days were killed by their own
people. They were viewed as mercy killings."

Nemesis and Nike slipped to my upper arms, radiating
soothing emotions my way. I shifted uncomfortably, having
no trouble picturing the upcoming battle with Scott. For
Warhounds, family meant just about everything. Even if
that family *had* disowned his mother and her half-mortal
mutts. "Wait, that doesn't mean the killer *has* to be a Hound.
Anybody who knows their arcane history could have done
this. I mean, if you read that in some mortal book, it *has* to
be fairly common knowledge."

Cass stared down at his suddenly clenched fists. A muscle

worked in his jaw, and Trinity and I shared a questioning glance. Had our baby-faced detective left some crucial detail off of his résumé?

"Okay, so I stretched the truth a little. I didn't read the stuff about Cats and Hounds in any book." He inhaled and exhaled deeply. "And I didn't get lucky guessing that the catnip was in the vic's mouth—I smelled it."

Wait. Pretty much the only beings who could outsmell Furies magically speaking were . . . Nah. Couldn't be.

"I'm not exactly a hundred percent mortal." He lowered his voice, no doubt to make sure only Trinity and I could hear. "My great-grandfather was a Hound. Full-blooded." Oh, that only made me like him more. Mr. Innocent *had* lied on his résumé. I couldn't blame him one little bit, with all the anti-arcane sentiment I'd come across during my years on the force.

Still, Cass could get in *big* trouble if anyone besides Trinity or me found out. Ever since the Peace Accord that ended the Great War between mortals and arcanes—which mortals referred to as the "Time of Troubles"—all those who had more than one-sixteenth arcane blood running through their veins were subject to disclosure laws that were supposedly meant to benefit us—just like the so-called "one-drop" rule was supposed to benefit Native and African Americans way back when.

And that *totally* explained the flash of amber light I had seen in his eyes when he sniffed out the catnip. While half-blooded arcanes took after their arcane parents, if their descendents married individuals with primarily mortal blood, those arcane abilities became more diluted with each generation. I was willing to bet that the enhanced sense of smell was the only thing Cass had inherited from his Warhound ancestor. That and his oh-so-youthful glow. No wonder he'd been able to pass for so long.

"Ooookay, don't take this the wrong way, but Trin and I

didn't just hear that." His white pallor warmed up several notches, and he released his clenched fists. "But hypothetically speaking, explain how what you didn't just say relates to our case."

"The counting coup habits of both Cats and Hounds have been pretty much edited out of history, as far as outsiders are concerned. Especially for those who intermingle with mortal society. They have to act civilized, at least on the face of it, though there are still bloodthirsty members of both races who engage in the old ways from time to time." His expression grew inscrutable as he glanced down at the Cat's corpse again. "Great-Grandfather made sure that all of us with any drop of his abilities were raised knowing everything about Hound history, just in case we'd ever need it."

I met his gaze unflinchingly. "So what you're trying to say is you don't think any other arcane races besides Cats or Hounds would have known about the tongue and catnip thing."

He shook his head. "And I highly doubt that a Cat would have done this to another of his kind."

Trinity arched a brow. "Are you so sure about that?"

"I have to agree with him, Trin." Much as I didn't want to. "Based on what I know about Cats, and what Cass just told us about the whole counting coup and catnip thing . . . Odds are we're looking for a Hound as the perp."

And with my luck, tracking him down was going to lead to a second *off-again* phase with my own not-so-cuddly Warhound. Oh well, there was always my backup lover, Jack Daniels.

CHAPTER TWO

I WAS SNUGGLED UP WITH JACK D THAT EVEning watching my favorite sitcom when a key turned in the front door. My pulse picked up speed because only one person had the key to my Cambridge townhouse. Scott. My currently on-again lover. The empty snifter clinked when I set it down on the mahogany coffee table and smoothed my hair. Honey blond, since I was in mortal form, the perfect contrast to the hot pink nightie I hoped would get Scott in an insanely good mood *before* I broached the topic of serial-killing Hounds.

My assumption was confirmed when the masculine scent of Scott's cologne wafted into the living room seconds after the front door slammed shut. I closed my eyes to enjoy the fragrance he knew drove me crazy, and he struck, crossing the room in record time and straddling my legs on the leather sofa. My eyes snapped open and caught sight of a mind-blowing hunk with burnished bronze skin, chiseled muscles, shoulder-length auburn hair, and glowing yellow eyes. Those unearthly eyes burned with inner fire as he leaned forward and nuzzled my neck.

"Well, good evening, sugar," I purred in an imitation of a smooth-as-molasses Southern drawl. "Wasn't sure you'd make it by tonight."

He gave me a knowing smirk and nipped my lips with his own. "After that picture you texted of you on your couch? Fat chance of that."

Which I'd very well known—and he very well knew I had.

Instead of 'fessing up, I wrapped my arms around his body and nudged him next to me on the couch. His amber eyes darkened when I drew him in for a long kiss. Which led to a make-out session I would have given an 8.0 on the Richter scale. Scott had magic hands, hands that raised white-hot lines of heat wherever they touched bare skin. When his fingers snaked down to tug on my satin panties, however, I forced myself to scoot back a few inches. I was not above smooching him into a better mood; but I needed to get business out of the way before we moved on to pleasure. More's the pity, as my screaming hormones raged at me.

Scott's nostrils flared, no doubt scenting the change in my pheromones, or however that Hound crap worked. "Something wrong, baby?"

"No, no. Not between us. But you remember those two Cat vics I was telling you about the other day?"

He nodded. "Yeah. Bizarre as hell, with how damned hard they are to kill. Well, permanently kill."

My turn to nod. "Exactly. We found victim *numero tres* earlier today."

His eyes widened. "No shit?"

"No shit. And there's no doubt that all three are related."

"Meaning . . ."

"Meaning that Boston has its first arcane serial killer prowling the streets. Or alleys, I should say, since that's where we keep finding the bodies."

He frowned. "Harp's gonna have a fit when she hears this."

A few months ago, hearing him mention his former lover (okay, so a one-night stand didn't really warrant the term *lover*) would have had me spitting with jealousy, but he'd spent the past weeks illustrating just how platonic their relationship had turned out to be—while ours was anything but. Even weirder, though, I'd actually started to *like* the hot-blooded Latina shape-shifting Cat. And before anyone can accuse me of stereotyping Latin Americans, the hot-blooded part comes mostly from the whole Cat thing. That gutsy, take-no-prisoners personality along with her sharp instincts, wicked intelligence, and drive to succeed had recently propelled her to join me in the record books: I was the first official arcane member of the Boston PD (of *any* PD), she the first arcane Special Agent in the FBI. Her part in bringing down my bitch-of-a-mentor's plot to re-fan the flames of war between arcanes and mortals had not gone unrewarded. Although, if you asked me, losing the higher pay rate and lower stress level of an hourly consultant wasn't *really* a reward.

Okay, so maybe I *hadn't* shaken off every ounce of feminine jealousy. Sue me.

I cleared my throat before launching into the segue I'd rehearsed while nursing the whiskey. "You know that mortal saying *Cat got your tongue*?"

His eyes narrowed slightly, just enough that I could tell he suspected where this might be going. "Yeah. One of my da's favorites." His mortal father, Morgan—100 percent Irish born and bred—had immigrated to Boston with his older brothers after their parents left their nest egg as an untimely inheritance. He'd served on the mortal side during the start of the Great War decades earlier—ironic, since Scott's mother, Liana, had fought on the arcane side.

"Seems the killer flipped that saying around on the vic. Had his tongue ripped out and replaced with . . ." I let my voice trail off and watched for Scott's reaction.

He didn't disappoint me, either; he clenched his fist, gritted his teeth, and ground out, "Catnip." No question mark at the end of that most-distinctly-*not*-a-guess.

Even though I'd expected it, hearing him so easily fill in the blank on that sentence made my heart sink. Before today, I wouldn't have had the first clue what word would have best completed it. And not to brag, but that meant that the vast majority of other arcanes wouldn't have, either. As a Fury, it was my job to know juicy little tidbits about all magical races to help protect them or—like now—use against them to wreak justice and, if need be, vengeance on those who commit murders as heinous as the three now being investigated. *Hell, Cass is right. Only another Cat or Hound would have known about the catnip . . .*

Scott, no slouch in the brains department, made the obvious connection. "You think a Hound's behind this."

I winced at his flat tone of voice. "Not necessarily." The wishy-washy tone of *my* voice made me wince again.

He snorted. "You already know as well as I do—or you wouldn't have enticed me here under false pretenses—that the two races most likely to boast a killer with *that* particular MO are Cats and Hounds. And as Da would say, not bloody likely a Cat would count coup against another Cat. 'Bout as likely as a Hound collaring another."

Now *that* had been a rough period in Warhound history. Anubis, their patron god—as Celtic goddess Epona was their patron goddess—had become enraged when a faction of his followers in ancient Egypt sided with enemy priests attempting to overthrow the Pharaoh that Anubis favored. He not only allowed the faction to be enslaved by a third group of priests vying to get *their* favored candidate on the throne, he actually forged the magical collars used to subdue his own people. Yeah, there was a *reason* I had no desire to run into that particular deity again anytime soon. He made *me* look like a forgiving pussy cat.

"Hey, no false pretenses. I really *was* lonely." He arched a brow. "Okay, so I had ulterior motives besides seeing you in mind, but that doesn't make me any less lonely." I shifted just so, causing one of my negligee straps to cascade from my shoulder to midway down my bare arm. Scott's eyes followed along for the ride. I smirked. "And let he who is without ulterior motives of his own cast the first stone."

"Touché." His hand skimmed to my arm, slid the strap back in place one slow inch at a time, and then settled on my shoulder, caressing one of my most erogenous zones.

My eyes fluttered open, closed, and open again. "Mmmm. What?"

He laughed softly. "Problems, baby? I'm not distracting you from your case, am I?"

"Case?" I shook my head to clear it and slid back on the couch until there was a good foot of space between us. "Hey, you did that on purpose!"

"Yeah? So did you."

He had me there. I ignored his valid point and cleared my throat. "You're right that the two most likely pools of suspects are Cats and, yes, Hounds. But you also know good and well that I can't afford to entirely rule out either group until I get some hard evidence. So, would you mind looking at the crime scene photos and giving me your opinion as a Warhound?"

"Sure." Those amber eyes of his grew even brighter—not a good sign for my departmental budget. Damn mercs. "Just as soon as you hire me on as a consultant."

Double-damn mercs. "Fine. But just you, Scott—not the Shadowhounds as a whole."

He shrugged. "Okay by me. Most of them are on other assignments at the moment anyway."

My face softened as I thought about one other Shadow-hound in particular. Patrick "Mac" MacAllister. Husband to Elliana Banoub, Scott's second-in-command in his family-run mercenary enterprise. Mac was also half-Sidhe, half-Fury (yes, the first *male* Fury), son of Allegra, my mother. Which, of course, made Mac my youngest brother: my eighteen-year-old chronologically but thirty-year-old genetically youngest brother. Yeah, made my head spin just thinking about it.

"Ellie and Mac?"

He let out a frustrated sigh. "We got another lead on Sean's whereabouts that didn't pan out." Sean Murphy, Scott's baby brother, had vanished under mysterious circumstances just after we laid down the smack on the mad scientists responsible for both my mother's and best friend's abductions.

"So now they're just holding down the fort at HQ," Scott continued. HQ referred to the smoke-infested, pub-like room plus windowless office nestled at the back of Liana Murphy's arcane antique store that Scott's mercenary group used as its base of operations. Scott's father, Morgan, had founded the Shadowhounds from that room several decades earlier—the same year Liana cut ties with her family, the high-and-mighty Banoub clan, and used the trust fund money she'd squirreled away to open Hounds of Anubis. She may have given up her inheritance and social standing for love, but she sure hadn't given up her wits. She and Morgan had done just fine without the support of her family's billions, *thankyouverymuch*.

I *still* found it amusing that her favorite niece, Elliana, had followed in her footsteps a year ago, throwing over *her* social standing in the Banoub dynasty to marry my brother after jilting her intended husband—who turned out to be a cheating dog in all ways figurative *and* literal. Ellie was another person who was slowly but surely growing on me. Like old, stinky cheese.

"So," I pulled a sour face. "How much is this going to cost me?"

"You mean *besides* the hot sex?" He wiggled his eyebrows in that appealing way of his.

"Whether you get the hot sex depends on how much you try and gouge me for. Remember: The PD is footing the bill for this one, *not* the Sisterhood." And the PD's pockets were nowhere *near* as deep as the Sisterhood of Furies, my immortal superiors.

Fortunately for *both* our raging hormones, Scott knew that and was too honest to price gouge me. Or too smart— he *did* want to take advantage of my ulterior motives to satisfy his own, after all. He named a reasonable consultant fee, and we shook on it. I'd take care of filling out the official paperwork the next day. Really just a formality, since I was the city's Chief Magical Investigator.

I slid the coffee table closer to the sofa, booted up my sleek new laptop (courtesy of my baby brother, the techno-guru, who'd taken one look at my last POS and sneered), and logged on to the magical-case-management software that my big brother, David, had designed for me with help from Mac. David and his wife, Jessica, ran a software empire and had pulled some strings for me to get the database up and running so quickly. They'd also taken a huge loss on the project in order to make it fit into the start-up budget the PD had given me to get its first official Magical Crimes Unit off the ground. Nepotism was most certainly alive and well in the MCU.

Hey, whatever gets the job done. 'Bout time we got the PD's magical investigations out of the Dark Ages. Even if both brothers dragged me into the whole process kicking and screaming. Amazing how much less I hated computers now that I had a top-of-the-line model rather than a bargain store reject.

I called up the crime scene photos Trinity had scanned in just hours ago. Scott remained silent while I scrolled through the pictures, until I got to a close-up shot of the victim's wide-open mouth—and sightless Cat-slit eyes. He let his breath out in a very feline-like hiss and stayed my hand on the wireless mouse. My gaze locked on his and saw the recognition in his eyes. *Oh shit, he knows this guy.*

"Harp's gonna have more than a fit when she hears this, Riss." My pulse skittered, since that could only mean *she* knew this guy, too. "His name's Bryant Wilkins, and he was Harper's fiancé in college."

CHAPTER THREE

BARELY AN HOUR LATER I HAD DITCHED THE hot pink negligee for my red leather uniform. Scott and I waited for Harper outside the branch of the city morgue that housed arcane corpses. Her job for the FBI made her no stranger to after-hour telephone calls summoning her to check out a body, but this was the first time her duty was to ID the corpse rather than investigate its murder. Of course, she didn't know that yet. Neither Scott nor I had the heart to break the news over the phone, especially since she lived by herself. Way more tactful to just tell her I needed an assist on a case and give her the morbid news in person. On the selfish side, I was glad that she was the one who would ID the victim, rather than his immediate family members. At least we could spare them *that*.

I don't know who was more surprised—Scott or me—when Harper showed up so very *not* by herself. And judging from the possessive way the golden-eyed, dark-skinned Adonis held her hand, we could have broken the news to her over the phone. No way she'd been alone at her place when she got my call. *Wait . . . dark skin and yellow eyes. Holy shit. Harp's bagged herself another Hound!*

This time, Scott won the *Who's more surprised?* contest hands down. He did a double take when he caught a good look at Adonis's face. His mouth and eyes widened comically before he managed to choke out, "Penn?"

Harper had her own moment of shock when Scott stepped forward from the shadows next to me. "Mutt?" She flushed and shot me an accusing look. "You didn't tell me *he'd* be here."

I motioned to Adonis "Pot? Kettle? Hel*lo*!"

Her normally tan skin grew even more flushed. "Yeah, well—"

The mysterious Penn seized the opportunity to get a word in edgewise. "You do not seriously believe I would allow Christabel to leave my condo in the middle of the night to come to the gods-forsaken *morgue* alone?"

My lips trembled from the effort to hold back laughter as I switched my attention to Harper. "*Chris*tabel?" Scott had let it slip that Harper was actually her middle name, in honor of her mother's maiden name, but he'd always refused to reveal the Cat's true first name. Now I could see why.

She shot me a *drop dead* look while patting Penn on the arm. *Down, boy,* I thought with an inner sneer, but managed not to roll my eyes. Barely.

Scott spoke up again before Harper—oh, calling her *Christabel* was going to be *way* more fun than calling Elliana *Ellie*—could. "Do I even *want* to know why the hell you're holding hands with my pompous asshole of a cousin?"

I could really *go for a tub of popcorn right now . . .*

Penn's gaze zeroed in on Scott, and he frowned, narrowing

his eyes as he sized up the other Hound. Recognition suddenly hit. *"Murphy?"*

I couldn't resist a sardonic, "And here I thought that was my special nickname for Scott when he's being an ass."

Adonis nodded as if I'd confirmed something for him. "So. The half-breed in charge of the Shadowmutts."

Oh no, he didn't!

I flashbacked to a few months previous when Scott had to restrain me from kicking the shit out of Ellie for a similar snarky comment about my missing best friend (and sister Fury), Vanessa. This time *I* was the one throwing myself between Scott and one of his smart-ass cousins. I shifted Nemesis and Nike into physical form, drawing magic through them to amp up my Fury strength to keep Scott from tearing into Adonis. Though with the other Hound's decided lack of charm, tact, and self-preservation, I wasn't 100 percent convinced he was worth the effort. Still, letting Scott rip him apart would mean a whole lot of paperwork that I didn't want to deal with in the middle of a murder investigation.

Harper had her hands equally full holding Penn back from Scott. She whispered to him fiercely, showing that she hadn't completely lost her backbone as I'd suspected when she'd let Penn—who could be none other than *the* Pennington Banoub, Elliana's eldest brother and the financial genius currently heading up the Banoub family dynasty—pull his macho man routine and call her Christabel.

Once certain that Scott wasn't going to break my hold, I drawled, "Now, now, boys, don't make me get out the water hose."

My words had a similar effect to the threatened hosing. They stopped struggling and settled for scowling at each other in that testosterone-laced way men have. Would have been sexy if I didn't have other things going on. Like, you know, stopping a serial killer.

"Can we count on you two to behave, or do I need to break out the cuffs?"

They threw even deeper scowls my way but remained tight-lipped. I nodded at Harper, and we stepped back from our menfolk. She focused on me. "Not that I wouldn't just *love* to catch up on old times standing on the street outside the city morgue in the middle of the freaking night, but would you mind telling me what kind of FBI help you need so desperately that I just *had* to come down here now?"

The part I'd been dreading. The hesitation in my stance must have clued Penn in that I was about to give *Christabel* bad news, because he settled his arm around her shoulders. She just arched a brow. "Harp, I'm sorry to be the one to tell you this, but I asked you down here to ID a murder victim."

She had trouble processing that for a second. Then her mouth drew open slightly, and she let out a choked "Ohhh."

I rushed to reassure her. "He's not a family member. But Scott thinks it's a past"—feeling the heat of Adonis's gaze on me had me amend my original phrasing to—"acquaintance of yours. From college."

Harper steeled her expression and her spine, then nodded. "I see. Cat, then?"

"Yeah. The third victim of three, discovered just today."

Her mouth widened again. "Wait. The third of three. You mean those other two Cats we heard about—"

I nodded grimly. "Are definitely related to Vic Number Three."

"And I know—knew—the latest vic." Not a question, so I didn't give an answer. Adonis pulled Harper closer and leaned down to brush his lips against her head. The tenderness of the gesture had me revising my opinion of him ever-so-slightly upward. "Well then, let's get this over with. At least I can spare his family having to see him before they can clean him up."

Gods, was I ever glad of *that*. And if we had any chance in hell of sparing them the knowledge that his tongue had been ripped out, I would move mountains to make that happen.

"Come on. Sahana's waiting for us."

ARCANE MEDICAL EXAMINER SAHANA PATEL hummed a subvocal tune that only other arcanes—or spooks—could hear. The corpse on the examining table vibrated in time to her seven-note melody, which rose and fell and rose again. Intermittent flashes of black energy danced in the air around her, looking like visible bursts of static electricity. Her song reached a discordant crescendo and the dark energy exploded, raining down in crackling sparks, each spark echoing one of the seven notes in concert. The sound should have been ugly and harsh, but in reality, it took my breath away.

Sahana sagged as the answer she so painstakingly coaxed from the corpse via arts both magical and mundane came to her. I stepped forward quickly, dragging my eyes away from the fading Raga-song and catching Sahana before she could fall. She didn't register surprise, although I knew she'd been too caught up in her work to notice me enter the autopsy room. The high from working her unique form of magic still held her in its grip.

I broke the silence between us, knowing from personal experience it would help ground her in the here and now. "COD?"

She let out a soft sigh. "Magical poisoning. His blood is tainted with it. The toxicology reports showed that clearly, but not what kind. Too rare."

"But your song?"

Her dark red lips curved and wide-set onyx eyes glittered. "Coaxed the poison's magical makeup from the blood. Now, comparing it against our databases to match the signatures will be child's play."

I shook my head with a bemused expression. "Magical autopsies and rare arcane poisons. Just what every parent wants their child to play with."

She let out a bark of laughter, the harsh sound at odds with the typical melody of her voice. "And the very sort of toys that a Bhairavi Raga cuts her teeth on from the cradle."

Poor Sahana. She possessed the rarest—and deadliest—form of Raga magic. The power to harness musical notes to read the signs of death left behind when otherwise immortal arcanes died. While most of us lived to a very ripe old age in the centuries, if not millennia, some of us met untimely ends at the hands of others. Murder most foul. The flip side to the more benign abilities that had made her New York's most valuable arcane medical examiner before she transferred here was that she could, if she so chose, coax a healthy body into hastening itself to an early grave.

Which was the reason that Bhairavi Ragas were relentlessly drilled in the mechanics behind and ethics of their gifts from an exceedingly young age. Most of them tended to become introverted, distancing themselves from just about all others and becoming virtual hermits. Others, like Sahana, honed their inner strengths and macabre senses of humor to harness their gifts to the benefit of arcanekind. She wasn't the first of her kind to serve as an arcane medical examiner for a mortal municipality, but in my opinion she was hands down the best.

"So, not to rush you along or anything, but we're ready in the waiting room to ID Jove Doc 21-5."

She nodded and re-covered the corpse marked *Jove Doe No. 21-3, Aegir.* The designation meant the poor sap who'd been poisoned to death was the third unidentified arcane male corpse of the twenty-first week of the year.

I rejoined Harper and the boys in the waiting room. The Cat stood in front of the window that separated the waiting room from the viewing room, fingers clenched and breathing more ragged than usual. Penn hovered a few feet away. He looked like he wanted to get closer but had been rebuffed. I wouldn't be feeling all that lovey-dovey if I were in her shoes, either.

Scott nodded as I crossed the room to stand next to Harper. She didn't say anything, just let out a sigh, eyes glued dead ahead.

Unfortunately, pun intended.

The door to the viewing room opened, and Sahana wheeled in a gurney covered with the customary white sheet. Footsteps heralded Penn drawing closer to Harper and Scott stepping up behind us while the gurney rolled across the other room. Sahana stopped just shy of the two-way window, expression suitably solemn, and folded the sheet back to reveal Jove Doe's head. I gave her an approving nod. Harper definitely didn't need to see the mess the corpse's abdomen had become. Fortunately, we couldn't see into his mouth, either. Sahana had managed to work it closed once more.

Recognition hit Harper like a punch to the stomach. She staggered a crooked step back, brushing up against Scott behind her and Penn to her right. Her lips trembled and tears welled in her eyes, though she brushed them away seconds later with an expression gone fierce.

"Oh, Bryant, I *will* find who did this to you and make him pay."

Investigative instinct made me ask, "What makes you so sure it's a *him* who did this?"

Her eyes glinted jade green under the room's dim lighting, signaling she danced on the cusp between mortal form and Cat. "Trust me. Only a very strong male arcane would be able to take out three other Cats so easily and in such quick succession. And you know damned well statistics show that serial killers are nine times out of ten male. Even among arcanes."

I nodded thoughtfully, then motioned for Sahana to

re-cover Jove Doe—make that Bryant Wilkins—once more. Harper turned on me sharply. "I want in, Riss."

My breath rushed out. "Ah, Harp, that's probably not a very good idea, considering your relationship with the vic."

Penn's nose flared at that statement. His head whipped toward the sheet-covered corpse, and jealousy swept across his face.

Harper narrowed her eyes. "That didn't stop Scott with Sean, or you with Vanessa, now did it?"

I winced because I didn't really have a comeback for that one. Even knowing I had been the only Fury available to investigate my best friend's disappearance—and the corpse magically disguised as hers that had washed up in Boston Harbor three years later—didn't make me feel like I had a leg to stand on. Besides, Harper and I were more alike than either of us cared to admit. If I didn't involve her in this investigation in some sort of official capacity, she'd just go behind my back and conduct her own. *Been there, done that, got the T-shirt.*

"Okay, you're in. But only as far as *I* say, and only if you follow my orders explicitly. I won't have you compromising my investigation because of your feelings for one of the victims."

Penn gritted his teeth. "Christabel, I don't like this, not one whit. And who was this—this *Cat* to you that you feel so honor-bound to involve yourself in something that's not your affair?"

Harper whirled on Penn, looking angry with him for the first time, despite all the asinine comments he'd made since I'd met him. Admittedly not that long ago, but he'd gotten quite a few zingers off in a short time.

"Just what do you mean by *this Cat*, hmm? That Cats don't deserve avenging or protecting? That I'm the only Cat worth your time? Or are you just playing with me, is that it? Everything you said about the feuding between our

species being outdated was just smooth-talking your way
into my bed?"

Penn's mouth dropped open. He looked like nobody had
ever talked to him like that before. I was willing to bet that
wasn't too far from the truth. "Christabel, no, you know
that's not what I . . ." Passion colored his cheeks red and
his eyes a dark shade of yellow that bordered on orange. He
reached out and grasped Harper's arms with both hands. "I
love you, Bel. I asked you to marry me last night, and I
meant it. You're the first woman—of *any* species—I've
proposed to. And the last, no matter what answer you give."

Oooh, I was really jonesing for popcorn again . . .

Scott, on the other hand, didn't appear nearly as enter-
tained. His fingers dug into his palms so tightly that his
normally dark skin went two shades paler. For an instant,
jealousy writ itself large on my *own* face, but I shoved the
green-eyed monster mercilessly away. Scott wasn't pissed
off at Harper because he was jealous. He was pissed off
she'd fallen into bed with one of his hated Banoub cousins.
The very clan that had disowned his mother because she'd
married—in their opinions—beneath her station.

Sure, I might have to remind myself of that a few more
times to actually believe it, but hey—baby steps.

Tears shone in Harper's eyes again, and for a moment I
wasn't sure if she was going to punch her lover for admitting something so personal in front of others or go all
mushy-gooey on us. Thankfully, she did neither.

"The answer, you insanely jealous and infuriating man,
is yes! Gods, yes. This proves just how short life can be—
even for *us*—and I won't waste another single second. I
don't care *what* our families say."

Harper threw herself into Penn's arms and proceeded to
go hot and heavy. And by the looks of it, humid. Scott's scowl
reappeared. Uh-oh. Someone was about to blow a gasket.

I grabbed his arm and dragged him out of the room,

giving the other two a chance to get the raging hormones out of their systems. He muttered under his breath with each step; his voice rose several decibels once the waiting room door shut behind us. Something about "stupid, gullible kittens getting in over their heads with lying, cheating, backstabbing pure-bred shitheads who wouldn't know the meaning of love if it bit them in their miserable, snotty asses."

On the plus side, at least he was stark, raving mad at someone else for a change.

"Why don't you tell me how you *really* feel, Murphy?"

He did a double take when I used his surname, something I usually reserved for moments when he pissed me off. "I—she—can you believe what just happened?"

I couldn't resist a moment of perversity. "The irony of Harper accepting a second marriage proposal right in front of her first fiancé's still-fresh corpse?"

"What? No, the fact she's betraying me with one of *them*."

My brow arched in a fairly good imitation of his freakish eyebrow raises. "*Betraying* you? Isn't that just a little overdramatic? Considering it was *just* a one-night stand and all." Okay, so I couldn't resist throwing his own words back in his face. I'm a Fury, not a saint.

Thank *all* the gods and goddesses. Talk about nonexistent sex lives.

"She's my *friend*, Riss, and friends just don't—"

"Let other friends find love in unexpected places? Like, say, between a Warhound heiress and a mortal mercenary?" Boy, had the world turned completely upside down? Here *I* was reading the riot act to *him* for letting anger get the best of him. His lips tightened mutinously, and I could tell that he was too pissy to listen to reason anytime soon. Quick, time to distract him before he turned that pissiness on me.

"So, what do you think now that you've seen one of the vics in person?"

He allowed himself to be redirected, not nearly as excited

about our role reversal as I was. "She's right about one thing." No need to ask which *she* he meant. "Had to be a wicked-strong arcane to take out three full-grown Cats that easy."

One could have made a damned good argument that none of the Cats had died an *easy* death, but I got his point. "So, we're most likely looking at a killer who's another Cat, unlikely as that might seem, or one of the hybrid Sidhe clones, a Giant or half-Giant, maybe . . ." My voice trailed off when he met my gaze unflinchingly. "Or a Hound."

The nerves in his jaw worked but he just gave a terse nod.

"And knowing what we know about the counting coup and catnip thing, the two most likely pools of suspects are Cats and Hounds. Though the odds of a Cat doing that to another are pretty freaking low." My eyes narrowed at the sudden flash of insight stabbing through me. I turned to stare at the door separating us from the unlikeliest of love-birds still locking lips in the waiting room. "Do you think . . ." He arched a brow. "How common is it for Cats and Hounds to marry?"

Interest colored his eyes a darker shade of amber. "Not very. I can count on both hands the times I've heard of mixed couples being able to actually get to the altar without one or both families doing something to crack their wedding bells."

"So. Maybe we should find out for sure whether anyone else knew about Harper and Penn's relationship, and whether the other vics have any ties to *Christabel*. It seems awfully convenient to me that Boston's first arcane serial killer would just *happen* to pop up just as they start to go public about their relationship."

His lips twitched at my saccharine use of her first name, but he refrained from commenting out loud. Never let it be said my Hound was stupid.

CHAPTER FOUR

AN UNPLEASANT HALF HOUR LATER FOUND
the four of us crammed into my upgraded but not-so-
spacious digs, courtesy of my promotion to head of the
Boston MCU. The new office smelled superior to and had
a better view than my old one, along with the brand-new
desktop computer donated by my brother and sister-in-law,
but had barely enough room for one chair behind the desk,
two on the other side, a battered bookcase, and a tiny table
with four more chairs hugging it that served as the conference center for the Magical Crimes Unit. Four other offices
lined the hall, housing Trinity and the other two permanent
members of the unit, along with the newbie detectives—
like Cass—that came and went when they couldn't adjust to
life on the arcane side. Cass, I hoped, would actually stick.
The biggest perk, as far as I was concerned, was our closer
proximity to the magically protected holding cells, the

interrogation rooms, and most important of all, the coffee machine on this floor.

Harper stared at the array of crime scene photos spread before her, face growing paler with each image she shuffled through. Jove Does 18-4 and 20-1 didn't look any better in death than Bryant Wilkins had, although at least they hadn't had their tongues cut out and replaced with catnip. I still hadn't worked up the courage to share that little tidbit with Harper.

Finally unable to take any more, she jerked the pictures facedown and let Penn take her into his arms. Normally I wouldn't have allowed a civilian—arcane or not—into my inner sanctum or to view grisly crime scene photos unless he was a suspect or relative, but I just didn't have the heart to watch Harper go through something like this alone. Especially considering the less-than-understanding mood my own Hound was currently in.

I let her mourn for a couple of silent moments before breaking in gently. "Familiar to you, Harp?"

She gave a jerky nod, face still buried in Penn's chest. Her voice was muffled but audible when she spoke out loud. "Carlos Mendez and Simon Xavier." The names clearly didn't mean anything to Penn, but Scott let out his breath sharply. "B-boyfriends from high school. The only two I dated seriously."

This time it wasn't jealousy I saw in Penn's eyes when they met mine. It was, pure and simple, fear. Someone was systematically—and violently—eradicating past lovers of his brand-new fiancée. Apparently in chronological order. Possibly to send a brutal message to one or both of them: Cats and Hounds are *not* to mix. The logical assumption would be that someone from Penn's family was offing the Cats to warn her off from him, but there's that whole saying about ASS-U-ME-ing I try to live by. Some jealous psycho stalker *could* be offing Harper's ex-boyfriends on the way up the ladder to the juiciest prize: newest flame and Warhound tycoon, Pennington Banoub.

There was no gentle way to ask my next question, so I just spit it out. "How many people know you two are seriously involved?"

Penn's body stiffened, and Harper whirled to face me. Her mouth opened, then closed, and then opened again when realization hit. "You think someone's trying to break us up."

"I think it's a damned good possibility someone is not at *all* happy you two are bridging the species divide between Cat and Hound. Just how long *have* you been seeing each other?"

Mr. Adonis growled and leaned toward me in a threatening manner. Which, of course, set off *my* Hound, who growled and leaned toward his not-so-beloved cousin. *Hmm, a dogfight instead of a catfight.* Harper and I shared an amused expression in wake of all that figuratively bristled fur and raised hackles. Yeah, she was definitely growing on me.

She patted Penn's arm soothingly, which calmed him enough to back off. Physically anyway. "If you're trying to suggest that one of us is in any way involved—"

Busy soothing my own savage beast—Scott—I glanced over my shoulder and let out a snort. "Down, boy. If that's what I thought, I wouldn't *suggest* it at all. I'd flat out accuse you, and we'd be in an interrogation room. What I *am* suggesting is that someone *else* is pissed off about you two being involved, and going to no small lengths to make that pissiness known."

His features grew thoughtful instead of confrontational. "Harper and I have been together for more than a year." Scott muttered something under his breath. "Though we've only started making it more open over the past few weeks. For most of that time, only a handful of trusted people knew that we were seriously involved."

From Scott's sour expression, I was willing to bet that

Harper had hooked up with the other Hound not too long after his own one-night stand with her. According to him, they'd been casual friends for several years before that, growing closer once they admitted that romance was not in the cards for them. Probably a big part of the reason he was so resentful that she had taken up with his detested cousin. Not only did it sting that she'd done so, but it had to be even worse that she'd kept it secret for more than a year, only confessing to him after she accidentally outed herself by showing up at the morgue with her new beau. Penn's comment about only *trusted people* knowing had only rubbed salt in the wound.

Scott's extreme bitchiness was starting to make a little more sense.

I forced my brain back to the professional rather than the personal, jotting down notes on my steno pad. "I'll want the names of every person who *did* know of your involvement the entire time. Even more importantly, you'll need to give me all the details of your becoming more open about the relationship over the past few weeks. Names of people you told, places you went to openly, that sort of thing. Basically the who, what, when, where, and how of your love life." Harper nodded, fierce determination in her eyes, though Penn seemed way less than thrilled. My next comment would probably thrill him even less. "Most important of all, though, is for you to make me a list of all of your exes, Harp. I need a chronological list going back to high school along with basic details like when you were involved, how serious you were with them, and how long you dated. We'll start with the most serious exes, since that seems to be the killer's focus, and we'll work our way down from there."

Penn's gritted teeth spoke volumes for how he felt about *that. Whew, if I were Harper, I wouldn't write up that list while lover boy's around.* Granted, my love life over the past couple of years had been pretty stagnant—except for the on-again portions of my relationship with Scott—but the ten years prior to *that* had been about as unsaintlike as it could get. Partly because I was a red-blooded American woman, with all that entailed, and partly because Furies were no strangers to raging hormones and emotions of *all* kinds.

Harper took a deep breath, grief and tension written even larger on her face than before. "Is it okay if I e-mail all this to you? I need—I just have to get out of here." I nodded sympathetically. "I'll get you that last list first, since . . ."

Her voice trailed off, but any one of us could have finished that sentence: *since one of them will be the killer's next victim.*

"You know we're both here if you need us." I elbowed Scott in his side. He muttered something that sounded halfway appropriate. "Harp, I really am sorry about all this."

"Yeah, you and me both, Riss. Sorry for every one of the men I've dated . . ."

She jerked to her feet and rushed out of my office before anyone could say anything, guilt chasing her as surely as any physical demon could have. Penn nodded to me, purposely ignored Scott, and hurried after his fiancée. Leaving me behind to ponder her parting words and be extremely grateful that she hadn't been romantically involved with Scott for more than twenty-four hours. The guys the killer was going after were long-term boyfriends—as far as I knew, no one other than me, Harper, and Scott knew they were anything more than pals. At least, that's what I had to hope.

I HAD TO SAY ONE THING FOR HARPER: THE woman had an impressive track record, based on the list she e-mailed the next morning. She put even me to shame, which was saying something. Then again, fortunately for the MCU's resources, only eight of those relationships fell under what I would have called the *serious* category—and three of *those* could be checked off the list by virtue of being dead.

That didn't count Penn, but I was willing to bet the killer would either save him for last—or turn out to be someone who cared about him too much to off him. Besides, now that he and Harper knew about the threat waiting in the wings, they wouldn't be taken unawares like the others had been.

Scott padded up behind me, the aroma of freshly brewed gourmet coffee teasing my nostrils and making me lean back in my office chair with a happy little sigh. He set a large mug—one of the few surviving from my mother's failed ceramics hobby years ago—on the credenza next to my desk, leaning down to plant a kiss atop my bedhead hair. "Morning, sunshine. You're up and at 'em early."

I reached up to pat him absently on the way to snatching the coffee mug. After taking a long, slow gulp and giving another, zestier sigh, I smiled. "The jackass neighbor woke me up by revving his motorcycle at oh-gods-early, and I decided to check e-mail on my way back from cussing at him. Harp e-mailed the list of potential vics."

He sipped his own coffee as he read over my shoulder. "So. Five that seem to be in the highest-risk category. Leaving off"—his voice grew derisive—"His Highness Pennington Kazemde Banoub."

Bitter much? Wisely, I kept that thought to myself. "And if we go by chronological order, the two she dated in the year following her breakup with Bryant Wilkins would be in the most immediate danger, and the two she dated in the couple of years prior to hooking up with His Highness being in the least immediate danger."

Scott tapped the laptop monitor. "And leaving good ole

Vic the Slick smack dab in the middle of the road. As usual."

I read the line he indicated before turning to look up at him. *Victor Esteban, dated seriously for eight months five years ago, close friends ever since breakup.* "Vic the Slick?"

My Hound rolled expressive amber eyes. "He's a scrawny little guy, about as feminine as a guy can get and still be this side of straight."

"Ahh, metrosexual."

"Takes a comb and hair gel everywhere, spends as much time in the john as a woman, and has been known to cart around a purse. If that's what you call it, then yeah." He did fake quotation marks in the air. "Flaming *'metrosexual.'*"

"Man bag," I corrected while adding a few notes behind Victor Esteban's name.

"Say what?"

My lips twitched with the effort to hold back laughter in the face of Scott's incredulity. "Man bag. Not purse. That's what they call bags that guys carry around."

"Whatever. He and Harp are tight, real tight. I bet he numbers among the *trusted people* who knew when she started screwing around with Prince Asswipe."

Okay, this time I couldn't just let it pass. "Hmm, feeling a little bit jealous, are we?"

"*Jealous?* Of a prissy little guy who's shorter than *you*?"

"Watch it, buster."

His lips twitched. "No offense to you."

"Whatev. Look, I'm sure Harp had her reasons for keeping you in the dark." Another mutinous twist of his lips. Pretty damned ironic, really, considering how he'd kept *me* in the dark about his sister Amaya's abduction but *had* told Harper about it. Fortunately, we'd recovered Amaya. "Did you ever think about the fact she was trying to protect you?"

Incredulity etched itself across his face. "*Protect* me? Why the hell would *I* need protecting from *her*?"

A couple clicks on the mouse and the battered body of Bryant Wilkins stared out at us sightlessly. "From the crazies out there. Those who think that Cats and Hounds shouldn't mix on even a platonic basis. Though there *is* one little difference between you and this *Vic the Slick* guy." When he smirked and opened his mouth to make an undoubtedly smart-ass remark, I hurried on. "Be*sides* his height. I'm talking about the fact he's a Cat. Which should have put him at *less* risk than you from backlash if someone found out about her relationship with *His Royal Highness*."

He looked a little less cranky and a little more intrigued. "How do you figure?"

"Well, if we were dealing with your garden-variety brand of racist fanatic, they'd be striking out at the Hounds in her life to scare her away from them, rather than starting with the Cats. That would be the *logical* thing to assume anyway. Harper and Penn wanted to keep their relationship as much on the down-low as possible. The best way to do that was to (A) limit the number of people they told about it, and (B) tell those they considered at highest risk of endangering it as little as absolutely possible."

A grunt, and then his hands settled on my shoulders to caress absentmindedly. "I think I like the way your mind works, baby. 'Cause in this equation, her telling Vic the Slick as much as she did actually means she likes me more."

I rolled my eyes. Leave it to a ridiculously alpha-type Hound to reach *that* conclusion. Still, if that's what it took to get him *out* of his whiny funk, it sure as heck worked for me.

"Fortunately for us, Trinity commandeered our newbie detective to help inform Bryant Wilkins's next of kin about his murder before the two of them start digging into Bryant's activities over the past few days. Harper's e-mail said she's planning to go along with them for moral support. That leaves you and me the task of interviewing and offering protection to the highest-risk of Harp's exes."

His eyes lit up with that avaricious gleam that didn't bode well for the MCU's bottom line. "Gonna take more manpower than the PD boasts to handle *that* job."

What he meant was more *arcane* manpower. Which, right now, consisted of exactly three official officers—*moi*, of course, and the remaining two permanent members of the MCU: a husband-and-wife pair of nightowls. Literally. Kale and Mahina shape-shifted into humongous predatory owls who owed their abilities and existence to the Hawaiian goddess Hina. My recent hiring of those two to handle the night shift so I could sleep most nights through was hands down one of the brightest moments I'd enjoyed since forming the Magical Crimes Unit.

Though moving closer to the coffee machine still ranked pretty high up there.

"And I bet you know just the right people for the job. Who just *happen* to be related to you by blood."

"Well, not *all* of them are related by blood."

*Yeah, those are the ones who married in*to *the family. Like I will someday.* Wow. Where the hell had *that* thought come from? We'd only been in the *on-again* phase of our relationship for a few months and were taking it slow. He came over to my apartment some nights, I went over to his others, but neither of us had permanently moved belongings to the other's place like during our passionate eighteen-month relationship. Nothing was yet set in stone.

At least, that's what my brain said. My heart, on the other hand? Not so much.

"Yeah, yeah, yeah, Murphy. I see your ultimate plot. Ensure job security for your never-ending assortment of relatives by sleeping with the head of the MCU."

He shot me a sexy wink and an even sexier grin, white Hound's teeth gleaming. "Seems to be working so far."

I laughed at that, because he *did* have a point. "Come on, lover boy, we've got people to see, things to do, and asses to protect."

And for once, those asses to protect didn't include either one of ours.

CHAPTER FIVE

HARPER HAD THIS ON ME: EACH OF HER EXES was hotter—and more successful—than the last. Unintentional on her part since she's *so* not the gold-digging type, but true nonetheless. Take the first two victims, Carlos Mendez and Simon Xavier, her high school boyfriends. Both had been fairly average in looks and subsequent careers: Carlos a lower-level CPA in a mortal-owned firm and Simon a dental hygienist for the area's first arcane dentist. Both lived low-key lives from an arcane point of view. Neither would have inspired fireworks-inducing passion at first glance. Bryant Wilkins, however, seemed a step above in areas both physical and financial. A fitness guru, he'd double-majored in business and physical education, and later opened the first of what would become a regional chain of fitness centers. I'd been able to pull publicity photos of him off his company website and whistled at the tall, well-built hottie staring back at me. Dark blond hair, deep blue eyes, and a perfect white smile that might have been worked on by good ole unassuming Simón. *You definitely traded up on that one, Harp.*

Then I remembered how all had been brutally sliced and diced without regard for looks, finances, or loved ones who might mourn their loss, and scowled at the photos of Exes 4 through 6, the ones Trinity and I had deemed most at risk via an earlier teleconference. I was praying they could give me some new insight into the killer we were up against. Barring that, hopefully Scott could get a feel for which of his Shadowhounds would make the best security fit for each.

"You casting for a porno flick, or what?"

I blinked and looked up to see Scott smirking at me as he eased his siren red sports car (clichéd but oh-my-gods-sexy) into a parking space at the top level of a garage I hadn't noticed us enter. He saw my confusion and nodded at the glossy photos spread across my lap.

"Oh hardy har, Murphy." I fought back a flush since my thoughts hadn't been too far from his line of thinking. Stuffing the photos back into a manila folder, I glanced around to orient myself. The open-roofed parking garage clued me in to the fact we'd left Boston proper and found our way out to the 'burbs. Or as 'burb-like as it got in the metropolitan area surrounding Beantown. "Meritton Enterprises?"

Scott nodded. He pocketed his keys and climbed out of the Ferrari with surprising grace, considering how big he was in comparison to the delicate-looking car. I pushed the passenger door open and leapt up to do the same, only to stumble as my knee buckled. White-hot pain licked its way from the center of my knee outward, and I cursed, long and low. Scott was at my side in an instant, concern on his face, but he caught one look at the fury in my eyes and wisely kept his hands—and sympathy—to himself.

Every damn time I start to think this blasted knee is getting better . . . But Gianna, the Oracle who saved me from certain death months before, had warned that just wasn't going to happen. I'd used magic to seal myself away from agonizing pain during a fight with evil cloned Sidhe—once thought extinct—in order to save Scott's life, rather than channeling magic through my Amphisbaena to heal the wound then and there. Because of that not-so-little choice, magic masked the pain for a time while the injury grew exponentially worse during the rest of that fight for life. Scott's sister, Kiara, a Warhound who specialized in magical poultices and remedies, kept me stocked with spellworked bandages and creams to hide the pain and allow me to function despite the ravaged knee. But her remedies seemed to be fading, and more and more, I found myself turning to alcohol to take the edge off. What was I going to do if *that* stopped helping? Move from Jack and Coke to just plain coke?

No, it's just the stress you're under. I gritted my teeth and rolled my eyes. Not even *I* could believe my halfhearted protestations anymore. If things kept going like this, I was going to have to break down and crawl back to Gianna for another opinion. I might be stubborn as hell, but I wasn't stupid.

But time enough for that later. Right now, I had a serial killer to bring down.

I cleared my throat and brushed nonexistent dust from my dark blue jeans. With my promotion to Head of the MCU had come the need to blend in with mortals on occasion, rather than my usual shock and awe routine with the Fury getup. Today I'd opted for dressy jeans, a deep blue blouse, and mortal form for the planned day of interviewing Harper's exes. No sense in scaring the shit out of everyone until absolutely necessary.

My cell phone buzzed inside my jeans pocket. I took it

out and checked the number. Unknown caller, so back inside the pocket it went so I could focus on the task at hand. They'd leave a voice mail if it was important.

Scott steered the conversation away from my near fall. "Meritton's expecting us?"

I nodded. "Yeah, Trin made the phone calls for us. She had time before sitting in on the latest autopsy with Sahana." We'd decided one of us should be there for that, especially since the lab results for the first two Cats were supposed to come in today.

We made our way to the elevator in the middle of the garage, rode the empty car to the ground floor, and passed through a tunnel into the lobby of Meritton Enterprises. I let out a low whistle at the gleaming granite walls, expensive slate flooring, and shiny accessories surrounding us. Apparently, business was *very* good for Paul Meritton. Which went along with my unscientific theory that Harper's exes just kept on getting better with age.

An overly chipper male receptionist directed us to—where else?—the top floor and a secondary, even plusher-looking reception area. A chic woman in a stylish but no-nonsense suit introduced herself as Paul Meritton's executive assistant, Clara Danvers, and offered us various and sundry beverages (though none alcoholic, more's the pity). At our polite refusal she ushered us down a hall and through a solid wood door.

Paul Meritton, CEO and sole owner of Meritton Enterprises, jumped to his feet and rushed over to welcome us the moment we stepped over his threshold. I'll admit it, my knees—both this time—got a little weak when he turned the full force of his megawatt smile our way. *Holy . . . he should be a supermodel, not heading up a medical supply corporation.*

Because *damn*, he was sexy. Coal black hair, olive-toned skin indicating Greek heritage, and warm brown eyes that could have been the template for bedroom eyes. He wasn't as tall or muscular as his direct predecessor, Bryant Wilkins, but *whoa*, was he way more gorgeous. His cheekbones were to die for, his long eyelashes needed no mascara to make them fuller, and his unblemished complexion could have made angels weep. I tried to find a flaw in his physical features and just kept coming up empty.

I can't believe Harp broke up with someone so gorg—

Then he spoke, and the mirage wavered. "Chief Holloway, Mr. Murphy, so marvelous to meet you both." The high-pitched voice that came out of those perfect lips would have sounded *so* much more appropriate coming from the assistant he turned his attention to. "Clara, cappuccinos. Now." The charming expression he threw our way turned to barely disguised derision when he glanced at the other woman.

So, there's reasons one and two. A voice that could make angels and *devils weep, and rude to boot.* It was actually a relief to find that his interior wasn't as perfect as his exterior. And further illustrated that age-old adage about appearances being deceiving.

He gathered up every ounce of his charm and guided us into decadent visitor chairs placed across from his high-end office chair. It was easier to see through the snake oil façade masked by his breathtaking good looks after having witnessed his shoddy treatment of his assistant and okay, after hearing that godsawful, nails-on-chalkboard voice. Something about the light in his eyes when he focused on me had the hair on the nape of my neck standing at full alert. I frowned but couldn't quite put my fingers on whatever was bugging me.

"Now, then. Your partner mentioned something about a murder investigation, but I didn't quite catch how exactly she thought *I* could be of assistance to *you*." Raised brows and a half smile indicated doubt that someone of *his* caliber could be in any way associated with something so distasteful as a murder investigation.

I kept my expression bland but polite. "We have reason to believe that a serial killer is prowling the streets of Boston, Mr. Meritton."

He acted suitably surprised, though that could have been exactly that—an act. "How horrible. But that relates to me exactly how?"

"An *arcane* serial killer."

"An arcane—but we haven't had an arcane serial killer in I don't know how long."

Try "ever."

Out loud, I said, "Yes, and what's more, this killer seems to be preying upon one arcane race in particular."

This time his expression didn't appear feigned. Apprehension made his mortal-seeming brown eyes flash unnatural yellow (not all Cats have green eyes in arcane form like Harper's) and back again. "He's killing Cats?"

Typical to assume a serial killer was male, especially among law enforcement, but I took note that Meritton had assumed the same thing Harper did. "He or she." He rolled his eyes, making it clear what he thought about *that* suggestion. "And not to unduly alarm you, Mr. Meritton—"

The snake oil salesman slipped back into place. Complete with creepy, flirtatious smile turned my way. As if we were alone in the office—maybe even in the entire building. "Please, call me Paul."

I continued smoothly, though inside I was dying to look at Scott to see how he was reacting to Meritton's not-at-all-subtle flirting right in front of him. "But we have reason to believe that you are at no small risk from this serial killer."

Another arched eyebrow. "And that reason would be?"

"All three of the victims had one trait in common. One which you share as well. A past romantic relationship with the same woman."

Apprehension grew into outright fear. He pushed back in his chair, and a bead of sweat welled up on his forehead. "Wait. Are you telling me that all three of these men screwed the same woman? Someone I screwed as well?"

Oh yeah, Mr. Charming had disappeared entirely in light of the revelation he actually *could* be associated with a murder investigation. "All four of you share an ex in common, yes."

"Who? What *woman*"—he spat the word—"could possibly be worth killing over?"

Scott shifted in his chair and I resisted the renewed urge to look at him. Boy, Meritton was on a roll here. Hitting on a Hound's current lover, bad-mouthing a past lover . . . Not that the gorgeous but slimy man had any clue to either of those facts.

"Does the name *Harper Cruz* ring a bell?"

His sneer grew even more pronounced. "That whore is the reason three good men have died? Three Cats?"

I slammed the low but solid heel of my red leather boot onto Scott's foot to keep him from leaping across the desk. "Ms. Cruz"—I enunciated the *Ms.*—"is the thread tying all three victims together, yes. And we have every reason to believe this killer will strike again, that the killer is taking out exes of hers in chronological order, which means that you are at very high risk of being next."

The sneer disappeared entirely. Meritton licked his lips and took in a deep breath of air. For the first time since we entered, he turned his full attention on to Scott. "I want to hire you." Well, guess he knew exactly who "Mr. Murphy" was. My lips trembled with threatened laughter, but I did the honorable thing and told him the MCU would be hiring Scott's mercs to serve as bodyguards on his behalf.

The two of them settled into the business of working out the exact timing and details and paid little ole me no heed, so I stood and wandered around the spacious room. Meritton's assistant bustled in with gourmet cappuccinos—which I just *had* to sample so as not to appear rude—and then out again. The floor-to-ceiling bookshelves that took up an entire wall caught my eye. I set down the coffee mug and wandered closer, letting my eyes roam across the book spines. The typical business books you'd expect to find in a CEO's office occupied one shelf. Books specific to the medical industry took up another. I browsed two more mundane shelves before coming across something much more interesting: esoteric arcane history books. Esoteric because I, big arcane history and cultural buff that I was, had only read a bare fraction of the books. Hell, I'd only even *heard* of a handful of the many I hadn't read. My gaze went to the still-haggling Meritton before settling back on the bookcase's upper shelves. Well, well, well, Mr. Meritton was definitely a collector.

My cell phone buzzed again, but my attention had been caught by a slim, dull-colored book titled *Treatise on the Cultural and Theological Divide Between the Bastai and the Anupu'mesu*. The word *Bastai* had me backtracking in light of the current circumstances. The Bastai—meaning Cats like Harper who could trace their roots (however far) back to the Egyptian goddess Bast. The Anupu'mesu—*Anupu* being an ancient name for Anubis, *mesu* being loosely translated in ancient Egyptian to *children*. So specifically those Warhounds descended from Anubis rather than the Celtic goddess Epona.

My spider sense started tingling. I plucked the gray-covered book from the shelf, noting from the magical *buzz* shooting up my fingers that no expense had been spared to protect its pages by magical means. Interesting. Not all of the arcane-centric books on the shelf had been so well preserved. In fact, most of them *hadn't* been, or my skin would have started crawling the moment I got close to the bookshelf. Considering that magical preservation along with the book's subject, I started thumbing to the table of contents.

Like most cops, I could speed-read with the best of librarians. I ran my gaze along brief but pithy chapter titles such as "History of the Bastai," "Worship of Bastai in Ancient Egypt," "Prominent Pharaohs and Their Ties to the Anupu'mesu," and so on. About halfway down the page, however, my eyes widened and air whistled out through my teeth. Oh. My. Gods. "Bastai Counting Coup and Anupu'mesu Response to Same."

My pulse picked up speed. That title could mean one thing and one thing alone: the Bastai proclivity for ripping out enemy tongues and the Warhound reciprocation using catnip. The fact that one of Harper's exes had *this* particular book could have been coincidence. Or a mere stroke of luck for me since it could provide invaluable insight into the killer's mind. But what *was* Paul Meritton? Innocent bystander who just happened to own a rare treatise on an equally rare kind of serial killer's MO? Or bitter ex-lover who variously lusted after and scorned women, and had gone over the edge after discovering that his *whore* of an ex had started sleeping with the enemy?

My fingers tapped the table of contents page while a dozen thoughts raced through my mind. One way to get a feel for which theory might be closest to the truth presented itself, causing me to turn and stroll back to Meritton's desk, expression oh-so-casual. I waited for an end to their discussion—which had been winding down over the past couple of minutes—and took advantage of a lull in the conversation.

"Quite a collection you've got over there, Paul." It almost hurt me to call him that like he wanted, but I took one for the team. I even smiled and subtly batted my eyelashes at him, and that hurt a hell of a lot more. Scott's eyes narrowed and fire lit inside, until I shifted slightly so he could read the book's cover. Then realization set in and his anger dissipated.

Good boy.

Meritton blinked at the abrupt change in topic, and then *he* caught sight of the book in my hands. His reaction— pleased recognition and an eager grin—wasn't what I expected. "Oh, yes, I see you're a bibliophile after my own heart." He stood and stepped toward his bookshelf, seeming interested in his collection as a whole rather than the specific book I held. "Spent a pretty penny collecting these—all first editions, of course. You won't find a private collection to rival mine, and very few arcane museums house such a trea- sure trove of magical culture and history."

"So you're a—closet historian?"

His eyes sparkled with the first sign of true warmth I'd seen since walking into his office. "My undergraduate degree was in arcane anthropology. I switched tracks in graduate school to an MBA, which was when I met . . . Harper." His tough-guy façade cracked enough that I real- ized he actually had, in his own way, loved her during their time together. Maybe still did. Enough to kill over her, despite how shocked he'd sounded at that suggestion just moments before? Perhaps that had been his intention all along. Maybe he was, even now, playing me.

Still, he either didn't immediately recognize the book I held or didn't want to tip his hand by reacting. And that *could* work to my benefit.

"I have a bachelor's in history as well as criminal justice. I've seen a lot of the public collections you just mentioned— and a few of the private as well." I waved the one in my hand as if it were an afterthought. "The others in the Magi- cal Crimes Unit would salivate to get their hands on even *one* of these books."

He smiled and made a magnanimous gesture. "Then

you must take the book as a gift. Consider it a donation to start the MCU's own private collection."

Wow, that was easy enough. "Oh, I couldn't . . ." I kept my voice eager, with just a hint of flirtatiousness. *Oh Jack, how I'll need you to wash away this dirty feeling later . . .*

"Truly, I insist. Don't worry, I'll make sure my accountant writes it off come tax time." He winked and walked toward me. Took a lot of willpower not to back up as far and fast as possible. "Besides, I have to show my appreciation to the Boston Police Department for being so diligent in watching out for its citizens, arcane as well as mundane." He said that with a straight face and not the slightest trace of irony. Man, he *was* a good actor.

Scott was between Meritton and me before I could blink. He made it look natural and smooth and *not* as though he was marking his territory to keep the interloper away, waving his PDA in the air. "It's all set, Meritton. My cousins will be in the lobby by five o'clock to rendezvous with you. They know the details we discussed. All I ask is that you don't try and give them the slip, and they will keep you safer than a newborn kitten in its mother's care."

Ha! Look at that—Scott was actually learning diplomacy, using a feline analogy instead of canine. I'd say I was rubbing off on him, but honestly, I was still working on that whole diplomacy thing myself.

Shocking, I know.

Meritton nodded at Scott. "Believe me, this Cat prefers to use as few of his ninety-nine lives as possible. And I have no intention of seeking out Bast's final embrace anytime soon."

I reached into a pocket and pulled out one of my fancy-schmancy MCU business cards, holding it out until he accepted it. "My cell number is on there, Paul. Please feel free to call me if you think of anything that could be helpful to my investigation, or if you notice anything out of the ordinary." I nudged Scott's arm with my shoulder. "You'll be in good hands with the Shadowhounds, speaking as a former client. They're the best at what they do."

His lips twitched as if he wanted to smile, but he simply said, "Indeed. Now then, I have a meeting I need to prepare for so please forgive me if I leave it to Clara to show you out."

A dismissal if I'd ever heard one. Not that I minded. Meritton might have been a looker, but my ears had gotten more than enough of that chipmunk voice. "Thank you for your time. And please, don't hesitate to contact me should you need to."

He made his smile and voice feel like a sleazy—and unwanted—caress. "Certainly, Chief Holloway. You've not heard the last from me."

Unfortunately, instinct told me that was all too true. The sole question I had, however, was whether he would be speaking as a potential victim or the killer himself.

CHAPTER SIX

EX-LOVERS 5 AND 6 HELD TRUE TO MY trading-up theory: Both were, impossible as it seemed, even better looking and more successful than Paul Meritton— thankfully minus the squeaky voice and misogynistic tendencies. Though they took more convincing than Meritton to accept the offered protection. Ex Number 5, Aaron Vega, because the former Marine (yes, folks, they allowed us to kill and die for them long before they accepted us as full-fledged members of mortal law enforcement) worked private security himself. Ex Number 6, Beacon Hill tycoon Ward Rockefeller (yes, distantly related to *those* Rockefellers) just seemed blasé about the whole situation. Too blasé.

"What do you mean, that won't be necessary?" I tried to moderate my tone as I stared across the table at the corporate shark who could have given Andre Carrington a run for his money in moral ambiguity. Tried, but failed, since I couldn't understand his refusal to grasp the seriousness of his situation.

"Simple, Chief Holloway. I have neither the time nor the inclination to be followed around and spied upon by anyone—whether official police officers or"—he smiled apologetically at Scott—"mercenaries working on the police department's dime." His hand shot up to forestall my next point. "Or even on my own dime. It's simply out of the question."

Scott and I exchanged wordless glances that said a lot. Like, *Either this guy's a moron, or he knows something we don't. Or both.* I turned back to the moron. "Mr. Rockefeller—"

"Please, Chief, call me Ward. *Mr. Rockefeller* is and always will be my father." His lips curled around the *Mr. Rockefeller*, and he made his voice upper-crust snooty to the extreme. "I *do* appreciate your concern, but again, my answer is no. You have delivered your warning, and I choose to refuse your offer of police protection. Last I checked, that was perfectly well within my constitutional rights. Even as an *arcane*."

Interesting. The way he spat out that last word indicated extreme displeasure. I was willing to bet with the mortal authority, though no big surprise there. Half the time *I* was pissed off with the mortal authority, and I worked for them. Still, it was worth noting.

Scott brought that point up himself when we were en route to Harper's downtown condo. "Rockefeller seemed remarkably *un*concerned by the news he could wind up our serial killer's next victim, don't you think?"

"Considering the crime scene photo I tried to spook him with, hell yeah. That photo would have sent most executives crying *wee, wee, wee* all the way home."

"And yet it barely fazed him."

I tapped the manila folder on my lap and pursed my lips. "Had it been Aaron *Semper Fi* Vega, I wouldn't even think twice. But coming from Ward the businessman? Definitely weird."

"Could be he watches gory slasher flicks when he's not dismantling companies to sell for sickening amounts of money."

"Maybe. And maybe he's not worried because he knows he has nothing to fear."

We exchanged another pointed look before he turned his attention back to the road and I pulled out the little steno pad I kept on hand. Most of the pages contained brief notes written in shorthand and doodles in the margins. The last page with writing, however, contained my so-far-sketchy list of suspects.

1. Harper's family—all of them. Have Trinity research most likely culprits.

2. All the Banoubs except Ellie (probably) and Penn (maybe). Research myself.

3. Paul Meritton—misogynistic and had book on coup-counting. Coincidence or wreaking vengeance on woman who dumped him?

My fingers tapped the notepad while I considered. Adding Paul to the list—despite the fact he was a potential victim—didn't make me feel bad in the slightest. I could easily picture him in the role of teaching an ex-lover a bloody lesson about rejecting his sexist ass. The thought of adding Ward Rockefeller to the list for the mere fact he'd been amazingly unworried about the Cat-murdering serial killer had me hesitating for some reason. *Because he's a high-and-mighty Rockefeller? That didn't stop you from putting the Banoubs on the list.*

But there had also been his outright disgust with the mortal authorities. A slim thread to hang suspicions on, but better to consider him and clear his name than to write him off now and be blindsided with his guilt later. Like I'd done with Stacia . . .

Thinking about my former mentor brought a scowl to my face. I scribbled Rockefeller's name as Suspect Number 4 on the list out of sheer spite but couldn't push away Stacia's ghost so easily. Stacia Demetriou, an Elder so old she'd probably been around when they first erected the Palladium (the arcane version, not the mortal), had taken on my Fury training when my mother couldn't. I only found out a few months ago *why* my mother disappeared and left me an orphaned, Fledgling Fury: Crazy-ass Stacia had manipulated a group of mortal scientists into abducting my mother, experimenting on her, raping her, and ultimately getting her pregnant with the first male Fury. My half brother, Mac.

I softened slightly at the thought of my baby brother. Thankfully he'd broken through the brainwashing Stacia and her cronies pulled on him and busted my mother out of the prison they'd held her captive in for two decades. Only with his help—and my mother's—had we tracked down my missing best friend and sister Fury, Vanessa. Too late to save her life, but just in time to rescue her bred-in-captivity daughter, my adorable niece, Olivia. My brother and his wife, Jessica—Vanessa's biological sister—were in the process of officially adopting Olivia as their youngest daughter. Big sister Cori, just shy of sixteen years old and showing every sign of following in the footsteps of *both* her aunts, heartily approved.

And I know, it all sounds like a soap opera—or Jerry Springer episode. Arcanes have all the angst, betrayal, and drama that mortals do. Just add magic, stir, and watch the fireworks explode!

There's a reason the powers-that-be gave Furies so many

souped-up powers—and bound us to them through blood, oaths, and the Sisterhood: to even the score of us being out-numbered by all the other arcanes out there we were sup-posed to keep in check. But even with my super strength, speed, and shape-shifting abilities, I'd barely managed to take out the traitor who had miraculously taught herself to channel both Fury and Harpy abilities without going batshit insane. She'd claimed—before I killed her crazy ass—I had the same strength of will that allowed her to ride on the other side of Rage as a Harpy without giving in to insanity. Forgive me if I wasn't in a rush to test that little theory.

Not only were Harpies the mortal enemies of Furies, they murdered their Amphisbaena when Turning from Fury to Harpy and morphed into white-haired, yellow-eyed shells of their former selves, losing all ties with the Sisterhood and their mortal families. Yeah, not in a rush to lose everything that means anything to me, thanks.

Especially not now that I had won back the thing that meant the most to me of all—my relationship with Scott.

Speaking of the golden-eyed devil, he took advantage of my distraction to park on a darkened, quiet level of a down-town parking garage and pounce, sweeping my notebook and folder from my lap to the floorboard and pulling me toward his hard, warm chest. Surprise formed my mouth into a wide O, which he invaded with demanding lips and tongue. I pretended outrage for about two seconds, making a halfhearted attempt to push him away. The knowing light in his eyes called me a liar, and I gave in to the lust pulsing between us. Gods, would this raging inferno between us ever cool off? I sure as hell hoped not.

We made out like two teenagers in the backseat of a bor-rowed sedan, and damned if that image didn't turn me on even more. Especially in light of the fact we were parked in a public garage in the middle of the afternoon in downtown Boston. Someone could walk by and catch sight of us necking at any moment. A scandalized businessperson coming home from the office. A security guard patrolling the dimly lit garage. Pennington Banoub could walk right up and tap on Scott's windo—

Pennington Banoub walked right up and tapped on Scott's window. *Speaking of golden-eyed devils . . .*

This devil's eyes glinted with perverse amusement, a perversity I wanted to slap right off his handsome face. He didn't even *try* to look innocent. Good thing, too, because that was one emotion he could *never* pull off. Well, gee, I guess he and his cousin *did* have something in common after all, considering the way Scott attacked me in public. My own eyes narrowed at that thought as Scott failed to react to the sudden interruption with the heat I would have expected. *Why, you little shit. You* knew *Penn was walking up to the car . . .* Another woman might have gotten pissed off at being branded by one Hound to antagonize another. Sadly, the Fury in me reveled in it all too much. Not that I would ever admit that to either of them.

I leaned over Scott to shove his door open and into Penn's side. Hard. I arched a brow at his grunt of pain. "Enjoying the show much?"

The fact he ignored the pain long enough to grin wickedly only endeared him to me. *Ah, hell.* How could I dislike someone with a streak of mischief so much like my own?

"Definitely enjoying the scenery anyway." He wiggled his eyebrows and looked me up and down. Even though I knew he was doing it just to tick off Scott—which worked— I found myself flattered. The appreciation on his face wasn't feigned.

Yeah, yeah, yeah. So Furies are impossibly vain. *I* didn't create us that way.

Scott moved to assert his dominance over the other

Hound, shouldering me back and growling. Penn smirked and stepped back, but only to give us room to exit the Ferrari. I scrambled across the driver's seat seconds after Scott and grabbed his shoulder to keep him from doing anything rash. Like knocking his cousin's lights out—permanently.

He turned a growl my way, and I shot him a *down, boy!* look. "Behave yourself," I muttered under my breath, even though both Hounds could easily outhear me. Then I glanced back at Penn and frowned. "Wait. You just get here, *alone*?"

Seeing as how he'd agreed not to go anywhere solo for the next few days, that fact pissed me off far more than his ogling my assets. He apparently sensed—and respected—my rising Rage, because he wiggled a small, gift-wrapped package and rushed to reassure me. "No, I've been upstairs with Christabel. Just came out to get something from my car."

Curiosity piqued, I admired the elegant silver-and-white paper. "What's that?"

He smiled mysteriously. "You'll see. Now, if you two kids are finished necking, I don't want to leave Bel alone any longer than necessary."

Christabel. Gods, I was going to have *so* much fun with that one. Later. Like after we caught the psycho killer stalking those poor guys unfortunate enough to be her ex-lovers. *Including Scott* . . . Gods, I hoped no one knew that. But seeping worry had me questioning how sure I could be of that.

My hand tightened on his arm, and he shot me a questioning look. I forced a smile and took off after Penn, not wanting to verbalize my fear that the killer would somehow find out about his one-night stand with Harper. The only thing allowing me to keep my Rage under control as far as that went was convincing myself that neither of them would have gone around blabbing about *that* little interlude.

*Get a grip, Marissa. Focus on what you can control—
nailing this bastard to the wall. Keep Scott close until you
do, and you have nothing to worry about.*

Yeah, if only my overprotective Fury instincts reacted
so easily to silly things like *logic* and *reason*. Then again,
if they did, Furies probably wouldn't be such effective hunting and killing machines. Oh, life's little trade-offs.

My brain returned to cataloguing potential suspects
(something I *could* control) on the walk to the lobby of Harper's building and the elevator ride to her floor. Elevators still
made me leery—after being ambushed by a human sorceress in one—but living in Boston made developing a downright phobia of them impossible. One of the very few benefits
to my magical Rage was the ability to channel a tendril to
beat back the fear and focus on the suspect list.

I'd been to Harper's place a few times over the months
we'd gotten to know each other and had to admit she had
much more elegant taste than me. She opened the door to
Penn's knock and ushered us through the wide foyer that
separated the entryway from the large, spacious area con-
sisting of her living room, dining room, and kitchen. Deco-
rated in crisp white with bold slashes of black and teal, the
open floor plan was modern and more put together than
anything I could have managed in my own townhouse.

My feet had barely crossed the threshold into Harper's
living room when I started picking up weird vibes from our
arcane version of Romeo and Juliet. They kept exchanging
surreptitious glances I caught from the corner of my eye.
The weird part was they would then look in my direction
and quickly away again. As if they were planning to ambush
me or something.

And the way my life went, that might not be far from the
truth.

I tensed and crossed my arms over my chest, stopping in
the middle of the floor and causing Scott to bump into me.

"Riss?" Harper and Penn—both preparing to sit on a long white sofa I would have spilled whiskey on in a heartbeat—cast guilty looks in my direction and froze.

Ignoring Scott's questioning tone, I tilted my head at Romeo and Juliet. "I should have *known* something was up when you seemed so insistent about having us over for dinner tonight."

Harper tried—and failed as miserably as Penn would have—to look innocent. "What are you talking about, Riss?"

"Don't pussyfoot"—ha!—"with me, Christabel." Okay, so I couldn't resist. "I'm a Fury *and* a cop, and I know a sting operation when I see one. So spill it."

Penn jiggled the gift in his hands again. *Is that for Harper?* The Cat in question took the package from her fiancé as if she expected it, answering that question. Which could only mean . . . *It's for* me? *Okay, just why are they trying to butter me up?* I was sure I wouldn't like the answer to that question—and I was right.

Harper cleared her throat and stepped toward me. "Penn and I were thinking." I didn't like this already. "We don't want to give this bastard power over our lives, but at the same time, we want to see him caught more than anything. So, what if we killed two birds with one stone? Took back control of our own futures and set a trap for his psycho ass all at once?" Well, *that* didn't sound so bad. "We took more than a year to admit our love publicly, but we're not doing that with our engagement. In fact, we want to move the wedding up. Way up. To next month."

What the—wait. That could actually work. Trinity, Scott, and I could investigate all the major players behind the scenes leading up to the wedding and "And we want *you* to be our wedding planner." She settled the package in my hands. *What. The. Hell???*

I blinked. Then tilted my head to the other side. Looked

behind me to Scott, and then back to Romeo and Juliet. No, I hadn't suddenly woken up from some bizarre dream. Harper really stood there with a straight face and said she wanted *me* to be her *wedding planner*.

Harper took advantage of my shocked silence to tap the gift. "Open it."

Still unable to formulate a coherent thought, much less a sentence, I ripped into the elegant wrapping paper and found myself staring down at a thick paperback entitled *Wedding Planning Made Easy*. And for once, found myself just as speechless as a creepy dummy doll.

"JESUS, RISS, FOR THE DOZENTH TIME, NO, I did *not* know about Harper's crazy but brilliant scheme!"

I paused in the act of unlocking the door and looked over my shoulder. "Wait. You think her plan to have *me* be her *wedding planner* is brilliant? When did she slip you the Kool-Aid?"

Scott rolled his eyes. "Think about it, Riss. You're a shape-shifter. So you assume a disguise, come up with a cover story, and get instant access to everything and everyone involved in the wedding. The bridal party, relatives, guests, caterers, entertainers—you get the perfect excuse to poke your nose into everything associated with the bride and groom. Because they're supposedly *paying* you to make sure their perfect little day goes off without a hitch."

"So you think it's a great plan and I should roll with it?"

He leaned against the doorway and shrugged. "I think it's got potential. Trinity and I could pose as your assistants easily enough. We're much less newsworthy than the Chief Magical Investigator and, thus, easier to disguise without magic."

"Oh no, Murphy. You don't get off so easy if I have to go through with this stupid idea." I poked him in the chest. "Harper and I discussed that while you were in the little boys' room. You, my dear, are now Groomsman Number Eight. Congratulations."

Horror seeped into his gorgeous features. "Oh hell no, I'm not being groomsman to that . . . that—" His brows shot straight up. "Did you say *eight* groomsmen?"

I fought back a snicker as his horror ratcheted even higher. "Eight out of ten. You know how Cats and Hounds are serious about that whole *be fruitful and multiply* thing. Look at it this way: You're not *really* his groomsman; you'll be acting as his bodyguard during wedding-related events. It *could* be worse: Your pal Vic the Slick is stuck being her man of honor to avoid a brawl between all her sisters and cousins."

Scott shuddered. "Gods, you couldn't *pay* me to stand up there with *nine* bridesmaids."

While I'd valiantly held back a snicker, I couldn't fight off the smirk that came over my face. "Would the thought of playing the part of 'Groomsman Number Eight' go down easier if I remind you that I *am* paying you? Well, the MCU is anyway."

"Only if you promise I don't have to start being *nice* to that jerkoff."

"Why would you start being nice at this late date?" I shot him another smirk and finished twisting the key in my front door. Magic rushed over my skin, cataloguing me as being on the *allowed* list, and then set a dozen magical alarm bells shrilling painfully. Scott's supernatural hearing had him clapping hands over his ears and letting out an inadvertent whine. I reacted instantly at the warning that *someone* had breached my home's very expensive magical defenses some-time over the past twelve hours. Nemesis and Nike hissed into action when I shifted to full Fury form, twining their way from upper shoulders to lower arms and mentally demanding I let them down. Which I did.

They promptly slithered into the townhouse to take point. Scott grabbed my arm and bit out a choked, "What the hell, Riss?"

"The alarm. Someone got in while we were gone." I didn't have to specify that *someone* had been an arcane. We both knew the alarm wouldn't have reacted so violently to mortals.

"The Cat killer?"

"Maybe." Unease trickled down my spine in the form of shivers. "Stay here while I check it out."

"Oh hell no, Princess."

I rolled my eyes since he couldn't see them. "Fine, come on in with me and get zapped into unconsciousness by the defenses just like whoever broke in did."

He cursed up a storm when I darted into the house but wisely stayed on the other side of the threshold. Stubborn but not stupid—just one reason we made such a perfect match. When we didn't want to kill each other.

I kept my body low, following the magical trail left by Nemesis and Nike, and checking each room on the lower level, though I found nothing out of the ordinary. I frowned. How did whoever broke in stay conscious long enough to get in and back out? It would take someone with an insane level of magical ability to counteract the defenses I'd had installed after my bout with arcane and mundane assassins just months earlier. Unless whoever it was had broken into an upstairs window?

Sure enough, I circled back around through the dining room to the front entryway and found a spitting Nemesis and Nike slithering their way along the stair banister. They allowed me to scoop and carry them rather than fall behind my headlong flight up the stairs. My office and guest bedroom were both empty, as was the guest bathroom between the two rooms. Which left only *my* bedroom—and wasn't *that* a chilling thought?

I hurtled through the open doorway only to find yet another empty room. Everything seemed to be in its usual place, although the room seemed a bit chilly thanks to the breeze pouring in through the open window—

Wait, I never *leave my windows open* . . .

My eyes narrowed. Well, that explained *where* the intruder had entered and exited, but not *how* they had safely gotten in and out. Or *what* they'd been after. Dre Carrington and I were definitely going to have a *little chat* about his supposedly infallible security experts, however.

I slowly pivoted, letting my gaze take in the room's contents one last time before heading back toward the hallway, which was when I caught sight of the paper that had fallen to the floor. My pulse picked up speed as I bent down, retrieved the paper, and quickly skimmed it.

The message was short and not-so-sweet. *Since you can't be bothered to* answer *your phone, get yourself to Salem NOW Marissa Eurydice Holloway. Nan's awake.*

I froze as those last two words sank in. To anyone else, they might have seemed innocuous, but for me they heralded a miracle: My grandmother had *finally* awakened from a decades-long coma.

CHAPTER SEVEN

SCOTT WAS JUST AS SHOCKED TO HEAR THAT my grandmother had woken up from her twenty-two-year-long slumber as I had been. He also insisted on accompanying me to nearby Salem so I could hear the details from my mother. While Mom spent most of her time "Realmside" these days, recementing old ties to sister Furies, my brother and sister-in-law maintained a cozy suite for her in the attic of the home David and I grew up in.

By the time we stood on the front porch to ring their doorbell, it was well past nine o'clock. Normally I might have felt guilty for barging in on them that late without calling ahead first. Well, guilty toward David and my niece Cori anyway. Vanessa's sister, Jessica, and I might have called an uneasy truce after I finally solved Vanessa's disappearance and rescued her daughter, but that hadn't made us into sudden BFFs. And admittedly, tweaking her nose had been my main reason for not bothering to call ahead.

The door swung open before I even had a chance to ring the bell. A harried-looking, *slightly* older-looking mirror image of myself jerked me inside and patted me down as if to make sure I was in one piece. Rather roughly patted, which clued me in to just how exasperated my normally polite mother really was.

"It's about time you got here, Marissa Eurydice Holloway." I winced as every child—no matter how old—did when confronted by a parent using their full given name. She paused in her harangue of me to throw Scott a thousand-watt smile. Sometimes I thought she liked *him* more than me. "Hello, Scott dear. Come on in."

She turned back to me once Scott stepped into the entryway and shut the door behind him. "Do you have any idea how long I've been trying to get in touch with you? *Why* in the names of all the gods did you not answer your bloody cell phone?"

Uh-oh. A tiny bit of her childhood brogue—she'd been raised in the late 1800s in Scotland—slipped back into her voice. Wow. She was *really* ticked off. Not quite the reaction I expected to the news that Nan had awoken from her seemingly endless coma. Annoyance I hadn't answered her calls sooner—that made perfect sense. But anger that bordered on Fury Rage seemed way overkill.

"Mom, I'm sorry. There's a nasty arcane serial killer on the loose right now and—"

She waved that off as if it weren't a shocking development (which it was) and clenched a hand on my arm. "Something's wrong with your Nan, Marissa."

I frowned. "What do you mean *wrong*? I'd call waking up from a magical coma pretty right myself."

Mom bit her lip so hard blood trickled down her chin.

"That's just it, Marissa. She woke up an entire *week* ago, but the Oracles only admitted that to me this morning. Just before your grandmother waltzed into the Palladium and slapped that fox-faced bitch in the middle of a Lesser Session."

I winced. There were two ways to take a seat as an Elder—get enough votes from the Greater Consensus (made up of all the Elders) to gain a vacant position. Or the much bloodier old-school method: Challenge an active Elder to a duel and win the seat if the other Fury yielded—or died. Guess which option started with a bitchslap during an open session? Ding, ding, ding. And trust Nan to challenge not just *any* Elder, but the current Moerae, Ekaterina, who served as nominal head of the Lesser Consensus.

"Okay, granted, that doesn't sound like Nan at all. She always seemed to hate politics."

"She *did*! You get that from her, you know. But I think you're missing the other, equally important point there."

"Which would be?"

"*Where* was your grandmother for the past week, *why* didn't she come to either of us to let us know she was safe, and *how* am I supposed to make sure she *is* safe when she's refusing to see me?"

Her voice rose several octaves on the last sentence. *So we know where I get* that *trait from.* Not that I could blame her for the skyrocketing tone. This all sounded suspicious in the extreme. "You tried to talk to her after the Session?"

"Of *course* I did. I may not have a seat on the Lesser Consensus just yet, but word of the mighty Muriel's return traveled fast. The minute the session let out, I ran through the crowd to see her, but she wouldn't talk to me. Her daughter! Two Elder Megaeras cut me off from her like . . . like blasted bodyguards and informed me—her daughter—that my presence was neither required nor desired. Me—her bloody daughter—not required!"

My own jaw dropped open—and not just at the colorful language Mom had reverted to. Two Elders on the Lesser Consensus had supported Nan in her challenge of the current Moerae? They had then dared interfere with two of the most sacrosanct Fury relationships—mother to daughter and mentor to student, since Nan had trained Mom over a century ago. Either one of those kinships should have granted Mom immediate access to Nan. That both together *hadn't* meant . . .

"Someone is either impersonating Nan"—not as improbable a concept for me to consider after the dead Sidhe disguised as Vanessa's corpse—"or someone managed to wake her from the coma where the Oracles failed and is pulling her strings like a puppet. Coercion, maybe, or just plain taking advantage of a disoriented coma victim."

When Nan's only sister, Medea, Turned Harpy, Nan vowed to track her down and put her out of her misery. An ambitious task, to be sure, since Harpies bore absolutely no resemblance to the Furies they had been. Against all odds, Nan succeeded, but at great cost to herself. Newly Turned Harpies were particularly vicious and Medea had been no exception. She fought Nan tooth and claw. When it was obvious Nan had the slight edge over her, she lashed out in a magical kamikaze move that would have made a Phoenix proud. Medea died while Nan survived—if living in a persistent vegetative state could truly be called surviving.

Mom took a deep breath and nodded, a miserable light in her eyes. "I think you're right. As if there weren't enough strife in the Sisterhood, now this. But who would go through the trouble of coercing Nan just to take a stab at the Moerae's seat? The chances of getting her to wake up after all this time were exceptionally slim."

Scott spoke up. "Maybe it was just a crime of opportunity." When we both looked at him curiously, he went on. "You said she woke up a week ago and escaped from the Oracle's hospice. Why not check with them to see if they notified the Sisterhood when she first escaped. I can't imagine them keeping that info from both the family *and* the Elders."

I pursed my lips thoughtfully. "Good point. They probably didn't want to alarm the relatives until they exhausted every resource to find her. And if we find out *who* in the Sisterhood was first contacted . . ."

"You may be able to track down whoever is pulling your grandmother's strings now," he finished for me. "At the least you'll have someone to question for more intel."

Mom folded her arms across her chest and gave a determined nod. "I knew I liked you for good reason, Scott dear." She glanced at me. "I know you must focus on bringing your killer to justice for now. I am not without allies among our sisters. We will handle questioning the Oracles and whoever they first informed of Nan's awakening. Just make sure you answer your bloody cell phone next time I call."

Awww, so she *had* paid attention. That gave me enough warm fuzzies that I ignored her cell phone crack. "I—are you sure?" She gave another nod, but my heart was still torn. Every one of my Fury's instincts screamed at me to track down the ones responsible for my mother's current heartache and for sowing discord among the Sisterhood. But the cop in me felt the full weight of my duty to keep Boston's arcanes safe from the psycho currently stalking the city streets. Right now was definitely one of those times when being a Fury sucked far more ass than it kicked.

I COULDN'T COME ALL THIS WAY WITHOUT checking on the two little girls most precious to me—my nieces. Although, granted, Cori couldn't accurately be called a little girl much longer. Her sixteenth birthday was just around the corner, and thinking about *that* just made me feel old. I was also starting to get more than a little nervous, truth be told. I'd always been so sure she'd follow in my footsteps as a Fury, but she still hadn't manifested those abilities. If she didn't Fledge sometime in the next year, odds were that she never would.

And wouldn't *that* just make Jessica the happiest mother on Earth?

I scowled at my own pettiness. First of all, Jessica had cooled toward magic considerably since I used it to find Vanessa and rescue Olivia. Second, with the danger this family always found itself in, Jessica would probably be secretly relieved to learn her eldest daughter would be better able to protect herself.

I shook those morbid thoughts away, left Scott in the capable hands of my mother, and tiptoed upstairs to Olivia's nursery. The chubby-cheeked infant had a thumb shoved inside her mouth and sucked at it vigorously. I blew Olivia a kiss and softly shut her door before moving toward the end of the hall. Music thumped steadily, growing louder the closer I drew to Cori's room, but not loud enough to disturb her parents or baby sister.

I smiled affectionately. One thing you could always count on from my elder niece and that was consideration for others. Something that would come in handy during her life as a Fury—*if* she became a Fury.

There you go again, idiot. It doesn't matter either way.

Although an ugly little voice inside whispered that, at least a little, it *did*.

Annoyance had me knocking on her door more forcefully than intended. The music immediately lowered a few notches, and footsteps hurried across the room.

Cori was apologizing before the door swung fully open. "Sorry if I woke Liv, Mom—" She broke off when she recognized me. Pleasure lit her features, and she grabbed me in a bear hug. "Aunt Riss! Grandma finally got a hold of you, I see." She tugged me into her bedroom and closed the door. The neon green and purple décor remained the same as I'd last seen it a month ago, although several different celebrities lined the walls—all male, ridiculously young, and amazingly gorgeous. I recognized an up-and-coming Orpheus pop star who made the phrase *tall, dark, and handsome* so much more than a tired old cliché. Even if he *was* young enough to be my—much younger brother.

Eat your heart out, Dre Carrington.

Cori folded her arms across her chest and gave me a look borrowed from her straitlaced mother. "If I went an entire day without answering my cell, Mom would *so* ground me for a week."

My lips twitched from the warring urges to laugh or curse. Neither of which I actually did. "Good thing I'm not fifteen or living under *my* mother's roof, then, smarty-pants. Speaking of which, how's school?"

She settled atop her bed in a careless heap and gave an equally unconcerned shrug. "Same ole, same ole. Though ever since it became public knowledge you're my aunt . . ."

I arched a brow. "Yeah?"

"The mean girls who used to give me constant grief don't bug me nearly as much. Kinda nice, I guess, though it'd be better if I could intimidate them myself."

I thought back to when my sixteen-year-old self first Fledged and how I'd nearly gotten expelled taking out new-found Rage on one of my own *mean girls*. "Oh, trust me, that never ends well for newly Fledged Furies. This way you don't have to worry about possible criminal charges."

Her eyes widened. "I have *so* got to hear that story some-time." She let out a breath and her spirits deflated. "Though now I'm starting to think that's all Fledging will ever be to me—someone else's story."

"Now, Cori, you know I didn't Fledge until after I turned sixteen."

"Which *I* turn in exactly six weeks. And I haven't shown the *slightest* sign it's coming like you did ahead of time. What if—what if it doesn't? What if—what if I take after Mom and Dad rather than you?" She spat that last out as if it were a fate worse than death.

Gee, I wonder where she could have possibly *gotten that impression?*

I shoved aside the niggling sense of guilt and plopped down next to my niece, gathering her close for another bear hug. "Cori, sweetheart, you are an *amazing* person just the way you are. You are your school's star softball player, you have a fantastic circle of friends, and your family thinks the world of you. Including me. If you never Fledge into a Fury, that won't change how any of us feel about you. *Especially* me."

"But—"

I placed a finger over her lips. "No buts, young lady. All anyone wants from you is for you to be *yourself.* Whether you Fledge or not, *you* are the one we love and are proud of. You are going to grow up to be a kick-ass woman who becomes whatever it is she wants to be."

"And I *want* to be a Fury!"

I stroked her hair and sighed. "I know, sweetheart. I wanted the same thing. Let me tell you this much, though— worrying about it won't change a thing. It'll just make you into a quivering, neurotic mess. And *that* I know from experience."

She gave a disbelieving chuckle. "I have a hard time picturing *you* as a neurotic mess, Aunt Riss."

"Oh, baby girl, picture it. It's happened way more than once. Though if you tell anyone else that, I will categorically deny it."

Her laughter when I stuck out my tongue sounded much more relaxed and like her usual cheerful self. I vowed to make sure I didn't put any pressure on Cori that might make her think I'd love her any less if she *did* take after her parents rather than her aunts. Gods knew we had plenty enough to worry about in our family without taking on that stress as well.

THE SHITSTORM SWIRLING INSIDE MY FAMILY and the Sisterhood shoved every bit of remaining resistance to playing Harper's wedding planner out of my head. After reassuring myself that both my nieces were safe in their bedrooms and chatting briefly with David and Jessica, I became a woman on a mission. I would learn how to fake it enough to make it as a hoity-toity girly-girl until we could bring down a killer. And *then* I was taking my built-up vacation to clean house—I mean Palladium—with my mother. Trinity could handle things in my absence, especially with Scott's arcane muscles to back her up.

Sleeping in my bed curled up with Scott that evening, I made a mental note to contact my old pal—ha!—Dre Carrington to have my defenses upgraded yet again. Granted, there may not *be* a security measure capable of keeping out Elder Furies, what with their nifty travel power the rest of us could only lust after. Still, if anyone could, it would be the very finest in arcane security—the ones employed by Dre's narcissistically paranoid (and filthy rich) ass to keep him safe. I had firsthand knowledge of that fact, seeing as how it had been *his* sorceress who ambushed me in that elevator.

Nothing against my mother personally, but if something was rotten in the state of Furydom, I didn't want *anyone* able to break into my home and take me by surprise. Not even Elder Furies.

My helicopter brain kept whirring all night, and I got very little sleep, which meant I was up even earlier the next morning. Scott tracked me down in the breakfast nook, where I was hunkered down with coffee, low-fat bagels, and *Wedding Planning Made Easy*.

"Okay, you *look* like my delectable lover; you even *smell* like my delectable lover. But no *way* would she be reading that book and eating *low-fat bagels*. Who are you and what have you done with my Sugar Princess?"

I barely glanced at him as I turned to the next page. "Good morning to you, too."

He clutched his chest dramatically before sitting across the table. "Okay, now I *know* you're not the real Riss because you didn't throw food at—" *Splat!* A piece of cream cheese–slathered bagel hit him square in the face.

My smile would have done an angel proud. "What was that, baby?"

He wiped the food off with a growl, but the curve to his lips belied the threat in his voice. "Seriously, when did you start keeping low-fat food in the house?"

I curled my own lips, though not in amusement. "Since Trin hit the big 3-0 and decided to drag me along on her health kick."

"And you're actually going along without a fight?"

Tapping the mug holding my gourmet, full-fat, overcaffeinated beverage, I smirked. "Nah. I ran out of Pop-Tarts and haven't had time to shop. I didn't feel like hitting Dunkin' Donuts at the crack of dawn, and the bagels were stuck in the back of the freezer."

He let out a guffaw. "Okay, *there's* the woman I know and love." I couldn't help the goofy smile that settled over my face. "So really, you're actually reading that thing? Last I saw, you'd dumped it in your recycle bin."

"Yeah," I said morosely. "I'm *really* reading this thing. I have to close this case before I can help Mom figure out what's up with Nan. If learning which fork goes where and how to organize dress fittings for ten gets me access to potential suspects, then gods help me but that's what I'll do. Besides, I only have to learn enough to fake it around wedding guests while I investigate potential suspects. It's not like I'm going to be *really* planning this stuff. Harper and her sisters have that part covered."

I had another reason for giving in to the undercover wedding-planner operation, and he was sitting right in front of me. My overactive imagination the night before had delighted in reminding me over and over again that Scott had been involved with Harper, however briefly, which meant that he very well *could* be in danger from this luna-tic. The chance was slim—very slim—but not nil. I loved him too much not to do everything in my power to protect him. Besides, it wouldn't be the first time I'd gone under-cover in a role I didn't enjoy, and I doubted it would be the last.

He noticed me rubbing my throbbing knee and frowned. "Kiara's new potion not helping?"

Shit. Time for yet another deliberate misstatement. Okay, lie. "It's helping. My knee just aches when I sleep on it wrong."

He actually accepted that explanation without argu-ment. Wow. I must be getting better at hiding my true feel-ings from him. Not sure if that made me relieved or very, very sad. With everything going to hell in my life except for him, I decided to settle on relieved. I *would* tell him about my knee getting worse again and my failed attempts to self-medicate with good ole alcohol. Later.

"What's the plan for today?"

I pushed my empty coffee mug away. "First, I want to touch base with Trinity at HQ. Get her impressions from the family members she spoke to, and see if Sahana has any more findings or test results for us yet. After that, she and I need to convince Cappy that sending the two of us in undercover is, in fact, as brilliant a scheme as you seem to think." Good ole Cappy. Fortunately he'd come out of the magical trance a Sidhe clone had put him under relatively unscathed. The Sidhe clone, on the other hand, hadn't been *nearly* so lucky.

Scott gave a sudden grin. "So, how's Zalawski doing these days?"

I rolled my eyes at the mention of my archenemy on the force. Before I'd been promoted to chief of the newly formed MCU in addition to my post as Chief Magical Investigator, Trinity and Zalawski had been the mortal detectives assigned to assist my magical crime investigations. Only problem was Tony "the Asshole" Zalawski and I hated each other more than—well, more than Cats and Hounds. He'd taken great pleasure in my unwarranted suspension during Vanessa's investigation, and I'd taken even greater pleasure in transferring his ass *out* of the MCU the minute it was formed. Unfortunately for my inner sense of vengeance, though, the little weasel hit the ground running.

"He's been promoted twice in his new unit. And what a surprise he's such a frigging genius working as an under-cover drug dealer."

Scott's lips twitched, but he held back his smile. "Yeah, I'm sure acting like a sleazy hard-ass is a real stretch for him."

That brought the sunny back to my face. I grinned, marked my spot in the *Wedding Planning Book from Hell*, and focused on finishing off Trinity's bagels so we could get down to business.

Once we were both dressed (this time I went all out in my red-hot Fury leather), we headed downtown. My early bird ways meant we got there before Trinity, though not by much. She sauntered into my office soon after loaded down with a tub of low-fat yogurt and a box of granola. Granola, for gods' sake.

I wrinkled my nose. "You have *got* to be kidding me! I already ate your taste-deficient bagels this morning." Scott looked over his shoulder, saw that Trin had brought enough health food to choke a horse, and burst out laughing.

Trinity stuck her nose in the air and leaned against the doorway. "Back off, beasts. This is *my* breakfast for the week." Yeah, 'cause we were *so* in danger of attacking her over bird food. Her expression sobered. "Did your mother ever track you down?"

I nodded, expression souring. "Yeah. I know all about Nan."

Trinity jiggled the granola box. "Allegra didn't give many details, but she didn't seem overly thrilled by your grandmother's miraculous recovery."

Hel*lo*, understatement. "Long story short, Nan woke up a week ago; Oracles only 'fessed up yesterday—after Nan bitchslapped Fox Face in open Session."

"'Kay, so I don't know that much about Fury politics, but that can't have been a good thing for a former coma patient's health."

I gave a bark of laughter. "She basically challenged Ekaterina to a duel for her Lesser Consensus seat. Potentially to the death. And she refused to speak to my mother yesterday."

"I thought they were really close."

"They were. Which is part of the problem. Anyway, Mom's checking into what the hell's wrong with Nan while I work on closing this case so I can give her backup. Assuming you won't mind holding down the fort here?"

Trinity patted her shiny deputy chief badge she'd earned along with her assignment to the MCU. "I think I can manage," she remarked drily. "So, we better get our wheels on if you want to actually use up some of your PTO. Though Cappy may have a coronary from the shock when you put in *that* request."

My mouth took on a sardonic twist. "Funny you mention Cappy and shocking requests, Trin." I picked up the *Wedding*

Planning Book from Hell and tossed it at her. "How do you feel about the high-society event-planning biz?"

She scrambled to catch the book without spilling her bird food. *"Wedding Planning Made Easy."* Her eyes widened and she raised a brow. "There something you two need to tell me?" She moved the book and food to the front of her stomach and mimed a baby bump.

"Gods, no!" I burst out at the same time Scott said, "I wish!" I threw a pen at him. "No, Trin, I would have mentioned something like that *before* we reached the wedding-planning stage. Assuming I chose to make an honest man out of my baby daddy. Have you already forgotten the Addams Family proposal scene in the morgue?"

"Well, hell. Why would *you* need a wedding-planning book for *their* engagement?" She paused. "Wait. Shocking requests to Cappy. You with a wedding-planning book. I smell a sting operation in the air."

That's my girl! And where I had been horrified by the thought, she looked positively gleeful. "Think you're up to playing assistant to my J-Lo routine?"

She gave me a *Girlfriend, please!* look. "The day I can't keep up with *you* in the acting department is the day I turn in my badge."

Which, knowing her the way I did, would happen the day after I 'fessed up about my knee problems. Trinity could give a Fury lessons in the stubbornness department. Probably the reason we worked so well together.

I gestured to her breakfast-turned-fake-baby-bump. "Better eat if you're gonna. We've got a full day of autopsy reports, undercover authorization requests, and sucking up to supervisors to get going with."

"Sounds like my kind of day," she drawled before heading toward her own office.

Sadly, I didn't think she was kidding.

* * *

TURNED OUT I WAS SURROUNDED BY CRAZY
people. Captain Robert "Cappy" Peterson thought "Special
Agent Cruz's" undercover operation was an "absolutely
brilliant idea." There went my last shred of hope we'd have
to come up with some other harebrained scheme. Unfortunately (or fortunately, depending on how you looked at it), I
was slowly warming up to the idea myself.

They totally *slipped me the Kool-Aid when I wasn't looking.* Though, really, the more I'd thought about it, the better
an idea it seemed. Acting as the wedding planner meant I
could mix and mingle with the wedding guests—all potential suspects—and nobody would really think twice about
me getting a little nosy in the process. And whether the
killer proved to be a jealous ex, a would-be lover, or a racist
psycho willing to do anything to keep the couple from marrying, the wedding events should serve to rile that person's
temper something fierce.

After getting the okay from Cappy, we turned our attention back to Sahana, who'd had her hands full with an
autopsy when we went by her office that morning. She'd
cleared her lunchtime so we could discuss her opinions on
the Cat corpses now that she'd had a chance to go back and
examine everything from the perspective that all three
cases were linked. We caught up with her in an empty
interrogation room, Trinity munching on what looked like
rabbit food while we arcanes shared an extra-large pizza. I
considered offering her a piece but selflessly concluded
that would be insensitive toward her newfound healthy
lifestyle.

Once we'd demolished lunch, we turned to the grislier
subject of autopsy reports. Sahana passed out several
sheets of paper for us to review. She waited about five seconds before jumping in. Excitement lit her usually serious

features, an excitement that was contagious. *She has something!* Finally, a break in the case.

"So I went back and double-checked, but you were right that neither of the previous Jove Does had their tongues removed or catnip placed into their mouths. *However,*" she drawled à la Trinity, a satisfied smile playing at her lips, "when I viewed the magical makeup of the catnip while in Raga song, I noticed something ve-eee-ry interesting. It matched the makeup of an unknown substance, traces of which had been found in the blood of all three Cats."

I blinked. Hadn't been expecting that. "Wait, are you saying they were all poisoned?"

Scott shook his head emphatically. "The Bastai may hate catnip for what it symbolizes, but it's not poisonous to them."

Sahana set a paper with a chart full of bars and text on the table. She tapped one of the lines. "Normally, no. But this was no ordinary catnip. It appears to be a magical hybrid that I can't find in *any* of the books." She raised a finger in the air. "True that none of your vics died from this toxic-to-them catnip. The dose was way too low for that. However . . ."

She let her voice trail off dramatically. Hooked, line and sinker, I bit. "What?"

"My theory is that all were drugged with this catnip to first weaken them so they could be overpowered; and second, break down their bodies' normal abilities to regenerate upon death."

My pulse picked up speed. "Wait. Are you saying that this *catnip* is not only some kind of Kitty Cat Kryptonite, it automatically takes them from ninety-nine lives to *game over*?"

"Well, I'd have to test it on a volunteer to be a hundred percent sure—but I don't think anyone's going to rush in for *that* case study." We couldn't help chuckling at that visual.

"I was hoping you might see if Special Agent Cruz would be willing to donate some blood and tissue samples so I could compare how *her* samples respond to the catnip versus the samples from the corpses I've already tested. I don't have any Cat friends myself or I would ask them."

I jotted a reminder in my notebook. "No, Sahi, I'm sure she'd be happy to do that. And you've done *great*! We've been stumped on how the perp put their lights out permanently without decapitation or incineration."

Trinity nodded enthusiastically. "Yeah, *great* work indeed. Although . . ." She bit her lip and shot me a reluctant look.

Sheesh. Somebody *always* had to go and rain on my parade. "What?" I sounded much less eager to hear the conclusion to *that* dramatic pause.

"Well, if someone used the catnip to drug our vics, and the drug weakens Cats considerably . . ." Ah hell. I *really* didn't like where I suspected she was going with this. "Doesn't that mean that a female *could* have pulled these murders off?"

Effectively doubling our already-sketchy list of suspects. Yeah, at least she hadn't disappointed: I hated that conclusion every bit as much as expected.

CHAPTER EIGHT

IF SOMEONE BROUGHT MY IDEA OF HELL TO life and sent me there, it couldn't have been worse than my debut as Sierra Nieves, Wedding Planner to the Stars and new transplant to Boston, Mass. My first mistake had been trusting Harper's FBI associates to create my alter ego, which turned out to be even worse than my already-low expectations. She was, quite simply, a Diva with a capital D. Double D's, actually—which I was reminded of every thirty seconds when one of Harper's uncles let his gaze fall from my eyes to my overly ample assets.

Remember you're playing a role, I chanted to myself in the middle of the expensive catering venue, where five dozen of Harper and Penn's "closest" family members had gathered for the hastily arranged engagement party. That none of the Cats or Hounds had yet killed each other was a very *good* thing. That I was about to let nerves and Rage get the better of me and kill several Cats myself was most certainly a *bad* thing.

Though it sure would have made me feel better.

"That old man looks down your shirt *one more time* and I'm coming in there." Scott's voice groused through the wireless earpiece that connected me to Trinity on the far side of the room and to Scott and Cass in an undercover van down the street. We'd decided that, for this first operation, it would be best to keep the risk of bloodshed down by having Scott sit out rather than mingle as one of the groomsmen. Especially in light of the room full of uptight Banoubs already itching for a fight they couldn't (so far) indulge in. The two boys also had a bird's-eye view of whatever I saw thanks to the camera disguised as a brooch pinned to my suit jacket.

My lips twitched from the urge to laugh at Scott's comment, though Uncle Number 2 (or was he 3?) wouldn't appreciate the humor. I turned the threatened laugh into a cough. "Excuse me." I batted my eyelashes and edged away. "Frog in my throat and I really need to visit the ladies' room." *Before I Fury out and shove a frog down* your *throat.* Don Juan wannabes my ass—more like Don Lotharios.

Trinity cut me off as I made my way toward the high-end powder room, otherwise known as the ladies' room. "You trying to make a run for it already?" she asked with a smile.

"Ha. Don't I wish?" I jerked a thumb over my shoulder toward Don Juan Lothario. "I figured it wouldn't exactly be diplomatic for me to rip apart one of Harper's uncles."

"Hmm." She pretended to consider that for a moment. "You're probably right. Then again, it might liven up this joint."

Trinity *did* have a point. It was dullsville at the moment. Hounds were sticking with Hounds on one end of the room while Cats stuck with Cats on the other end, and never the twain did meet. Then again, considering that the two races had been at war for countless millennia, that might not have been such a bad thing. Just then, out of the corner of my eye, I caught sight of someone I *really* didn't want to talk to headed our way. I held out hope until she made direct eye contact and nodded. "Shit," I muttered under my breath.

"What's wrong?" Scott asked in my ear at the same time Trinity looked around and said, "What's up?"

"Don't look now, Trin, but Mama Hound coming our way at ten o'clock."

Needless to say, Trinity looked. *Mama Hound* in this instance referred to Neema Banoub, famed matriarch of the Banoub clan. She also happened to be Scott's maternal grandmother and a right royal bitch to boot. I'd been unlucky enough to encounter her a handful of times before this and only spoken with her on one of those occasions. Of course, she didn't even know that *I* was *me*. She thought that I was the Double-D Diva herself, Sierra Nieves, Wedding Planner to the Stars.

Gods, I can't even think *that with a straight face. I can't* believe *they actually thought that was a good pseudonym to run with.*

Though I *did* have to give them bonus points for snappiness. Sierra Nieves did sound like a name someone would pick if they were going to work for the stars—or in a strip club. We had wanted to craft a cover that would appeal to both the Cats and the Hounds. Most of Harper's family members were Latin Americans, as was the persona I currently wore, and she also had the benefit of being half-Hound and half-mortal, which would give me a good excuse to hang out with Scott more than might otherwise be seemly and give me something in common with Penn's family—even if they *did* tend to sneer at "half-breeds."

Of course, what would appeal *most* to the Hounds in the crowd was that she had worked with celebrities for years and was wealthy in her own right. When it came to the Banoubs, money *did* talk. Loudly. It was one of the reasons Liana had given up most ties to her family when she married Scott's father. Morgan didn't have more than two pennies to rub together when they fell in love, and that had made him a most ineligible bachelor in Neema Banoub's eyes.

Of course, seeing how well Liana and Morgan had done for themselves in the years since might have caused some of the Banoubs to rethink their actions of four decades earlier. The Murphys had become, hands down, the preeminent supernatural mercenaries in Boston, and Liana's prestigious boutique, Hounds of Anubis, was *the* place to go for arcane artifacts and odds and ends such as Kiara's magical remedies. I guess that old mortal saying that hindsight is 20-20 wasn't too far off the mark.

Trinity looked back at me and arched a brow. "Uh, I assume by Mama Hound you mean Penn's mother?"

"Grandmother," I corrected, eyes glued on the high-society maven gliding through the crowd.

"Okay, grandmother. What's so bad about her coming over to talk to us?"

I shot Trinity an *Are you kidding me?* look. "Don't tell me you've never heard of Neema Banoub? The phrase *right royal bitch* was created just for her."

Trinity's lips twitched. "Isn't that a really bad pun?"

I shook my head. "No, it's a really *true* pun. She has *got* to be the biggest bitch I've ever met, and that's saying something. And the one and only time we ever spoke did *not* end well."

Her lips twitched again. "Well, luckily *you*, Miss Sierra Nieves, have never met her and vice versa. Maybe she'll like you this time."

"Ha. You know how badly I get along with Zalawski?"

"I think all of Boston knows how badly you get along with Zalawski."

"Well, take that and multiply it by ten, and you might wind up in the neighborhood of how poorly Neema Banoub tends to get along with the unwashed masses."

Trinity couldn't hold back a snicker. "Unwashed masses? You, my dear, are *the* Sierra Nieves, Wedding Planner to the Stars. And filthy rich in your own right. Plus, you're a Hound. Why *wouldn't* she like you?"

I shook my head. "I'm only *half*-Hound. Trust me, that counts with these people. *Filthy rich* to a Banoub means counting assets in the billions, not millions. Not to mention, *the* Sierra Nieves is about as nouveau riche as it gets, which also matters to people like this." I would have gone into further detail, but Hound hearing being what it was, I let my voice trail off and waited for Neema to close the distance between us.

Trinity, perceptive as usual, began talking about the innocuous subject of head counts and the current supply of fancy-schmancy hors d'oeuvres and even fancier-schmancier cocktails being served by the tuxedoed wait staff. Technically speaking, we were the ones in charge of this party, and it was our job to discuss those little details, boring as we might find them. Boring as *I* might find them anyway. Trinity seemed to be thriving on this undercover operation.

Neema, flanked on each side by her *acknowledged* daughters—Liana's two sisters who *weren't* in the proverbial dog house, one of which I presumed to be Penn's mother, whom I'd never met—barely glanced at Trinity before turning her attention to me. Piercing golden eyes raked me up and down, found me wanting, but she deigned to speak to me anyway.

"Miss Nieves." She gave a snooty nod. "I am Neema Banoub, grandmother of the groom, and I would like to have a word with you, if you please." *Or even if you don't.*

I would have given Trinity an *I told you so* look if not for Neema's hawk-eyed gaze. No sense offending her at the

very first event of this month-long wedding extravaganza—
unless I found out she had anything to do with the serial killings in my city. Then, *nothing* would stop me from offending
her with extreme prejudice. And pleasure.

"Oh, Mrs. Banoub, what an honor to meet you. Would
you like to go somewhere a little quieter?"

She accepted my fawning air as if it were her due, and,
well, since all her life she'd been treated that way, I guess it
was. I took her single nod as acceptance of my suggestion,
murmured a pretend request to Trinity, and with a dramatic
sweep of my arm, ushered the three women through a quiet
hallway and into the little office reserved for event planners.

Once I seated them comfortably and poured each a
glass of mineral water, I settled on a plush chair and smiled
winningly. "Now then, Mrs. Banoub, please tell me what I
can do for you?"

Neema turned that supercilious look on me again. "What
you can do for *me* is make sure that little—" She bit her
tongue when one of her daughters gently touched her arm.
"Ahem. What I mean to say is that it is critically important
that this—this *affair* go off without a hitch. My grandson
may be marrying that *young lady*, but that doesn't mean I
will accept an event beneath the Banoub standards. Now,
while my grandson hired you without giving me so much as
a say in the matter, I *am* paying for this wedding and as such
expect to be kept informed every step of the way."

I opened my mouth to give a polite response, but she just
took a breath before marching on. "I've done my research,
and you come highly recommended by two of my West Coast
acquaintances."

Damn. Maybe letting Harper's FBI associates create my
fictitious persona hadn't been such a catastrophe after all.

"Because of that, I won't insist my grandson hire someone else. However, I would prefer to reach an understanding
with you. Since I will be paying for the vast majority of this

affair, I expect it to live up to *my* expectations. Which, let me assure you, will be quite high indeed."

Gods, I had a headache already. Between Harper's lecherous uncles and Penn's hands-on bitch of a grandma, I wasn't even sure Jack could get me through this month.

Still, I did my best to placate Neema. After all, she really *was* paying for most of this shindig. Keeping her pleased meant that Sierra Nieves got to keep this job—which meant I got to keep my cover, and keeping my cover meant I was that much closer to finding the Cat killer and, in turn, helping my mother kick some Fury butt. I soothed Neema and her daughters as best I could. Though, really, she only had *a few* little *concerns* and *suggestions* to ensure the upcoming *nuptials* lived up to the Banoub family name. Penn had warned me she would want to get her white-gloved hands all over every aspect of the wedding plans, so I made her think she would get the final say on every teeny-tiny detail without actually promising she would.

Over the course of the schmooze fest, Neema introduced her daughters as Zahra, the groom's mother, and Rashida, his aunt, who were charming in the extreme, although both said little in comparison to their mother. Toward the end of the impromptu chat session, Penn's mother murmured something to *her* mother about someone waiting to speak with them. They stood to leave, though—to my surprise—Penn's aunt stayed behind.

I arched a brow. "Is there something I can help you with, Rashida?"

She leaned back in her chair and narrowed her eyes slightly. "Come, let us drop the pretenses and speak frankly. *You're* a Hound." Her conspiratorial expression indicated she was conveying a high honor upon me by including me in her little club. "I'm sure you feel just as strongly as do the rest of us that this entire wedding is a disaster in waiting. We shouldn't have to sit here and pretend otherwise."

Hmm. This was an interesting side to Penn's aunt I hadn't expected to see. I decided to play along. "Oh, what a relief to find someone unafraid of cutting to the chase. I *do* have to say that in all my years of planning weddings I have seen some unlikely pairings, but this has to be the most scandalous of them all."

Rashida's slim golden necklace jingled with the force of her nod. "Exactly! You understand perfectly that one of those *creatures* shouldn't be allowed to steal away one of our best and brightest bachelors. The mere thought makes me want to vomit." Her face screwed up in a most unattractive way.

I made a polite sound of agreement and let her continue with her rant.

"The only thing I can think of is she cast some sort of spell on my nephew. He's always been such a *good* boy who knew the proper way to perform his duties to the family. I can't believe he would have fallen in love with one of those . . . *things* . . . willingly. Unless magic was somehow involved." She kept raving for the next several minutes, face and demeanor growing increasingly ugly as she did. Spittle flew from her mouth, and I began fearing for my own safety. Good thing Sierra wasn't half-Cat!

By the end, she must have realized just how ugly she sounded, because she caught hold of herself, smoothed her expression, and gave a tight smile. "You'll have to forgive me. It's just that I feel very passionately about this subject. And it's such a relief to know that we have an ally in you, Miss Nieves."

"Please, call me Sierra. And just let me know how I can help you."

Her smile grew slightly feral. "Let's just say that I would be *very* happy indeed if you found any way possible to discourage my nephew from actually going through with this farce of a wedding. Without appearing to do just that, of course, and all while maintaining the highest standards expected of a Banoub event."

Why don't you just ask for the sun and moon while you're at it, too?

"And as a token of appreciation, you can expect to receive twice whatever my mother is paying you for the wedding planning alone—whether or not he actually calls it off."

Huh. Penn's aunt was *so* against him marrying a Cat that she would pay off the wedding planner to do her best to sabotage things. Her little tirade proved she *was* more than passionate about this subject, but was she rabid enough to take the leap from sabotage to murder (or as was more likely, murder for hire) just to scare her nephew away from Harper?

One thing was for sure. Aunt Rashida was definitely going on the suspect list.

The ironic thing about people like the Banoubs was that you didn't actually have to outright agree to go along with their plans. As long as you didn't voice an objection, they just assumed that of *course* you were going along with whatever they wanted. Rashida was no different. She looked at the priceless concoction of gold and diamonds encircling her wrist. *Bet that watch costs more than I make in three months.* "For now, you'll have to excuse me. I have other matters I must attend to."

Like plotting another murder?

She stood and left the room without a backward glance. I waited until the door shut behind her and let out a deep breath. I was starting to understand why Scott had such a depressingly low opinion of his Banoub relatives. Well, other than Ellie. She wasn't quite as pretentious or obnoxious as the rest of them—not since she'd shown the exceptionally good taste of marrying my baby brother.

Speaking of Scott, I pulled out my cell from a jacket

pocket and dialed his number. Not that I didn't trust Trinity or Cass: I just wanted to pick his brain in private. After all, he *was* related to "these people." Even if most of the time he hated to admit that.

His smooth-as-silk voice sent shivers down my spine when he answered the phone, "Hey, baby." Gods, how *could* he do that to me with just two simple words?

I did my best not to let him hear just how much he affected me. "So, Murphy, what do you think?"

"I'm damned glad my mother got away from those people when she did."

"I think *that* goes without saying. But as fascinating as I find your family history, I'm talking about the actual topic at hand. You know, the whole serial killer thing."

"Well, color me biased, but I definitely think not-so-good-ole Aunt Rashida just made herself look very suspicious. Then again, I wouldn't put *anything* past, what did you call her, Mama Hound? I've heard stories about her over the years that would turn your hair gray."

I reached a hand up to my hair even though he couldn't see the gesture. "Furies don't *get* gray hair," I mock groused. "Not unless they want to."

Amusement laced his voice. "Well, how in the hell am I supposed to grow 'old and gray' with you if you don't let your hair go gray?"

Earlier lust-fueled heat turned to gooey, sappy warmth that went straight to my belly. Just when I thought he couldn't get to me any more than he already had, Scott went and proved me wrong. For now, however, I let that sentiment slide by without comment. First we had to get through this investigation. *Then* we could start thinking more seriously about the future. Well, after we dealt with his pretentious relatives, my injured knee and budding addiction, and my own family issues . . .

"Focus, Murphy!"

"Yeah, yeah, yeah. I think we should at least consider both of them, Rashida in particular. That was some hate fest she went on just now."

A very good point, and the conclusion I'd already reached, though it felt good to hear him echo it since he (theoretically) knew these people better than I did. "All right, so we'll add them both to the list. For now, I guess it's back out into the fray for me." I ended the call and crossed the room. My hand had barely closed around the doorknob when the door came flying my way. Fury instincts kicked into overdrive, and I managed to avoid a painful collision with solid oak.

"Ay, perdóname! Lo siento mucho."

Whoa. Speaking of lust spearing straight to the belly . . . five feet eight inches of sheer animal magnetism had just crossed my path. And whereas Harper's lecherous uncles had been Don Juan wannabes, the man himself now stood in front of me in all his glory. Thick, wavy black hair fell down his shoulders and made me want to run my fingers through it. His dark brown eyes reminded me of my favorite chocolate. His burnished skin was so smooth it could have made Scott envious. And that voice! It dripped with the faintest hint of a Spanish flavored accent and hinted at all sorts of naughty things. He may not have been overly tall or muscular, but da-aaa-mn.

Though I could have done without the leather-stitched man bag over his shoulder.

No sooner did that thought cross my mind than I put two and two together. Gorgeous good looks, impeccable fashion sense, a hairstyle that looked too perfect to be mere happenstance, and the man bag. This could only be Vic the Slick.

My brilliant deduction was confirmed when Scott muttered in my ear, "For crying out loud, Vic. Lose the effing purse already!"

I didn't have to channel magic to understand what Don Juan had just said. Eight years of high school and college Spanish courses (plus a semester studying paranormal creatures in South America during grad school) meant I had no trouble following along. Convenient, since Sierra Nieves was supposed to be fluent in her own right.

I steered the conversation back to English for benefit of the little ears listening in via the wireless mike. "No, no, how stupid of me to get so startled!"

He held out his hand and, to his credit, actually kept his gaze firmly on my eyes rather than my girls. "Not at all. Please allow me to introduce myself since we haven't formally met. My name is Victor Esteban, and I am Harper's man of honor. You must be the supremely talented and of course lovely Sierra Nieves." He didn't say it but I almost heard the echo, "Wedding Planner to the Stars!" in his voice.

"Oh, how wonderful to meet you finally, Victor. Harper's told me so much about you."

"All good, I hope."

"Well." I returned his flirtatious smile. "*Mostly* good."

Perfectly sculpted lips pulled back into a smile. "Now, being *all* good would be rather boring, wouldn't it?"

I ushered him inside the little office and closed the door behind him. "Is there something I can do for you, Victor? I trust that everything is going smoothly out there?" I played the role of Sierra Nieves to the hilt, smiling and twirling my hair and giving off come-hither vibes. Victor reacted tit for tat in the flirtation department. I have to admit, every time Scott made a frustrated sound in my ear, I fought back a snicker. Considering the many times he'd made me green with envy over the past few years, it only seemed fair.

Victor, every inch the gentleman, pulled out my chair before seating himself. He waved a reassuring hand. "No worries there, Sierra. Everything is going impeccably with the engagement party. My only regret is that I missed the first half."

"Oh, that's right. Harper *did* mention you were in California testifying at some sort of trial." I made my last few words sound slightly inquisitive.

He flashed another smile. "Yes, I do a lot of consulting work in the medical industry and, to supplement my income, also serve as an expert witness for corporations."

Interesting. I'd have to do a little more digging to see just what sort of medical consulting he did. Did he have an MD? That might warrant putting *him* on the suspect list, since a doctor who was also an arcane would have the necessary knowledge to best incapacitate—and permanently kill—a Cat. In this case, a *fellow* Cat.

"That sounds positively fascinating, Victor. I'd *love* to hear more about it."

"Perhaps we can get together for lunch sometime this week? To discuss my role as man of honor, of course." *Of course.*

"Are you just going to flirt with him all night or try and rule him in or out as a suspect anytime soon?" If I could have picked the sour grapes out of Scott's voice, I would have made a fortune on the resulting wine.

Still, he *did* have a point. "A good idea, since we will be working together so closely over the next few weeks to make Harper's day as perfect as possible."

"*Ay, querida*, I very much look forward to working with you." His expression sobered. "Which brings me to why I selfishly cornered you. I'm sure that, by now, you have heard of the murderer who stalks our city streets?"

"Yes, I read the headline in the *Herald* this morning. Very tragic and very scary." Yeah, and if I got hold of whoever leaked the fact the three Cat corpses had been tied together before we'd wanted that news getting out, Sahana might well have another autopsy to perform.

"Tragic indeed. I knew each one, at least in passing, and all were very fine men. It's also devastating to see what Harper is going through now." His voice thickened with emotion. "If I could get my hands 'round the neck of whoever is causing her such pain . . ."

He seemed to care for Harper an awful lot, considering he was an *ex*-lover. Then again, she cared enough about him in turn to name him her man of honor. I echoed that sentiment out loud, though less accusingly.

He smiled fondly. "Harper and I have known each other since we were little *niños*, you must understand. We actually made a try as a couple a few years ago, but *ay*. What an ill-fated attempt it was. Some people are meant to be friends rather than lovers."

Okay, that sounded reasonable, especially in light of the fact Scott had said pretty much the same thing about his dismal one-night stand with Harper. "Ohhhhh?" I drew the word out with curiosity. "So it ended badly, then?"

"Oh no, quite the contrary. We both realized our mistake and parted ways as lovers amicably." Another quick smile. "Trust me, Harper would never have named me her man of honor—even to stave off bloodshed between her sisters and cousins—had we not remained on good terms after the breakup. We make far better friends than lovers. Which is why I wish I could choke the life from whoever is causing her so much grief now."

I made an appropriately sympathetic sound.

"Now then, the reason I wished to speak with you was to discuss the matter of security."

I kept my expression politely interested. "Security? I do believe that aspect is being handled by the groom. He's paying a pretty penny to make sure no crazies have access to any of the events. Especially considering all the threats that have poured in since the engagement announcement ran in the papers." My poor Night Owls were going to have their hands full running down those threats to see if any might be credible enough to consider as potential suspects. Assuming their shift stayed as quiet as it had the past few evenings.

Victor made a sour face. "It amazes me that, in so many ways, the mortals are so much more progressive than we arcanes. Look how far they've come in racial relations over the past decades. We've had centuries to settle our differences, and yet we're still so stuck in the past."

"So you're not one of those who feel that our two kinds shouldn't mix?"

"Please. As a medical researcher, I place my faith as much in science as magic and far more on the present than the past. I say it's time to let bygone feuds become just that. Bygone."

"Indeed. Oh! What was it exactly you wanted to know about security?"

Victor frowned. "In light of the fact half of the guests will be Cats, I would like to hire on extra security as a wedding gift to Harper and Penn. Since you *are* the wedding planner, I wanted to let you know. I'd prefer not to worry the bride and groom, however."

"You think it necessary to hire on yet more security?"

"I think it would be reckless not to. The security Penn has hired will be keeping an eye out for the more obvious psychos rather than focusing on someone more subtle, like a serial killer. The Bastai in Boston are a relatively small group compared to the Hounds. The odds that the killer may choose one of the wedding guests to strike out at are not overly low."

He had a point. And the more eyes we had peeled open for danger, the better. "So who exactly did you have in mind? I would have to have complete faith in the security service you chose, of course."

"Of course. I've had a new but excellent security force

recommended to me. Alabastros is a private mercenary group much like Penn's Shadowhounds. I'll have them fax over their particulars to you. No, wait, why don't we meet for lunch tomorrow, and I can hand the information to you personally?" He leaned forward and swept my hand up in his own. "We can discuss their qualifications while getting to know each other in a more intimate setting—"

"Riss, you need to get rid of that bozo ASAP."

I gritted my teeth and resisted the urge to cuss Scott out soundly. Mustn't *break my cover. Though I am going to break* someone *a little later.*

Cass's voice sounded a half beat after Scott's, cluing me in to the fact Scott wasn't just playing green-eyed monster. "Kale and Mahina just called in. They've found another body."

CHAPTER NINE

NAUSEA HIT ME STRAIGHT IN THE GUT. NO need to ask whether or not the body belonged to a Cat. I just wondered which one of the men I'd met over the past week now lay in ruins in some run-down alleyway. And how to get rid of Don Juan gracefully.

Trinity took care of the second concern for me. She burst into the office, all smiles and apologies, babbling about some catastrophe going down. Victor took the hint immediately. He excused himself with a reminder that we really should "do lunch" sometime soon. The moment he was out of sight and sound, we scurried toward the parking lot and her shiny new Spyder. Even with panicked concern riding me, I had to take a moment to admire the sleek lines of electric-blue sex on wheels.

Once we buckled up, I asked the question I'd been fearing, "Do we know who it is yet?"

Trinity shook her head at the same time Cass spoke over the headset. "All Mahina said was we have another Cat corpse under a Dumpster just off Beacon Street."

My heart sank because that told me all I needed to know. Only one of Harper's exes both worked and played near Beacon Street, and only one had been arrogant enough to turn down any and all offers of protection. Rich and powerful—and now dead—Ward Rockefeller. Once word of *this* murder leaked out, all hell really would break loose. Not only was he a wealthy, well-connected arcane, but he also had blood ties to one of the most prominent mortal families in American history.

Well, a morbid voice inside me whispered, *guess that means we can take him off the suspect list.* While part of me hated myself for thinking that, my more pragmatic side realized that if I didn't hold on to some sense of humor in this situation, one of two things would happen. Either I would burn out like many other cops and have to quit the job that meant so much to me, or I would give in to the Rage burning in the back of my mind, rampaging through my list of suspects until I found the killer—all the while running the risk of turning Harpy

For now I had to focus on what I *could* do or I would drive myself nuts.

Trinity burned rubber *and* asphalt getting us from Back Bay to Beacon Hill in record time. Cass and Scott weren't too far behind in the undercover van although they didn't have a chance in hell of keeping up with Trin's Porsche. Brakes squealed as she slammed to a stop just short of the yellow crime scene tape blocking off curious onlookers from a narrow alleyway. I'd had the sense to shift from my Sierra disguise into partial Fury form (leaving off only the wings) on the ride over, and Trinity yanked off her wig, fake horn-rimmed glasses, and suit jacket before following me down the alley.

One thing leapt out at me as separating this scene from the others: I could tell with a single glance this had actually been the site of the attack rather than just a dumping ground for the body. I'd seen some awful crime scenes in my time, but this one made even me wince. A sizable pool of blood collected on the dirty concrete just off posh Beacon Street—the spot where the Cat had first been ambushed. Thick, crimson trails littered both the alleyway and the surrounding brick walls all the way from where we stood to a Dumpster several dozen feet in the distance. I picked my way along the ground carefully, keeping my eyes peeled for the slightest hint of evidence.

Kale knelt next to the battered Dumpster, high-powered flashlight trained underneath the half-ton container. The scattered lines of blood converged next to him and pointed the path to the body I presumed to be that of Ward Rockefeller. Reluctance to see him ripped to pieces like the others had me closing my eyes and cursing beneath my breath. It surprised me to feel sadness gripping me so tightly considering I hadn't known Rockefeller well—and hadn't liked what little I knew of him. Still, the thought of seeing the annoying but larger-than-life tycoon spread-eagle beneath the Dumpster like he was nothing more than trash himself just seemed horribly wrong.

I channeled tendrils of Rage, latching on to them like they were a security blanket. Sometimes that was the only way I could deal with the things I had to do. Hey, whatever worked, right? The only way I would be any use to Ward Rockefeller now was by pushing away my weaker emotions and focusing on the stronger ones that would help me find his killer.

Kale looked up when Trinity and I stopped just behind him. His long black hair, penchant for bright floral-print shirts, and *hey, brah* surfer demeanor caused many people to underestimate him, but when push came to shove, Kale was a damned fine police officer and no slouch in the fighting department. The only two (non-Fury) people I would trust more at my back during an investigation were Trinity and Scott.

He gave a small but sincere smile. "Hey, Chief, Nananana. You made some tracks to get here that fast."

Trinity rolled her eyes, but I knew she enjoyed the Hawaiian nickname Kale had given her in honor of her new "baby." Mahina, who came from a different island than her husband, pronounced the word more like "Lana-lana," but either way, it made me give an inward shudder. I'd not yet met the spider I liked. Unless you counted the Porsche.

I crouched beside him, steeling myself for the sight to come. "What do we have?"

Just like that, Surfer Dude disappeared. "Caucasian male Bastai apparently beaten and bludgeoned to death, though we haven't come across an obvious murder weapon. Mahina fished his wallet out of his pants pocket and ID'd him as thirty-eight-year-old Ward Rockefeller." As expected. "The perp roughed this guy up way more than the others, and that's saying something. MO seems a little off, too."

Trinity gestured to the blood and guts surrounding us. "The killer did him here and left him rather than transporting the body. Could mean his usual plan got messed up somehow."

I nodded. "Killer hears about Harper's pending nuptials and goes berserk, maybe."

"Maybe. Or he knew about the engagement party tonight and wanted to rain on their parade."

"Hey, Kale. The tongue missing again?"

He motioned under the Dumpster. "We didn't want to disturb the vic too much before you got here, other than ID'ing him. I'll leave that determination up to you, Chief."

"Gee, thanks. How thoughtful of you."

Mahina walked up and laughed. "That's my man for you. Considerate to a fault. He also has this thing about catnip."

"What, that it smells worse than skunk musk?"

She grinned my way. "Cats don't seem to mind it so much."

I pointed under the Dumpster. "I think that a few would disagree with you."

That statement had us all sobering and focusing our attention on what mattered. Examining the evidence in hopes we might find something to nail this bastard to the wall.

"Stand back," I cautioned before summoning Nemesis and Nike to life. The twin serpents hissed and twined around my arms, one moment static tattoos painted across my skin and the next living, breathing reptiles whose chaotic thoughts flooded my mind. Their tongues flicked out, in, and then out again, and negative impressions bombarded me. Apparently they didn't care for the smell of catnip any more than Kale or I did. *Tough!* I thought at them. Amusement replaced annoyance, and they responded to my request for enhanced strength.

Magic flowed through them and into me, and I grabbed hold of the half-ton Dumpster, lifted it straight up, and set it down a dozen feet from its previous resting spot. Cass and Scott finally put in their appearance. They ducked under the crime scene tape, Cass flashing his badge at uniforms as he went, and moved toward us. Somehow, just meeting Scott's gaze for a moment gave me the strength to turn back to the body on the ground and do what needed doing.

Good gods, where *did his face go?*

Bile stung my throat, but I fought back the urge to throw up. The other Cats had been maimed and torn in many places, but their faces had still been recognizable. Ward's quite simply wasn't. The skin on his face hung in bloody tatters that made me think of shredded legal documents covered in spilled ink. His eyes . . . or make that eye, since one was missing . . . dangled from its socket by a slender cord of ligaments. I actually didn't have to do anything to discover whether his tongue had been removed and replaced with catnip—his mouth had frozen wide open in terror, clearly revealing the pungent leaves stuffed inside that I could now smell clearly.

I turned from the horror and zeroed in on Mahina since she'd been the one to call us in. "Who found the body, and how did they find it under the Dumpster in the dark like that?"

She kept her voice businesslike. "Anonymous caller phoned it in from—big surprise—a pay phone just a few blocks away."

"The killer." She nodded, though I hadn't made it a question. "How long ago?"

"Just over an hour. Dispatch sent a regular unit, but when they saw the violence of the crime scene and the fact the vic was in an alleyway, they asked Kale and me to take a look in case it was linked to the other Cat murders."

Which, of course, it was. *You bloody son of a bitch. I'm going to stop you, one way or another.* Nemesis and Nike soothed me the only way Amphisbaena could, sending me mental pictures of the psycho cowering before us and covered in his own blood for a change. The Fury in me reveled in that image.

"All right, boys and girls, this asshole is really starting to piss me off. Nobody gets away with doing this to *our* people in *our own city.*" I glanced at Scott. "Vic wants to hire extra arcane security for the wedding, and after this . . . I think he's right."

My Hound didn't waste time arguing. "Absolutely right. My people can only do so much. Do you know the group he wants to hire?"

"He's faxing the information over to me. They're newly

formed, but he said they came with excellent recommenda-
tions."

"Good. Send the info my way once you get it. I'll make
sure they're up to our standards." One less thing for "Sierra"
to worry about.

I glanced back at Mahina. "Any luck running down those
threats that came in after the engagement announcement?"

She cleared her throat. "Most of them came from the
typical arcane racists and don't seem particularly credible."

I arched a brow. "*Most* of them?"

She hesitated, pursing her lips before speaking up again.
"Only one of them really sets off my creepy meter." Something we in the MCU had come to respect greatly. "It's the
most coherent of the bunch and gives away details I'd expect
only someone closely tied to either the bride or groom to
know."

"How'd it come in?"

"Not via telephone or e-mail like most of the others.
Someone went to the trouble of cutting up newspaper letters old-school-style and sending it snail mail. Gonna take
a lot more work to track down the sender."

Great. An actual viable lead and of *course* it had to come
in via the least traceable method. "You keep working that
angle and let me know if I need to request more resources
from Cappy."

She nodded. "Aye, aye, Riss."

I let out a deep breath and glanced around the crime
scene once more. The dull throb of my knee, which had
been bugging me all day, became a steady, outright burst of
pain. I cursed inwardly. Like I didn't have enough crap to
worry about without my injury giving me fits again. *Gonna
have to bite the bullet and find* someone *who can help me
fix this.*

As much as Kiara's potions and spell-worked bandages
had done for me over the past few months, they had their

limits. She wasn't a full-fledged Healer, and she wasn't a mundane MD. It was really starting to look like I needed somebody who was both. Of course, that severely limited my options since there weren't too many arcanes who could call themselves magical Healers *and* licensed medical doctors. Still, I had decent connections in both worlds. Surely I could find *someone* that could help me.

Scott picked up on my exhaustion and the frayed edges of pain around my eyes and mouth. In his typical way, he didn't bother beating around the bush expressing that fact, either. "You look like shit, Riss. Let's get you home so you can catch some Z's."

Trinity and Mahina exchanged amused glances, and Kale smirked. Wisely, though, he kept his male mouth shut.

It was proof of just how tired I really was that I didn't comment on Scott's missing tact and just nodded. After giving a few last-minute instructions to the other members of the MCU, I let Scott lead me away from the blood-bathed crime scene. We didn't speak much on the drive home in the undercover van I'd commandeered for the night, just held hands as we each became lost in our own thoughts. My mind raced, picking through the various clues and pieces of evidence we'd gathered over the past couple of weeks, trying to make sense of the senseless and decide who should be Suspect Numero Uno. The pounding of my knee didn't make that an easy task. Beating that out as a distraction, however, was my growing worry for the man sitting next to me, softly caressing my fingers with his own. The man I was learning to love more each day—even when he drove me up the wall—and that terrified me even more. The thought that I could lose him when I'd only just gotten him back . . . It made my heartbeat pick up speed. It made sweat break out on my brow. It made me feel a depth of fury I hadn't felt in months, not since Vanessa died in my arms. Losing her had been like losing a piece of myself, and with Scott, I knew it would be ten times worse. I'd lived through losing him once. Going through that again—permanently—would kill me.

Rage reared its ugly head, and razor-sharp talons exploded from my fingers without conscious intent. Scott let out a hiss of pain, and the scent of blood had my already-blurry vision going even hazier. *Shit!* I hadn't lost control like this in years—not counting my reaction to Vanessa's death.

"Uh, Riss, you okay, baby?"

The love and concern in his voice nearly did me in. Tears pricked my eyes, taking my vision from blurry to blinded, and I had no choice but to jerk the van over to the side of the road. Through my tears, I could just make out the sight of my townhouse a half-block away. Ironic that I'd steered us here on instinct and found an actual legal parking spot to boot.

My voice sounded more forlorn than I could remember when I shook my head adamantly. "No, Scott, I'm *not* okay." My breath came in quick pants as I fought to clear my vision. He pulled my hand—the one that had sliced into his—up to his face and kissed my fingers tenderly. I could see that my unexpected vulnerability touched him. His eyes glowed with tenderness and love. So much love.

More than I deserved by far.

"I understand," he said softly. "It wasn't easy to see someone we were just talking to a couple of days ago torn up like that. And so soon after Vanessa. That had to be hard for you."

I bit my lips hard enough to draw blood. "You're right, Scott. That *was* hard. But it's not what has me so worked up right now."

He tilted his head. "Then what is it, baby? How can I make it better?"

"That's just it, Scott. I don't think you can. I'm worried about *you*."

Confusion marred his features. "What are you talking about?"

I rolled my eyes. "Have you forgotten the fact you had a past relationship with Harper? You know, the woman whose ex-lovers are being brutally picked off one by one? What if the killer finds out about you and her? What if I get called to another crime scene, and instead of some anonymous Jove Doe or guy I barely know, it's you?" My voice broke.

"Riss, you know I can take care of myself."

I gave him a pointed look. "Yeah, just the way Vanessa could take care of herself. Just the way my mother took care of herself. Just like all of those Cats *should have* been able to take care of themselves. As you reminded me recently, not a one of us is infallible, Scott. Immortal we may be, but not indestructible. And that includes you."

He tried to reassure me, but I barreled on without letting him speak. "What if this killer gets you alone and drugs you? What if he does to you what he did to Ward Rockefeller and I can't stop it? Don't you know that would kill me, too?"

Suddenly, just like that, something inside clicked for me. This was exactly how my father had felt every time my mother went out on another Fury mission. This feeling was what David felt when he'd had to watch *me* follow in her footsteps and go off on my own life-risking endeavors. And this feeling was precisely the reason Scott hadn't fought harder to keep me from breaking up with him after Vanessa's disappearance, when her smarmy ex-boyfriend Dre Carrington forced Scott's family to work for him. Terror that I would share Vanessa's fate and he'd have to live with that loss.

I had no idea why this came as such a revelation to me.

Intellectually I'd always understood these things, but nothing hit you upside the head with a clue-by-four quite as hard as firsthand paranoia.

Scott pulled me across the bench seat and into the shelter of his embrace. His magic fingers trailed across the bare skin of my tattooed arms, whispering up, down, and up again. He leaned forward to press soft kisses along my forehead, murmuring comforting little nothings in between kisses that somehow managed to make me feel better.

Then again, that could have been the wakening hormones talking.

"Riss, I love you, and I *know* you love me, but remember what my trying to protect you two years ago cost us both. We lost years that we could have been together. We *have* to focus on that, on living our lives the way *we* choose to and not letting some psychopath push us into running scared to suit *his* twisted purposes."

"Scott, I don't think I'm strong enough to lose you again. Not like that. I mean, I could take it if things just didn't work out between us. It would hurt like hell, sure. But I can*not* bear the thought of walking up to a crime scene and seeing *you* beaten to a bloody pulp." My voice hitched and tears stung my eyes again.

He pulled me tightly to the warm, hard planes of his body. "Riss, if we work together, if we channel all of our resources into finding this guy, you won't have to. Besides . . ." He planted one more kiss on my head. "Nobody else knows about Harper and me. You're the only person I've told." That might have given me a warm, fuzzy feeling if he'd voluntarily told me instead of me browbeating him into it.

I pushed back slightly. "Okay, I'm glad that I'm the only one *you* told, but what about Harper?"

He shook his head. "Trust me, no way Harp went and blabbed about that to anyone. Cats *don't* kiss and tell."

I rolled my eyes. "Unlike Hounds, you mean."

He growled playfully. "I know I'd like to kiss and tell with *you* right now."

It shouldn't have been so easy for him to get me in the mood. I'd had the day from hell, and the night had only gotten worse. Feeling frisky should have been the last thing on my mind. But the magic of being with Scott was that he could get my body revved up in a way no other man ever had. I looked into his eyes and gave in to the desire burning between us. What better time than now to reaffirm our love for each other, to physically express our emotions and laugh in the face of the psycho obsessed with Harper who didn't know the meaning of the word *love*? By the enthusiastic way he led me out of the van, into the townhouse, and up to my bedroom, Scott agreed wholeheartedly.

CHAPTER TEN

TWO WEEKS PASSED IN A BLUR OF RUNNING down investigative leads that turned into dead ends, putting in appearances at wedding-related events, and keeping tabs on my family members as much as I could manage. Fast-forward to my idea of the *perfect* Saturday morning: trapped inside a high-end bridal boutique with one bride, nine bridesmaids, and her mother and aunts while figurative feathers ruffled over who should wear what dress style and one particularly pain-in-the-ass cousin complained loudly over Harper's chosen color. Though what was so offensive about midnight blue was beyond me.

Yeah, just the way I wanted to spend what should have been a rare day off.

Dear cousin Camilla cornered me for the umpteenth time when I let my guard down for five seconds, whining about how sallow "such hideously dark colors" made her skin look. I was a few straws past the camel's-back-breaking limit, so I pasted a saccharine smile onto my lips. "Sallow skin, oh the horror! We simply *can't* have that." I tapped a pen against my trusty clipboard, tilted my head to the side, and faked a sympathetic look. "Penn's sister Elliana *is* the same size as you. While she's not on the best of terms with the groom's grandmother, I'm sure she would be more than willing to step in for you. With such gorgeous dark skin, sallowness will certainly be no problem for *her.*"

Camilla's eyes widened, and she opened and closed her mouth several times before managing an uncharacteristically quiet reply. "No, that's okay, I—I'll make it work. I know a makeup artist who does wonders." She scurried away before I could make good my threat to replace her as Bridesmaid Number 6.

I couldn't help the smirk that crossed my lips. Gods, the only thing getting me through this day (other than the promise of quality time with Jack later) was the fact I was dealing with the bride's and groom's families separately: the bride's in the morning at the bridal boutique and the groom's in the afternoon at the tuxedo fitting. There'd initially been talk of having Penn's female relatives along here as well, but smarter heads had prevailed. Thank *all* the gods and goddesses. Twice.

A chuckle caught my attention. I turned and caught sight of the not-so-tall but wicked-dark and handsome Victor Esteban. He smiled, appreciation gleaming in his eyes; although, as usual, he played the perfect gentleman and kept his attention focused on my face rather than my girls. "Well played, Sierra." He nodded at the retreating back of Bridesmaid Number 6.

I allowed my smirk to shift into a self-satisfied smile. "After dealing with high-maintenance relatives like that for more years than I care to remember, I've learned there are three basic types of bridesmaids. The selfless ones who are there to make the bride's day easier, the more common bridesmaids who are there for the bride but aren't afraid to tell it like they see it, and the temperamental prima donnas like Camilla who will bitch and moan about every tiny detail having to do with them. Funny thing, though. The moment you mention replacing them as a bridesmaid they suddenly become all sunshine and roses."

Vic stepped closer, and his shoulder pressed against my arm. Tiny sparks of heat flashed from his body to mine. I flushed at the sensation. Seemingly unmoved, he glanced down at the clipboard in my hands. "Well, color me impressed. Care to organize my life a little? I am absolutely hopeless when it comes to that sort of thing." He gave a heavy sigh. "Though you are obviously so busy you may not be able to fit me in. Don't you allot for any *me* time in your schedule?"

I rolled my eyes. "Don't think I've had any of *that* since I started establishing my clientele here in Beantown. If I'm lucky and we manage to finish on schedule here, though, I may actually get to enjoy an hour or two for a real, live lunch."

He gestured to the bride and nine bridesmaids in various stages of undress around the large fitting area we had claimed for our own. "Harper choosing a color and fabric but allowing each woman to select her specific dress style was a stroke of genius."

I glanced around and nodded. "True, that's becoming a trend among some brides. I actually love the practice because it takes away the worry of offending any bridesmaid who might not have the right body type for a particular style, while at the same time retaining the sense of cohesion and theme most brides aim for." Yes, I had studied my wedding planner's guide well.

His dark eyes smoldered as they peered into my own

again. "Well, if things go as smoothly when Harper tries on her gown as they are going with the bridesmaids, perhaps you *can* steal away an hour or two for yourself—and me. Lunch at the eatery of your choice, my treat."

Damn, this man was sexy. The chemistry between him and *Sierra* practically sizzled in the air. If it weren't for the fact I knew Scott was listening in on the wireless headset, I might have allowed myself to sink a little further into Sierra's persona and flirt like hell in return. One small favor from the gods, at least. Scott was so busy running a background check on Vic's new security force that he hadn't made any jealous jabs at *Vic the Slick* yet.

As conflicted as I felt over my attraction to Victor, I couldn't pass up the perfect opportunity to grill him for more information. While he wasn't at the top of my suspect list, I couldn't afford to discount him completely. Plus, as not only one of Harper's exes, but a current close friend, he could provide a treasure trove of valuable information not readily available elsewhere. The sudden rumbling of my stomach made the decision for me.

I tapped the pen against my clipboard again and gave a sunny smile. "I think I just might take you up on that offer, Mr. Esteban."

He responded to the flirtatiousness in my voice with a smile of his own. Just at that moment, however, a loud spatter of Spanish intermixed with English broke out across the room. We both whirled and saw—what a shock—Camilla exchanging heated words with Harper's youngest sister, Marisol. I let out a vexed noise and started to move over to break up the fight.

Victor laid a hand on my shoulder before I'd gotten more than a step away. "Allow me." He rolled his eyes in a mirror of my own gesture moments before. "Camilla may be a pain in the ass, but she also has a slight infatuation with me." He nodded toward Harper. "The consultant's bringing over Harper's gown now, and I know you'll be of more use to her than I will."

I could have kissed him then and there for saving me from going another round with Bridesmaid Number 6, but he was already halfway across the room so I stepped over to the blushing bride instead.

Although, from the gritted teeth and tight-lipped expressions on the faces of all four women, Harper's red cheeks were more likely due to anger or frustration than excitement over trying on the gown in which she'd say the words "I do" to her hunk-a hunk-a burning love. I swooped in, gathering the gown in question from the intimidated bridal consultant hesitating in the face of bristled Cat fur, and swept Harper toward the nearest changing room.

The wedding gown Harper had ordered the week before and had rushed here at great expense looked worth every single penny. Since we were less than two weeks away from the big day now, we had our fingers crossed it would fit well enough to only need minor alterations. My thoughts were so what a *real* wedding planner would think and so far from what *I* would normally think that I couldn't help shaking my head and smiling. Obviously, Trinity's enthusiasm for undercover work was rubbing off on me. I was really losing myself in this role and, unexpectedly, enjoying myself more than anticipated.

My gaze fell upon Victor across the room. He and *Sierra* had been spending an *awful lot* of time together lately—when Scott had been preoccupied with a high-maintenance client of his and I couldn't find the heart to turn Victor down. I'd open my mouth to say "No" and he'd touch my hand and somehow I'd find myself saying "Yes" instead. All part of my carefully crafted cover story, I told myself. *Suuuuure it was.*

Harper gave me a grateful look as I rushed her away from her bickering mother and aunts. She tucked an arm in mine, all but scurrying along beside me when her relatives burst into furious Spanish again. Either they'd forgotten I could understand every word they said, or they simply didn't care who heard them arguing in their language of choice. Once Harper and I stepped into the oversized closet of a room and closed the door, she collapsed into a cushioned chair. I gave her a sympathetic look. "That bad?"

She gave a huffy breath. "Worse. I would *so* prefer to elope, but both our families would disown us for sure. Especially considering the hot water we're already in for 'marrying beneath' ourselves and 'sleeping with the enemy.' If I have to listen to that selfish cow bitch about midnight blue making her skin look bad *one more time*, I just might say *to hell with it* after all and ride off into the Hawaiian sunset with Penn. Alone. Blissfully, blessedly, alone." Her eyes took on a dreamy cast. "Mmm, Hawaii. Can't wait to see those gorgeous sunsets Mahina told me about. That's the only thing getting me through this nightmare."

"Take me with you?" I quipped.

She smirked. "Not on your life. It's gonna be just Penn, me, and the heavenly beachfront property he's rented for the honeymoon. One of the few benefits to marrying a Banoub." She let out another huff. "Bast knows I need to focus on the upsides right now because the downsides more than outweigh them."

"That what your aunts bitching about?"

"Them, my mother, my uncles, just about anybody with the slightest claim of blood or affection to me. I've heard countless reasons why I shouldn't be marrying one of *them* from dozens of people who know nothing about *him*. Or how freaking amazing he makes me feel. The way everyone's carrying on, you'd think we're some modern-day Bonnie and Clyde committing the crime of the century getting married. That we're vowing to *burn, pillage, and plunder* rather than *love, honor, and cherish*." She shook her head. "I envy you and Mutt."

I blinked. "*You* envy *us*?"

"Hell yeah. Things are a *lot* less complicated for you two. Your family and his haven't been sworn enemies for the past few thousand years. If you post an engagement announcement in the papers, death threats aren't going to pour in like crazy. I can tell how much you love each other, and nobody thinks less of either of you for that. You don't have to keep secrets from each other, either. You're like open books in your relationship."

"Yeah, sure, open books." Hopefully my voice didn't sound as unconvincing as my inner thoughts did. I considered her words and realized that, in some ways, she was right. Scott and I were lucky that our arcane races hadn't been at brutal odds for thousands of years. Contrasting that to Harper and Penn, our relationship *did* seem uncomplicated: until you threw in not so little considerations like my worsening knee, growing dependence on alcohol to get through the days, and my continued failure to find Scott's missing brother . . .

For a moment, I found myself envying *her.* Then thoughts of the serial killer preying upon her ex-lovers crossed my mind, and I winced.

I turned my attention back to the uncomplicated task at hand: adjusting the folds of Harper's ivory gown so we could open the door for the big reveal of the bride in all her glory. And glorious she truly looked. The bell-capped, corseted bodice hugged her curves in all the right places, and intricate beadwork grew progressively heavier from the top of the gown as it worked down to the cinched-in waistline. The A-line skirt of the gown, in contrast, was starkly simplistic for the most part, with just a light dusting of beadwork along the gown's short train.

Harper stared at herself in the mirror, mouth falling open and tears glittering in her eyes. She truly *was* a breathtaking bride.

My voice sounded suspiciously husky when I spoke again. "Forget about everything else for this one moment, Harp. What's important is that you and Penn love each other and are pledging that love in front of all the gods and goddesses." A few tears leaked out and trailed down her cheeks, sparkling in the bright overhead lights like diamonds setting off her beauty. "And damn, you look so freaking amazing; you are going to make that selfish cow seem so sallow in comparison she'll bitch about the wedding pictures for decades to come!"

That had Harper bursting into laughter, reaching back, and catching my hand in her own. She squeezed. "Thanks, Riss. I know we got off to a shaky start and we haven't been friends that long, but everything you're doing for me really means a lot. I'm not sure how I can ever thank you properly."

"Don't be ridiculous. Without your help, I never would have tracked down Vanessa in time to say good-bye and save Olivia." And dammit, now she had tears pricking at *my* eyes.

She smiled slightly. "True, but working on *that* investigation was a lot less sucktastic for me than this one is for you. I'm not sure I could handle my family if I wasn't related to them by blood, and as for Penn's family . . ." Her voice trailed off, and she gave an exaggerated shudder. One I wholeheartedly wanted to echo.

"Come on now, let's show you off. You're gonna knock their socks off."

And hopefully afterward, over lunch, Vic could help me fit enough pieces together that I could knock the socks off the Cat killer—permanently.

* * *

"WELL, CHIEF, YOU *SURE* HAVE EXPENSIVE tastes!" Cass's voice quipped in my ear as he got a bird's-eye view of my surroundings through the ever-present—and fake—brooch pinned to the lapel of my designer jacket.

He *did* have a point; although, more accurately, *Sierra* was the one who had chosen the upscale Italian restaurant in which to allow Victor to wine and dine her. Mc. Whatever. Had my cover been a mortal planner for the rich and famous, I'd have been stuck munching on the rabbit food required to maintain my svelte disguise, but fortunately for me she was a Hound. Meaning plenty of cheesy pasta, garlic bread, and all the cannoli I could eat!

Victor smiled across the candlelit table, forking up a good portion of that cheesy pasta from his plate. "I have to say your impeccable taste continues to impress me. You've just introduced me to my new favorite *ristorante*."

I gave a careless shrug. "It's hard to find a *bad* restaurant in the North End, but Rigazzi's is certainly among the best. Though in the interests of full disclosure, I *am* related to one of the chefs by marriage, so I got the inside scoop before I moved here."

"And what *did* bring a successful event planner all the way from La-La Land to humble Boston, Mass.?"

"What usually causes someone to completely uproot themselves and trek across the country?" My shrug this time was fatalistic. "*Love*." I gave a sour spin to the word.

He clenched his fingers around the fork. "You have a boyfriend already? I'm crushed."

"*Had* a boyfriend. Until I came across him indulging in a little—shall we say—coed naked filing with his trampy little secretary. A *mortal*, no less, and *such* a cliché."

Victor shook his head, sympathy followed by outrage on my behalf washing across his face. "What a *pendejo*. To cheat on someone so alluring with a lowly subordinate." Sadness replaced outrage, and he touched his glass with a wistful expression. "I lost someone very precious to me not that long ago. I would give anything to have Sylvia back now. That your man did not feel the same means the *pendejo* did not deserve you, *querida*."

I stared down at my pasta plate, allowing vulnerability to leech into my voice. "You're right, he didn't. And *I* didn't deserve to give up so much only to lose it because of him. They say that living a good life is the best revenge, and I agree. So I busted my butt to establish an illustrious clientele here while still consulting for my Hollywood patrons on the other coast." A tight, pleased smile passed my lips. "And the *pendejo* mysteriously lost a good third of *his* illustrious clientele from *both* coasts."

He gave an appreciative chuckle, then raised his wineglass toward me. "A woman after my own heart. Another appropriate mortal saying in regards to vengeance is that it's a dish best served cold. Here's to cold dishes and living a good life." I clinked his glass with my own, and we grinned at each other.

"So. Tell me more about yourself, Victor. All I know other than the fact you're very charming is that you act as an expert witness in the medical field."

"I'm sure you'll find it as painfully boring as everyone else does, but I'm a nonpracticing MD involved in research and development on a consultant basis. As you mentioned, I fill my résumé out by serving as an expert witness in malpractice lawsuits."

"That doesn't sound at all boring. Though what exactly is your field of expertise?"

"I focus on the pharmaceutical end of the industry." My breath caught in my throat, and I leaned forward. Could he be an expert in blending mundane plants with arcane—like a heretofore unknown brand of magical catnip? "Mostly developing artificial drugs meant for the treatment of serious diseases such as AIDS, cancer, and diabetes. Did you know that arcanes are over sixty-five percent more likely than mundanes to develop diabetes later in their lives? Many believe that's because here in the mortal realms, arcanes are eating diets that are even worse for them than mortals, and the need for drugs to effectively treat diabetic arcanes is growing."

He gave a self-deprecating laugh. "Told you it was excruciatingly dull." Cass made snoring sounds in the headset, and I had to bite my lips. Vic must have seen them twitching because he touched my hand with his. "You have a lovely smile, Sierra. One of the things that most attracts me to you." His dark eyes smoldered, and my skin physically tingled where he touched it. It was strange how physically attracted I felt to him, even when I knew without question that my heart belonged to a certain Warhound.

Scott joined in with his two cents. "I don't know *how* he gets any play with those tired old lines of his. But much as it pains me to admit, it's highly doubtful he's our guy."

Frustrating that I couldn't ask it myself, but Cass took pity on me. "Why not?"

Computer keys started tapping from Scott's open mike. "Been doing some digging on Vic. He had an alibi for the time that the first Cat was murdered, and it's doubtful he could have had time the other night to get from the airport to Beacon Hill, beat the snot out of Rockefeller, head back home near BU to spruce up, and make it to Back Bay in time for canapés. Dammit."

I heard the words in my ears, some part of my mind even registered them, but my attention was focused on Victor's bedroom eyes and full, kissable lips. The warmth where our hands touched had to be one of the most erotic sensations I'd ever experienced. Which, considering the fact my official lover could hear and see everything I could at that moment, should have had me squirming with guilt. And yet, oddly it didn't. I fumbled for something to say or do and came up empty. Victor leaned forward slowly, almost as if he was moving in for a kiss—but was just moving in for a closer look at the wine list. Scott's low growl through the headset showed he was finally taking the Cat as a serious threat. Which made Victor push back and frown.

"What was that?"

I blinked dazedly. "I—ah, what?"

"I just heard some sort of buzzing sound—are you still wearing your headset?"

My hand touched the slim earbud and a guilty expression crept across my face. "Oh, yeah. Didn't bother taking it out since we're heading straight to the tuxedo place after this. Must have been interference from a cell phone just now." I deliberately pressed the *mute* button on the device. Now, they could still hear what went on around me, but their inconvenient and ill-timed comments couldn't make Victor suspicious. "There, power off and problem solved."

Fortunately for Victor's personal safety and my relationship, the hot and heavy moment between Cat and "Hound" had been ruined. He caressed my hand before turning back to his lunch, and I gave an inner sigh of relief. True, he was now even lower on the suspect list, but the last thing I wanted to risk was blowing my cover. It only took one person blabbing to the wrong person at the wrong time to bring everything tumbling down like a house of cards.

And unfortunately, I spoke from firsthand experience.

CHAPTER ELEVEN

EXPECTING THE AFTERNOON TO GO MORE smoothly than the morning had been incredibly naïve of me, something I couldn't claim to be very often.

Victor walked me from the North End to the formal-wear shop just inside Chinatown where Mama Hound planned to hold court over the selection of tuxedos. Since she was footing the bill for the tuxes—and most everything else—there'd been no way to dissuade her from attending what *should* have been an all-male (besides me) event.

Not that I hadn't tried.

The first sign the afternoon was going to lead to large amounts of self-medication that evening came when Victor ushered me across the store's threshold. An unsmiling, tight-lipped Scott met my gaze from the corner where he stood with the other groomsmen. Other than a slight bobble as I walked across the room, my composure didn't crack. I pulled Sierra's persona around me like well-wrought armor and prepared to do battle. Shame sparked where it had failed to earlier. Victor was *so* not my usual type that the chemistry between us kinda freaked me out. Granted, he was handsome as hell and dripped enough sex appeal to make a movie star jealous, but still. Was my stupid unconscious mind trying to tell me something? Was it my Fury nature rearing its unbridled head? Was it panicking at all the wedding brouhaha going on around me? *Oh please. Just because Harp is marrying* her *Hound doesn't mean you have to rush off to do the same thing.* Or could I just be overthinking things? I'd shared powerful chemistry with men other than Scott before, so was it such a shock to have it happen again? I just had to play things as cool as possible. Once this case was over, I'd go back to being *me*, Sierra would die a quiet death, and Victor would be none the wiser. I had *nothing* to worry about.

And maybe if I told myself that often enough, it might start to ring true.

Scott didn't speak when I stopped in front of the gathered groomsmen, just narrowed his eyes when Victor stepped up beside me. *Oh hell. Could this* get *any worse?*

Yes, yes, it could.

The "dulcet" tones of Neema and Rashida Banoub sounded from the back of the store. I mentally gritted my teeth, gathered up the groomsmen, and herded them toward the voices. *Please, gods and goddesses, let Penn be there already.*

For once, luck was with me. A resigned-looking Penn stood on a pedestal while his grandmother and aunt criticized a harried-looking tailor as he fiddled with Penn's tuxedo. His mother—obviously the submissive personality of *that* group—sat on a cushioned bench watching the fireworks. Despite her demure pose, something about her expression when she caught sight of Victor had chills rushing down my spine. If looks could kill, Victor wouldn't have to worry about the serial killer at all. I reconsidered my opinion of Zahra as a nonthreat. Maybe Neema and Rashida *weren't* the only Banoubs in the room to watch out for . . .

Speaking of the Banoubs, Mama Hound and her Alpha Daughter noticed me and beckoned imperiously. I shot apologetic looks at the groomsmen (and man of honor) before rushing over to soothe ruffled feathers. It was easy to lose myself in the mundane task of supervising the tux fittings for the next couple of hours, especially since that meant not having to think about sexy devils like Victor, fuming lovers like Scott, and the growing pain in my knee from all the torture I was putting it through. After three hours standing at the bridal boutique, walking to and from the North End for lunch, and another two hours here, disguising my pain from everyone else—especially Scott's watchful gaze—was becoming harder than expected.

As the hours ticked by, however, Penn turned my attention from my knee to his increasingly erratic behavior. He blew up at his grandmother and aunt midway through his fitting and engaged in a very loud argument with them—something I'd *never* seen him do. Usually he remained excruciatingly polite and respectful toward them. Seeing him verbally eviscerate them caught everyone off guard, even the tyrants themselves. His snappish attitude extended toward his three youngest cousins when they started goofing off, though really, who could blame men in their early twenties for getting bored after two hours of mostly standing around doing nothing? Apparently Penn could—and he did, quite vocally. I finally stepped in and escorted him to a smaller changing room to calm down. I had just about succeeded when his body stiffened and he glared over my shoulder at whoever had entered the room.

"Sorry, Sierra, but Mrs. Banoub asked me to fetch you. Something about the cummerbunds not being the exact

shade of blue as the bridesmaid dresses." I started at the
sound of Victor's amused voice and then had to wonder
why Penn looked so pissed off at the sight of his wife's man
of honor.

Victor hesitated at the entryway. Penn growled loudly
enough to put Scott to shame, muttered what sounded very
much like a heated insult in Egyptian-flavored Arabic, and
stalked away without even looking at me.

Whoa, something *struck a nerve right there.*

The question, then, was whether all the stress was getting to Penn—and Victor was a visual reminder of the
killer making his life a living hell—or whether I needed to
take a closer look at him *and* his mother.

Victor barely moved aside in time for Penn to storm past.
Looking sadder than I'd ever seen him, Victor watched the
other man stomp down the hallway toward the main fitting
area. Always a sucker for a man in touch with his sensitive
side, I patted his shoulder. "Sorry, I'm sure he's just stressed
out. Prewedding jitters and all that jazz."

He sighed and shook his head. "I'm afraid there's more
to it than that, *querida.*"

I tensed my body. "I didn't know there was bad blood
between you and the groom." If Harper had left out such an
important piece of info, she and I were going to have one of
my famous little "chats."

"Not between Pennington and me directly." Victor gave
me a serious look. "What I tell you now must go no further. I
wouldn't want Harper to think I was trying to come between
her and the man who brings her so much happiness."

"Of course."

"Harper wasn't the first Cat that Pennington had a secret
relationship with."

Okay, that came as a surprise, sure, but didn't explain the
Dr. Jekyll and Mr. Hound 'tude Penn suddenly had going on.

"When his old flame decided she'd had enough of dating

a Hound incognito, she left him for one of her own race, a former boyfriend. Pennington became furious after he found out and barged into her home to confront her—and found her new lover there. Needless to say, fur flew, and at the end of it all, the Banoubs paid a pretty penny for the cover-up and hospital bills."

Now *that* could certainly explain the *Hulk, smash* routine.

Dammit! I was supposed to be narrowing down my suspect list, not adding to it. And I liked Penn. He and Harper had a good thing going (other than the serial killer and their pain-in-the-ass relatives), and I didn't want to be the cause of bringing that to a screeching halt. Which investigating— and arresting—the groom-to-be would sure as hell do. *Gods, I need some Excedrin. And Jack. Lots and lots of Jack.*

I'd make my dearly departed alcoholic father proud yet.

Not the time to think about the skeletons in *my* closet. "So the Banoubs have reason to resent Cats for hurting one of their own."

Victor paused before laying a hand on my arm. "No, *querida*, the Cat didn't hurt one of their own. Pennington sent his old flame's lover to the hospital with so many broken ribs it's a wonder he didn't damage anything vital."

Oh, lovely. Now I really *would* have to seriously consider Penn as a suspect. And if I found out he was guilty, risk losing the new friend I was coming to care about so much. Even if she *had* slept with my boyfriend once upon a time.

Some of my unease must have shown, because Victor drew me into his arms and rested his cheek against my forehead. He leaned in to kiss me.

It was ridiculously hard to tug away from his embrace, but I somehow found the strength to do just that. "V-Vic." Gods, was that *my* voice sounding so shaky and uncertain? "We can't do this."

Disappointment crossed his face. His fingers tightened on my arms, but then they relaxed and he nodded. "You're right. Anyone could walk in and you're working. I'm sorry. I shouldn't have taken advantage of you like that."

I latched on to the excuse he provided. "Y-yes, exactly. I can't afford to alienate clients like the Banoubs. And if Mama Hound walked in here right now . . ."

He let out a loud bark of laughter. "Mama Hound? Oh, that's so appropriate for her."

My hands couldn't resist touching his arms once more before I pushed away and moved to the empty doorway. I ignored the sense of cold and loss that washed over my skin when it was no longer in contact with him. *What the hell, Riss? Maybe you're getting in way too deep here. You are* not *Sierra Nieves, and you do* not *want Victor Esteban.*

No matter *what* twisted signals my body might be sending out . . .

THE REST OF THAT AFTERNOON PASSED BY in a merciful flash. One by one, Mama Hound pronounced each groomsman's tuxedo satisfactory, and the men scrambled off as quickly as they could, until only Penn, Victor, and Scott were left. *That* could have led to big trouble in little Chinatown if not for the fact that Scott had already agreed to escort Penn to meet Harper and the bridesmaids at the already-in-progress cake and food tasting. Something that I got to sit out of, thanks to Trinity.

Scott's eyes threw daggers Victor's way and sent sparks skittering down my spine when he shot me a heated glance before following Penn outside. I looked down at my trusty clipboard, pretending to write down some all-important note, but really stalling long enough to make sure Scott wouldn't get the chance to blow our cover by confronting Victor. *And to think I once thought it would be hot to have two men lusting over me at the same time . . .*

Not so much. More like a big, huge pain in the ass. Especially considering one of them only wanted a fake "me" that didn't exist, and the other should damned well know none of this was real. No matter *how* it might sometimes feel.

Victor held the door open for me and followed me out into the late afternoon sunshine. I blinked until my eyes adjusted. My knee gave a very loud protest when I carelessly stepped down onto the sidewalk, and I barely managed to hold back a girly squeal of pain. Victor's hand latched on to my upper arm to steady me. I smiled gratefully, caught once again by the sheer magnetic heat that poured from his body to mine whenever we touched.

"Careful there, *querida*. Now then, the gentleman in me insists on seeing you home safely. Especially in light of the arcane killer prowling our fair city's streets."

Well, *that* would prove awkward—my cover didn't extend to having a fake apartment set up for visitors to see. I sure as hell couldn't let him take me back to my own townhouse in Cambridge and risk a nosy neighbor screwing things up. Neither could I let him know that Cass waited just down the street in the van to take me back to the PD so I could go over the day's events with Trinity once she finished up at the cake and food tasting.

"That's very—noble of you, Victor, but really, it's not necessary."

His lips took on a stubborn set that reminded me of Scott in one of his moods—or myself, come to think of it—and I floundered for a valid reason he couldn't take me home. Cass came to my rescue. "Tell him you're meeting another client downtown."

I could have kissed him—though no way Scott would have looked past *that* one. Before Victor could insist, I smiled and patted the hand still resting on my arm. "I'm headed back downtown to meet another client."

Victor's features relaxed into an easy smile. "Absolutely. At least let me walk you to the train."

Cass's voice buzzed in my ear. "I'll circle Boylston until you get rid of the alley cat."

I resisted the urge to roll my eyes. Scott had apparently been talking to my rookie way too much.

We engaged in interesting but unimportant banter during the ten-minute walk, until something occurred to me. With his medical degree and contacts in the arcane and medical fields, he could well provide the answer to my current debilitating pain problems. Surely *he* knew of someone, preferably several someones, who straddled both the magical and scientific communities the way he did.

I opened my mouth to pose that burning question, then remembered that little ears were listening to our every word and hesitated. True, it was just Cass listening right now rather than Scott or Trinity, but still. This wasn't something I was ready to share with others just yet—especially not those closest to me. Those who would worry the most . . . not to mention try to talk me *out* of rushing to my mother's aid the minute this case was closed.

My left hand reached up toward the headset controls and hovered for a moment as guilty conscience warred with pride. Pride won out, and I shut off the mike *and* the earphones this time. I practiced my apology in my head, *I'm sorry, not sure what caused the technical difficulties. They just stopped working.*

Scott might not buy it, but Cass would—if he wanted to stay in the MCU for any particular length of time. Besides, not like anything was going to jump out and attack us between here and the Boylston T (what most Bostonians called our subway system) stop. Though, if they did, I could more than handle things, especially with a Cat by my side.

"Victor, I've been wondering . . ."

He tilted his head and smiled. "What deep thoughts have you been pondering in that pretty head of yours?"

"A . . . friend of mine"—yeah, that was smooth—"has a medical condition that several arcane Healers have attempted to treat and failed. A strictly mundane doctor would have even worse luck treating her condition, but she is growing desperate to find a treatment that will, if not cure her condition, at least alleviate her pain. I—I hate to see her suffer so, and I wondered if there might not be other arcanes like you. Arcanes with medical degrees who could help her."

His expression became suitably solemn. "It is hard indeed to watch those we love suffer. What a good friend you are for wanting to help her. I *do* know several practicing arcane physicians who could certainly be of more use to her than me."

My pulse picked up speed, and I squeezed his hand tightly. "Oh, Victor, I can't tell you how much that would mean to me! And to her."

By this point, we had reached the entrance to my T stop. He pulled me into an empty store alcove and jotted down several names and numbers on the back of a business card. "I can vouch for any one of these physicians, although they do, of course, have different specialties. Your friend will need to call each to find out if they correspond to her specific condition. Even if none of them do, they will be able to recommend others just as capable." He pushed the card into my hand, then brought my fingers up to his lips and brushed a kiss against each one.

Gods, but he was hot *and* sweet. Such a devastatingly heady combination. Part of me screamed that it was wrong, but another part of me just couldn't help reveling in the sensation.

"I don't know how I can thank you for this."

His smile grew wolfish. "Have dinner with me tomorrow night and we'll call it even."

I laughed, trying to think of a polite way out of it without breaking my persona as Sierra. Then he kissed my hand again, and refusal became the last thought on my mind. "Of course. That's a small price to pay for the gift you've given me. And my friend."

He dropped my hand and gave my lips a quick brush with his own. "And now, *querida*, I really should let you get to your appointment. I've risked your professional reputation one time too many today."

If you only knew the truth!

"Again, thank you so much for these names, Victor."

"Until next we meet, then, sweet Sierra, allow this to serve as a token of my affections." He reached into his ever-present "man bag" and withdrew a single long-stemmed, bloodred rose, pressing it into my hands with an intense smile.

Okay, despite the fact that roses usually made my allergies go haywire, I couldn't help the electric pulse of pleasure his simple (if not particularly original) little gift inspired. As I smelled the rose, I felt clearer all of a sudden. Stronger. Refreshed. He watched while I walked off in a daze, feet barely touching the ground and a goofy smile on my face. The farther away I got from him, though, the more I found myself regretting accepting his invitation for dinner. Sure, I'd been playing the role of Sierra—who had no reason *not* to accept his advances—but for a few moments I'd been enjoying the idea as much as the real Sierra would have. If, you know, she existed. Now, separated by physical as well as temporal space, the thought of dining with the too-slick-for-words Cat didn't seem nearly so attractive. I mean, he couldn't compare with Scott in a *million* years.

I decided to find a way to break the "date" later, headed toward the subway turnstile, and ducked down the hallway to the exit where Cass was supposed to meet me. That reminded me I'd never turned the wireless back on, so I reached up to do just that. The sound of footsteps scraping along the concrete in my wake made me postpone my shift back into partial Fury form. No rush anyway. I could just as easily switch inside the van. Unease pricked my skin when I heard a door slam shut somewhere ahead. Odd. This narrow hallway led straight to a one-way exit onto the street, and nobody had passed in front of me.

The unmistakable stench of sulfur teased my nostrils, and I froze. Harpy. At least one in front of me, if not another behind. I couldn't be sure since the odor came from only one direction. Victor's rose fell from my hand as I thought, *What the hell? Why would Harpies be following* Sierra?

The logical answer was they wouldn't. Not unless my cover had somehow been compromised. In which case, worrying about blowing it by shifting was an entirely moot point.

Instinct had saved me more than once, and right now it screamed at me to shift; so I did. Fury magic washed away Sierra's form in an instant. Shimmering charcoal hair whipped around my head in the slight magical breeze shifting always summoned. Nemesis and Nike slithered their way along my skin, changing from ink-drawn tattoos into living, breathing reptiles. They sent questioning thoughts my way at being summoned in a dimly lit hallway that stank of Harpy, and I flashed back images of a potential ambush. And proving themselves to be the perfect familiars for me, that possibility excited rather than worried them. Their eagerness transferred to me, and I started moving forward again.

I neared the steep flight of stairs leading to the exit below and paused, trying to determine whether the footsteps behind me belonged to a Harpy like the ones coming up the steps did. Still impossible to tell. I would prefer the odds stacked against me to the alternative—having an innocent mortal stumble across a Harpy and Fury catfight.

Though, really, if a Harpy had accepted another contract against my life when their new queen, Serise, had sworn lifelong friendship with me (though not the Sisterhood as a whole), she and I were most definitely going to have words.

Inspiration struck, and I shifted to full Fury form— adding the ridiculously large wings to the shimmering hair, glowing green eyes, and Amphisbaena. Magic stirred at my command, forming a sudden draft of air that helped me launch straight up. I twisted my body to look behind to find out whether I was being trailed by friend or foe—only to find out the cavalry had arrived before I'd even known I needed it.

Relieved, I floated back to the ground a dozen feet away from the woman striding along the corridor. Matching charcoal hair, red leather uniform, and Amphisbaena tattoos worked into her skin marked her as another Fury, although her tattoos were emerald-hued where mine were crimson. She stepped a few paces closer, and I saw her clearly enough to recognize her as someone I actually knew. An African-born Megaera who had trained closely with Vanessa. A heartbeat later I placed her name.

"Gods, Durra, am I glad to see you." I angled my body so my back faced my sister rather than the Harpy now running full-tilt up the staircase. The yellow-eyed, white-haired skeletal woman burst over the top of the stairs and scurried our way. I shifted slightly to the left and gave a warning. "We have compan—"

Agony exploded in my back, and I staggered forward, eyes widening in shock as spell-worked silver exploded through my shoulder. Pain and confusion increased, and I tried to figure out how the Harpy had gotten behind me fast enough to stab me in the back without my sister stopping her. And that's when unpleasant reality intruded. The Harpy hadn't tried to kill me—my sister Fury had.

CHAPTER TWELVE

DAMNED GOOD THING I'D MOVED INCHES TO the left just before she struck, or her immortal-killing blade would have sliced through my heart and done just that. Killed me.

Nemesis and Nike put two and two together a heartbeat before I did and launched themselves in the air toward Durra. Her own Amphisbaena remained in tattoo form, probably because they would have flipped out when their scummy Fury tried to murder a sister. Just thinking that thought had Rage kicking into overdrive, separating me from the worst of the pain so I could contemplate a little payback. I turned my back to the subway wall and kept an eye on my girls as they advanced on a now-retreating Durra. Once satisfied they could hold her off for the moment, I assumed a fighting stance while the Harpy jogged the last few feet separating us. She passed beneath a yellowish light fixture, and I got a good look at her face only to recognize the single living Harpy I trusted—their new Queen.

"Brace yourself, Fury," Serise spat out, yellow-green eyes glowing with a Harpy's uncontrollable Rage. In Serise's case, that was only half true. What separated Queen from subjects was her ability to tap into the combined magic of all Harpies to control her emotions when needed. That and access a whole hell of a lot more strength than any Fury could ever hope to.

I didn't have the slightest clue what Serise was talking about, but that didn't stop me from obeying. She slammed me back against the wall. I couldn't help it this time. Pain burned along my body when my open wound hit rough concrete, and I screamed. The echo of my shriek had just faded when an explosion boomed from the bottom of the stairwell where Serise had just been. Where I *would* have been if I hadn't paused at the top of the steps. Where Durra would have no doubt shoved me had I not flown *toward* her rather than away.

Which meant that more than one Fury was involved in this little plot.

Magic concussed the air, shooting straight up from the explosion on the lower level and knocking all three of us off our feet. Serise landed between Durra and me. Both women shook their heads to clear them and spat at each other like cats. I knew that, for whatever reason, Serise was there to protect me from my sister Fury. Injured as I was, there would be no shame in sitting back and letting her fight this battle for me.

But that was *so* not my style.

Nemesis and Nike took advantage of my lying dazed on the floor and returned to their normal perches on my arms. I channeled magic through the serpents, funneling energy to my body's charged-up healing abilities rather than cutting myself off from the pain in order to fight. Stubborn I might be, but I tried not to be stupid, and I'd learned my lesson all too well with my knee injury—which meant pulling up my big-girl pants and fighting through the pain. Rage made it just bearable enough to leap to my feet, hop over Serise before she could get up, and land a flying kick to the half-standing Durra's chest. Her eyes widened comically, and she toppled over like a domino, head cracking against the concrete with a most satisfying *thunk*.

My girls hissed encouragement as I planted a foot on each side of Durra's exposed neck and squeezed. Her fingers scrabbled against my booted ankles, trying to find purchase but sliding across the slick leather in vain. I felt the vibrations from her own boots kicking the concrete as she struggled to get enough leverage to break my hold. Too bad for her that she didn't have the twin impetuses of pain and Rage feeding her as voraciously as I did.

She must have realized the futility of her position, because she stopped struggling, met my pissed-off gaze, and managed to choke out, "P-please."

I bared my teeth. "You *dare* raise silver against a sister and expect mercy?"

"F-following orders."

Serise stirred behind us, but she didn't intervene. Just waited.

"Whose orders?"

Durra struggled to respond, but the bluish tinge taking over her lips meant low oxygen supply was making that kind of hard. I relented ever so slightly, easing up on my orthopedic chokehold so she could speak more clearly.

"Elder."

Oh, like *that* was specific. "*Which* Elder and why?"

Her teeth chattered, and she clenched them, obviously reluctant to speak out against whoever sent her. Maybe even magically compelled not to. I tightened my hold, and suddenly she became more willing to fight that reluctance.

"The Megaera."

I relaxed my hold on her out of sheer dumbfounded shock. While the Sisterhood as a whole was democratically governed by the Conclave of Elders, each class of Furies had one Prime sister who ruled over the class with pretty much ironclad authority. Rather than being democratically selected, that sister inherited her station when the previous Prime died. She gained her predecessor's knowledge, memories, and special magical ability unique to that class of Furies. And while each Prime was, technically, an Elder, they owed their allegiance first and foremost to their class rather than the Conclave. Kind of like the mortal state versus federal government system.

The three classes guarded the knowledge of who the current Prime was fiercely, both so no class could manipulate another's Prime and to prevent other arcanes from striking out against them. Hearing that I'd somehow pissed off *the* Megaera enough for her to send assassins after me sent icy terror skating through my belly.

Oh bloody hell. This has *to be related to the shit going down with Nan.*

Didn't it?

A little inner voice cautioned me not to jump to conclusions, something I'd been trying to cut down on lately. Came with that whole learning from previous mistakes thing.

"The Megaera's name, Durra."

Outright mutiny lit in her eyes this time, and *she* bared *her* teeth. "You know I can't tell you that, Tisiphone."

That stung, having her call me by title rather than name. She and I had never been particularly close, but she and Vanessa, on the other hand, had . . . Wait. Vanessa. My best friend had once confided that Durra had made a pass at her after she'd broken things off with Dre Carrington. While

Vanessa had been insanely flattered, she was every bit as straight as me. Could it be coincidence that the Fury in love with my murdered best friend just tried to murder me? I didn't care that *the* Megaera had ordered it—for a Fury to raise silver against another would take either an intense personal grudge or severe crime on the intended victim's part, and I had committed no such crimes.

"Tell me this isn't about Vanessa."

I heard Serise's breath catch at that name. She'd been held captive and impregnated right alongside my sister, then helped Vanessa escape and protected her until my mother and I arrived. Vanessa had died in my arms soon after, but Serise had done everything she possibly could to help her. One of the reasons I trusted the Harpy where I would no other.

Rage flashed in Durra's eyes and she sneered. "You deserve to die just like *she* did, in agony and betrayed by a sister."

I wanted to stagger at the poisonous accusation but couldn't. She'd just get free and try to finish what she started. "What the hell is *that* supposed to mean?"

Serise stepped forward to murmur in my ear. "Sirens. The mortals will be here soon."

Great. Just what I needed—a ton of mundane red tape and paperwork over something I still didn't understand myself. "Explain yourself. *Now*." Okay, maybe I dug my feet together a little more forcefully than needed. The bitch had just tried to kill me and accused me of betraying my own best friend. Sue me.

"We know the truth, Tisiphone. No *way* Stacia acted alone."

"So you think that *I* helped butcher my best friend, not to mention hold my mother hostage for twenty years? Are you all out of your ever-loving minds?"

Her lips twisted into a fierce line that indicated nothing I said would make a difference. Serise made an impatient noise, one that said we really *should* get the hell out of Dodge. I stared down at my sister, aching to find something to say that would convince her of the truth and my innocence. I'd been a victim of Stacia's insanity just as much as Vanessa and my mother. Maybe even more so, considering the fate she'd planned for me from pretty much day one.

"If you can't give me her name, then tell me how you tracked me here. I haven't shed blood without burning it properly and I was in disguise just now, so *how* did you find me?"

She rolled her eyes before replying in a silken voice, "Other bodily fluids work almost as well as blood when it's not available, *sister* dear, especially for powerful Elder Furies."

"But I haven't left any of *those* lying around eith . . ." My voice trailed away as an image flashed into my mind. Me, handing off an empty (or nearly empty) coffee cup to a snot-nosed rookie, and watching him chuck it into the Dumpster as we examined the third Cat victim's corpse. Jeez, the Megaera could run a tracer spell on another Fury using trace amounts of *saliva*? Holy hell. Now I'd have to be paranoid about destroying disposable cups as well as my own blood.

Rage stirred, insisting I finish choking the life out of the traitor at my feet, but that wouldn't solve anything. The Megaera—whoever she was—would just send others after me until I either convinced her not to or raised enough political clout that she had no choice but to back off. Both of which were going to be pretty damned hard in my current predicament.

Hell. Now I *really* had to solve this gods-bedamned case and get back to the Palladium—not only to help my mother with my grandmother, but to save my *own* ass. *Fucking Fury politics.* As I'd said before and would no doubt say again, they made mundane politics look like a trip to Disney World.

I hopped back a step, freeing Durra in one smooth motion. "You couldn't be more wrong about me, Megaera." Two could play the empty title game. "Not that I expect you to believe me." I motioned to Serise. "You go back to your murder-happy Prime and tell her trying to off me in the dark is going to piss off a whole hell of a lot of people—not just Furies. Tell her to grow a pair and come at me the right way—and to watch her own back. Vanessa would *never* have disrespected the Sisterhood like this, and she would be absolutely ashamed to call either one of you sisters."

Durra scrambled to her feet, eyes shooting me even more daggers than Scott's had thrown Victor's way earlier. The slightest bit of shame seemed to pass over her face with my last sentence, but it was absurdly short-lived. She spat at my feet and disappeared.

Which left Serise to grab my arm so we could do the same.

SERISE GUIDED ME BACK THE WAY I'D COME and into a restroom on the subway station's main level, where she directed me to shift into a less obvious form than my Fury guise. She surprised me by smoothing out her own features into something approaching an average mortal's: platinum blond hair instead of bone white, brown eyes instead of unearthly yellow-green, and blue jeans and a T-shirt instead of the black leather uniform most Harpies wore. I had no clue that they retained the ability to shapeshift once they'd left behind their lives as Furies. Then again, as far as I knew, I was the first Fury in millennia to enjoy anything close to friendship with one of their kind.

The shape-shifting ability was definitely something to file away for future reference. Pseudo friendship only went so far. Serise had her sisters to protect and I had mine. Well, minus the backstabbing bitch Durra and whoever the hell *the* Megaera was.

Once we could more easily blend in with the chaotic stream of mortals flooding out of the station, we did so, pretending to be as confused and terrified as the people who had no clue what caused the explosion in the stairwell. Terrorist strike, or so most of them assumed, and really they weren't far off. The terrorists just happened to be arcane rather than mundane, and their weapon of choice had been magic instead of C4.

Serise set a ground-eating—and completely silent—pace. A dozen questions burned in my mind while we put distance between the station and ourselves. *How* had Serise known about the assassination attempt in the first place? *Why* had she risked her own life and the neutrality she enjoyed in order to save my ass? *Who* had sent her to save me, and was that Fury in danger herself? My heart skipped a beat when I realized the likeliest Fury to be in a powerful enough position to learn of such an attack, want to save me from certain death, and trust Serise to send her to do just that was my mother.

I couldn't bear the silence anymore once fear started eating its way through my stomach. I grabbed Serise's arm and gave her a pleading look. "My mother?"

Her lips twisted in what passed for Harpy affection. My mother had been through an even worse ordeal than Serise, held hostage by the same crazy-ass mortals led by my even crazier-ass mentor, Stacia, for twenty hellish years until Mac managed to free her. "Is safe. Another of your sisters—also a Megaera—warned her of the attack, but that Fury couldn't risk angering her Prime."

"So Mom hired you instead." No need to ask how Serise found me like I'd asked Durra. If my mother hired Serise, she had also provided enough of her own blood for the

Harpy to magically track me with it. Furies, unfortunately, could only use the blood of the person being tracked rather than that of a relative.

Serise's eyes met my own. "She offered to pay, but I refused."

That had me blinking. Harpies were, by their very natures, both avaricious and bloodthirsty in the extreme, something that made them even better mercenaries than Scott's Shadowhounds. They *never* took jobs for free.

Maybe Serise and I are better friends than I thought . . .

She shot that theory down with her next words. "It seems you Furies are not the only ones with an uprising in the works. Some of my own sisters have made threats against me. Your mother arranged for Rinda to spend time with her half sister in safety until I can execute the ones moving against me."

We'd discovered via methods both magical and medical that the two infant girls shared the same paternal DNA, although we hadn't yet identified the Warhound who'd provided it.

I frowned. "No offense, Serise—I appreciate the fact you kept me from walking into that explosion and all—but how can it be safe for Olivia to have Rinda anywhere near her if Harpies are out to get you?" And what was my mother thinking anyway? Neither my brother nor my sister-in-law could channel the slightest bit of magic, and Cori hadn't yet manifested her Fury abilities. If Harpies came after the infant half sisters, there would be little they could do to stop them.

Serise gave a tight grin as we ducked onto a quiet residential street not too far from Chinatown—and Boston's magical Underbelly. "Sisters loyal to me are leading the known traitors on a wild-goose chase as we speak, and your mother sent two Furies she trusts implicitly to guard both babes. Once I see you to the safe house, I go to help guard them myself." One of her hands rested on her barely rounded belly, and I remembered something easy to forget. She carried yet another modern-day marvel inside her—the second Harpy child ever conceived biologically. Before Rinda—and the unborn baby who would likely become Calaeno's namesake—Harpies had only ever been created magically when a Fury lost control of her Rage, murdered her Amphisbaena, and Turned.

I narrowed my eyes. "Why would Harpies move against you anyway? Not only were you Calaeno's chosen successor in line after 'Penelope,' but you're carrying a miracle inside you that may well allow Harpies to become a saner, stronger arcane power in their own right. Why jeopardize that?"

Her eyes glinted yellow-green before solidifying into their disguised mundane shade. "Do you not remember Penelope's plan to murder me and claim Rinda as her own to solidify her claim to the throne?"

"Ohhhh." Now *that* made *way* too much sense. "So if they kill you now, while you're theoretically more vulnerable, they can adopt Rinda and rule in her name until she grows up." Assuming they *let* her grow to full adulthood.

"Exactly so."

She nudged my arm and left the sidewalk, hurrying along a private walkway toward a narrow brick row house wedged between two others. I didn't recognize the neighborhood or this particular home, but the cop in me memorized the address and searched the surrounding area for any sign of threat. All was quiet around us—ridiculously quiet, really, considering it was six in the evening and we were close to Chinatown and the Belly—but that seemed mere happenstance rather than an ambush in waiting. Still, we held our limbs loose and unimpeded, ready to strike out with deadly force should that prove necessary.

Which it usually did.

This time, however, we made it into the safe house without incident. Serise knocked sharply at the front door, which opened before her third knock finished echoing. A man I didn't recognize ushered us inside. My back itched when I walked past him, making it *really* hard to let him stand behind me. I wasn't quite sure whether that was residual nerves from being *stabbed in the back* not a half hour earlier or him setting off my Fury instincts all on his own. I decided I didn't care and whirled around just as he slammed the door closed—only to find he wasn't himself anymore.

"Hi, Mom." She had as grand a sense of drama as I did— which explained a lot, really.

Mom—aka Allegra MacAllister Holloway—barely nodded her mortal head in my direction before turning a serious gaze on Serise. "There's been a change in plans. Our sisters will meet you at the second safe house rather than the first." I took my cue from her and returned to mortal form myself.

Serise stiffened. "The first?"

"Was compromised. My son and his wife had to evacuate along with their daughters and yours. I realize that wasn't part of the original plan—"

The Harpy Queen slashed a hand in the air. "Now that I have children of my own to care for, you needn't explain your actions to me. All will be kept safe until you send for them." Her lips twisted. "The last place anyone will look for your loved ones is in the midst of Harpies."

Mom's body relaxed. "My thanks, Your Majesty." Apparently my mother was deeper into political mode than I'd guessed. Whether that boded well or ill, I had no clue.

Serise turned back to me. "Try not to walk into any more ambushes, Fury. I may not be there to save you next time."

I arched my brow sardonically. "I seem to recall saving you *and* your daughter from an ambush not so long ago."

"Which is the other reason I took this job for your mother without pay." Damned if she wasn't starting to develop an actual sense of humor. "For now, I must join the others."

Proving she hadn't strayed *too* far off the beaten Harpy path, she left without giving any pesky good-byes. One moment she was there, the next gone, leaving me to turn to my mother and ask the question burning inside my mind.

"What in the *hell* is going on?"

Now that we were alone, Mom grabbed my arms and pulled me to her, hugging tightly enough to hurt. I gave a grunt but didn't squirm. She needed this closeness, confirmation that I *hadn't* been killed in the ambush after all. Although I wasn't quite sure why she'd gone to the trouble of sending Serise to save my ass when she'd journeyed all the way from the Fury slice of the Otherrealms to here.

She finally pushed away, though her eyes still drank in the sight of me hungrily. Wow, she'd *really* been scared for me—I could tell that by the way her lips trembled and her deep blue eyes shone with unshed tears. "Hell isn't too far off the mark, Marissa." She raked a hand through her elegantly coiffed hair. "The Sisterhood is in utter chaos these days, much as the Elders manage to hide it from others. Your grandmother continues to refuse to see me, and her challenge to Katya still stands."

"Katya?" I blinked when realization hit. Katya, aka Ekaterina, current Moerae (basically the chairperson and CEO of the Sisterhood's ruling council, the Conclave) and major pain in my backside. "You're on a familiar name basis with Fox-Faced Bitch now? Thought you two hated each other."

"We did. We do. Probably always will. But she knows as well as I do that something isn't right with Nan, and she's smart enough to realize I *will* gain Stacia's seat on the Conclave any day now." Her lips pressed together in an even-grimmer line, if that was possible. "Things are more dire in the Conclave than you know, Marissa. Someone is stirring up strife now, not only sister against sister, but class against class. Alecto against Megaera; Megaera against Tisiphone."

My stomach knotted up at the pointed expression in her eyes. "So you mean I may not have personally pissed off the Megaera after all?"

She gave a vexed sigh. "My allies in our own class are doing their damnedest to uncover the identity of the Prime Megaera so we can either pressure her into backing down—or take her treacherous ass out. Without knowing who she is, it's impossible to say for sure, but it seems far more likely you were selected because of your class and ties to both Nan and me."

Which meant that the Megaera had used Durra's unrequited love for Vanessa and Rage that I'd been unable to save her to con the other Fury into raising silver against a sister. *Bitch.*

"She wants to make an example of me. Send a warning to all Tisiphones in her twisted power play."

Rage burgeoned in the wake of dread. Striking against me for personal reasons was bad enough—but that I could almost understand. Sending an assassin after me for political reasons, on the other hand, was something else entirely. Add to that the fact someone was trying to hurt my mother in the vilest way possible—through the loss of a child—and it was a wonder physical steam wasn't spewing from my ears.

I reached out, taking one of Mom's hands in my own. "You focus on finding out what's wrong with Nan and forcing the vote for Stacia's seat. We *need* you on the Lesser Consensus. Serise will keep our family safe, and I can take care of myself here, especially now that I know they're gunning for me. And when I have this damned serial killer taken care of, I will join you in the Palladium to watch your back while we find out once and for all who is scheming against us. If it's a fight they want, then a fight they shall have."

Mom squeezed my fingers and gave a predatory smile of her own. "That's my girl!"

Like mother, like daughter indeed.

CHAPTER THIRTEEN

I HAD TO AGREE TO STAY FOR THE NEXT FEW days in the safe house Mom had on loan from Serise before I could convince her to return to the Palladium. *She* had to assure me bodyguards waited for her there before I agreed to let her go alone. One positive thing about Mom now being an Elder Fury—phenomenally cool travel powers that meant she didn't have to take the train ride from hell younger Furies in the area were stuck with.

At least we had *something* to look forward to about turning one hundred.

Once I saw Mom safely off, I faced the music and called Scott's cell. While he couldn't have known for sure I would be in that particular T stop at that exact moment, somehow I knew he'd be worried nonetheless. Then again, who could blame him with my magical assassination track record lately?

"Where the hell are you?"

The stark fear in his voice made up for the angry words. "In a safe house arranged by Mom. She just left so this was my first chance to call."

Some of the panic evaporated, though he still sounded concerned. "Your mom? Then the attack *was* aimed at you. Who have you managed to piss off now?"

His attempt at humor was appreciated even though it fell a little flat. "Oh, nobody special. Just the Megaera."

Silence met my own deflated joke. Scott knew more than most other arcanes did about Fury society (and politics) by virtue of his line of work and relationship with me. I didn't have to explain who *the* Megaera was—or how much hot water that put me in.

Finally he managed to respond. "Just when I think you can't inspire another gray hair, you prove me wrong."

I laughed—Scott's deep red hair was as shiny and gray-free as my own. Hooray for being immortal! While you *could* be horribly murdered (say, stabbed in the back with a spell-worked silver blade and thrown into a magical explosion), you'd look young and fabulous all the while. The thought of how close I'd come to cashing it in earlier had me closing my eyes and taking a deep breath. What if I wasn't so lucky next time? He deserved to know the truth about my knee and budding addiction.

"Scott, I'm sorry."

"You're—sorry. For what?"

My pulse thudded in my ears. I took another deep breath, steeling myself for the admission to come. "Sorry—that things between Vic the Slick and Sierra are getting so hot and heavy. You know that's just an act on my end, right?"

Kinda sorta. And *a* truth, though not the one I'd intended. Evidently near-death experiences didn't completely wipe away one's inner wuss. *Okay, baby steps then . . .*

He took a breath of his own on the other end of the connection. "Yeah, I know. So, I was that obvious, huh?"

I grinned. "The smoldering eyes, the brooding lips, the clenched fists when we walked in together—yeah, just a bit."

"Oh well, at least I managed to hide the daggers shooting from my gaze."

Not so much. I thought it but didn't want to rain on his parade—not with him being in such an upbeat mood. Well, considering . . . Considering the fun fest that was my life. "Scott, things are really going to hell in the Sisterhood. Mom thinks the Megaera chose me to set a political example."

"Fucking Fury politics."

My heart went *pitter pat.* "My sentiments exactly. She's gone back to kick some political ass and take some Megaera names—one in particular—but it's probably going to take us both to bring this thing to a head."

"Which means we need to close this case."

Warmth spread from my head to my slightly curled toes. *We.* Not *you.* Just knowing he had my back the way I had Mom's gave me strength. That unwavering loyalty and sense of responsibility for others mirrored my own—a big reason I'd turned to him for help several short months ago despite our messy breakup. No matter what happened between us, we would always have each other's back. If that's not really love, I don't know what is.

My voice grew husky with my reply. "Speaking of which, how'd the tasting go?"

"We got there just in time for the cake."

"Lucky you. Trin?"

"Said to tell you everything went smooth as molasses, sugah."

"Never knew you could pull off such a convincing Southern drawl, Yankee Boy."

He snorted. "Says the woman whose father's family has been in New England since the *Mayflower.*"

More like the Salem witch trials—which, admittedly,

wasn't all that far off. "Okay. The final dress fitting in a few
days shouldn't be too traumatic. Guess Sierra's next big
hurdle to jump will be the bridal shower. In the meantime,
we need to keep running down leads as fast as we can. I
still can't believe the wedding's just over a week away." My
mind spun with a half-dozen details still to be dealt with
before the Big Day. Assuming that not only the killer let
things get that far, but that nobody else threw any major
wrenches into the works.

"I'd like to touch base with Sahi tomorrow on the autopsy
results for—Rockefeller." Guilt twinged at the thought of
the man I'd been unable to save, but I forced it aside. "See if
he was hit with the same cocktail as the others. And we
have *got* to figure out just where that stuff is coming from
and exactly how it works." I rubbed my eyes as weariness
overwhelmed me. So much to do in such a short space of
time—and that wasn't even factoring in the Fury shitstorm
still waiting for me.

He must have heard it in my voice. "Give me your address
and an hour. I'll be there with pizza and your favorite PJs."

Okay, maybe I'd been wrong before. Pizza and comfy
PJs—now *that* was love. Not to mention, the best offer I'd
gotten all damned day. *I just might have to keep him
around for good this time . . .*

EVEN ON A SUNDAY MORNING, SAHANA COULD
be found elbow-deep in some poor bastard's chest cavity
while she hummed her eerie Raga song. The morgue was
like a 24-hour diner—open 365 days a year—and Sahi was
its fearless manager who kept everything running like
clockwork. It helped that she was Hindu rather than Chris-
tian (Sundays were just another day for her) and that she
moved to Boston specifically to get some breathing room

away from her meddlesome family. As she'd confided to me before, she loved them like crazy, but that's exactly what they did—drove her out of her ever-loving mind.

I watched her work her magic through the narrow viewing window, sipping on the hot cup of Starbucks coffee Trinity had been kind enough to provide this early weekend morning. Of course, neither Scott nor I mentioned that we'd already had a healthy dose of caffeine on the way over. Never let it be said that Yankee manners could be put to shame by good old Southern hospitality.

Speak of the devil and she shall put in her two cents. "How long do you think she's gonna be?"

I tilted my head. "Judging by the pitch of her voice and the hairs raising on my neck, I'd say she should be done any . . . second . . . now."

My dramatic pauses for effect were timed perfectly. Sahana's body drooped a few seconds after, a clear sign she'd found the answers she'd been seeking, which was my cue. I handed off my cup to Scott. He and Trinity crossed the hall to Sahana's office door while I slipped inside the autopsy room. Sahana managed a weak smile when I put my hands on her arms and guided her to the stainless steel sink so she could wash away the less savory traces of her career field.

"Sahi, Sahi. If you're going to push yourself this hard, you have *got* to have someone in the room with you. A lab tech, a uniform, that cute guy your mom's always trying to set you up with. *Some*body. One of these days you're gonna lose yourself in the Raga song and then what?"

She paused in the act of lathering her hands with harsh yellow soap. "I expect the same thing that will happen when you keep pulling twelve-hour shifts without taking any days off, Chief."

"Touché," I muttered before shoving a wad of paper

towels her way. "But at least I'm getting better at delegating. And seriously, why is there never a lab tech around to help you?"

Sahana finished patting her hands dry with precise movements—whether due to her exhaustion or innate perfectionist tendencies I wasn't sure—and leaned against the heavy-duty sink. Her eyes narrowed as she looked at me, and something . . . *hungry* . . . rippled across the pupils. My heart skidded fitfully, and the hairs along my neck rose straight up.

"Because it wouldn't do at all for the Chief Arcane ME to suck the very life from her mortal lab tech's flesh and bones unintentionally, now would it?" She said it in an off-handed, conversational tone that made it all the spookier.

I took an unconscious step backward, and she blinked, her expression returning to its usual pleasant manner. As a colorful friend of mine used to exclaim, shit fire and save *all* the matches. Intellectually knowing Sahana's powers over life—and death—were like a powder keg just waiting to be lit and witnessing a little bit of that explosion in waiting were two very different things. I realized something else in that moment. The way I felt inside right now was the way people had been reacting to Sahana her entire life. It was one of the reasons Bhairavi Raga almost always retreated from the outside world and lived exceedingly hermetic lives, and *the* reason Sahana often immersed herself in her work for the PD. People drew away from her out of fear.

Well, not me. I gritted mental teeth and arched a sardonic brow. "So, what? Was that supposed to make me wet my pants? I've eaten scarier things than you for breakfast, sugar." Little white lies when the situation called for it: the mark of true friendship.

Surprise lit Sahana's eyes, and her lips slowly curved

upward. First chance I got, Sahana was *so* coming with Trinity and me for a girls' night out. Right now, however, we had other things to focus on.

"Seriously, though, as Chief Magical Investigator, I'm going to have to insist we hire a couple of arcane lab techs to assist you where mortals can't. The last thing the PD wants to do is lose its exceedingly valuable arcane ME to something that is entirely preventable. And the last thing *I* want to do is lose a friend through mortal personnel's unwitting ignorance."

She let out a relieved-sounding sigh. "You can do that?"

I shot her a pointed glance. "Notice how the MCU went from Trin and me to number five full-time members, two part-time members, and arcane consultants as we need them? They didn't just hand that to me—I had to fight for them. Same as I'll fight for what *you* need."

"Gods, Riss, I can't say how much it would mean to me to have some lab techs I don't have to worry about—about—"

"Breaking?"

"Well, yeah."

I patted her on the shoulder. "You don't need to tell me what it would mean because I've felt the exact same thing myself. Buying me a few cocktails when we go out to paint the town red next month will do nicely."

Laughter burst from her lips. "Can't remember the last time I went out with friends."

"Which is *precisely* why Trin and I will be dragging your ass out, whether you like it or not."

"Oh, I'll like it just fine, don't worry." Her expression sobered. "Speaking of Trinity, I assume you're here for an update on the Rockefeller case."

I simply nodded.

Sahana pushed away from the sink and led the way across the hall. After exchanging greetings with the other two, she unlocked her office door and ushered us inside.

She wasted no time in pulling out a manila folder overflowing with papers and setting it down on the desk between us. "Ward Rockefeller was definitely drugged with the same hybrid form of catnip as the previous Cat victims. However, unlike those victims, there was a high enough concentration flowing through his veins before death that he would have died with or without the beating that followed his being drugged."

I tilted my head thoughtfully. "Well, that confirms our theory that something pissed the killer off enough to change his MO. He attacked Rockefeller in the same place he dumped the body and then placed a call to 911 to make sure the corpse would be found."

Trinity took up my theme. "He shot Rockefeller up with enough of the drug to completely incapacitate him in seconds, rather than more slowly. And he didn't play with Rockefeller the way he did the others. Just systematically and brutally beat the hell out of him."

My gaze focused on Sahana again. "You were going to test the drug on the blood samples Harper gave you?"

She tapped the folder on her desk. "The tests I ran confirm my suspicions that this hybrid catnip neutralizes the Cat's innate ability to self-regenerate. Smaller doses of it seem to weaken those abilities without permanently wiping them out, but at higher or sustained concentrations . . . complete cessation of regeneration is inevitable."

Scott let out a low whistle, one I was tempted to echo. If word of *this* got out . . . anyone with a grudge against Cats would be granted a shortcut to rubbing the cause of that grudge out in an instant. I shifted uncomfortably at the logical next step in that equation. A rival group who had been at war with the Bastai for countless years could poison their enemies with this drug and then easily wipe out the entire race. Genocide on a horrible and horribly simple scale.

Something I would go to *any* lengths to prevent. I leveled

a grim stare on Sahana. "Have you shared these results with anyone else?"

She gave me an insulted look. "Do I *look* insane to you, Riss? Bhairavi Raga I may be, but that doesn't mean I like to *cause* death. Leaking word that there's a handy-dandy drug that negates the Bastai ability for self-resurrection would be like signing a death warrant for them as a species. *One* arcane race driven to extinction is quite enough in any generation."

My breath rushed out in relief. Good to see she had reached the same realization I had—and shared my feelings on the matter. While Bastai fought like the wildcats they resembled in shifted form, what gave them a true edge against other arcane races was their ability to recuperate from fatal wounds, especially considering they couldn't take damage nearly as well as races like Warhounds, Giants, or Furies. Too bad I couldn't yet share the news with her that the Sidhe were no longer quite as extinct as we all once believed. For the next little while, the public had to believe the Sidhe who'd been rescued were half-breeds. They couldn't afford the truth getting out until their numbers grew great enough to grant them a measure of protection.

We discussed her results for another half hour, along with how they impacted the criminal investigation. She handed the overflowing folder to me and told me I now held the only evidence of what her test results had proven about the hybrid catnip—basically washing her hands of the headache and leaving it up to me to decide what to do with that evidence. Whether to risk it falling into the wrong hands or destroy it to make damned sure that would never happen; one of which would be betraying a fellow arcane race and the other of which would be betraying the mortal laws I was sworn to uphold.

No pressure or anything.

The beauty of my partnership with Trinity was that she

would respect whatever decision I made and neither rat me out to other mortals nor guilt-trip me if I made the decision to destroy the test results. She trusted me as much as I trusted her, and she was just as invested in keeping the peace between mortals and arcanes as I was. Still, it was a ridiculously huge decision to make on my own. For now, I wanted to lock the documents under spell and key, deal with the immediate task of finding the killer, and consult with those I trusted before deciding one way or the other.

In the meantime, I had *more* than enough trouble to keep me occupied.

BRIGHT AND EARLY MONDAY MORNING, I CON-fronted one of those troubles head-on: finding a specialist to help me with the agony that was my knee. On the plus side, I didn't have to book my arcane doctor's appointment under an assumed identity, since Marissa Holloway *could* be the "friend" Sierra had mentioned to Victor. Add the referral from Victor to my status as Chief Magical Investigator and wonders were worked. Not only did the third physician on Victor's list specialize in arcane orthopedics; his receptionist also recognized my name and rearranged his schedule to get me in that very day.

There's something to be said for friends in high places.

Not that I'd ever be willing to throw over Scott in favor of his high-and-mighty cousin's clout. I scowled at the thought. The teens sitting across from me on the T gave me weird looks before scrambling to another seat farther down the subway car. For a moment I wondered how scary elegant Sierra Nieves could manage to look, weird face or no, but then I remembered that I was actually out in public as myself today. Well, as one of the average-faced mortal disguises I wore when I wanted to travel under the radar. No sense taking undue risks when the Megaera Prime might

have other sisters on the warpath and out for my blood.
Scott was tending to a Shadowhound emergency and may
have *somehow* been under the impression I was sticking
around the PD. Guilt stirred but I stubbornly choked
it down. If all went well during my appointment with
Dr. Silvina, I could finally come clean to Scott about the
true extent of my knee injury and the steps I was taking to
overcome it. No, *really*.

A half hour later I squirmed atop a paper-covered examining table and stared down at my bare legs. My hands kept
tugging my cotton blouse lower, but nothing helped the sensation of being exposed. The nurse had left behind a paper
gown she actually thought I was going to slip into. Ha. I
donned those flimsy scraps of "fabric" exactly once a year
when forced atop that feminine torture device undoubtedly
invented by some man, and my yearly physical wasn't due
for another few months. All Dr. Silvina needed to see was
my freaking knee so he could live with me in my T-shirt
and panties. Or not live—the choice was his.

Anxiety rode me relentlessly by the time Examining
Room 3's door swung open. A wizened old man who stood
maybe half my height strode into the room, skin an odd
shade somewhere between asparagus and olive green, and
head glaringly bald in the room's harsh lighting. A closer
look showed that he was neither old nor human, facts that
the color of his skin had me placing a few seconds later.
Dr. Silvina was a *Goblin.* And unlike my old "pal" Allaz-
zar, purveyor of illegal, hybrid, magically enhanced weap-
ons (also known as "weps"), a full-blooded Goblin.

He was also used to his patients' initial shock that he
worked in such a non-self-serving career field, apparently,
because he wagged a finger in my direction and made a
clucking sound. "Now, now, Inspector Holloway, you of all
people should know not to judge a book—or doctor—by its
cover." His gaze flicked from me to the paper gown I'd

thrown on the floor in a fit of pique, and a smile tugged his lips upward. "Although perhaps in your case, what I've heard about Furies isn't too far off the mark."

Something in his voice reminded me of my father's father, who I hadn't seen since I was eight or nine. I'd worshipped the ground Gramps walked upon for those brief years, so no surprise that the resemblance had me relaxing slightly. "You'll have to forgive my lack of manners in staring, Dr. Silvina, and I'm sure you've heard this more times than you care to remember, but . . . I've never seen a Goblin Healer, much less a Goblin doctor."

"And here I am both. More than enough to shock you, I'm sure." He crossed the room to a wheeled metal stool parked next to a large wedge of wood I now identified as a step stool, which he used to climb and perch atop the other. Wheels squeaked as he spun his body to face the counter and take up a miniature laptop that didn't seem very miniature at all in his hands.

"All righty then." His fingers tapped across the digital notebook, and he glanced my way again. "The medical records your primary care physician sent over seem in order. Her last notation mentions that you sustained an injury via magical means that has responded poorly to all her efforts to treat it. Tell me more about that, Inspector."

My fingers clenched, and I took a deep breath, expecting to have as much trouble telling this story to Dr. Silvina as to the others I'd consulted over the past few months. Whether due to the fact he was so obviously arcane or his voice's similarity to Gramps, the story came spilling from my lips so quickly I barely paused for breath. It helped that he just sat there, listening intently, with no judgment upon his face, while I described my stupid decision to magically cut myself off from the pain and the consequences I'd been dealing with since that day. *Big* improvement over Gianna's lecturing.

When I mentioned her name, Dr. Silvina shook his head with a fond smile. "Oracle Gianna is indisputably a genius when it comes to Healing, but she is—like many of her peers—remarkably shortsighted when it comes to modern-day medicine and how it can be used to enhance rather than hinder or replace time-honored arcane Healing. I've had remarkable success in treating patients in similar circumstances to your own by utilizing magic to augment more mundane courses of rehabilitation, physical therapy, and where appropriate, orthopedic surgery. It really only makes sense, considering that the arcane body *is* both arcane and mundane at the same time." He rolled his eyes. "Although convincing some of my arcane counterparts is easier said than done."

My breath whooshed out, making me realize I'd been holding it in the first place. "So you're saying there's hope for my knee? Hope I can break my add— my need for arcane spells and mundane painkillers?" If copious amounts of alcohol counted as painkillers.

Dr. Silvina raised another admonishing finger. "Hope yes, Inspector, but this will be a long, frustrating, and agonizingly painful process. Even then, you may not break completely free of your dependence upon painkilling measures."

"But—but I won't become—won't become crippled?"

He wrinkled his long, pointed nose in distaste. "Absolutely not. Whoever gave you that pessimistic impression"— his indisputable genius colleague, Oracle Gianna—"was being unduly cautious to advise you of that fact. Although I suppose if they *only* tried arcane treatments rather than mixing them with the more mundane, they might have been right." His expression grew matter-of-fact. "I can't promise a complete cure, Inspector Holloway, but know this: We *will* improve the condition of your knee with time and effort. You will *not* become a cripple."

I'm not a bit ashamed to admit I hopped off the examining table, wrapped my arms around him, and placed an enthusiastic kiss right in the middle of his shiny, bald head.

Dr. Silvina did something else I didn't even known Goblins could do—blushed bright red. He mumbled something I couldn't quite make out, but I just grinned like an idiot and perched atop the table once more. No matter how much work was involved, no matter how long it took, no matter *how badly* it hurt, I would do whatever the good doctor told me if it meant avoiding the fate I'd come to dread so much. And take great pleasure in rubbing my success right in Gianna's supercilious face. Sure, other Furies wanted me dead and a serial killer was terrorizing *my* city's streets. All of that aside, I *would not* become a cripple. For now, that was all I needed to know.

CHAPTER FOURTEEN

THE REST OF THE DAY PASSED IN A BUSY but blessedly boring blur of going back over background info we'd gathered on the various victims over the past few weeks. Their activities leading up to the time of each murder. The names of any potential enemies who may have wanted to harm them. Lists of ex-lovers since that seemed to be an emerging theme in this investigation. And of course, any threats made against them in the past, whether overt or otherwise. Unfortunately, no common thread jumped out other than the fact that all had been romantically involved with Harper.

By the time I neared the safe house's front stoop that evening, I wanted nothing but to curl up on the sofa with Jack and Scott—in that order, since Scott had texted earlier that he'd meet me at our temporary home sweet home with carryout in an hour or two. I rubbed my knee irritably as it throbbed, and I dug into my jeans pocket for my keys, only to have the front door swing unexpectedly open.

Instinct had me jumping back and preparing to shift before my conscious brain caught up enough to register that the person in front of me was friend rather than foe: Serise wearing her ordinary mortal disguise. My pulse slowed to a dull roar, only to pick up speed when the next logical worry struck. "Where the hell is my family?"

She jerked me inside the foyer and slammed the door much as my mother had before. "They're sleeping safely upstairs with two of my sisters guarding them."

"Two? Last I heard you had a half dozen with you."

Her lips twisted grimly. "I did, along with two Furies loyal to your mother. My two are all who remain."

My body sagged against the front door behind me. "Oh gods, Serise. You mean they *all*—"

"Sacrificed themselves so your family and my children could get to safety, yes."

She kept her voice emotionless, but I knew her well enough to spot the flash of anguish in her eyes. To lose four of the sisters she was pledged to protect in one fell swoop must have hurt like hell, especially for such a wildly emotional race as Harpies, and yet she would not allow herself to openly grieve them. Not in front of outsiders anyway, which was what I was—no matter how friendly we had become.

Grief for my own lost sisters flared, but I could do no less than a Harpy and pushed aside my own sorrow for the Tisiphones who had given their lives to protect my innocent—and fragile—family members. "They found the second safe house."

A statement rather than a question, but she nodded anyway. "Late last night, but I couldn't risk contacting anyone while we tried to lose anyone trailing us. Not even you or your mother. This was the only safe place I could think to bring them." She made that admission with a haggard expression, hands curling protectively over her belly. "I—it makes no sense how they keep tracking us so easily, not with all the precautions your mother and I put into place. Not unless"—her expression soured—"unless your enemy sisters are working with mine and have a relative's blood my 'sisters' can use to trace."

I frowned. "I don't see how they could be using a relative's blood. You had all of my blood relations with you except for Mac, my mother, and me . . ." Horror widened my mouth and eyes. "My gods, no. Surely *Nan* wouldn't be helping them . . ."

A tired voice echoed in the air unexpectedly. "Unless, of course, your Nan's not really your Nan."

I pushed away from the door and searched for the owner of that voice. "Mom?"

She materialized midway between Serise and me, staggering before I managed to catch her in my arms. Exhaustion was evident in every line of her face and in the boneless way her body collapsed against mine. Her skin seemed a strange grayish-white hue I couldn't ever remember it being.

"Jesus, Mary, and Joseph!" I did an unintentional impression of my sister-in-law. "You look like death warmed over, Mom." Showing just how true that observation was, she didn't even make a snarky comeback, just heaved a huge sigh. My protective—and practical—instincts kicked into overdrive. "Serise, get something sugary to eat from the kitchen. And a lot of it."

She leapt into action while I half carried my mother to the living room sofa and helped her sink into its cushiony depths. A sense of helplessness washed over me as I watched her struggle for each breath. I hadn't seen a Fury this magically and physically drained in—well, ever—and it terrified me. The thought of losing Mom so soon after getting her back . . . *No, don't even* think *like that. She'll be just fine once she gets some sugar into her.*

Furies were a bit like hummingbirds in that respect: Sugar helped replenish our depleted energy stores, especially when we overexerted ourselves like Mom obviously had. Okay, make that two respects: We can hover midair and fly backward much like the tiny winged wonders.

Serise bustled back with an entire family-size box of Pop-Tarts, ripping into an individual package and handing it straight to my mother, who devoured the twin pastries in thirty seconds flat and held out her hands for another. The next couple of minutes consisted of her chowing down the sugary-sweet goodies and Serise opening the next package until finally Mom's color started to look a little healthier. Only then did I finally ask the questions burning inside me.

"What did you mean, Nan's not really Nan? Have you found something out? Is someone impersonating her like the Sidhe did with Nessa?"

Mom finished cramming the last few crumbs inside her mouth, swallowed, and shook her head. "Not exactly. It's Nan's body all right, but I'm afraid she's not in control of it."

I blinked. "Whoa, okay, maybe you need to back up and get me up to speed."

"I've been doing some digging since we talked on the phone last, trying to figure out if someone else had a hand in Nan coming out of the coma. Turns out someone besides you and I had been visiting her regularly in the two decades since she killed Medea."

My breath caught. "Who's that?"

She hesitated before replying. "Stacia."

Of all the names she might have said, few—if any—could have surprised me more. True that both Nan and Stacia were Tisiphones, like the two of us, and equally true that each had been maternal figures to me. But Mom and Stacia had been mere acquaintances before my mother's disappearance, and I'd never heard that Stacia had been close to my grandmother. In fact, thinking back, I'd always gotten the impression Nan hadn't cared for her much. Then again, I'd been ridiculously young when Nan fell into her coma: It was way before I joined the Sisterhood, way before Stacia took my Fledgling self under her wing. It was just an impression I'd gotten from the few times Stacia's name came up in conversation between Nan and Mom.

One of those conversations tickled at the back of my brain, since it'd taken place just a week before Nan's fateful fight with her sister. I closed my eyes and channeled ten-drils of magic to enhance faulty childhood memory.

Mom and Nan had sat across from each other at the breakfast nook in the kitchen, unaware I had tiptoed into the formal dining room to peek in on them. So rare to have them both home at the same time; even rarer for me to catch them unaware and in mortal form. Sometimes I liked to just watch them when they didn't know it. Mom so blond and lovely; Nan red-haired, fiercely handsome rather than conventionally pretty. And in mortal form, so much easier to eavesdrop on.

Hey, I'd been like ten years old and curious as hell. Sue me.

At first, they'd spoken of boring things like the house-hold routine, how I was doing in school, David being away at college, and my parents' upcoming anniversary, when Nan was going to take me on a weekend getaway so Mom and Dad could enjoy one of their own. But then they men-tioned a name that immediately caught my attention. Great-Aunt Medea.

"Stacia believes she knows how to track down Medea."

Nan had frowned down at her cup of coffee. Even then, I'd loved the strong, rich scent of the gourmet blend she preferred. These days, tasting it sent me into paroxysms of delight. "I know I swore I'd track down Medea at any cost, and I will, but I don't know how wise an idea it is to trust Stacia in this matter."

Mom had given a frown of her own. "You don't trust Stacia?"

"Not so much that, necessarily. She's a damned fine Tisiphone, and she serves us well on the Lesser Consensus. But her feelings for Medea, *those* I don't trust at all."

A deep sigh from Mom at that. "You can't blame her for grieving when Medea Turned Harpy. If something ever happened to . . ." Mom's voice broke slightly, and she amended her statement. "*When* something happens to Geoffrey, I know I'll go a little crazy myself."

"Yes, but you don't have a pattern of going more than a little crazy like Stacia does. You weren't there that day when she managed to take out the mortals who killed her Wing of sisters. Crazy is putting it mildly. Imagine what she might do when confronted by Medea Turned Harpy. It's going to be hard enough on me to put Medea out of her misery. No telling what could go wrong if we allow Stacia to go with us."

Looking back on that conversation with the added wisdom and experiences of my adult self, some of the missed nuances suddenly made a whole lot more sense. Whoa. Stacia and Medea had been lovers—something nobody had ever even hinted to me before. Things had been serious enough between the two women that Stacia had done something crazy after Medea Turned. I made a mental note to find out exactly *what* she'd done just in case it wound up being important down the line.

My eyes narrowed at the next leap in logic. Nan must have convinced Mom *not* to trust Stacia when they went after Medea because, as far as I knew, the two of them confronted Medea alone. *How* they found my great-aunt I'd never heard for sure. All I *did* know was that poor Mom witnessed her mother kill her aunt at the cost of a coma that stole decades of Nan's life. Knowing Stacia—and her unique brand of crazy—the way I now did, I could say with confidence that would have pissed her off in the extreme. Nan made the most logical target for that anger. So why, then, would Stacia visit Nan regularly in the years to come?

I shifted uneasily as a dozen possibilities flicked through my mind, each more sinister than the last, each I might once have claimed to be more *impossible* than the last. But after the hard truths I learned about my former mentor, I could no longer put *any*thing out of the realm of possibility where Stacia was concerned.

Not even that she was somehow manipulating Nan from the grave.

I voiced that possibility aloud. "You don't think that Stacia . . ."

Mom twisted a foil wrapper in her hands and pursed her lips. "I'm not sure *who* is influencing her now or how they're doing it, but I *am* certain that someone *is* doing so. I also find it highly suspicious that she is allying herself more closely with sisters loyal to the Megaera class rather than her fellow Tisiphones . . ."

That had my eyes blinking triple-time. "Whoa, whoa, whoa. Back up there. *The* Megaera?"

She frowned. "I said the Megaera class, yes."

I shook my head violently. "No, not the class. *The* Megaera. That makes perfect sense."

"I'm afraid I don't—wait. You think the *Megaera* is the one manipulating your grandmother now? But—But . . ."

"You said yourself that things are going to hell in the Sisterhood. Durra claimed the Megaera ordered her to make that hit on me, and I've seen nothing to indicate anything contrary to that. Think about who could gain the most by pushing for a civil war to break out in the Sisterhood now, Mom. Which class hasn't had a sister serve as Moerae since the War ended?"

"Has it *been* that long since a Megaera sat as Moerae?" Mom's expression morphed from disbelieving to considering as she thought over the past few decades. "Two Alectos, then a Tisiphone, another Alecto, and now Katya. My gods, Marissa, you're right. The last Megaera to serve as Moerae was Hazuki."

Hazuki, the Japanese-born Fury who finally succeeded in brokering peace between mortal and arcane more than thirty years earlier. Her time as Moerae had been productive but short-lived: An unknown group of disgruntled arcanes assassinated her not too long after she ironed out the Accord. My mind whirled as it pieced together a dozen different odds and ends of information garnered since I'd become a full-Fledged Fury, trying to make sense of the senseless chaos that seemed to be sweeping across the Sisterhood like a raging flood.

"You don't think that the Megaeras believe that . . . that a *Tisiphone* was responsible for Hazuki's assassination, do you? And that we've secretly conspired to keep them from being voted in as Moerae in the years since?"

"Gods, Marissa, I don't know. You've certainly been more active in the Sisterhood the past couple of decades than I have."

"Well, it certainly makes more sense than anything else I can come up with. What other reason could they have for waking up Nan and pushing her to challenge Ekaterina for her seat? Why would they want to go after me and, more bizarrely enough, the *mortal* members of our family? What could possibly be worth risking civil war among the Sisterhood if not gaining political power over the Furies as a whole?"

My brows furrowed as that thought tickled at the back of my brain. Civil war seemed to be brewing not just in the Sisterhood of Furies, but also among the Harpies. Stacia had once plotted to gain control over both the Furies as herself, and the Harpies in her guise as Calaeno's second, Penelope. She'd been the only Fury in history with the

ability to channel Rage as both Fury and Harpy without first
slaughtering her Amphisbaena. Now we learned that she'd
been not only obsessed with manipulating me to follow in
her footsteps but had also been secretly visiting Nan over the
decades since Nan killed her lover-Turned-Harpy, Medea.
Only I still couldn't understand *why* she would have visited
the comatose woman she believed killed her Megaera
lover . . . And then sudden realization blindsided me.

"Oh. My. Gods. Maybe *Stacia* was the reason Nan stayed
in a coma all those years. During her visits she could have
cast any number of spells prolonging Nan's slumber. The
perfect little revenge." Mom met my shocked gaze with one
of her own. "Stacia's death was probably the reason Nan was
finally able to wake up. But now, for gods know whatever
reason, Nan's wreaking havoc against the Sisterhood. It's as
if she blames us all for what happened to her . . ."

And gods, as I knew from firsthand experience, hell had
nothing worse than a Fury scorned . . .

SCOTT CHOSE JUST THAT MOMENT TO PUT IN
a not-so-timely appearance by slipping quietly through the
front door and into the living room. Fortunately for the
overly distracted Mom and me, Serise hadn't been taken
unaware by his arrival, having apparently catalogued who
and what he was way before we did and choosing not to
interrupt the thread of our conversation to warn us. Which
meant, of course, that he arrived just in time to hear my
cheerful observation.

"Whoa, hold up a minute. Your psycho mentor caused
your now-psycho grandmother's decades-long coma? Anubis, Riss, *how* do you manage to get caught up in this kind of
shit all the time?"

I blinked up at him for a moment before realizing he
actually *was* there and not just some figment of my over-

wrought imagination. And then loyalty to Nan kicked in. "My grandmother's not a psycho, Murphy."

He reached out to pull me into his arms and pressed a warm, comforting kiss atop my head. "I see we have unexpected guests. Care to fill me in on what's going on, baby?"

I did just that, spilling out the latest details in a hurried rush while Serise brought a second box of Pop-Tarts to my mother. Once I'd finished, he let out a long, low whistle and hugged me even closer, both signs of just how worried he had become. And hell, I couldn't blame him. Part of me was shaking in my figurative—*and* literal—boots as the enormity of the situation hit me. Somehow, in some way, Stacia *was* manipulating Nan from beyond the grave. I had no doubts whatsoever that she had put this little drama into motion. Perhaps she had cast one final spell upon her death that set about the miraculous reawakening months later; there was no telling what someone as devious and powerful as Stacia could have managed.

I'd be stupid *not* to be terrified.

Once Mom had finished off the second box of Pop-Tarts, I pushed away from Scott and turned my focus back to her. "You've been pushing yourself way too hard, Mom, and that's not going to help any of us in the long run."

She stood and narrowed her eyes. "*Someone* is controlling your Nan and will stop at nothing to kill *all* of us. The Megaera is pushing for civil war among the Sisterhood. I do what I must there, just as you do here."

I bit my lower lip hard enough to draw blood. "That's all well and good, Mom, but if *you* kill yourself from magical overexertion, then who will there be on the Conclave to speak out on our behalf? Ekaterina?" My voice grew scathing. "Please, she'd just as soon let me die as save me. I *have* to solve this case down here before I can come to the Palladium to watch your back. If I can't trust you to take care of yourself in the meantime, then—then I'll . . ."

Her expression softened somewhat, and she took my hand in hers. "Marissa, I understand that you have to fulfill your duties to the mundane police force. Your oaths to the Sisterhood demand you do so, if not the pledges you made directly to the mortals. I trust you enough to believe that you *will* solve this case and help me before it's too late. Just as I trust both you and Serise to watch out for our family in the meantime. Now trust me to handle myself until you *can* come watch my back."

I heaved a long sigh, both because she was right and because her words echoed sentiments expressed by both Scott and Trinity in the past. Sometimes I really *did* let my Fury need to protect others overwhelm my common sense and come off as if I didn't trust those around me to take care of themselves. Which was *far* from the truth, but still. Letting my mother go back into that nest of vipers alone was going to take every ounce of self-control I had. Kind of like when Scott had trusted me to go after Vanessa's daughter alone with only two Harpies as protection from a small army of evil Sidheborn clones.

Scott's gaze met mine in that moment, and I knew he could tell exactly what I was thinking. And yeah, payback most assuredly *was* a bitch . . .

CHAPTER FIFTEEN

THE REMAINDER OF THAT NIGHT WAS SPENT drawing up lists of those we could trust implicitly and planning out schedules for my family to be protected at all times. Scott assigned a pair of his cousins to help in the guarding without my even asking, something that relieved my mind somewhat. Shadowhounds were both fiercely loyal and totally kickass. Dre Carrington sent over two of his best sorcerers to magically shield the safe house from the strongest of tracer spells. Expensive as hell to hire them on an emergency basis, but well worth it. Mom waited long enough to make sure their protection spell passed muster—and kiss both her nieces—before returning to the Palladium. After a good night's sleep, I threw myself back into the investigation with a vengeance, determined to crack the serial killer case once and for all.

Once Scott's cousins showed up to bolster Serise and

her sisters, Scott dropped me off at the PD before heading off to tend to the high-maintenance client who was starting to get on everyone's nerves. Mahina cornered me a couple hours later, skipping into my office with a big grin on her face and one of those manila folders I was coming to hate in her hands. Weird for her to look so upbeat considering the normally nocturnal woman was working daylight overtime. Even my growled "Now what?" didn't dampen her spirits; she kicked the door shut and plopped down in a guest chair without an invitation.

"Remember that death threat I thought was the most credible?"

I nodded grudgingly.

"So it's untraceable by mundane means. No envelope to test for DNA. Forensics worked every other angle they could think of and came up empty."

"By the disgustingly smug look you're wearing, I assume it was only untraceable by *mundane* means and you have something more helpful to tell me. Otherwise, don't hold your breath waiting for a holiday bonus this year."

While Mahina and her husband had worked with me for mere months, they'd both quickly adjusted to my *occasional* (ha) moodiness and *slight* (double ha) sarcasm. Pretty much par for the course where Furies were concerned.

She ignored my bitchiness and tossed the manila folder in front of me. "I had a sorcerer friend of mine run some tests on the paper and newsprint letters making up the threat. He was able to divine that the paper is some expensive kind of parchment made only in—get this—Egypt and imported to one and only one store in, but of course, the Belly. Apparently the paper was spell-worked to prevent divination of its owner's identity but *no* spell can completely wipe out an object's origins. He also divined that the letters came from fancy magazines rather than cheap newspapers."

My crankiness evaporated, and I jerked the folder open, revealing the death threat entombed in a Ziploc bag along with the sorcerer's printed findings, a list of magazine names I vaguely recognized, and Mahina's handwritten notes on the Underbelly establishment selling the parchment. I did a double take when I read an oh-so-familiar name: Hounds of Anubis.

Finally! A lucky break in this gods-bedamned case. I closed the folder and pulled my cell out of my pocket. "Remind me I owe you a disgusting bonus come December, Mahina. Freaking fantastic work."

Her smile grew smug, but I couldn't blame her. "I'll hold you to that, Riss."

I jabbed in Scott's number and waited until he picked up. "Hey, handsome. If you're done holding your client's hand, I need you to meet Mahina and me somewhere ASAP."

"Oh yeah? I'm up for a threesome with two hot chicks. Where we hooking up?"

"The store where our new number one suspect bought the parchment paper he or she used to send a not-so-congratulatory note to Harper and Penn."

"Ah, the death threat Mahina thought might pan out."

"Exactly. And the parchment came from your absolutely favorite store ever."

"Well, what a stroke of luck for you, Chief Holloway. It just so happens I know the owner of my absolutely favorite store ever. I can pull some strings if you make it worth my while."

"You pull the right strings with *me*, and I'll make it all worth your while." Mahina choked on a sudden fit of laughter she tried to disguise as a cough. I pretended I hadn't forgotten she sat across from me and winked. "Seriously, though, can you meet me at Hounds in, say, a half hour?"

"Make it closer to forty-five minutes and I'll be there."

I glanced at the wall clock and nodded, even though he

couldn't see me. "One o'clock at your mother's shop, then. It's a date."

"Make sure you both wear something sexy," he teased before hanging up.

I smiled and shoved the cell phone back in my pocket. *See, Dr. Silvina said you're* not *doomed to become crippled, and you have a huge break in the case. The day's looking up already!* My inner Pollyanna conveniently ignored the fact that nine hours remained in the day—more than enough for things to take another giant skydive.

Since Trinity and Cass were holed up somewhere researching hybrid pharmaceuticals (a relatively new field blending science and magic to create new medicinal drugs)—trying to figure out where the hell the killer catnip came from—Mahina and I commandeered the undercover van for our "date" in the Belly. I remained in my own mortal form since the tinted windows eliminated the chance someone would catch sight of me during the short drive. We stopped for cappuccinos on the way. Caffeine made pulling massive amounts of overtime just bearable enough to endure, and Mahina was a Starbucks gal after my own heart.

Thanks to our pit stop, Scott beat us to Hounds of Anubis by moments. He stood on the front stoop, chatting with Elliana—Penn's sister—and Mac, my genetically engineered baby brother. Mac was the first to catch sight of Mahina and me after we parked at an empty meter. He trotted down the stairs, heading straight my way for our habitual bear hug. I inhaled the scents that marked him as both male and Fury, a sharp contradiction, and hugged him back. "Hey there, little bro."

"Hey there, big sis."

Mahina showed no surprise at our greeting. While we'd not yet come clean to the world about Mac's Fury abilities, neither had we hidden his relationship to us entirely. Most thought he was the part-Sidhe son Mom bore while in captivity, which was only half the truth. The brainwashed Sidhe *had* raped her repeatedly, trying to get her pregnant, but the mortal scientists controlling them had only succeeded once they genetically *and* magically manipulated Fury egg and Sidhe sperm, and artificially inseminated her. I could never forgive them for what they'd done to her by force, but one blessing had come of the debacle. Mac.

I'd always wanted a little brother or sister—preferably a fellow Fury. That I'd gotten one when I'd given up hope, and in a shockingly male package, just showed what an ironic sense of humor most of the gods possessed.

Scott came up to claim a hug of his own. He planted a big wet one on Mahina's cheek, which had her smirking and threatening to tell her husband. We all laughed at that, because Kale was about the most easygoing guy in the world and trusted in his wife implicitly. For good reason: Night Owls mated for life.

I looked up at Scott. "Done holding the hand of your high-maintenance client?"

He made an ugly face. "Yeah, got him settled down for now. Until his next bout of paranoia strikes and he demands another face-to-face. Like we aren't stretched thin enough right now guarding the potential Cat victims and assisting the PD, I have to go personally babysit some jackass Orpheus who's convinced his fans are out to get him."

I couldn't resist. "So you're working for Dre Carrington again?"

He swatted me on the butt. "That's low, even for you. No, this is some new hotshot pop star who's barely old enough to vote, which means he knows *everything* even when he knows *nothing*."

"Okay, other than the young thing, still sounds like Dre to me."

Elliana piped up from behind. "Who knows, maybe Dumb and Dumber are related."

Mac laughed. "Sure would explain a lot."

His wife scowled. "Yeah, though at least Dre has eyes only for himself and that Sidhe girlfriend of his. This new twerp, on the other hand, is lucky I didn't cut out his eyes and shove them up his ass."

"Ahh, charming as always, I see, Ellie."

Mac threw an arm around her shoulder before she could give me shit for using the nickname she hated. I smiled sweetly and turned my attention back to Scott. "Your mother inside?" He nodded. "Okay. Let's go see if we can get a name for our prime suspect."

I waited for the others to go ahead and got my brother's attention. He hung back, turning an inquisitive expression my way. "What's up, Riss?"

"You talk to Mom lately?"

He shook his head. "Nah, Elle and I've been busy juggling assignments to keep up with the new intake of clients courtesy of you. We visited her at David's a couple weeks ago and spoke on the phone last week." His gaze suddenly sharpened. "Is she okay?"

I filled him in on the Fury shitstorm currently in the works. He listened, expression growing darker the more I spoke, and cursed when I told him about the subway explosion aimed at me along with the attacks on the rest of our family. Once he heard that Mom had gone back to the Palladium—alone—he exploded even more furiously.

"Gods damn it, Riss, we should *be* there with her right now." He raked a hand through his spiky red hair, flattening most of it. "Bloody freaking hell."

I touched him on the shoulder. "I know, Mac, and I'm doing everything I can to solve this case so I can go to her. And *she's* doing everything she can to pave the road for you coming out so we can induct you into the Sisterhood. Although once we *do* get you in, the name's gonna have to change." My attempt at humor didn't do much to soften his demeanor. I sighed and let my hand drop. "I know you want to do more, and, trust me, I wish you could. But the way things stand right now, admitting the truth about you would only paint a big red *X* on your back and put *two* of Mom's children at risk. She'd be so busy worrying about both of us she'd be in more danger herself."

"Your being right doesn't make this any easier."

I noticed Elliana hovering in the store's doorway and nodded in her direction. "Your wife looks put out with me right now. We better not keep her waiting."

He gave me one of his brotherly *Don't change the subject* looks. "Don't think we're not going to talk more about this later, *big sister.*"

I winced at his tone. "Yeah, I know. Just—not right now, okay? Give it a few days."

"You have until the wedding ceremony next week. By then, your case should be done one way or another, and we can focus on Mom and—Nan." He said the name wistfully, since he'd never seen Nan in anything but pictures and home videos. The Oracles who cared for her in the Otherrealms scrutinized each visitor to their hospice carefully. No way they'd miss his blend of Fury and Sidhe abilities when they scanned him, and their ties to the Sisterhood meant they'd have no choice but to report him. Which could well lead to the civil war we were so diligently working to avoid.

Though the crap with Nan might make all that a moot point soon.

"Deal." He eyed me for another few seconds as if he could see whether I was just humoring him written on my face before heading toward his wife. I brought up the rear but paused in the doorway when the sensation of being watched struck. My eyes scanned the street and buildings around me. Nothing out of the ordinary caught my attention.

"Great," I muttered under my breath. "Now *I'm* becoming paranoid."

Although, is it really paranoia if people truly *are* out to get you?

SCOTT'S MOTHER, LIANA, WAITED FOR US IN the elegant office she maintained just off the store's main showroom. Mac and Elliana bade us farewell and returned to Shadowhound HQ in another part of the building, leaving Scott, Mahina, and me to sit across from the Murphy family matriarch. Having spent so much time in the company of her mother and sisters recently, I couldn't help noticing she'd gotten her no-nonsense demeanor from those Banoub women, but there the resemblance ended. They tried to demand what they didn't give and what they most certainly hadn't worked for. Liana, however, earned respect just by being herself.

Not that I'd ever admit that to her. She *was* her mother's daughter in some ways, after all. Give her an inch and she'd take a hundred miles.

Liana smiled serenely when we turned down her offer of tea, then she zeroed her gaze in on me. "Scott tells me I may be able to help you with the case you're working on."

"Yes, I believe so." I accepted the Ziploc-encased parchment from Mahina and passed it over the antique Chippendale desk. "This is one of the death threats made against Harper and Pennington, one we feel must be taken seriously and thoroughly investigated. Does anything about it look familiar to you?"

She turned the clear plastic bag over in her hands before giving in to the urge to read the letter. I'd already memorized the filthy, hate-mongering words staring up at her. Her eyes were filled with grim determination when she finished reading and met my gaze. "I may no longer be on speaking terms with the majority of my birth family, but I wish none of them ill will. Especially not Elliana's brother. My nephew corresponds with me via e-mail regularly. Has done so for years."

Well, that bumped him up another few notches in my esteem. I'd never realized that. Judging by Scott's sudden scowl, neither had he.

Liana turned the bag over again and raised it closer to her eyes. She nodded to herself. "This *letter* is attached to a rare brand of spell-worked parchment I import from Egypt."

I leaned forward and gazed at her intently. "Don't take this the wrong way, Liana, but why do you sell parchment designed to hide its owners' identity from magical divination?"

She blinked. "I don't. The spells worked into this brand of parchment preserve the paper from the degradations of time or messy spills."

"So whoever purchased this already-expensive parchment from your store spent even more money having it spell-worked even further."

"They must have." She narrowed her eyes and flipped open the slim laptop sitting in front of her. "While I don't remember everyone who purchases this parchment personally, my records will indicate the dates on which we've sold packages and— if the purchasers paid with credit, as many people do these days, I may even be able to provide you with names."

"How far back can you check?"

Liana smiled primly. "As far back as you need me to check, though for now I'll limit it to the past year. I can go back further should that prove necessary."

I nodded. Sounded good to me. Her fingers tapped over the keyboard, she clicked the mouse a few times, and the printer behind her spat out the results of her search. She sped-read the paper as she turned. Her face grew pale, and she jerked her gaze toward me. Liana was hard to rattle—I'd only seen her *this* shaken when I revealed that the Amaya being held prisoner by Dre Carrington was actually an amnesiac Sidhe disguised to look like her eldest daughter.

She pulled herself together and handed the paper over. "We've sold more than twenty packages of that parchment over the past year, although only half that number were paid for by credit card. You'll notice that the last two packages were sold to the same person a month ago." My eyes reached that line the exact moment she said the name out loud. "To my nephew, Pennington Banoub."

SCOTT AND I IMMEDIATELY LOOKED STRAIGHT at each other. To my surprise, he appeared troubled by this news, rather than pleased. Then again, resenting your wealthy cousin for how his side of the family treated your mother was a long way from wanting to believe him to be a psychotic serial killer.

I raised a hand. "Hold on a second. Just because Penn bought the parchment—even if it turns out to be from the same batch—doesn't mean he was the one to send in the threat. Someone could have stolen the paper in order to make it look like he was the guilty party. Or . . ." My voice grew thoughtful. "He could have bought the parchment for someone close to him."

Scott's eyes widened in realization as he no doubt remembered the racist tirade I was currently thinking about. "Like his grandmother, mother, or . . ."

We finished that thought in unison. "Aunt Rashida."

Liana flinched at the mention of her sister. Her bitchiest, least favorite sister, I was willing to bet. "I—yes, it's entirely possible Penn bought the paper for his grandmother or aunt during a visit to Elliana when I wasn't present. I remember both of them collected stationary like some women collect shoes."

It went without saying they would collect expensive and/or rare stationary like the heavy, cream-colored parchment the death threat had been "written" on. I let out a breath. "Well, speaking to Penn about this should be nice and fun."

Scott let out a bark of laughter and shook his head. "You better let me play *bad cop* on this one, Riss. I'm less likely to kill him if he tries to deck me."

Which was a sentiment I couldn't really argue with.

I reclaimed the death threat, handing both it and the inventory printout to Mahina. "Liana, I know this goes without saying, but as a police representative, I have to say it out loud anyway. Please don't mention any of this to anyone. Not even your husband. It could compromise our investigation."

She nodded, fingers clenched on the desk before her the only sign of her emotional turmoil. "Gods know Morgan has kept his work secret from me more times than I could count. Not knowing this won't hurt him any."

Seeing her fight to hold her true feelings inside made me realize that, no matter how long she'd been at odds with her family, she still cared for them. Learning that one of them was, at best, a racist sending death threats against her nephew and, at worst, a psychotic serial killer was eating her up inside. Add all this to the fact that her youngest son was missing, and Liana was in a whole lot of pain.

"It takes a whole heck of a lot to keep a Murphy man down," I said. "One of their charms." Or one of their biggest flaws, depending.

She glanced at her son with a fond smile. "Indeed."

I pushed back my chair to stand. "Thanks so much for your help, Liana. If we need any further information on the parchment paper, I'll let you know right away." She nodded and I turned to Mahina. "Why don't you head back to your place for some sleep? Scott and I can handle the confrontation—I mean conversation—with Penn, and we need you and Kale as fresh as possible to hold down the fort tonight."

"Sounds good to me, Chief. Mind dropping me off on the way?"

"Not at all."

We bade Liana farewell before trooping to the undercover van and piling in—after Scott performed a thorough physical check while I scanned it magically. With crazy-ass assassins on the loose (again), better safe than sorry. A half hour later, Scott and I pulled into Harper's parking garage, although we made a far less impressive appearance in the white whale of a van rather than Scott's shiny red sports car. Which, of course, was pretty much the point.

According to a text exchange between Scott and Harper, Penn and one of his brothers had dropped her off at work earlier but were supposed to pass time at her place before picking her up later. I was just about to shut the engine off when my cell phone buzzed insistently. Having learned my lesson *not* to ignore the damned thing unless in the middle of a crisis, I flipped it open and said hello.

"Riss." Trinity's voice sounded more subdued than usual in my ear. "There's been another attack."

My fingers clenched around the phone. "Attack—not murder?"

"Yeah. Paramedics just rushed Meritton to Mass General."

Relief that Meritton had been attacked rather than one of Harper's more sympathetic exes morphed into guilt—though at least the obnoxious executive hadn't been declared DOA. He still had a fighting chance, unlike Ward Rockefeller.

I checked the dashboard clock—3:12. "Give us ten minutes."

Scott grabbed on to his *oh shit* handle when I reached

over him to flip on the LED visor light and turned on the van's police siren. "Who?"

"Meritton." I reversed sharply and exited the garage, tightening my fingers around the steering wheel. "He's alive but that's all I know."

He sensed the frustration in my voice. "Meritton may have the voice of a chipmunk, but he's smart, Riss. He'll be able to give you details about the attack."

"Yeah, if he makes it." For once, civilian vehicles got out of the way promptly as I sped toward nearby Massachusetts General Hospital, one of the first facilities in the country to develop separate arcane emergency facilities.

Which did not go unremarked upon by Scott. "They get him to Mass General breathing, and he'll make it."

"I've never had a case like this where the perp continues murdering victims right under my freaking nose. It's like he's taunting me to stop him and I can't."

"We'll catch him, baby. We will."

I forced myself to take several calming breaths, focusing again on his use of the word *we*. With Scott beside me, I felt like I *could* do anything. I'd always felt that way—the main reason I'd gone to him for his help with Vanessa even after I'd broken things off with him and had no right to expect it. It also helped to remind myself that this jackass killer was the one thing standing between me and helping my mother in the Otherrealms. We had leads pouring in now, and with a potential witness to question, things were looking up. They had to be. Believing anything else would paralyze me with self-doubt, and that wouldn't help anyone.

Trinity met us near the nurses' station in the Arcane Trauma Unit, an unexpectedly chipper expression on her face. "He's gonna make it. The paramedics said he's out of it and has superficial wounds on his arms and torso, but nothing life-threatening."

"Thank the gods. I'm assuming the 'out of it' means he was drugged like the others."

She nodded. "Yep. They pointed out a puncture wound on the side of his neck that could be the injection site."

I tilted my head. "Side of the neck as opposed to the back like the others. Could be Meritton heard the perp and turned just enough that he didn't get a full dose of the drug. Probably didn't hit the intended vein, either."

Scott whistled. "Lucky bastard."

Trinity nodded. "There's a mundane unit securing the crime scene for us. I spoke to the senior officer, and he said that, unlike with the other attacks, this time the victim put up a fight, lending credence to a decreased drug dosage. Hopefully the perp will have left behind some DNA to make tracking his ass down easier."

"So when do we get to talk to Meritton?"

An unfamiliar voice sounded from behind. "He's asking for you now, Chief." We whirled and caught sight of a beefy, middle-aged doctor handing a medical chart to a nurse. "You *are* Chief Magical Investigator Holloway?"

Some people recognized me more easily in Fury form than mortal—obviously this doctor didn't have that problem. "Yes, I am."

The doctor—Cyrus Gideon, according to his name tag—nodded at Trinity. "Inspector LaRue explained that Mr. Meritton may have been attacked by the same person responsible for the serial killings going on in our city. Normally I would advise against a victim under the influence of an unknown substance speaking with police, but he's becoming more lucid already and is adamant he see you now. If you'll both follow me?"

I asked Scott to keep an eye on the entrance to the arcane unit, and he agreed, leaving Trinity and me to troop after Dr. Gideon. It was a short walk to a brightly lit room featuring two emergency gurneys, one of which held a thrashing, cursing Paul Meritton. Several exasperated medical personnel—mostly arcanes—were in the process of trying to calm him down with very limited success. Only when his gaze fell upon me did he finally settle down.

"Chief Holloway, told you that we'd meet again." His eyes seemed glassy, but he didn't slur any of his words. "Luckily for you it happened sooner than expected."

Same ole Meritton, at least: squeaky, high-pitched voice and overweening sense of pride. Some things even a brush with death couldn't beat out of a person.

I couldn't resist asking, "Paul, what happened to your security detail?" A stubborn expression came across his face, and I shook my head. "Don't tell me you gave them the slip?"

He scowled. "I needed some alone time, for Christ's sake. Ten bloody minutes without someone staring at me or telling me what to do. Is that too much to ask?"

Trinity took over the *good cop* persona. "Of course it isn't, Mr. Meritton, but what's important right now is catching the person who attacked you so you can get your privacy back for good. Can you tell us anything about what happened?"

"Of course I can." He shifted on the gurney, glaring at the medical staff poking and prodding him. "Would you leave me alone for a gods-damned second so I can *think*?" I nodded, and they slipped out of the room, seeming relieved rather than annoyed at having their work interrupted. Meritton turned his attention back to Trinity. "I took the private exit from my office and stepped into the back for a cigarette. Just needed to *breathe* for a minute. Yeah, I know it wasn't the smartest thing in the world to do but . . ." He looked suddenly exhausted and unsure of himself. "My father was just diagnosed with a disease the Oracles aren't sure they can treat. They give him six months if he's lucky, and there's not a damned thing my millions of useless dollars can do about it."

Well. Even misogynistic assholes had their soft spots. I found myself glad for the Meritton family that they wouldn't have to face the loss of *two* of their members in such a short period of time and managed to keep my voice more even-tempered. "So you stepped outside in the alley to sneak a smoke, and then what?"

"Nothing at first. Was on the second cigarette when I had the feeling someone was watching me. Had time enough to curse myself and turn for the door when that shithead *stabbed* me in the neck and started wailing on me. I got a little woozy but was able to give as good as I got—the money I spent on that black belt in tae kwon do didn't go to waste, I can assure you—and we made enough noise the bodyguards tracked us down and scared off the shithead."

"Did you get a good look at your attacker?"

"I tried, but whatever he shot me up with made my vision blurry. All I could tell was he wore black clothes, biker boots, and a ski mask so I couldn't have made out his face anyway."

"Height? Build? Race?"

"Hard to say. More than five six, less than six foot. Average build. Race I couldn't say, because he had on that mask and gloves." He frowned as if just recalling that detail. "Yeah, leather gloves the same color as the jacket, although he had slits in them where his claws came out."

That had both Trinity and me leaning forward eagerly. "Claws?"

"Yeah. Funny how I just realized that. The whole thing happened so fast." He gestured to the bandages on his arms and chest. "He clawed the hell out of me, but I was doing the same thing to him so I guess we're even."

Trinity and I exchanged glances. "Would you say your attacker was a Cat, then?"

Meritton hesitated. "His claws were more like a Cat's than any other type of shifter, but his eyes . . . they weren't colored or slitted like a Cat's, and our pupils *always* slit if we shift enough to get our claws out. Mine sure as hell did." He gestured, and I consciously noticed what my subconscious had already picked up on. His eyes were still greenish-yellow with the telltale slitted pupils of the Bastai.

"Do you remember what color his were?"

He squinted in concentration, before nodding confidently. "Yellow. Not like a Cat's, more orange-yellow. Like a—"

We said the last word in unison. "Hound's."

I cursed under my breath, since that wasn't what I wanted to hear. Instead of a civil conversation with Penn about the parchment paper he'd bought, we might be dragging his ass back to the MCU for an interrogation. Because, just like his cousin Scott, Penn possessed amber-yellow eyes typical of many Hounds. Add that to his link to the parchment paper the death threat came in on, and things weren't looking too good for Mr. Adonis.

Harper was *so* going to kill me for cracking her wedding bells . . .

CHAPTER SIXTEEN

SCOTT CONVINCED ME NOT TO BREAK OUT the sledgehammer just yet, reminding me that another Hound could be the culprit. I would have put my money on dear Aunt Rashida except for that whole keeping-an-open-mind thing.

Trinity made a face when I suggested she ride back to Harper's condo in the undercover van with us, and I rolled my eyes. "What, you too good to ride in anything but your *Porsche* now, Nana-nana?"

She had the grace to flush and give in, knowing I would give her never-ending piles of grief otherwise. The dashboard clock read four forty-eight by the time we made it back to Harper's parking garage. Her text had indicated she'd be working until six thirty or seven, so we'd have just enough time to *chat* with her fiancé before he had to pick her up. Hell, depending on how the conversation went, we might just be able to pick her up on our way to an MCU interrogation room.

Not exactly a ride I'd be willing to take in this (or any other) lifetime.

The three of us stepped out of the van and headed to the entrance to Harper's building, only to stop when Scott grabbed my arm and pointed to a Lexus SUV pulling into an empty space a couple dozen feet away. "Isn't that—"

"Penn's *fine* brother, Tariq," Trinity finished before I could. She met my amused glance with a defensive, "What? He's single; I'm single—there's no crime in looking."

"No, there's not." My eyes narrowed when the logical realization hit. "If Tariq is pulling into the garage *alone*, that means Penn is upstairs. Alone."

Scott shook his head in disgust. "What an idiot."

Trinity blinked, making the connection as well. "Meaning not only did he put himself at risk staying alone in Harper's place, he may have no alibi for the attack."

Gods save me from those who refused to save themselves. "Bingo. So, lover girl, care to distract Tariq long enough for Scott and me to catch his brother by surprise? Give us, say, ten minutes if you can."

She smoothed the lines of her jacket over her curve-hugging black slacks. "Sugar, there's no *if* to that statement. Ten minutes are all yours."

Poor Tariq. No way could he see the potential heartache coming his way. Then again, knowing my partner the way I did, he wouldn't want to run even if he *could*.

Penn couldn't see the trouble breathing down his neck, either. When he nonchalantly opened Harper's door without uncovering her peephole or asking who was knocking, I had to clench my fingers to keep from wrapping them around his beefy neck. Here we were, running ourselves ragged to keep him safe, and he couldn't be bothered to take the most basic of precautions to secure his *own* ass. That indicated one of two things: more than enough arrogance to get himself killed or lack of worry because *he* was the killer. Possibly both.

He didn't seem overly surprised to see us. Interesting. "Marissa, Murphy." Of course he sneered the second word. "I'm afraid Christabel's not home yet."

My tone was deceptively conversational when I replied. "Thanks for sharing, but we already knew that. We're here to speak with you, not her."

"Well, come on in, then."

He stepped back and let us pass through to the living room. I chose to remain standing this time, manila folder held at my side and eyes glued on him as I tried to read his emotions. He didn't seem overly concerned that we'd paid an unexpected visit to see him at his fiancée's home. No accelerated pulse, no quickened breathing, no beads of sweat breaking out where they shouldn't. Either he had no clue what had just gone down, or he was a damned good actor.

That second option got my blood pressure boiling. "So, care to explain what the *hell* you're doing here alone when you know there's a psycho killer gunning for Harper's lovers stalking the city streets?"

Penn scowled and shot me a stubborn look. "That's not really your concern, now is it, Chief Holloway?"

Oh, from "Marissa" to "Chief Holloway." Our boy was too arrogant for his own good indeed. He needed to be cut down a peg or two, and fortunately I was more than up for the task. "Actually, *Mr.* Banoub, it is *entirely* my concern considering that we're in the midst of a serial murder investigation and you have now made both my life and your fiancée's far more stressful."

"I've been perfectly safe while my brother's been running wedding errands for me. I had the most cutting-edge of arcane and mundane security systems installed several days ago—I knew the moment you stepped into the hall and that you were friendly."

Friendly was pretty much the last adjective I'd use to describe my feelings for him in that moment. *Frustrated*, maybe. *Disgusted*, sure. *Fed up with*, oh yeah.

"While I am overcome with joy to hear *you've* been perfectly safe, Pennington, I can't say the same for Paul Meritton. Perhaps you've heard of him? One of Harper's exes—who was attacked a couple of hours ago not *all* that far from here. By someone who could fit your general description, come to think of it. Luckily *you* have an alibi, since you've been with your brother all morning. Oh wait. You *don't* have an alibi because your brother needed to go *run errands*."

He had the sense to go pale and fall back onto the pristine white couch behind him. "Oh gods, another murder?"

Interesting that he said *murder* rather than *attack*. The killer should have known he'd botched things with Meritton: None of the superficial wounds he'd suffered were life-threatening, and the drug dosage had been way too low to put him in any danger on that front, either. Even more interesting, Penn looked every inch his typical clean, well-pressed self, with no signs that he'd been in a recent life-or-death struggle. No scratches or cuts, no bruises or black eyes. Well-groomed fingernails without a trace of blood or skin beneath them. Even if he'd taken the time to wash up and change clothes after the attack, there should have been *some* mark on him after a fight with a full-grown Cat, especially since there'd been nowhere near enough time for him to visit a magical Healer *and* get back here to clean up.

I leveled a tight-lipped expression his way, staying silent long enough to make him squirm before responding, though not to his question. "Can anyone verify you've been here the entire morning, Pennington?"

Color flooded back into his cheeks, and he shoved to his

feet. "You can't possibly think that *I* had anything to do with this!"

My brow arched meaningfully. "Is that a 'no, they can't'?"

He cursed under his breath, turning pleadingly from me to his cousin. Which spoke to his desperation, since he never failed to disparage Scott at every single opportunity. "Murphy, *you* know I'm not a murderer. No Banoub would—"

Scott smiled coldly. "Oh, so *now* I'm a Banoub? Don't look at me to save your ass, cuz. You got yourself into this mess, you can damned well get yourself *out* of it. Or not, it doesn't really matter to me so long as Harper's safe. Something she hasn't been for a moment since hooking up with *you*."

Penn's face paled again, and his body sagged from the force—and truth—of Scott's words. "I swear I had nothing to do with Meritton's attack. If I had a problem with one of Harper's exes, I would take it up with him face-to-face, man-to-man. Not attack him from behind and drug him senseless."

"Like you did with your last Cat lover's old-flame-turned-new?"

His cheeks flushed. "*Who* told you about that?"

"Never mind my sources, Penn."

He let out a loud sigh. "Yeah, like with Jillian. Though *he* attacked *me* when I went to get my grandmother's ring back from her."

I let that information sink in for a moment, adding it to all the other bits and pieces floating around. True that, in many ways, Penn made the *perfect* suspect. His recent outbursts over the smallest stressors. The fact he resisted the idea of hiring a full-time bodyguard and had conveniently sent his brother out to run wedding-related errands just before another Cat was brutally attacked. Not to mention his link to the parchment paper used for the most credible death threat.

Speaking of which . . . I opened the folder in my hands, withdrew the Ziploc-wrapped parchment, and dangled it in the air, rear side facing him. "Does this look familiar to you?"

He stepped closer and peered at the parchment intently. At first he seemed puzzled, but then recognition lit in his eyes. "Looks like the stationary Aunt Rashida asked me to get the last time I visited Elliana at Hounds of Anubis."

Bingo. I flipped the paper around so the text spelling out the threat showed clearly. He mouthed the words as he read them, his expression growing darker the further along he read, until his lips pressed into a furious line and his fists clenched at his sides.

"I can't—she wouldn't—no." He shook his head as denial replaced anger. "My aunt would not say such ugly things." Oh, but she would—as "Sierra" had already witnessed first-hand. "She would never hurt me like that. Besides—" Penn seemed to grasp at straws as his worldview that family was all and the Banoubs stood on a lofty pedestal was challenged. "She would never have the strength to torture and kill all of those men."

Now that *last* statement was one I could actually agree with, but I had two words for him: *hit men.* Having been on the wrong end of murder-for-hire contracts more than once, I was living, breathing proof that money could buy the brawn that nature did not grant. And money was not the slightest bit of a problem for Rashida Banoub.

I didn't share any of that with Penn. No sense upsetting him even further, and I didn't want to risk him warning off his aunt before I could confront her myself. So I settled for distracting him instead.

"This cutting-edge security you installed. Can it verify you remained here in the apartment all morning?"

Excitement lit his features and he nodded. "Yes, it can! There's video surveillance not just in the hallway, but at each of the windows and the common areas as well. The security logs will also show I activated the system and didn't deactivate it except for when I let you two in."

Well, *that* was one less thing to worry about. Though Mr. Adonis was exceptionally lucky he'd had the damned security systems installed or he'd be heading back to the PD with me whether I believed in him or not. I couldn't appear to favor him over other potential suspects just because he was Scott's cousin. *Especially* because he was Scott's cousin.

"I'll need copies of the video and security logs before I go. And, Penn, don't make me tell you again. Until this case is solved, neither you nor Harper is to be alone for a *moment*. Not to pop downstairs to check the mail. Not to sneak outside for a cigarette. Not even to buy wedding presents for each other. I don't care how rich or powerful you are, I don't care how safe you *think* you are, this killer specializes in taking out wealthy arrogant bastards who believe they can handle themselves. Don't risk your life—and Harper's— because you think you're somehow special. The morgue's full of people who thought that. Are we clear?"

"I—yes, we're clear. And you're right. Gods, I've been a fool."

Not to mention ridiculously lucky. I slipped the Ziploc bag into the folder and eyed the nearest clock. Exactly ten minutes had passed since we'd left Trinity, which meant—

Penn's body stiffened when a soft chime echoed through the apartment. "Someone just stepped off the elevator." He hurried to a small, discreetly mounted plasma screen on the wall between the living room and kitchen. "It's just my brother. Oh, and your partner."

Punctual to a fault. One of the things I loved most about Trinity. Hey, *one* of us had to have that quality.

She also didn't skip a beat when Scott and I dragged her out of the apartment before she really set foot in it—after one final admonition to Penn to keep his lips zipped and stay with someone else at all times. Of course, I had to tweak her nose on the elevator ride to the lobby.

"Tariq seemed *really* disappointed you left with us so soon."

Her expression was decidedly smug when she leaned back against the elevator wall and drawled, "Not *too* disappointed, sugar, seeing as how we have a date for the weekend after the wedding."

I burst into laughter and held my hand out to Scott. After grumbling a bit, he reached into his pocket, pulled out a twenty, and slapped it into my palm. Trinity and I exchanged a grin. "Well, at least you made the *smart* bet, Riss."

"Actually, we both knew you'd wrap him around your pretty little finger. Scott just figured Tariq would make you as Sierra's assistant and ask you to be his date for the wedding."

She thrust her head into the air and *hrmphed*. "As *if*. I've not yet blown my cover when on assignment, and I sure don't plan to start now. Besides, people generally see what they expect to, and he had no cause to think mousy Miss Jones would show up here."

Oh so true about people seeing what they expect to see. One of the reasons arcanes had been able to hide their presence from the vast majority of mortalkind for so many millennia.

I filled Trinity in on what we'd learned from Penn and my next plan of attack: confronting Aunt Rashida about the parchment paper used for the death threat. Rashida was a smart—and rich—cookie, though, so I wanted to arm myself with as much ammo as possible before skipping into the lion's den.

"I'm gonna e-mail Mac the list of magazines Mahina's friend divined from the death threat letters and have him do some digging. If Rashida has subscriptions to most of those magazines . . ."

A grin spread over Trinity's face. "Brilliant. Absolutely brilliant." She got that sneaky look I loved so much as another thought occurred to her. "If she's the one who sent that threat in, she doesn't know the reporter failed to save the envelope before handing it over to police."

And *that* was further proof why I kept her around. "Not too shabby yourself, Trin. If she *somehow* gets the impression we retrieved, say, a hair from when she sealed the envelope and can easily make a DNA match once we get a warrant . . ."

"She may get flustered enough to let something slip."

Scott shook his head, looking torn between admiring and appalled. "Remind me to never get on your dynamic duo's bad side."

In unison, she and I replied, "We don't *have* a bad side."

To which he rolled his eyes and said, "Of course you don't."

Smart man.

WHEN MY BABY BROTHER CAME THROUGH for me, he really *came through*. Not only did his techno magic prove Rashida Banoub possessed a subscription for *every single one* of the magazines on the diviner's list, she also paid dues to a radical organization associated with the one political magazine on the list, *Divergence*. The organization, Citizens for Arcane Divergence (the CAD), seemed to have a twofold mission: separation of the arcane races from mortalkind and, still further, separation of the arcane species one from another. The CAD sought to establish an arcane nation here on earth—something that just wasn't happening without another war—and taught a tenet favored by one of the mundane world's biggest villains: racial purity.

They abhorred intermarriage not just with mortals, but between the arcane races themselves. Finding out that Rashida Banoub was a card-carrying member came as absolutely no surprise after her tirade the night of Harper and her nephew's engagement party.

Scott and I left the safe house bright and early the next morning for Rashida's high-rise apartment in one of the oldest, poshest buildings in the Underbelly. Technically, it wasn't even *in* the Belly—the citizens of this haute couture neighborhood had seceded from the Belly years ago and "modestly" named it Avalon, after the Isle of the Blessed associated with Arthurian legend. Which I'm sure sits really well with the residents of the *true* Avalon, one of the few Otherrealms still alive and kicking.

Rashida's butler—I kid you not—ushered us into the penthouse suite, down an artwork-bedecked hallway, and into the *salon* where his employer waited for us. That's what he called it, too, the "saah-lon." Scott and I pointedly avoided meeting gazes since bursting into laughter would have ruined the grim atmosphere we were going for. Our hostess stood when we entered the room, dismissing the butler with a nod and finally deigning to look directly at us. Scott earned a slightly curled lip before she turned her gaze my way. She recognized me (as myself) right off the bat; but in Boston, most arcanes did.

"To what do I owe this unexpected—pleasure, Chief Holloway?"

Man, she did the ice-queen routine better than Ekaterina— and that was saying something. "I'm sure you're familiar with the investigation coinciding with your nephew's upcoming nuptials, Miss Banoub." I called her "Miss" rather than "Ms." deliberately—she'd recently gone through a nasty divorce— to see if I could get a rise out of her. Disappointingly, her poker face would have done Lady Gaga proud.

"Of course. Such a horrible thing going on right now.

An arcane serial killer." She shook her head. "You never saw such things before the War."

Translation: before we high-and-mighty arcanes started mingling with the riffraff mortals. Like immortals didn't engage in countless bloodthirsty and violent acts long before we started traveling the fairy paths to the mortal realm.

I forced any sign of derision out of my voice while withdrawing the plastic baggie from its folder once more. "The War changed many things for us all, Miss Banoub. Now then, I won't waste your valuable time by beating around the bush." She glanced blankly at the bag dangling from my hands until I turned the text in her direction. Recognition sparked in her face for a moment, but she shoved it aside in favor of that winning poker face and met my eyes silently. I gave a small smile. "I must say I'm shocked to learn that a lady of your class and breeding knows some of the filthy language used in this letter."

Frost painted her words even colder than her pinched face. "I'm sure I don't know *what* you're talking about, Chief Holloway."

Derision dripped from my lips this time. "Of *course* you don't, Miss Banoub." I tossed the Ziploc bag to Scott, taking note of the way her eyes warily followed its sharp arc from me to him. Papers rustled as I drew two of them from the folder and let them flutter to the antique table resting between her and me. They landed slightly skewed but face up and clearly legible. The first contained a typewritten account of how we traced the parchment paper from the death threat to her—something that had her lips tightening and her fingers trembling. The second paper was our coup de grâce, however: the diviner's list of magazines used to spell out the death threat along with the corresponding list of Rashida's magazine subscriptions—all of which appeared on the first as well.

I had to give her credit. Despite growing noticeably pale after skimming the second paper, she showed little other emotion; she simply raised her gaze to defiantly meet mine.

"The jury will find your subscription to *Divergence* and your membership in the CAD *most* incriminating, Miss Banoub."

Her body jerked as her ice-queen façade cracked ever so slightly. "Jury? What in Anubis's name are you talking about?"

"The jury for your trial, of course." I dropped all pretense of courtesy, letting the crackle of Rage color my voice. "You see, *Rashida*, my partner is applying for a search warrant right now based on the evidence in front of you. A warrant for your DNA. Once we link your DNA to a hair found on the envelope that threat was sent in, the DA will have *no* trouble indicting you for terroristic threats against a protected class. From there, it will be a short hop, skip, and jump to linking you to whatever goons you hired to carry out the killings. Cue the second jury for your murder trial."

"M-murder?" She sagged onto the sofa behind her much the way her nephew did just the day before. Her hand settled atop her chest as she fought for breath, seemingly on the verge of a breakdown. "I—you—no, you don't understand!"

"Understand what, Rashida? Why you murdered those poor, upstanding males whose only crime was to be from a different race than your own?"

"No!" she shouted, cheeks flushing with sudden color. "I would *never* murder anyone, much less good boys like those who—who . . ." Her voice trailed away.

I blinked as comprehension flooded my brain. "Who date within their own species as the gods intended?"

She either failed to catch or didn't care about the sarcasm in my voice on the last few words. "Exactly. *If* I were going to hurt anyone in this unsavory situation, it would be that feline bitch, not one of her unfortunate ex-lovers."

My lips twitched at the juxtaposition of "feline bitch," though I managed to fight back an outright chuckle. "So you expect me to believe you *aren't* against the other arcane races as a whole?"

"I'm not!" she insisted, sweeping a hand toward the list of magazines in front of her. "*Divergence* caters to arcane races of *every* stripe, Chief Holloway, and the CAD boasts members of every species as well. We stand for racial pride and purity, not hatred or genocide."

Scott spoke up for the first time, waving the note. "It doesn't get much more hate-filled than this nasty piece of work right here."

Rashida refused to glance his way or acknowledge him directly, simply locking her gaze on mine and launching into another theoretical. "*If* I admitted to sending that death threat—which I am most certainly not doing at this point— my motive would have been passionate conviction in my beliefs. A far cry from the jealous rage necessary to systematically butcher Cat after Cat."

She *did* have a point. Her ice-queen persona seemed to suggest someone far more inclined to sending in vitriolic— but supposedly anonymous—death threats rather than engaging in torture and murder. Even if one degree removed through a hired assassin. Not that I'd say that to her.

My lips twisted in a saccharine smile. "It doesn't take jealous rage to hire a psychopath who delights in his bloody work, *Ms.* Banoub." I pretended to consult my notes. "Or should I call you Mrs. Nassar?"

Her fingers twitched on the desk before her, but she managed to keep her face remarkably composed. "As I'm sure you're perfectly aware, *Chief* Holloway, my divorce was finalized just last month."

I affected a surprised expression. "Oh, I do beg your

pardon. I hadn't realized your fourth marriage ended so soon."

"Fifth," she gritted out. "Which I'm sure you are equally aware of." Her fingers continued trembling as she removed them from the desk and crossed her arms over her chest. "Since you've brought up such a distasteful subject, let me point out the flaw in your theory that I hired some sort of assassin simply to come between my nephew and his . . . fiancée."

"Oh? What would that be?"

"I couldn't afford to hire a nickel-and-dime hit man from the dregs of the Belly, much less the sort it would take to pull off a series of perfectly executed murders, Inspector."

Scott and I shared disbelieving looks before I turned mine back on her. "Excuse me if I find that impossibly hard to believe, considering our current surroundings. Considering the family you come from."

"Five marriages. Five divorces, the first two of which were ridiculously expensive. Sure, I had ironclad prenups for each of the last three, but considering that my mother forbade me to marry the last of them . . ." Her expression hardened. "Let's just say I've been cut off from the familial purse strings for the time being. Why else do you think I asked my nephew to buy that stupid stationary for me?"

Well, color me surprised. Cut off from the familial purse strings or not, I'd never have guessed that Rashida was having the slightest bit of financial trouble. I'd have to have a forensic accountant verify that fact, but if it were true . . . She'd probably go down to the bottom of the list as a suspect. More's the pity.

I retrieved the documents in front of her and returned them to the folder with exaggerated movements. "All the same, I trust you won't be making plans to leave the Boston area anytime soon, Miss Banoub. Any effort to do so will be seen as a murderer fleeing justice, and I *will* come after your ass. As a Fury, not as Chief Magical Investigator. Understood?"

She stood, poker face intact once more as she realized I wasn't going to clap her in chains after all. "Completely understood, Chief Holloway. And just to make sure there's no further miscommunication between us, you can direct any future inquiries to my attorney, who will be in touch with you later today."

Touché, Ice Queen, touché. I thought it but didn't say it out loud. Sometimes I *can* exercise tact when called for. Made up for some of the times I failed miserably . . .

CHAPTER SEVENTEEN

LIFE AS SIERRA NIEVES RETURNED WITH A vengeance that afternoon when Harper and her bridesmaids met my alter ego for the final dress fitting. I found myself getting caught up in my role again, which amused me to no end. Who would *ever* have thought Marissa Holloway, unabashedly pragmatic Fury, would enjoy orchestrating dress fittings for ten extremely opinionated women?

Still, even I had my limits, and fortunately for my blood pressure, Penn took my warning to heart and waited for his fiancée in the bridal shop's lobby, accompanied by not one but *two* of his beefcake brothers, Tariq included. Probably a good thing that Trinity and Cass were handling a depressing but straightforward suicide that had been called in early that A.M., amazing undercover powers of Trinity's notwithstanding. Risking a blown cover twice would just be stupid. Not having to deal with the bride's aunts and mother helped my stress level, too. Harper's dress fit her like a glove with the slight alterations made by the boutique's seamstress, and even annoying cousin Camilla seemed happy with her completed gown. Truly a day for miracles. Maybe we'd catch the killer while we were at it.

Yeah, right, and the Megaera would extend an olive branch and offer restitution for the attack at the subway station.

Harper managed to snatch a private moment with me in her fitting room. "What happened when you questioned Rashida about the death threat?"

I rolled my eyes. "I can see your fiancé continues to follow directions in his usual manner."

She tilted her head and gave me a *whatever* look. "Like you expected him to keep that from *me*."

"Hoped for, maybe. Expected, not so much." When she pinched my arm, I grunted and surrendered with ill grace. "She didn't come right out and admit it, but I'm pretty sure she flipped out enough to send the threat. I *don't* think she had anything to do with the murders, however."

Harper finished changing back into her street clothes, giving a sigh as she settled atop a chair to slip on her socks. "That's pretty much what I expected. She's like a passive-aggressive version of my *own* aunts, really. Quick to anger, willing enough to threaten those standing against her, stubborn as hell, but not capable of cold-blooded murder."

"Unfortunately."

"Hey, that's my future aunt-in-law you're talking about."

"Yeah, yeah. I just meant unfortunately that leaves the actual killer still out there, free to run amok again." When her face fell, I reached over to give her a hug. "Hang in there, Harp. We'll get him—and soon."

Her lip trembled but she nodded. "I know we will." She began tying her shoelaces with sharp, determined movements. "Penn's taking me to Mass General after this."

"Whoa, you're going to visit Meritton? I got the impression that one didn't end on good terms."

"It didn't, but I just feel like—like—"

"Like you owe him a personal apology?"

She flushed. "It sounds silly when you put it that way, but—yeah. I do."

"Well, I can't tell you how you should feel in this situation. Nobody can. Just don't be surprised if he lashes out at you. He didn't strike me as the warm-and-fuzzy type."

"Bast's tail, but he is *so not*. Still, at least I'll feel I've done my part if he plays the prick and chases me out."

"Fair enough. So, you ready for the bridal shower?"

A charmingly ugly face met *that* question. "If I told you yes, I'd be lying. Two hours trapped at my mother's house with all *my* female relatives, all *Penn's* female relatives, plus the bridesmaids? Yeah, that's going to be so. Much. Fun."

I couldn't hide a grin. "Yeah, but just think: You have a wedding planner to blame if anything goes wrong or to break up any fights that start."

She perked up at the reminder. "True! And you don't have to worry about them getting mad at the *real* you or coming after you later because, hey, they think you're Sierra Nieves, Wedding Planner to the Stars!" Her hands waved in the air dramatically as she intoned Sierra's unofficially official title.

My turn to pull a sour face. "I should have known *you* came up with that stupid cover."

An expression of innocence she couldn't quite pull off dissolved seconds later as she gave in to laughter. "Actually, *that* part was Mutt's idea."

"Oh, he is *so* not getting any for the next month!"

Harper smirked at my bald-faced lie. "Sure, because Furies are known for their superior powers of abstinence. Good thing you all have to consciously will yourselves pregnant or there'd be little Furies-in-training taking over the world!"

Yeah, consciously will ourselves pregnant—or be manipulated by evil scientists jacking our bodies up with all sorts of drugs, magic, and other fun stuff. I smoothed my outer expression to keep Harper from pursuing a line of questioning I didn't want to think, much less talk, about.

"I've finalized all the arrangements with the caterer and Trinity's picking up the cake on the way to the shower. Is there anything else I can take care of for you?"

She shook her head adamantly. "No, Riss, you've done more than enough. Vic's just lucky you handled most of the arrangements since the shower's usually the maid of honor's albatross."

I had to fight to keep my true emotions from writing themselves all over my face again. I'd thought—okay, I'd hoped—that not seeing Victor for a couple days would cool my desire for him. No dice, however, as demonstrated by the spear of lust bursting through my body when he greeted me with a kiss to each cheek an hour earlier. Having Harper mention the supercharged sex drives Furies were infamous for helped assuage my guilt a tiny little bit. *See, Scott, it's not* my *fault he makes me feel like a bitch in heat. Blame the Fury hormones!*

Because that would go over *so* well with my Hound.

Hell, it wouldn't even go over with *me*. Sure, Fury hormones and supernatural Rage shaped our personalities, often goading us into acting on instinct rather than with deliberate thought, but that excuse went only so far. We each held final responsibility for our actions. Feeling something didn't mean we had to act on it. That this was the first time I'd found myself struggling with an overblown Fury sex drive for more than one man at once didn't mean I got to absolve myself of blame for how I reacted to it. No matter *how* much that realization sucked.

The Fury in me also refused to hide from the problem at hand. Ignoring my attraction for Victor would just make it stronger, more enticing. No, I needed to confront it head-on, take the bull by the horns—so to speak—and show my traitorous body who was boss.

I forced my attention back to the blushing bride. "All part of the full-service package you get from Sierra Nieves, Wedding Planner to the Stars!"

Harper shook her head with a grin. "Wow, we even have *you* drinking the Kool-Aid now."

"Scary, isn't it? But seriously, we should rescue your groom from the hundred and one bridesmaids you have running around in the lobby."

She gave a mock shudder. "Poor man. After he willingly sat through all this, I know he *really* loves me."

I didn't have to fake the smile that tugged my lips upward. The little moments in life revealed most clearly our emotions for those around us. Harper enduring hellish behavior from Penn's grandmother and aunt; Penn putting up with the now-constant companionship of his brothers, not to mention being overrun by bridesmaids; both focusing on the other in the midst of the upheaval going on around them, determined to live on their own terms rather than give in to the demands of a killer bent on destroying their relationship. Now *that* was love.

Harper led the way to the lobby, where we discovered Penn surrounded by two bridesmaids rather than nine, the rest having headed for the hills with their gowns. Penn and Harper trooped off with his brothers and her sisters, leaving me to take that bull—er, Cat—by the horns. Victor, no doubt remembering Penn's annoyance from the tuxedo fitting, hovered on the edges until the larger group exited center stage. He smiled once they disappeared from sight. "So, *querida*, alone again at last."

I opened my mouth to give him a polite brush-off, but his fingers brushed a stray lock of hair back, grazing the sensitive skin of my ear and setting off shivers along my spine. Liquid heat pooled inside my belly and good intentions went astray.

"I missed you yesterday, Sierra."

My pulse picked up speed. I stared into his dark eyes, transfixed. Oh, gods, *how* did he do this to me? How *could* he do this to me when I loved Scott so? It made absolutely no sense. "I—I missed you, too."

He captured my hand in his own, bringing it up to trace a searing line of kisses along the palm. "Please say you'll have dinner with me tonight."

I floundered for words, head saying "No" but body screaming "Yes!" *Just tell him . . . tell him no.* My mouth opened to say just that, but what came out instead was, "Of course." As he took me by the hand and guided me toward a luxury SUV parked at a nearby meter, images of Scott flooded my brain, but even that couldn't counteract the sheer, unadulterated lust pulsing through my body, clubbing my brain cells into submission and forcing me to follow where Victor led. Gods, that was so freaking *not me* that warning bells started ringing in my head at the same time my body made like a sheep. We reached the dark gray SUV, and something struck me right away. Its windows had been tinted the absolute maximum allowed under mortal law.

Something's wrong here; something is really *wrong. Think, Riss, stop feeling and* think*! Why do you feel like this each time you're with him? You love* Scott. My brain moved at a glacial pace, but at least it functioned. Doubt crept through my mind. What did I really know about Victor other than what Harper—and he himself—told me? A whole lot of nothing.

When Victor ushered me toward the passenger door, lips curved in a decidedly smug smile, inner alarm bells rang out. I'd learned to trust my instincts over the years, and in that moment, they screamed that I couldn't trust *Vic the Slick* as far as I could throw him. Okay, as far as a *mortal* could throw him. Maybe he wasn't a cold-blooded serial killer, but that didn't automatically make him trustworthy, either. And until I figured out *why* my hormones went haywire around him—and a way to counteract their temporary insanity—the wisest course of action would be to stay as far away from him as possible.

I forced myself to dig my heels into the ground and find my voice. "Vic, I'm sorry, but I really can't have dinner with you tonight. My—"

His fingers closed around my arm bruisingly, and he tugged me closer to the open door. "Hush, *querida*. Get into the car. I'm going to take you back to my place for the night of your life." He reached into his pocket and withdrew something small and dark in color that I couldn't quite make out and disquiet bloomed into outright fear.

Fortunately *that* just pissed me off. Rage stirred beneath the surface, and rather than tamp it down as I normally would, I fanned it from the barest spark to a blazing inferno. Clarity burned away all traces of unnatural desire. I glared into his beady little eyes, and suddenly he didn't seem all that attractive anymore.

"Take. Your. Hands. Off. Me. Now."

Surprise widened his eyes, followed quickly by annoyance and anger. Not that his anger could hold a candle to mine. "*Querida*, what's wrong—"

I held up a warning hand and took a step back. The hand holding the unknown object swung toward me, and I growled well enough to make any real Hound proud. His hand froze.

"Look, Victor, you need to just back off right now. Seriously."

"But, *querida*, I don't understand."

"Neither do I understand why you're so anxious to get me into that car. As I tried to tell you, my family needs me right now. So back. Off."

My cell phone chose that exact moment to ring, and I couldn't have asked for better timing. Victor looked like he wanted to smash the gadget to itty-bitty pieces, but I flipped it open before he could even think about going through with it.

"Hello." The phone beeped a couple times, signaling a dangerously low battery. I scowled since I knew good and well I'd charged it the previous night.

A burst of static sounded in my ear followed by a tinny voice. ". . . Riss . . . Cori's gone . . . her anywhere. Need to find her."

I frowned. "David?"

Another buzz of interference and then, "You gotta find her, Riss!"

Definitely my brother's voice begging me for help. And oh gods, it sounded like something had happened to Cori. My pulse pounded in my ears. What if the Megaera had gotten hold of her and was even now planning to use her as a hostage? Or even worse, what if they'd already killed her—*No! She's fine. You'll find her and get her back to them.*

"David, I'm on my way now. Just stay calm."

The cell phone beeped insistently as I slammed it closed and shoved it into a pocket. Victor's expression seemed more concerned than annoyed now, but it didn't fool me. Something was *definitely* not quite right with Vic the Slick.

"Something you need to keep in mind, *Victor.* My family comes first for me. Always have and always will. And if you *ever* try to force me to do something against my will again, you better reconsider because *nobody* uses me. Nobody."

His mouth opened and closed several times, but I didn't wait for a response; I simply turned away and took off toward the safe house. Whoever had snatched Cori had sure as hell better hope she escaped before I caught up with them.

* * *

I HALF RAN TWO BLOCKS BEFORE DUCKING into an alleyway and shifting into Fury form, trusting the darkness to shield me from prying eyes as I launched into the air and flew straight toward the safe house. Less than five minutes later I let myself into the safe house, only to find it in a state of uproar. Serise paced the living room floor, hand curled over her stomach and teeth clenched. David comforted Jessica on the sofa while one of Scott's cousins tried without much success to entertain the two baby girls crying in a playpen on the far side of the room. Scott's *other* cousin aimed a weapon my way until he registered my identity and lowered it. Serise's two sisters burst into the room from the rear of the house and calmed down upon recognizing me.

Jessica leapt to her feet and gave a relieved gasp. "Marissa! Thank God you're here."

Wow. I didn't get to hear her say *that* too often. If ever. "What *happened*? Where's Cori?"

She waved a piece of notebook paper in the air, and I snatched it. Cori's familiar feminine handwriting spelled out several hair-raising lines.

> *Mom and Dad: Please don't freak out when you read this. Some of my friends from softball camp are going to a movie nearby, and I just had to get out of here for a while. I'll be home before midnight. Promise!*

I let the paper flutter to the floor and met Jessica's anguished gaze with one of my own. "My gods, you mean she actually *snuck out*? Past two—no three—Harpies and two Warhounds? Not to mention her *parents*?"

The aforementioned Harpies and Warhounds had the

grace to look embarrassed, but Jessica just gave me a no-nonsense look. "David and I were bathing the girls down here when she snuck out from up there."

David broke in. "If you'll remember, Riss, you were a master of sneaking out of the house during your teenage years yourself. And we've been more worried about others sneaking *into* the house, not someone sneaking *out*."

Okay, so he had a couple points there, not that I'd admit it out loud.

I shook my head impatiently. "Whatever. When did you find the note?"

"Maybe fifteen minutes ago. She can't have gotten far, but we didn't want to leave the girls here to go look for her. Not until we spoke to you."

"No, no, you did the right thing. I want all of you to stay here and safe. Serise and I will track down Little Miss Sneaky and drag her ass back here in no time flat."

Serise gave a tight smile and strode across the room to me as I lifted my arm toward her. She slashed a thin line of blood into my skin and did her Harpy mumbo jumbo while a horrified Jessica looked on. David turned her away when he realized what we were doing, but the damage had already been done. Oh well, not like I ever took pains to hide what I was from the magic-hating woman. Besides, she'd best get used to it. Olivia would *definitely* manifest Fury abilities when she got older, and chances were that Cori would, too—provided she survived the ass-chewing when I caught up with her.

SERISE'S TRACER SPELL WORKED LIKE A charm, and we followed Cori's trail to a movie theater less than a mile away. I frowned at the crowds bustling inside and outside the large building and pondered the best way to extract my wayward niece without causing too large of a commotion. Not that I really cared if I mortified the almost sixteen-year-old girl in front of her friends; but I *did* care about drawing unwanted attention before I got her back to relative safety.

Then I caught a blur of motion near a side exit of the theater and realized someone else hadn't been too afraid to cause a commotion. I shot off toward the alley in a flash, trusting that Serise would guard my back. Voices grumbled angrily the closer I drew to the dimly lit stretch of asphalt, and my heart picked up speed when I recognized one of them as Cori's.

". . . don't care *who* you say you are or *how* good a friend you were to Aunt Vanessa. I'm *not* coming with you and you can't make me. So just back off!"

That's my girl! I let a small, proud smile curve my lips and then put on another burst of speed, determined to reach my niece before whoever she confronted could try and "make her" go with them.

"Calm down, sweetheart, and listen. The Elder Furies want to speak with you and they sent me to bring you to them."

"I don't care if the Moerae herself sent you to summon me. I'm not a Fury yet and I know my rights. You can't take me anywhere without a guardian, and you sure ain't my guardian, lady."

I finally caught sight of a scowling Cori with her back pressed against a grimy brick wall, hands crossed over her chest, and eyes narrowed. Standing just a few feet away from her was a shadowy figure I could just make out as wearing an all-too-familiar red leather uniform. I channeled a thread of magic to boost my eyesight and wasn't particularly shocked to recognize the face that went along with that voice as being Durra's. Several dozen feet still separated me from her so I didn't risk alerting her to my presence by crying out.

On the downside, that also meant Cori didn't know I was rushing to the rescue.

Durra apparently tired of reasoning with the stubborn teenager (I could have told her how futile *that* would be) and decided to switch to force. Her serpents hissed as she stepped forward, grabbed hold of Cori's arms, and began summoning the magical breeze that would allow her to take flight as I had earlier. I put on another burst of speed, but it was useless: I'd never catch up to them before she got my niece into the air.

Apparently Cori had the same thought and she liked it even less than I did because she totally gave in to her inner fury. Literally.

Cori gave a shriek of anger and threw back her arms, breaking away from Durra. Magic pulsed through the air, flowing across her body and shifting things a little here, a little there. Honey blond hair became charcoal gray. Deep blue eyes shifted to unearthly onyx facets. T-shirt and jeans were replaced with a sleeveless red leather vest and pants, battered sneakers replaced with red leather boots. Last, but not least, brilliant sapphire light washed over her arms, radiating from each shoulder down her arms and leaving in its wake rainbow-hued serpents with iridescent eyes. The serpents hissed, flicked their slender tongues, and twined their way from her upper arms to lower.

Oh my gods, she's finally Fledged!

Pride nearly overwhelmed fear, and I could do little but gape at her for several seconds. I'd *known* my niece would become a Fury, but never had I expected to be lucky enough to see her first transformation. Tears pricked my eyes, and I called myself all kinds of a fool but couldn't help it. What an honor the gods had bestowed upon me.

Fortunately, Cori didn't waste time on going all mushy; no, she got down to business. She shrieked again and kicked out with her booted foot, catching Durra off guard, since she'd been just as surprised by Cori's transformation as I had been. The Megaera flew back into the air and hit the opposite building's wall with a sharp impact. She grunted and fell to the ground in a boneless heap, eyes rolling back into her head as she fell unconscious.

Damn. That really is *my girl!*

Cori hissed as loudly as her serpents and advanced on the prone form of her enemy, raising wicked-looking talons that burst from her hands with little thought on her part. It didn't take a genius to know that if I didn't step in right away, Cori's inner Fury would have no trouble finishing off the woman who'd tried to snatch her. While that might make things easier in the short term, there'd be long-term consequences, not the least of them the tremendous sense of guilt she'd feel when her uncontrollable Rage wore off.

I summoned my own magical breeze and half jumped, half flew the remaining dozen feet separating us, slamming into my niece and forcing her back against the wall once more. She spat and clawed at me worse than any Cat might have done, once again inspiring a surge of pride. Damn, but she was going to make a great Fury someday.

"Cori, stop it. It's me, Aunt Riss."

She continued fighting for another few seconds until my words finally pierced the veil of Rage holding her in its grip. Once they did, she narrowed glowing green eyes and peered at me intently. I gave her a calm, reassuring smile and nodded. "It's me, baby. Now calm down and let go of the Rage. That's it, just take some deep breaths and forget about the woman behind me. Breathe in, breathe out. You can do it."

I heard Serise moving behind me and trusted her to make sure Durra wouldn't strike while I wasn't looking. I focused on talking my niece down from her Rage-filled ledge. It took several minutes, but finally she threw herself into my arms, sobbing, and slowly Fury magic receded, leaving once more only a blond-haired, blue-eyed mortal girl clothed in blue jeans and a T-shirt. With, of course, one unmistakable difference. Each of her arms now bore an apprentice Fury's rainbow-hued serpent twining from upper shoulder to elbow.

Cori was now, for better or worse, a Fury.

CHAPTER EIGHTEEN

OF COURSE, THE LAST THING EITHER SHE OR I wanted to deal with in that moment was her mother freaking out over her Fledging, so we decided the best thing to do for now was magically disguise her tattoos until things had calmed down some more. I'd have to tell my mother as soon as possible, of course, but for now we lost nothing by keeping her parents in the dark. They had plenty enough to worry about what with trying to keep all three girls safe.

Serise took care of preventing Durra from following us, and I didn't ask for details. She promised she hadn't killed the woman, and that was enough for me. She also agreed to keep quiet about Cori's transformation, for which I was grateful. Cori's parents let her have it when we got her back to the safe house, once they'd assured themselves she was unharmed. She kept glancing at me with a smile in her eyes, no doubt knowing how damned proud I was that she'd

Fledged, and then nodding at them with a properly chastened expression. I was *so* going to have my hands full mentoring that one.

And as the gods were my witnesses, mentor her I would. I had no clue how I'd work out all the logistics or when I'd be able to start her training, but no way would I trust her with anyone else. Mom, maybe, but she'd have her hands even fuller than I did once she was voted into Stacia's vacant Conclave seat.

The rest of that evening passed by uneventfully enough. Scott never showed up, but I didn't get too worried since my cell phone battery had gone completely dead sometime after David's last call. He'd undoubtedly called and left a message he'd gotten caught up with that damned client of his. If something worse had happened, Mom would have found out and put in another appearance.

I stopped by Best Buy bright and early the next morning to replace my defective cell phone charger and plugged it into my computer at the MCU so I could wade through several voice and text messages.

Sure enough, the first text came from Scott. Its header indicated it had been sent during Harper's dress fitting, but the damned cell hadn't sent an alert at the time thanks to the dying battery. *Needy client strikes again. Stuck with him all night. Call me at my place tomorrow PM.* Well, that explained why he'd never popped by the safe house the night before, something I'd barely noticed with all the hullaballoo going on.

Trinity had texted an update the night before on the suicide case, which had been as open and shut as expected, and sent another that morning asking where my lazy ass was hiding itself—using pretty much those exact words. I let her know I was already at the PD and then scrolled to the final message, fingers crossed I'd somehow managed to dodge the proverbial bullet for now. But then I noticed the minutes-old message was from Harper, clicked it open, and read five little words that sent my world careening off course once more.

He knows about the affair!

My pulse skittered. *Oh my gods, Scott!* Then I frowned. Wait. No way anyone could term my feeling an inordinate amount of lust for Vic the Slick as an "affair," even adding in the fact he kept trying to get me alone so he could engage in just that thing. So then what the hell was Harper talking about?

Only one way to find out for sure. I gritted my teeth and punched in Harper's number.

She answered before the first ring ended its electronic echo. "Oh gods, Riss, it's such a mess!"

The panic in her voice was very loud and very personal, and sounded like it had *nothing* to do with Scott and me. "Calm down, Harp, and tell me what's going on. What affair?"

"*What* affair? Mutt told me he *told* you!"

A lightbulb burst into life inside my tired brain. "You mean you *didn't* tell Penn about you and Scott?"

"Gods, no, Riss! He gets so insanely jealous. I *knew* he'd flip when he found out Scott and I dated even though it was before he and I even met. I'm not even sure how he found out!"

Okay, so technically this did have *something* to do with Scott and me, but relief that Scott had caused this disaster-in-waiting made me almost giddy, until my mind seized on one of Harper's words and shoved it to the forefront. Who referred to a one-night stand as "dating"? "I—it's not like you two dated long."

"Exactly! Four weeks is *nothing* in the scheme of things for an arcane!"

Yeah, nothing—unless you *lied* to a new lover by claiming you hadn't *dated* that person at all. *One-night stand my ass!* Rage churned in my belly, but self-reflection had me fighting it back. *What's worse—playing down a relationship that took place when you were broken up, or engaging in extreme amounts of lust for another man just because you're undercover?*

I kept my tone cautious. "Is he that mad? Has he—called the wedding off?"

"No, not yet, but—I'm scared, Riss. He stormed out of here mad as hell and threatening to beat the shit out of Mutt when he finds him. Tell me you're with him now so I at least don't have to worry about *that*."

Her faith that I could keep two riled-up Warhounds from killing each other might have warmed my heart under other circumstances. "I—wish I could, Harp, but Scott was babysitting that Orpheus again last night. I'm supposed to call him at his place this afternoon."

"It's almost noon now. Shit, Riss. Penn ran off without Tariq, and you know there's no love lost between him and Mutt's family."

I glared skyward. *Are you all even* trying *to help me out here? It's like you* want *to start another arcane war!*

"I'm shifting and taking off now, Harp. Meet me at Hounds of Anubis."

And maybe, if the gods got off their lazy asses to help a Fury out, I'd get there in time to avoid having yet *another* murder case on my hands . . .

HARPER MUST HAVE BEEN ON HER WAY TO Hounds when I called, because she pelted up to the building in Cat shape just as I landed and shifted from Durra's form to my own. It was pure self-preservation that I was impersonating the one Fury I knew none of the Megaeras would be after. Few others were present to witness our transformations—noon might have been a respectable time

of day in the mundane world, but here in the Belly it was
ridiculously early. Those who *did* catch sight of us recognized the telltale red leather of a Fury and wisely looked
elsewhere. Some things remained the same for immortals
as for mortals: Avoid getting caught up in police investigations if at all possible.

Neither of us wasted time on social niceties. "See Penn
on your run over?"

"No. Nothing from above?"

"Nope. Maybe we beat him here." A loud crash rent the
air, followed by raised voices and smaller crashes inside the
building. *There goes* that *idea.* I tugged on the boutique's
doorknob but found it locked despite the sign indicating
business hours started at noon. Not that locked doors had
ever stopped me before. Gods, we had to put a stop to this
as quickly as we could. Containment was the name of the
game at this point. The fewer people who knew that Harper
and Scott had actually dated (I bared my teeth just thinking
that), the safer he would be from the rampaging psycho.
Well, the rampaging serial killer. "Stand back."

She immediately hopped down several steps. I placed
both hands on the door and braced myself. While the building's *interior* doors had been spelled to recognize the magical signature of Furies—and allow them entrance to sealed-off
rooms—the exterior doors barred entrance to everyone unless
they had been keyed to the protective spells. Scott and I had
not yet reached the level of comfort in our relationship that
his family granted me unlimited access to the building that
housed both their livelihoods and homes. Not that it didn't
go both ways—he'd been knocked flat on his ass by my own
security system not that long ago.

Magic bubbled up from the floor beneath my feet and
surged through my body, pooling into a sapphire cloud that
clung to my hands. I murmured words that helped force
energy into the shape I willed it to become: a metaphysical

sledgehammer. Sparks flew when I jerked my hands forward and assaulted both the building's mundane lock and magical defenses. Physical pain seared my body each time I wielded that hammer against the door, but I simply grunted and continued striking until *success*! The door slammed open.

The front of the store stood empty. I led the way to the door separating Hounds of Anubis from the back room serving as Shadowhound headquarters, adrenaline surging through my system. No more crashes echoed from the other room, but that didn't mean a whole hell of a lot.

I paused at the door, taking the time to summon Nemesis and Nike into living form. Harper met my questioning glance with a nod of readiness and waved a Taser to show she had not come unprepared. One of the handy-dandy models that came with several arcane-specific settings and operated on a magical rather than an electrical level.

"You handle your idiot male and I'll handle mine." She nodded in response to my whisper, I shoved the door open, and we jumped into the room ready to kick some Warhound ass, only to walk into a scene neither one of us would have expected in a million years.

Scott and Penn sat at the beat-up table in the center of the room, locked in combat as anticipated, but not beating the snot out of each other. Instead, each had a hand clasped around that of the other, arms straining to force the other's hand to the table top and thus become the victor. Broken glass littered the floor around them, with several intact shot glasses and a very large bottle of whiskey giving silent testimony to the sources of the earlier crashes. Several of Scott's relatives stood around the room, cheering on Scott and jeering Penn, save for one person. Elliana clapped and hollered on his behalf more loudly than the others combined.

Harper and I exchanged looks again. Here we'd burst in, expecting to find our lovers locked in mortal combat, only to find them engaged in drunken *arm wrestling* instead. I wasn't sure whether to be amused, relieved, or pissed off. Neither, apparently, was she.

Scott's sister, Kiara—she of the healing hands and magical potions—happened to be closest to the door, so I scooted forward and jabbed her in the shoulder. She turned with a scowl, rubbing her arm, but relaxed when she recognized me. We'd become close friends during my first relationship with Scott, and unbeknownst to me, she'd continued to advocate on my behalf during our breakup. Of course, she'd gone for my figurative jugular when I first came back to Scott for help. He *was* her little brother, after all.

I jerked my thumb toward the arm wrestlers. "You the bookie or something? Thought people were killing each other in here. Almost busted down the front door trying to get in."

Her cheeks took on the hue of sun-ripened tomatoes. Liana must be away from the building entirely or her daughter would never have stopped to watch the show. I don't care how old someone gets, mothers never get less scary.

"Elle said those two have been going at it for a couple hours now. They drink and argue for a while, then start arm wrestling, then go back to drinking and arguing."

"She say what set them off?"

If possible, Kiara's cheeks grew even redder when she caught sight of Harper inching up next to me. "Um, wow, look at the time. Gotta open the shop or Mom will kill me." She scurried away before either of us could react, leaving us to shrug and move on to Elliana.

Oh gods, with the sheer number of people witnessing this shouting match, no *way* would we be able to contain this. Gossip spread among the arcane world just as quickly as it did in the mundane world. Okay, to be fair, even faster. Scott was *so* going to be on the killer's shit list after this.

I tried to drown burgeoning fear with sarcasm. "So, who's the house favorite?"

Ellie shot a sardonic look over her shoulder. "Like you can't tell."

My lips twitched. "Well, the Banoub name isn't exactly the most popular around here."

She rolled her eyes. "Tell me about it." Her gaze moved from me to Harper and grew sympathetic. "How you holding up, *chica*?"

"I've been better. But at least *those two* aren't beating each other bloody like I expected."

"It was kinda touch and go there for a while till I got them talking rather than growling at each other."

Getting two bristling Warhounds to go all verbal without throwing even one punch? Okay, that was impressive even for Ellie. Not that I'd ever tell *her* that.

Harper had no such qualms. "How did you pull off *that* miracle?"

"Threatened to sic Grandmother on the both of them if they couldn't settle things like grown men rather than oversized pups."

I blinked. That'd do it. Penn had been trained from early on to revere Neema Banoub whereas Scott would have wanted to avoid her invading the Murphy stronghold at any cost. Bad enough he had to put up with her in small doses in his role as groomsman.

Harper tilted her head, a calculating expression spreading across her suddenly feline face. "Hm. I'll have to keep that tactic in mind for the future."

Too bad that threat wouldn't work nearly so well coming from me. Scott knew good and well I loathed his maternal grandmother even more than he did. More's the pity. "So, how long they been arm wrasslin'?"

"About a half hour now. First they bitched at each other, then they got in a drinking contest, and now they're going for the best two out of three. Tied one-all at the moment."

Judging by the wordless grunts, the sweat dripping from their brows, and the strained looks on their faces, this one might end in a draw rather than a clear win, which would actually be healthier for both their egos. I kept my voice brusque. "While I'm glad the two *oversized pups* seem to have worked things out with relatively minor property damage, I'd really rather channel their skills in more useful—and sober—directions today. Like, oh, I don't know, tracking down a serial killer."

Ellie's eyes grew shadowed at the reminder. She burst into action, barking out orders to the catcalling (ha) mercenaries and clearing the room in thirty seconds flat. Penn and Scott paid little attention to their dwindling audience until I upended a bottle of booze (*not* my precious Jack) over their heads, at which point they howled out threats and turned to face their antagonist. Both fell silent when they recognized me. Outright guilt flashed across Scott's features—guilt I might have exploited if I wasn't wallowing in some of my own.

"So, now that you've worked *that* out of your systems, let's lay it all out on the table. Yes, Scott and Harper had a fling a couple years ago. Yes, they could have been more forthcoming on the exact nature of that *way* before now. No, we don't have time to open that particular can of worms. Can we all agree that stopping the killer before he strikes again is a little more important than dragging skeletons out of closets?"

Scott and Harper exchanged a quick, shamefaced glance but nodded wordlessly. Penn blinked bleary eyes in my direction, inebriated mind processing my words. Since *my* idiot male seemed to have no such difficulty, I realized he must have watered down his own drinks to make sure *one* of them kept his wits about him.

Penn shook himself suddenly—looking very much the

oversized pup as droplets of whiskey flew every which way—
and frowned at me. "So you knew already?"

"More like I guessed they had a—thing—but it's obviously past history now so nothing to worry about."

His shoulders sagged. "Guess it was stupid to think any
man—even a Hound—could satisfy a Fury *and* another
woman at the same time."

Since his sentiment so closely mirrored my own thoughts
on the subject, I had to choke back a laugh and force myself
to nod seriously. He reached an unsteady hand toward Scott,
who tensed until he realized the other Hound wanted to
shake hands rather than commit bodily harm against him.
"Just to be clear, you ever sniff around my mate again and
you're a dead man."

Well, shaky his hand and thought processes might be,
but he was sober enough to mark his territory the Warhound way. Mortal women might have gotten offended, but
we arcanes recognized it for what it was. Millennia of
magical instinct driving him to warn off a potential interloper, much the same as animals in the wild. Which, some
of the time, they *were*.

Scott accepted the handshake calmly. "No less than I'd
expect or deserve."

Harper cleared her throat and wrinkled her nose when
Penn stumbled to his feet and toward her. The man, quite
simply, reeked—inside and out—of whiskey.

I wasn't too shy to express that, either. "You two need
showers, stat, so we can stand to be in the same room as
you for more than five minutes."

Harper backed away from her fiancé. "Oh yeah. And
some coffee." When Penn nearly tripped over his own feet
trying to get to her, she amended that. "Lots and lots of
coffee."

Scott stood with much less trouble, wary eyes all on me,
no doubt braced for a bitch fest he couldn't quite believe

wasn't yet coming. Well, hundreds of how-to dating articles said to always keep them guessing.

I pointed to the door leading to the residential area of Murphy Central. "Seriously. You two go shower while *I* clean up *your* mess and Harper goes for coffee. Lots and lots of coffee."

He hesitated while Penn managed to get his hands on Harper and they exchanged murmured comments. "We good?" he finally asked with a pleading cast to his voice.

"For now." I caught another whiff of alcohol and waved him off. "But only if you go shower *now*, Murphy."

The sigh that racked his body was long, heavy, and proof of just how worried he had been. An hour later found both men clean, Penn mostly sober, and the four of us holed up in the tiny Shadowhound office just off of the former arm-wrestling arena. It also saw us locked in a fierce debate over where to proceed next in our investigation. Penn wanted us to just lock up all of Harper's exes—convinced that, if none of them turned out to be the killer, at least jail time would keep them safe while he offered himself up as the wedding-day sacrificial lamb to flush out whoever *was* the murderer. Needless to say, Harper didn't care for *that* suggestion at all. Plus, it was illegal.

Penn rolled his eyes when I pointed out we couldn't forcibly incarcerate potential victims, not even to protect them. He muttered something in ancient Egyptian—still going strong among Warhounds loyal to Anubis—something that had Scott trying to disguise a laugh as a cough.

I turned my baleful stare in Penn's direction. "Putting aside the legality issue, what if one of Harper's exes *is* the killer? Just because we *think* we've ruled them all out doesn't mean we couldn't be wrong. We want to catch the killer before he strikes again, not postpone his next attack until a time when we're not expecting it."

Penn closed his mouth on whatever argument he'd been

about to make and chewed on my words. Nice to know he *could* use his brain sometimes. Then again, the man *was* an acknowledged financial genius.

Harper pushed back from the wall she'd been leaning against. The office barely had room for a desk, two chairs, and a filing cabinet. "Much as I hate to say it, I think Riss has the right idea and we should be focusing on them as possible suspects rather than future victims."

I sat up straighter in my undersized chair. Harper had been resistant to the idea that *any* of her lovers—past or present—could be responsible for these killings. That reluctance likely had two sources: reluctance to believe any of them capable of cold-blooded murder and fear that she might have missed signs she'd been sleeping with a psycho. I wondered what had so radically changed her mind and asked just that.

She sank back against the wall, an unbearably sad smile touching her lips. "Remember when you said not to expect much from Paul since he didn't seem the warm-and-fuzzy type?"

I nodded slowly.

"Well, when Penn took me to see him, he acted like a Care Bear hopped up on meth, all sunshine and roses and concern for *us* and what *we're* going through."

"Okay, admittedly weird, but how do you get from there to murder?"

"Three things. One: He grilled me for details on the wedding like he actually cared—or was angling for an invite to make it easier to get close to us. Two: He lied to you about the reason he snuck away from his bodyguards that day—Paul hasn't smoked a day in his life, and in fact, he's allergic. And three: He knew about the tongues being ripped out—even though we never released that detail to the press."

CHAPTER NINETEEN

AFTER HARPER'S REVELATION, SCOTT AND I left the "happy couple" behind to head to Mass General so we could pay a little visit of our own to Paul Meritton—only to discover he had been released late the previous evening. A detour to his private residence proved no more fruitful—his palatial home stood dark and silent, without the normal hustle and bustle of household staff one would expect such an imposing estate to require. There wasn't even a single guard working the security gate, which told me all I needed to know.

"He's in hiding."

Scott tapped his fingers against the Ferrari's steering wheel and glanced up at the darkening sky. August afternoons tended to be hot, muggy, and prone to intermittent thunderstorms. From the looks of it, we'd be getting one of those in the next hour or two, which would mean cranking

up the convertible's retractable top. Something we both
would put off as long as possible. Neither of us enjoyed
being cooped up in steel cages on wheels when we could
have the open air hitting our skin instead.

"Think he'd be nuts enough to show up at his office
today? Seemed the workaholic type to me."

I pursed my lips. "Probably not, but that poor assistant
of his no doubt did. She can put us in touch with him if
nothing else."

He nodded and whipped the car in the opposite direction. One benefit to Meritton's excessive wealth: It took less
than five minutes to get from his home to his office. Mere
mortals might have made the drive in closer to ten. Thankfully, Scott was neither "mere" nor "mortal."

Perhaps unsurprisingly, Clara Danvers seemed to be
expecting us. She met us at the front desk before the receptionist had a chance to take our names. She murmured something I didn't quite catch to her fellow employee before turning
with a painfully polite smile. "Chief Holloway, Mr. Murphy,
how lovely to see you both again so soon, although under such
awful circumstances."

The woman certainly had an excellent memory. Then
again, that was what Meritton paid her for. "Indeed.
Mr. Meritton is in some ways a very lucky man."

She nodded. "None of us can believe such a horrible
thing happened so close to company premises."

No need to voice the usual empty platitude that it "could
have happened to any of us" since, really, it couldn't have.
One benefit to such a specific killer, I supposed, and the
major reason we didn't have an epidemic of mass terror
rampaging through the city. The mortal majority could tut-
tut about how horrible it all was without actually worrying
too much for their own safety.

"No need for worry," I drawled with a deep sense of
irony. "We have patrol cars cruising the area regularly for

the foreseeable future." She gave a remarkably unconcerned nod. "While I took Mr. Meritton's initial statement
in the hospital, I really need to ask him some follow-up
questions."

"I'm afraid Mr. Meritton is taking some long-overdue
time off to recuperate from his—ordeal."

I gave a polite smile of my own but kept my voice hard
as steel. "Only to be expected, of course, but it really *is*
imperative I speak to him as soon as possible."

No sign of surprise at my insistence, which meant Meritton had prepared her for this eventuality. Whether because
he'd expected he would fall under greater scrutiny as a suspect after becoming the killer's first (and only) survivor or
simply because it seemed likely we'd come up with more
questions for him remained to be seen.

"Of course. While Mr. Meritton is currently unavailable
in person—as I'm sure you can appreciate—he indicated a
willingness to speak with you via videoconference should
the need arise."

Videoconference? Was this guy for real? He expected
me to conduct a police interview electronically? Then I
remembered the size of the ego I was dealing with, and it
got a whole lot more believable.

"You can inform Mr. Meritton that the need *has* arisen,
and I can wait while you arrange the *videoconference*. Immediately. I'm sure *he* can appreciate the time crunch we're
under."

Clara Danvers let her no-nonsense assistant façade slip
enough to roll her eyes, as if saying her boss wouldn't really
appreciate it but she'd make sure he complied all the same.
Within fifteen minutes, she had Scott and me ensconced in
a private conference room in front of a sharp-looking laptop
computer with built-in webcam. A few clicks of the mouse
and keyboard, and Mr. Meritton's handsome but unappeal-
ing face popped onto the screen.

"I'll just leave the detectives here so you can enjoy your discussion in private, sir."

He waved her off as imperiously through the Internet as he did in person. Once the door closed behind Clara, he focused his attention on us. Or more specifically, on me.

"Chief Holloway. Have you nailed the bastard who attacked me yet?"

Funny how he managed to make himself seem like the primary victim here when three—make that four—other men had been beaten to bloody death where he'd been barely scratched. An uncharitable thought, but then Paul Meritton didn't inspire overly charitable emotions. He was an unabashed misogynist to boot, no matter the smooth demeanor he might sometimes affect, with varying degrees of success depending upon his mood. The outward appearance of a crazed, envy-ridden murderer? Perhaps.

"We have the vast majority of our resources working on this case, I can assure you, though we have not yet made any arrests." No flicker of surprise or even disappointment. "I *do* have a few more questions for you, however."

He shifted in the high-back black leather chair that was the only feature I could actually make out of his surroundings. "I will be happy to assist in any way possible. The sooner you track this bastard down, the safer I'll be."

I figured irony would be wasted on his oversized ego and bit back a sarcastic comment. At least he had one thing right: The sooner I nailed this killer, the safer Harper's lovers—including Penn and the man seated next to me—would be. As the bout of drunken arm wrestling had so amply demonstrated, I could no longer assume the killer wouldn't find out—or didn't already know—about Harper and Scott's intimate past. Though just thinking the words *intimate past* had me gritting my teeth. Okay, so maybe I was still a little envy-ridden myself.

"First, exactly how long have you been a smoker?"

He blinked. "I—what the hell do my smoking habits have to do with any of this?"

Aha, so I'd cracked his smarmy armor. "Humor me, please. I assure you that your *smoking habits* are relevant to the case."

Color bloomed in his perfectly chiseled cheeks. Had I never heard his squeaky voice or witnessed his asshole tendencies, I might have found it endearing to see such a gorgeous guy blush. Under the current circumstances, I just found it interesting.

He recovered himself quickly. "I can tell by your tone that you've caught me in my little white lie. As I'm sure you're now well aware, I don't smoke. It makes me physically ill."

Kinda like how his attitude made me feel. "Care to explain why you felt the need to tell a 'little white lie' to a police detective conducting an active criminal investigation?"

Meritton didn't skip a beat. "Because the real reason I slipped away from my bodyguards that evening was something I didn't want *anyone* knowing about."

Scott moved impatiently beside me but remained silent. Good thing Meritton could see only me in the webcam's viewfinder.

I vocalized Scott's impatience, though a bit more diplomatically than he would have managed. "And what activity did you engage in that required such absolute secrecy?"

"Waiting for my supplier."

My tongue skipped a few beats while my mind processed that statement. Whoa, wait a minute. Was he actually confessing to a sworn law enforcement officer that he'd been trying to buy *drugs* when the attack—the *alleged* attack— went down? That was just crazy enough to possibly be true. Who would admit illegal drug use to a cop except someone who didn't want to take the fall for murders they hadn't committed? Although, as I realized a heartbeat later, this killer might be smart enough to know that was exactly what a cop would think and use that against me.

Merriton must have caught something of my thoughts in my expression because he elaborated before I could ask. "My company enjoys a lucrative partnership with a supplier of experimental, but *not* illegal, pharmaceuticals we expect to be approved by the FDA in the next year or so. We're just waiting for the final testing to be wrapped up."

My brow furrowed. "And the reason you had to meet with this legitimate business partner in secret—leaving behind the bodyguards hired to keep you safe—is?"

He gave me a look that suggested I was being naïve. "Come now, Chief. Surely you of all arcanes are familiar with corporate espionage."

Against my better judgment, I became intrigued. "You mean you feared a competitor might have planted a spy in your security detail?"

Since he was related to most of that security detail, Scott muttered something rude under his breath. Too low for the laptop's mike to pick up, fortunately.

"It's not as unlikely a prospect as you seem to think. We've uncovered three spies in the scant year of our partnership. Now that approval is all but guaranteed, we anticipate finding even more."

I had to admit it made sense. Too much sense. My eyes narrowed when something else occurred to me. "Might these experimental, but not illegal, drugs happen to be of a—dual nature?"

His posture stiffened, and he cast the virtual me a suspicious glance. "*Why* would you ask that, Inspector?"

Oh, so I'd been demoted from "Chief" to "Inspector." Seemed I struck a nerve.

I leaned forward and made my voice as smooth as silk.

"Because, Mr. Meritton, each and every one of the killer's victims—including yourself—were shot up with the same hybrid drug. An interesting fact, wouldn't you say? I *do* find one thing even more intriguing, however."

He eyed me wordlessly, expecting but not asking for further explanation.

"Unlike the others, you received a small enough dose that you were only slightly impaired. In fact, it seems the amount you received served to augment your strength so you could fight off your attacker rather than succumbing to him as the others did."

"You needn't remind me just how lucky I was, Inspector."

Notice how he tries to ignore the hybrid-drug angle. "Yes. Unbelievably lucky, some might say."

He pushed back his chair and bared his teeth, visibly showing anger for the first time. "I'm not sure I like whatever it is you're insinuating."

"Okay, well then, let me stop insinuating and ask another question instead. How is it you knew what had been done to the other victims' mouths?"

"How did—Harper. That little bitch."

Scott growled plenty loud enough for the microphone to catch, but I didn't object. "That's Special Agent Cruz, Mr. Meritton, and she's the wrong species to be properly termed a bitch. But yes, she did let the cat out of the bag—pun very much intended—and I find it *beyond* interesting that you not only have access to large quantities of the exact type of rare hybrid drug used in these murders, but that you also know a detail never released to the press. One that only the killer could have known." Okay, so I was bluffing a bit about knowing he had the *exact* same hybrid drug as the killer. What he didn't know could only help me—I mean the investigation.

He was the one to do the teeth-gritting this time as he appeared to consider calling *me* a "little bitch." Wisely, he fought back that urge. "You're not pinning this on *me* due to your own raging incompetence."

Another growl from Scott, though this one had more amusement to it than anger. At least *one* of us found that funny.

"I've been called many things over the years, Meritton, but incompetent isn't one of them." Two could play the demoted title game. "I've also never railroaded *anyone* into confessing to something they haven't done. You *do* have to admit those two facts I mentioned are rather damning, however."

"The first fact is hardly damning considering the fact I supply the city morgue with many of its medical supplies. I have several—shall we say friends—working for the ME's office. As for the second fact . . ." His face assumed a more calculating expression. Several moments passed before his eyes widened, and he choked out an oath. "That son of a—" He shook his head and considered silently some more.

"Who, Meritton? And what?"

He waved me off much as he had Clara Danvers. Scott made more impatient rumblings next to me, but I just jabbed him into silence, eyes glued onto the laptop screen and Paul Meritton's beady little eyes, until finally, he spoke again.

"You really *should* look into Pennington Banoub's romantic past, Chief Holloway."

Oh, so Chief again, was it? Gods, but this man could turn it on and off like a switch. "Don't give me that BS, Meritton. I haven't found a shred of evidence pointing to his involvement, and you're not going to distract me from the fact *you* seem to have several strikes against you."

Meritton gave an impatient growl of his own. Not nearly as impressive as Scott's, but then, not many men were. "Listen to my words carefully. I didn't say *he* was involved, just suggested you carefully consider *his* romantic past rather than *hers* the way you have been."

I paused and chewed on his words. So he wasn't pointing an accusing finger in Penn's direction merely to save his own ass. That didn't explain why he was being so blasted cryptic all of a sudden. "Why the circular navigation, Meritton? Why not come right out and say whatever it is you want me to know?"

He tightened his lips into a narrow line before replying. "Because, first of all, I only have suspicions. And because, second of all, if what I suspect is true, my attack was meant as a ruse to get you doing just what you are—considering me a suspect. Next time I will not be so lucky, especially not once you look into what I've told you to investigate."

"If you feel you're in danger, you need to let me arrange protective custody for you."

His lips twisted sardonically. "The way you managed to 'protect' Ward Rockefeller? No thank you, Chief, I'd rather take my chances."

I wanted to join the Growlers R Us Club but managed to maintain my dignity. Just barely. "I can have you named an official suspect and arrest you on suspicion of multiple homicides, Meritton."

He gave a smug little smile. "Good luck finding me. I wouldn't suggest wasting the MCU's 'vast resources' hunting me down—or trying to anyway—when you would just be playing into the killer's hands. I have two final pieces of advice: Check on my alibis for the previous attacks to rule me out, and look into that other matter I mentioned."

"Wait, dammit, don't hang up yet. What if I need to ask you more questions?"

"Just do what I said for the love of Bast!" He gave an exasperated breath. "I swear by Her name I *did not* kill those other Cats or fake my own attack. And don't call me—I will call you."

The screen faded to black, the Internet-age equivalent of an old-fashioned phone slam. I let out a string of colorful curses in both English and Spanish, inspiring an amused chuckle from Scott. I turned my frustration in his direction, but he held his hands up in an *I surrender* gesture.

"What's so freaking funny, Murphy?"

He bit back another laugh. "Ah, nothing, I just think—"

"Just think *what*?"

"Okay, you just proved my point perfectly."

"That might make the slightest bit of sense if I knew what the hell your point *was*."

"Cursing in Spanish? You've obviously been spending *way* too much time playing the part of Sierra Nieves."

Damned if he didn't have a point after all, but he only knew the *half* of it . . .

WHILE I HATED TO DO THE EXPECTED (OR IN this case, demanded), Meritton's "advice" had actually been solid. Trinity and Cass agreed to verify the Cat's alibis for the previous attacks. Scott and I headed for Beverly, Mass., to track down one Jillian Matthews: high school administrator for an all-girls, mixed-race school; card-carrying member of the Bastai; and ex-lover of Pennington Banoub.

Stepping through the doors of Victory Girls' Prep made me feel unbearably ancient, immortal blood notwithstanding. Perky teenagers bopped to and fro along the halls in an endless line of pristine white blouses and matching plaid skirts. The blinding sameness reminded me of *Attack of the Pod People* until I noticed each girl did her best to show off her individuality through the judicious use of accessories. A lot could be said by the type of headband, necklace, knee socks, or combat boots (yes, really) one chose to wear. Add to that the telltale marks of arcane species like Cats, Hounds, Giants, and—surprisingly—several of the newly freed, pure-blood Sidhe born in captivity like my brother, and the school lost a bit of its scary sameness. Still made me feel depressingly old, though.

The school secretary seemed flabbergasted to have Boston's one and only Chief Magical Investigator (her words, not mine) show up at their "little school" to speak with Principal Matthews. I did my best to appear professional in the face of her outright fawning when what I *really* wanted to do was scream at her to get the freaking show on the road already. Finally, a five-minute monologue later, she ushered us into her superior's office.

I had to say, her office was smaller and way less ornate than I'd expected for someone who'd dated a Banoub. Then again, Harper's taste for designer clothing aside, her office wasn't what you'd expect, either, and she was getting ready to *marry* a Banoub. When I turned my gaze from the decor and onto the room's occupant, my surprise grew tenfold. Jillian Matthews was pretty, to be sure, but she stood about six inches shorter and forty pounds heavier than Harper or the typical supermodel type Penn was photographed with.

Which proved that yeah, we all have our preconceived notions and aren't always as open-minded as we like to think.

The woman stood and crossed the room with a polite but puzzled smile. "Good afternoon, Detectives. I'm Jillian Matthews, Victory Prep's principal. I trust that none of my girls has gotten into legal trouble." The fact she *said* it rather than *asked* it spoke of great confidence in her girls or her own competence as principal. Perhaps both.

I waited until the overfriendly secretary shut the door after she exited the office. "Absolutely not, Principal Matthews."

"Please, call me Jillian. Though I'm afraid I didn't quite catch your names."

"Marissa Holloway, and this is my associate, Scott Murphy."

She ushered us to plain but comfortable chairs before reseating herself behind her utilitarian desk. Stacks of paper and other items lined the desk as one might expect of a school principal, but in exceedingly neat and precise order. Not a huge surprise in someone who enjoyed administrating a bustling school the way Jillian Matthews appeared to, I supposed.

"Now, please tell me how *I* can help two of Boston's finest?"

I didn't correct her assumption that Scott was a police officer for two reasons: One, the truth might make her more reticent, and two, if I got my way, eventually he *would* become an official member of the MCU. Once Amaya felt up to assuming the position of Shadowhound leader her father groomed her for. Oh, and once I crossed the hurdle of talking Scott into it. Minor details, though.

"I'm sure you're familiar with the murderer preying upon Cats in the city."

She closed her eyes briefly before meeting my gaze with an expression of genuine sadness. "Of course. I knew one of the men well in high school and still can't believe he's gone. So awful for them all."

I made a mental note of that link. "I find it interesting that you know another man that has been linked to this case. Pennington Banoub. I understand that you might have reason to wish him ill . . ."

Little lines formed around her eyes and mouth as she made the connection. "If you're here to suggest *I* might somehow be involved in Penn's current troubles, then you can just call my attorney to discuss this further. First of all, I'm no fool, and second of all, there's a nondisclosure agreement in place."

"Oh no, sorry if that's the impression I gave. You are in no way a suspect, Jillian, but we *do* need to ask you a few questions about Penn and those past troubles you alluded to. We're just piecing together the backgrounds of the parties involved in the hopes we can find the right puzzle piece to crack this case. So we can prevent any more high school friends from losing each other too soon."

Her expression softened somewhat, although she still seemed hesitant. "But the NDA . . ."

"We have Pennington Banoub's complete cooperation in this investigation, and I can assure you we'll keep this conversation in strictest confidence—even from him."

She let out a pent-up breath. "Well, I would dearly love to help you catch Simon's killer. Fine, then, ask your questions and I'll answer if I can."

"Thank you. First, I've heard some details of your breakup with Mr. Banoub, but was hoping to get *your* perspective on the matter. Was he ever—physically abusive during your relationship?"

"Oh, Bast no! Had he even raised a hand to me, things would have ended much sooner than six months. No, he only got violent the once, toward my now-husband, and didn't touch me."

Good to know Harper wasn't marrying a domestic abuser than. A one-time fight brought on by the heat of passion was a much easier pill to swallow than a woman beater. Assuming, of course, that's how it actually went down.

"Could you tell me about that act of violence? Do you think he came to your place intending to hurt your husband?"

Her blond curls bounced with the force of her head shake. "No, I very much doubt that. He didn't even know Richard and I had reconciled at that point. Nobody did, not even Richard and me. After I called things off with Penn, Richard and I bumped into each other at a friend's birthday party, and, well, things between us reignited. We kept it secret at first, just in case things didn't work out a second time."

"So Mr. Banoub came to your place unexpectedly, then?"

She nodded. "To get his grandmother's ring. Richard answered the door instead of me because we'd ordered pizza and I was watching my favorite TV show. Richard's answering the door set off Penn's territorial instincts immediately, especially when he saw me on the couch wearing a silk robe that *he* bought for me. When I ran over to the door and he caught my scent mingled with Richard's, well. Things only escalated from there."

"He attacked your husband?"

She flushed slightly. "Ah, no, not exactly."

"Your husband initiated the fight?"

"Well, when Penn showed up unannounced and bristled at him, Richard's own instincts kicked in. He made a few insulting remarks toward Penn and demanded he leave. When Penn refused and insulted him in turn, I tried to get between them to stop it, but things had gone too far." She let out another breath and licked her lips. "A stupid part of me found it flattering that two men were willing to go to blows over me, but then reality set in. They nearly killed each other."

Interesting. The way Vic had told the story, Penn had beaten the snot out of the other man but walked away unscathed. I started to ask another question, but she shook her head with a rueful twist to her lips.

"Victor *did* warn us both that Penn would flip when he found out we reconnected so soon after the breakup."

My mouth snapped shut, and Scott shifted on the chair next to me. I didn't have to look to know he looked eager where I now felt sick to my stomach. What were the odds she was talking about a *different* Victor than the one so inextricably linked to this case? The man who had some strange power over me and I couldn't seem to stay away from even though that would be the *smart* thing to do?

Scott spoke up when words continued to fail me. "Victor?"

"Yes, the friend whose birthday party I have to thank for giving me my husband back." Her eyes went a little starry. "Victor Esteban."

My pulse went skittering madly—and not in a good way. Luckily Scott picked up my slack again. "Are you and your husband close friends with Mr. Esteban?"

"Richard is, but I'm actually closer to his girlfriend, Meredith."

He—wait. Victor had a *girlfriend* and was hitting on me? I mean *Sierra*. Rage tickled the back of my throat, which was absolutely ridiculous. The relationship with Victor—if it could even be called that—wasn't even *real*. What did it matter if he was a cheating bastard?

"Well, his girlfriend at the time. Richard's sister, Meredith. They later broke up."

The sense of relief flooding over me made no sense, and yet I couldn't deny it. Gods save me from my own insanity because it seemed I sure as hell couldn't.

Scott's voice was deceptively casual when he asked his next question. "How is it that the four of you became such good friends?"

Jillian smiled brightly. "Well, once upon a time, Richard and Victor were in business together. They're both doctors. I moonlighted as their business manager, and Meredith served as their pharmaceutical rep."

That had me breaking free of my temporary fugue. "Pharmaceutical rep?"

"Yes, Richard and Victor developed a new drug for treating diabetes that seemed promising and was quite lucrative for a time. Tests eventually showed it wasn't quite as effective as believed, and we all drifted our own ways careerwise once sales dried up. Though I understand Victor is making tremendous strides in the industry again."

My heart sank a little because intuition told me what was coming.

"He landed an amazing deal with Meritton Enterprises a year or so ago."

Scott's eyes glued on to mine when I raised my gaze. "Another diabetes drug?"

She waved her hand. "Oh no, he's moved on to a much more exciting area of research these days. Hybrid drugs."

Oh boy. No doubt we'd discovered the identity of Meritton's mysterious *supplier*, exactly what he'd intended when he "suggested" we dig into Penn's romantic past. Meritton had also indicated fear kept him from being more forthright with information but fear of what? Victor didn't strike me as the sort of person to become violent at the drop of a hat. Did Meritton merely fear Victor would shop his new miracle drugs elsewhere, or did he have good cause to fear physical retaliation? Or—the possibility I liked least but *had* to entertain—did Meritton actually believe *Victor* had something to do with the murders?

More importantly, did I?

That was now the $64,000 question.

Well, I'd have to let it stew and reexamine it later. Jillian's body language suggested she thought we'd taken up enough of her time, and really, she was right. I could think of no other burning questions to ask, so after I gave her my card and thanked her for her time, Scott and I made our exit. We got halfway to the car before he opened the conversation I'd been dreading.

"Looks like Vic the Slick is our new Suspect Numero Uno, then."

I forced back a sarcastic retort that Scott only *wanted* the killer to be Victor because he was so blinded by the green-eyed monster. At this point, considering how the bastard tried to force me into his car the last time I'd seen him, I wouldn't be too torn up to discover that Vic the Slick *was* the killer.

"I don't know that we can call him the *number one* suspect based on what little we have, but it's definitely a possibility we have to check into." He looked surprised that I didn't argue his point outright. Not that I was stupid enough to tell him exactly why.

Scott tilted his head as we reached the car and he keyed us in. "So where to now?"

I'd been chewing on that very thought during the first half of our walk to the car. "Where else? To track down a certain pharmaceutical rep and see what she has to say about *his* romantic past, just as Meritton suggested."

Scott's eyes widened. "Wait, you mean Meritton really wanted us to look into *Vic's* romantic past, not Penn's?" When I nodded, his gaze turned admiring. "That's my girl."

Oh yeah, I most certainly was.

CHAPTER TWENTY

SPEAKING OF GIRLS, I TOOK A FEW MINUTES to pop by the safe house and check on my family. Most particularly, she of the newly Fledged variety. Cori didn't seem too surprised to see me peek into the bedroom she was now sharing with one of Serise's sisters—the better to avoid her sneaking out again, my dear.

"You found the killer yet?"

I hated to burst the hopeful bubble in her voice. "Not yet, but we've had a great day of running down leads. We're on our way to run down another, but . . . I had to check in to see how you're doing." I shut the door snugly behind me. "No unusual bouts of Rage, I hope?"

"Nah, even though Mom and Dad grounded me for a week." She gave an eye roll. "Like I'm not already grounded until you and Grandma get all this shit sorted out."

I gave her a look her mother might have thrown. "Language."

"Aw, c'mon, Aunt Riss. Don't go all *Mom* on me now."

My no-nonsense expression inspired an uneasy flush in her cheeks. "Cori, I know I've always been the 'fun' aunt over the years—because, hey, that's what an aunt gets to do. But one thing you need to understand right now: As your senior Fury, that's pretty much what I am to you now. What we all are: extensions of your mother. And if I'm allowed to take you on as my apprentice, I'll be the most mothery type of Fury of all: your mentor."

"But, Riss, I thought—"

"The first thing you'll learn as an apprentice is not to think. At least, not when it comes to questioning your mentor. Not starting out. Maybe in a couple of years, once you've learned a thing or twenty."

"A couple *years*?"

I grinned. "Well, okay, so maybe you'll learn twenty things before two years go by. But I *do* want you to understand that things are going to change between us now. And you won't think all of them change for the better. But my job as a Fury is to teach you the skills you need to survive in your new life. No matter how *Mom*-like you think I am."

Her usual humor reasserted itself. "Buzzkill." We shared a laugh, and then she let out a sigh. "So, does Grandma know yet?"

I shook my head. "No, I thought we should tell her together. The same way we'll tell your parents."

She jumped up and gave me a tight hug. "I was hoping you'd say that. No *way* I want to tell Mom on my own."

I returned the hug, then pushed slightly away. "So, shall we call Grandma and give her the news before Scott and I have to head back out? Your parents can wait until I track down the killer so we have something good to outweigh what they'll see as the bad."

She nodded and we settled in to make the *easy* confession.

MEREDITH MATTHEWS DIDN'T PROVE TO BE *nearly* as easy to track down as her sister-in-law, though that didn't come as a huge shock. Medical representatives as a whole tended to be a very mobile breed, and she was no exception. Mac was kind enough to pull some of his electronic strings and gave us the name of the company currently employing her. Once we visited their downtown headquarters—and I flashed my badge—they gave us the addresses of the three doctors' offices she still had to visit and tried to reach her via cell to ask her to wait at her current location for us to arrive. Naturally, they couldn't get her to answer.

Equally unsurprisingly, we missed her at the first two locations and had to speed to Locale Number 3 to avoid missing her again. We finally had a spot of luck—she'd received her company's voice mails and waited for us in the now-deserted parking lot. *Sheesh, it's not even five o'clock yet.* Oh, to keep a family practitioner's business hours!

Meredith looked much more the expected type to hook up with a Banoub: gorgeous face, slim build, and legs that just wouldn't quit. She showed those off to good effect by climbing out of her sporty sedan and clacking toward us in three-inch heels. Not exactly practical footwear for an on-the-go pharmaceutical rep, but who was I—the woman who often wore tight red leather to kick ass in—to judge?

She held her hand out and wasted little time with pleasantries. "Chief Holloway, Mr. Murphy. My company indicated you needed to ask some questions. I'm afraid that I'm pressed for time right now, so please, ask away."

I wasn't sure whether to be put off by her abruptness or relieved she didn't go into Fangirl Overdrive the way Jillian's secretary had. "Ms. Matthews, thank you for accommodating us on such short notice. As you may have guessed, we're investigating the homicides of several male Bastai. One name has come up in several interviews—no, not yours—and we'd like to ask you some questions about that man."

Her brusque demeanor crumbled and a pale, stricken expression gripped her features. For a moment, I feared she was about to faint, but she stiffened her posture and gave a determined nod. "Victor."

Scott and I exchanged shocked looks, which did not escape her notice.

"If someone's name has come up regarding the murder of Cats and you think I can shed light on that person, it *has* to be Victor. Especially considering . . ."

She let her voice trail off, and I leaned forward, potential envy of her relationship with Victor replaced by sharpening investigative instincts. "Considering what?"

"Why, considering what he did to Sylvia, of course." When Scott and I shared another glance, she grew even paler. "You mean, everyone still thinks that was an accident?"

"I'm afraid I don't know anything about this Sylvia, Ms. Matthews, but please. If it might be at *all* relevant, please tell us." Although something about the name *Sylvia* was starting to ring a bell.

Her breath shuddered out in one long gasp. A dozen emotions danced across her face, the foremost of which was fear. Then that, too, disappeared, only to be replaced by sheer determination. "I've spent the past few months in hell, terrified he would come back and do to me what he did to her. I'm the only one *alive* who knows just how insane he's become. The only one who suspects the truth."

"What truth?"

"That Sylvia Rodriguez did not die of an accidental drug overdose. She was murdered by her lover—Victor Esteban."

BLOOD BEGAN POUNDING SO FORCEFULLY IN my ears I had a hard time hearing her last few words. Could one man so easily fool me? Not that I considered myself infallible—Fury bravado aside—but Vic inspired feelings inside me that only one other man had. If I had misjudged *him* so drastically, did that mean I was wrong about Scott as well? Ugly self-doubt wormed its way inside my soul, and *gods*, did it hurt.

Scott suffered no such qualms, of course. "What makes you so sure it wasn't an accident, and why do you think Victor was responsible?"

Meredith brushed shaky hands through immaculate brown hair. "When's the last time you heard of a *Cat* dying from an *accidental* overdose?"

Okay, she certainly had a point there. I'd never heard of that before, and if anyone in the city would have, it'd be me. Come to think of it, I vaguely remembered the Rodriguez case. Right around the time Vanessa's supposed body washed up in Boston Harbor—which explained why I only barely remembered it. My energy and emotions had been focused on finally finding those responsible for her abduction, and besides, the ME had ruled Sylvia's death accidental. She'd been a Cat in her late twenties found dead in her apartment with a crapload of illicit drugs in her system, her death due to an obvious overdose. Wait. Now I remembered why the name *Sylvia* seemed familiar. Vic had mentioned during lunch at Rigazzi's that he'd lost someone precious to him and he would have given "*anything* to have Sylvia back." A statement that seemed beyond morbid knowing what I knew now.

"As for why I think Victor was responsible . . . you know about his research into magically altered drugs?" At our nods, she took a deep breath. "When he first started that line of research, his intentions were pure. He truly wanted to find ways to help people by melding magical plants and energies with plants from the mortal realm, creating new drugs that could benefit all races. However, when it came time to test his results on human and arcane subjects, he hit a snag. Nobody wanted to be the guinea pig for an unknown medical researcher until he made more of a name for himself. Especially since he was arcane and not mortal. But Victor being Victor, he refused to give up. Instead, he started testing the hybrid drugs on himself."

I blinked. "That seems extreme. And dangerous."

"It was both. At first he developed— and tested—mostly benign drugs that seemed to have little effect on him. Of course, he didn't suffer from the ailments he was developing drugs to treat so all he could say for certain was that the drugs weren't toxic to arcanes. That, however, along with the reputation he slowly built, allowed him to find a larger pool of test subjects."

"So he was able to stop testing them on himself."

Her lips twisted as she looked at me without a trace of humor in her eyes. "He was *able* to, but he didn't. By then he'd become addicted."

"Addicted to—what? You said the drugs had little effect on him."

"Those in the early stages. As time went on, he became consumed by the thought of developing hybrid drugs that did more than merely treat specific conditions. He wanted to create drugs that would enhance an arcane's natural abilities. Make them . . . better."

Scott touched me on the arm. I could tell by the excitement in his eyes exactly what he was thinking. Victor could easily have created the hybrid catnip that subdued the Cat victims *and* a drug to enhance his own strength and speed to carry out the attacks. My lips tightened stubbornly. Just because he created them didn't mean he was the only one with access to the drugs or motive to commit the crimes.

Meredith interpreted our silence as encouragement to continue. "First he was addicted to the excitement and idea of his research. Eventually he became addicted to one or more of the drugs themselves, and he started to change. Became irritable and then downright volatile. He and I broke up but we got back together."

Now who did *that* remind me of?

"I loved him but he became impossible to reason with. When he went from a little jealous to a lot possessive and then extremely controlling, I had enough. Broke things off with him for good, though by then I feared how he would react if he thought I wouldn't take him back, so I convinced him it was *his* idea. As an extra precaution, I reminded him how close both he and I were to my brother. I truly believe those are the only things that kept me safe."

The more she said, the harder time I had reconciling her words with Victor's deeds. Sure, he seemed a little moody now and again—but who was *I* to talk? Also true he had been a little forceful with me once or twice when we'd been out. But it was a *huge* leap from there to controlling, murderous psycho. Wouldn't I *sense* it if he had that darkness in him?

Yeah, just like you sensed the whole lot of crazy in Stacia.

Scott caught my attention by asking another question. "But Sylvia Rodriguez wasn't so lucky, was she?"

Despair washed over her face though it did nothing to detract from her beauty. I bet she was one of those women who even looked beautiful crying. Couldn't say the same for myself. My skin blotched up worse than it did with a rash.

"No, she wasn't. It's like—like he was looking for a replacement for the one he never got over losing. Harper Cruz. I never lived up to his expectations, and he and Sylvia were even more on-again, off-again than he and I had been—though she had a higher tolerance for his addiction and attitude than I did. I tried to convince her to leave him once when I saw he'd progressed to physical abuse—bruises don't lie—but she refused. Claimed he was a brilliant genius *I'd* been too small-minded to understand. She was dead not even six months later."

The self-recrimination in her voice moved me. "There's nothing you could have done, Meredith. You tried to get through to her but she made her own choices. We all do." My own inner doubt weasels began scattering as newfound determination swept me up. Emotions and instinct be damned. If even half of what Meredith claimed was true, Victor Esteban was *not* the man I thought he was. Which meant he *could* be a cold-blooded killer.

And if that proved true, may all the gods and goddesses have mercy on his soul because I sure as hell wouldn't.

OUR NEXT ORDER OF BUSINESS WAS HITTING up Sahana to pick her brains on the Sylvia Rodriguez case. Unlike with mortal deaths, autopsies were *always* conducted when an arcane died. Some autopsies were more perfunctory than others—just the nature of the beast—but when an otherwise immortal being suddenly bites the dust, identifying the reason why is crucial. The percentage of arcanes who expire due to truly natural cases is exceedingly small.

"Hey, Sahi." She looked up from the takeout cornucopia spread out on her desk, and I shook my head. "How did I know you'd still be working this late?"

Sahana rolled her eyes. "Yeah, 'cause *you* don't do the same on a regular basis."

My arms shot up in an *I surrender* gesture. "You got a sec? We need to chat about the Cat case."

Sahana dropped the chopsticks she'd been expertly wielding—a skill I had yet to master—and motioned for us to sit. "Of course. I haven't unearthed anything new, though, I'm afraid."

"Actually"—I nodded toward Scott—"we're here to discuss something old. A death from a few months ago that *could* be linked to the murders."

She pushed her chair back slightly and tapped the desk with a pen she'd picked up. An unconscious habit that meant the gears in her brain had kicked into overdrive. "Hmm. Sylvia Rodriguez."

"Yeah. The only other Cat death this year. I remember you mentioning it to me before the MCU officially formed, but—well—my attention was admittedly elsewhere."

Her expression turned sympathetic without crossing the line to pitying. "Understandably so." She pulled the keyboard tray out from her desk and tapped away faster than I ever could. "Ah, just as I remembered. Thirty-two-year-old Latin American Bastai found dead in her home after a night of hard-core partying. No signs of foul play. Tox screens revealed extraordinarily high levels of alcohol and narcotics in her system. More than enough to kill her outright and then overwhelm her body's abilities to regenerate." Suddenly, her fingers stilled on the keyboard, and she raised widened eyes to stare into mine.

Adrenaline sent tingles flying along my skin. "You see something."

She nodded slowly. "Something that didn't mean much at the time. A small amount of an unidentified substance in her blood. I didn't recognize its chemical or magical signature at the time and thought the tests must have been off."

"But they weren't."

"No. I just didn't have anything to compare it with."

Scott reached the same conclusion a heartbeat later. "The hybrid catnip that nixes Cat regeneration."

"Precisely. Which confirms what you both apparently already suspected. Sylvia Rodriguez didn't die of an accidental overdose. She was murdered."

Even though my mind had been expecting that pronouncement, my heart still thudded painfully when she spoke the words out loud. *Oh gods, gods, how could I have been so stupid? I let my emotions—my gods-damned libido—blind me to the fact a monster was trying to seduce me! The very monster I swore to stop. How could he make me lose my mind for . . . him . . .* Rage roared to life when my conscious mind made the next logical leap. *That son of a bitch drugged me. He freaking drugged me!*

Red-hot fury flared and then cooled to ice-cold steel. I thought back over the past few weeks, dredging up every single Victor-related memory I could. *Electric sparks every time his skin touched mine . . . Unbridled lust consuming me whenever he was near . . . My mind wanting to say no to his invitations to spend more time with him after we ruled him out as a suspect—ha—but my body and hormones screaming out* yes!

Steely determination gave way, in turn, to shock and a sense of betrayal as profound as when Stacia revealed herself to be a traitor. The words escaped my lips before I could force them back. "My gods, I think he drugged me, too. Drugged me and made me w-want him. Made me *think* I wanted him." My voice skittered and I shot Scott an anguished look. "That bastard probably tried to date rape me. Would have succeeded if I hadn't gotten that emergency call from my mother."

SCOTT LET OUT AN EARSPLITTING ROAR AND leaped to his feet. Human teeth sharpened to inhuman

canines. Golden eyes glinted with the eerie fire that pre-
luded transformation. Barely audible growls passed peeled-
back lips. *Gods, Riss,* think *before you speak!*

I stood and reached out a calming hand, but he backed
away from me like I had the plague. Hurt speared through
me, ironic considering the sheer amount of pain already
overloading my senses. I once thought nothing could hurt
more than watching my dearest friend die in my arms and
then find out my mentor had been responsible. I thought
wrong. Realizing someone I trusted had drugged me into
lusting after him and then having my lover recoil from
me as if I were contaminated hurt even worse. Still, finding
out that my Fury nature wasn't what had caused those
feelings . . . at least that was a relief.

Sahana's arms wrapped around me, and she eased my
body away from Scott's. "Shh, sweetheart, let him get the
bloodlust out of his system."

Her whispered instruction dulled the mental agony
somewhat. Of course. Scott hadn't backed away from me
out of revulsion. He'd been afraid the surge of Warhound
anger very much resembling a Fury's Rage might overcome him and he'd hurt me. Severely. A Hound locked in
bloodlust was *not* a creature to be reasoned with. Lucky for
us all that Victor Esteban was nowhere nearby, or he'd have
been a dead man.

Though, really, now that we knew what we did, he was
pretty much *that.* A dead man walking.

Scott paced the few steps of clear space near the office
door like a caged beast, canines still visible, eyes still glowing, and growls still echoing through the confined area.
Several tense moments passed before the growls faded and
the goose bumps prickling my flesh receded. He turned to
me with a look of sheer anguish on his face. Anguish and,
shockingly, guilt. Which he immediately gave voice to.

"Anubis slay me, baby, but this is all my fault!" He started to cross the space between us but stopped, deep breaths racking his body as surely as inner turmoil.

My heart broke even more. "What the— Scott, *no*. How could it be *your* fault?"

"I *knew* something was wrong with that bastard, especially when you kept spending time with him even when you didn't have to. Even when we thought he couldn't be the murderer. But, gods, I didn't want to chase you away with what had to be plain old jealousy. Only it *wasn't*, and I wasn't there to stop that sack of shit. Wasn't there to *protect* you when"—his voice cracked midsentence—"you couldn't protect yourself."

Sahana sensed how much we needed physical touch and released me so I could throw myself into his arms. We clutched each other like we were drowning, desperate for something to hold on to in the midst of a howling storm. Scott stroked my hair when I buried my face in his chest and sobbed like a baby for what had been taken from us both. From me: trust and an unflagging sense of personal strength. From him: the Warhound need to keep his mate unharmed when she could not do that herself. And that only scratched the surface.

I somehow managed to pull myself together and took a deep, steadying breath. Scott sensed the change in my frame of mind and, after one final squeeze, let his hands drop away. He and Sahana listened as I found the courage to tell them everything I'd been trying to bury about the sheer firestorm of lust Victor had inspired in me every time he touched me, nodding wordlessly so I could get it all out in one frenzied rush rather than interrupting.

When I was done, they moved their gazes from me to each other, nodded once more, and spoke in unison. "He's the killer."

Hearing it out loud only solidified the truth in my own mind. Victor Esteban—no, Scott had it right with Vic the

Slick—was a drug-addicted, power-hungry psycho who had murdered the lover who jilted him without convincing him it was *his* idea. And now, there was no doubt in my mind he was *also* the envy-ridden killer preying upon the former lovers of the ex-lover he had never given up hope of winning back for himself. It *all* made perfect sense: The Cat victims also made the ultimate test subjects for his mad-scientist ways. He could inject them with as much of his drugs as he wanted since killing them was his ultimate goal anyway.

That clicked an inner lightbulb. "He experiments on them somewhere else until he's done with them. Probably tortures them to see how their bodies react. Then he delivers one final dose along with a fatal beating before dumping the body."

"Until Rockefeller."

My eyes blinked rapidly. "Yeah, until Rockefeller. He snaps because he realizes his efforts to break up Harper and Penn aren't working like he planned. Stops at Rockefeller's office, knowing what a workaholic the guy was, and goes all psycho on him. Doesn't have time to really clean up his mess because he has to get to the engagement party."

Scott picked up the thread. "He takes something himself to amp up his speed and strength, and cleans himself up—he'd just come from the airport so he had the clothes—before racing to the event in record time. It's dark out and he's really fast, so people either don't see him or don't believe their eyes if they do."

Sahana let out a breath. "He's spiraling out of control."

My voice was grim when I nodded. "Exactly like the drug-addicted psychopath he's become."

Her eyes widened. "He's been using hybrid drugs on himself this whole time."

"For years. We spoke to the ex-lover of his smart enough to make him think breaking up was *his* idea. He started using his drugs on himself in the year or two after his breakup with Harper. Meredith said she tried but failed to live up to his memories of Harp. I can only assume Sylvia failed even more in his drug-addled mind."

"So he killed her."

Scott snapped his fingers. "And his dual specialties in medical science and the magical arts allowed him to dress it up as an accident."

"Which I bought hook, line, and sinker," Sahana said bleakly.

Impatience had me snapping. "Oh no, Sahi, you don't get to blame yourself for *that* any more than Scott gets to blame himself for what happened to me."

"And no more than *you* get to blame yourself for Rockefeller's murder." I met Scott's narrowed eyes and nodded at his words. Victor Esteban had fooled a *lot* of people—some far wiser than myself—over the years. Wallowing in self-blame would do nothing to stop his madness or see him brought to justice.

"Time to set a trap for our *pal* Vic the Slick," I drawled with a tight smile. "And *this* time, the predator will become the prey."

MY FINGERS TREMBLED AS I RANG THE DOOR-bell to Victor's home and stepped back. I'd called him to ask if we could finally have our postponed dinner—this time at his place. Goose bumps pricked my flesh—not entirely due to the autumn evening breeze washing over my nearly bare back. Scott couldn't comprehend why I went to so much effort to look drop-dead gorgeous for the man who killed four men and tried to have his way with me. Trinity, once she'd gotten me to confide the details, understood all too well. If I let what he did to me change how I handled myself on the job—or in my personal life, for that matter—he would win; and I would start to die a little on the inside. I'd be *damned* if I let that happen.

I drew on the Rage bubbling below the surface to steady my nerves, allowing my gaze to wander from the door in front of me to the nearby window of Victor's double garage. No big surprise to see a flashy Mercedes Benz parked closest to where I stood, but the oversized dark gray van next to it didn't fit with his overly polished persona. I shook that observation away and focused on the role I needed to play. No way could I risk cluing Victor in to the fact we were on to him. He had to go on thinking that this was just another date between him and the new object of his obsession— Sierra Nieves. Only after I got him to make some sort of incriminating statement—whether regarding the murders or his drugging of me—could I let the guise of adoring new lover drop and do what I was itching to do: kick him where the sun don't shine.

Just thinking that put a smile on my face. Convenient because Victor chose just that moment to open the door.

A matching smile that struck me as overly proprietary crossed his face. "Good evening, *querida*. Come here." He reached out to touch me before I could retreat farther, a good thing for the ruse I was trying to pull off. The moment his fingers skimmed the bare skin of my arms, I realized the problem dressing so skimpily posed: Somehow, Victor was administering his lust-inducing drug via skin-on-skin contact, and I'd just made his goal a hell of a lot easier.

"It's okay, baby, we're here." Scott's voice came through the magically concealed earpiece, pitched low enough I could barely hear, which meant Victor had no chance of picking it up. Just hearing Scott helped me firm up my resolve. The cavalry in the form of Scott, Trinity, Cass, Kale, and Mahina waited a half block away inside our undercover van, with the added backup of Mac, Ellie, and several other Shadowhounds concealed throughout the neighborhood.

Even if this coldhearted bastard *was* drugging me, now I knew and had protectors nearby who wouldn't let him take advantage of me again. They'd stop him even if I couldn't. Just knowing that gave me the strength to do what I *could* and they *couldn't*. Get him to say something we could use against him in court.

The sparks skittering from his hands to my body confirmed my suspicions. Pleasure radiated along my shoulders and arms, and I gave in to the sensation. I had a role to play, and play it I would. For this one last evening, I *was* Sierra Nieves, Wedding Planner to the Stars and woman in love.

Victor tugged me into his arms and breathed heavily into my hair. I broke away and sat down on the couch. He sat down next to me and placed his hand on my knee. Thanks to his pharmaceutical manipulations, I didn't have to fake an enthusiastic response. "I knew you couldn't stay away, *querida*," he said, leaning in for a kiss.

I forced myself to tap into Rage just enough to give a teasing smile and then push away. "Good evening to you, too, *guapo*. While I'd love to spend all night gobbling you up, I haven't eaten since this morning, and I'm hungry for other things, too." Not a lie, either. I'd been too apprehensive to eat and only choked down donuts with my morning coffee because Scott and Trinity ganged up on me.

Victor smiled indulgently, took my hand into his, and led me into a candle-lit dining room. Bloodred roses— exactly the kind he had given me before—painted the snow-white tablecloth with brilliant splashes of color. Fine china and elegant wineglasses added further romantic touches to this seductive scene. Before, I would have been utterly charmed at the same time guilt burned inside for feeling emotions that betrayed my relationship with Scott. Knowing what I knew now, however, I just found it spooky.

He seated me at the table with an elegant flourish before sitting across from me and serving up a mouthwatering array of Italian food every bit as delicious as the meal we'd shared at Rigazzi's. One thing to say for the man—he really pulled out all the stops when it came to wining and dining the woman in his life.

Including the magical equivalent to GHB. Something best to remember.

Some sort of aphrodisiac to make sure the one he wants finds him impossible to resist. Guess he learned his lesson with Sylvia and makes sure no woman shatters his fragile little ego.

That helped me focus on why I was here, and I steered our dinner conversation in a roundabout way toward the wedding, along with the requisite worry surrounding the killer preying upon the bride's ex-lovers. Victor didn't seem to find this suspicious; in fact, he embraced the topic.

"I have every confidence in the security team I hired to keep us all safe. Unlike whoever that poor SOB Paul Meritton hired." He shook his head with an expression that didn't seem particularly sincere. "Then again, rumor has it he gave his security detail the slip, which is how the killer was able to attack him in the first place."

Wow, was Victor going to make this easier than expected? We hadn't made that detail public knowledge, so only the killer would know that. My breath hitched as I made another connection. Meritton had slipped away from his bodyguards in order to meet his supplier, who we now knew to be Victor. That meant that either Meritton had lied to us or Victor had set up that meeting in order to ambush him.

I tried to keep my tone casual. "He *left* the bodyguards he hired to protect him just before he got attacked? That sounds awfully suspicious."

Victor's eyes glinted with amusement. "Indeed. Not to mention the fact he suffered barely a scratch in the attack." His voice grew thoughtful. "I've never trusted him entirely."

"Oh? You know him personally?"

"Not so much personally as professionally. He's financing a side project of mine. Our relationship the past few months has become somewhat—strained."

I let my fingers caress the silky petals of the nearest rose and inhaled its unusually refreshing fragrance. *You should ask him what breed of rose this is. Not every day you find one that doesn't make you sick.* "So you think that *he* could be the one behind these murders?" If only *I* could so easily believe that. It wouldn't make Victor any less a murderer, but Sylvia's death *could* have conceivably been an accident he covered up out of desperation. *These* murders were sadistic acts of violence that could not be so easily explained away. Not even to assuage my own feelings of guilt for being fooled by the charming monster calmly eating pasta across from me.

His expression sobered. "I certainly think it makes far more sense for the police to be investigating *him* as a suspect than me."

Our gazes locked and my heart skipped a beat. Gods, was he on to us? Did he know my true identity? My body tensed as I gathered magical energy to burst into ass-kicking Fury mode before responding to him.

"Why on *earth* would the police be investigating you? That's—that's absurd."

"Precisely." Drops of merlot sloshed from his wineglass as he set it down forcefully. "I suspect that he faked his own attack in order to throw the police off his trail. Who knows what incriminating comments he made about me to get them sniffing around friends and ex-girlfriends of mine?"

Okay. So apparently one of *them* had spilled the beans to Victor that the police had been asking questions about him. Considering Meredith's very obvious fear of him versus Jillian's gratitude he'd been the reason she reunited with dear old Richard, it seemed safe to bet on the school principal as the big mouth. What I had more trouble deciphering was whether this was all a routine staged to make himself look innocent—or if *Meritton* was the one now pulling our strings. *Don't be stupid, Riss. No need to second-guess yourself.* He *is the one who is abusing his own hybrid drugs.* He *is the one who has the inside info on Harper's wedding plans and is close enough to her to learn everything he needs to know to attack her exes. And* he *is the one who uses drugs on unsuspecting women to get what he wants from them.*

Of course, another part of my psyche insisted on playing devil's advocate. *Yeah, but Scott said before that Victor couldn't have had time to pull off Rockefeller's murder. He had an alibi for at least one of the other attacks. And* who *is the one now in hiding, refusing to see you in person? Paul Meritton.*

I sipped the last bit of wine in my glass to gain another few moments to *think.* So now we were down to two viable suspects: Victor Esteban and Paul Meritton. Partners in a joint hybrid-pharmaceutical venture, which meant either of them had easy access to the type of drugs used in this case. Both were ex-lovers of Harper's. Victor still enjoyed a close, cordial friendship with her while Meritton openly expressed disdain and resentment toward her. Victor, however, abused the very drugs he developed and used them on others against their will. Meritton was the sole surviving victim and had suffered very minor injuries. He had also pointed the finger of suspicion in Victor's direction without obviously doing so. Was he really afraid *Victor* was the killer and would come after him again, or was *he* the killer trying to keep us focused on the wrong person?

Victor noticed when I set down my empty wineglass. "Here, let me top you off." He leaned forward and poured more merlot in my glass.

"It's very good wine," I said absently, mind still whirring.

"It should be. Cost an arm and a leg." He went to pull

back the bottle, but it slipped from his hand, knocked over the wineglass, and sent merlot splashing down the front of my light-colored dress.

I let out an undignified squeal and shoved back from the table. He apologized profusely and cursed himself before coming around to dab ineffectually at the wine-splotched fabric clinging to my curves.

"Victor, really, it's okay. No, stop, you're just making it worse."

His hands fell away and he looked distraught. Was this *really* the face of a heartless murderer? I didn't know *what* to think anymore.

"I need to soak this in cold water before the stain sets."

"Shit, of course. Let me find something you can wear. The bathroom door's right behind you."

I locked myself inside the spa-like room. My—make that Sierra's—face looked normal enough in the vanity mirror. No sign of the turmoil eating me alive on the inside. The purplish patches of wine across the front of my dress, on the other hand, seemed a fitting complement to my jumbled emotions. Gods, why couldn't any of this be easier?

Because you're not a little kid anymore and this is the real *world. It's hard and it's messy and sometimes it hurts. Now* deal *with it.*

A knock sounded at the door. I tried to pull myself together and moved to unlock the door, only to hear sudden commotion on the other side. Scuffling noises, the sound of flesh hitting flesh, and Victor shouting, "Keep the door locked, Sierra! Call 911!" Several more panicked shouts pierced the air followed by a single ominous thud.

Holy shit, what *is going on out there?*

Instinct kicked in and I threw the door open. Victor sprawled in a bloody, unmoving heap halfway between the bathroom door and his bedroom. I frowned as an unfamiliar odor tingled my nose, but the shadowy image of an

unknown figure disappearing into the bedroom caught my
attention. My first instinct was to run after it, but Victor
gave a low groan and I knew I had to check on him first.
Well, this *is gonna blow my cover all to hell.*

Magic answered my sudden call and washed along my
body, nipping and tucking like crazy until a midnight-
haired, emerald-eyed demigoddess in red leather stood
where an elegantly clad Hound had been seconds earlier. I
ducked down beside Victor only to find wide, glazed eyes
staring at me in amazement.

"You—you're a Fury?" His eyes rolled to the back of his
head and blood foamed from his mouth.

I channeled Rage to fight back fear and tried to clinically
catalog his injuries. Obvious claw marks riddled his body,
leaving his clothing in a shredded mess. Flesh and bone
could be seen through the tears in fabric and made me want
to puke. Gods, he was in *bad* shape. If he didn't get help
soon, he was going to die right in front of me.

No, not again!

Adrenaline surged, and I murmured the spell key to
unlock the magical camo hiding the headset serving as my
lifeline. A quick finger tap activated the mike, putting me
into immediate touch with Scott and company.

"Call an ambulance ASAP—Victor's been attacked and
is in *very* bad shape." Ignoring Scott's shocked outburst, I
hastened to add the realization that had just clicked. "Victor's not the killer after all. Paul Meritton is."

CHAPTER TWENTY-ONE

"THAT DID *NOT* GO THE WAY I THOUGHT IT would." I stared down the hospital hall at the friends gathered outside Victor Esteban's room in the ICU, Jillian and Richard among them, and rubbed my hands along bare arms to try and warm them. Nothing helped, however; the cold had sunk in too deep. *You're still in shock,* the clinical part of my brain pronounced. *Well, no shit there, Sherlock.*

No shit, indeed. I'd been so intent on finessing an incriminating statement from Victor that the thought he would become the killer's latest victim—fighting for his life inside a coma the doctors couldn't break through—had never occurred to me. Which had given Meritton just the opportunity he needed to strike. So Victor was an evil, manipulative slimebag, but he wasn't, apparently, a killer.

Scott inched over and placed his arms around me, which helped ease my shivers. A little. "You and me both, baby.

Shit, I was so convinced he *had* to be the killer . . . I still don't understand how Meritton got past all my Hounds, though."

Trinity turned her gaze from the gathering down the hall on to us. "To be fair, we were all prepared for Victor to make a break for it, not for someone else to break *into* his place."

Raised voices behind had us spinning and catching sight of an anguished-looking Harper running our way, Penn and Tariq struggling to keep up with her. She skidded to a stop in front of me and knew from my expression that it was bad. "Victor?"

Trinity answered when I couldn't find the words. "He's alive, Harper, but . . . in a coma."

Anguish increased tenfold, but suddenly disappeared. In its place came cold, hard resolve. "The wedding rehearsal tomorrow. We're gonna nail his ass there."

I managed to say, "*His* ass?"

She gave me her best sardonic look, which was pretty damned good indeed. "Paul *the Bastard* Meritton. It *has* to be him, based on everything Scott told me earlier today."

Scott probably should have kept his mouth *shut* a little bit longer, considering Harper's emotional ties to the case, but hell, I couldn't really fault him—or Harper. Penn, on the other hand, apparently disagreed.

Having just caught up with his runaway bride, he glared at his cousin and then turned his frustration my way. "Absolutely not. The wedding is *off*."

Normally someone would have made a joke about cold feet, but in this situation, humor was the last thing on anyone's mind.

Harper turned an angry glare on her fiancé. "Absolutely not," she turned his words on him. "We've not come this far to chicken out now. Don't you see, that's what he wants! That's why he attacked Victor—my man of honor—the night before the rehearsal. He thinks this will stop us, but it's not going to. I won't let it. I *can't* live like this anymore."

Penn's frustrated look melted away, and he pulled his now-crying lover into his arms, consoling her with softly murmured words and caresses. Seeing the moment of absolute love between the two made the icy shock gripping me fade away at last. I became every bit as much hardened in my purpose as Harper, and in that moment, inspiration struck.

"Nobody outside this hallway knows that Victor's so close to death."

Harper pulled back from Penn enough she could meet my thoughtful gaze. "Which means the killer doesn't know, either."

"Exactly. What if *someone* lets it leak to the press that Victor made it through the attack just as unscathed as Meritton and that the show is most definitely still going on. That Victor will be performing his duties tomorrow as planned. I doubt that the killer—that Meritton—will let the opportunity pass him by."

Penn frowned. "But Victor *isn't* unscathed, and he *won't* be performing his duties tomorrow."

"Ahh," I drawled. "But there's where you're wrong. Victor *will* put in an appearance tomorrow night. Or at least, a Shadowhound in Victor's clothing."

Scott made an approving noise beside me at the same time Trinity gave a low chuckle. "Oh, Riss, it's perfect. I'm sure he'll enjoy playing the part, too."

Harper took pity on her still-confused fiancé. "One of Mutt's mercenaries is . . . a master of disguise. By the time he gets done, Victor's own mother wouldn't be able to tell the difference between them. And he'll make the *perfect* bait tomorrow night."

"Abso-frigging-lutely." I let out a breath. "So, you sure you're up to this, Harp?"

She bared her teeth in not quite a smile. "Abso-frigging-lutely."

"Atta girl. Okay, so here's what we need to do . . ."

EXCESS NERVES GOT ME THROUGH MOST OF the next day, which was lucky considering I'd been thrust back into the role I thought I'd left behind forever. If we were going to lure Meritton out of his hiding place, however, the show did indeed have to go on. Part of that meant Sierra attaching herself at the hip to Harper and the master of disguise now posing as a hale and hearty Victor Esteban. My brother Mac.

While we had yet to "come out" to the world that Mac was the first male Fury in history, it had become fairly common knowledge over the past few months that he was part Sidhe. Most people assumed his abilities were limited to the illusionary powers of half-breed Sidhe rather than a full-blooded Sidhe's ability to shape-shift into that person's actual physical form. They assumed wrong.

Not that we were about to admit that today or anything. We had quite enough missiles to dodge, thank you very much. Including the five-and-a-half-foot-tall, hundred-and-twenty-pound missile barreling straight toward us in the exclusive Back Bay hotel where the wedding rehearsal was set to begin in little less than half an hour. Mac—I mean *Victor*—turned to me with a panicked look on his face. Seeing my normally composed baby brother fidgeting in his three-piece suit and midnight blue tie (okay, Victor's suit and tie) took me momentarily aback.

"Um, think I'm just going to check on Harper one last time, then," he said in that low throaty voice that used to drive me crazy but now—thank the gods—did nothing for me. I watched him skirt around elegant, fabric-draped chairs so he could avoid the "missile" while scurrying to the rear of the room where bride and bridesmaids congregated near the room's entrance—leaving me alone to face down an annoyed-looking Mama Hound.

"There you are, child, I've been trying to get a hold of you for hours."

Apparently not very hard, since I'd been here setting up things for tomorrow's ceremony and reception most of the day. I nearly opened my mouth to say that out loud but fought back my inner perversity just in time. "Mrs. Banoub, what a pleasure. How can I help you?" *Very good, Riss, you actually sound like you care about her latest disaster that isn't!* By the end of tomorrow—assuming the worst happened and we failed to flush Meritton into the open—I'd deserve an Oscar for playing this role all the way through. That or I'd be ready to voluntarily commit myself.

"You can start by telling me why that—that *man* is still involved in my grandson's wedding."

Her dirty glare at Mac's—Victor's—retreating back clued me in to who *that man* had to be, though I was a little confused by her sudden venom. She'd never seemed to care one way or another about Victor before now. I watched as my brother ambushed Harper, and then I caught sight of Penn and the groomsmen entering to take their places at the front of the room. All except Scott, who'd been intercepted by Trinity and was now heading back past Harper and Mac toward the hallway. That's when I saw Neema Banoub's eyes following their exit with eagle eyes and got another jolt. She wasn't bitching (ha) about Victor, but Scott.

"I—uh—I'm not sure what you mean."

She sniffed and curled her lip as she glanced back at me. "Why am I not surprised to hear that? You have not lived up to your sterling credentials throughout this farce, so why would you end your obtuseness now?" Her arm waved in Scott's direction. "That Murphy mongrel, child. The one my grandson decided to involve in this affair for some insane reason—only to discover the mongrel had just such a thing with his"—another lip curl—"Harpy of a bride."

Oh bloody hell. My worst fear confirmed—word had gotten out that Scott and Harper had had a *thing* in the past. Chances were that, if Neema Banoub had found out, the killer would have by now as well. Which meant Scott could be in as much danger here as Victor or Penn. Maybe more, considering he'd just ducked out of the bustling room with Trinity as his only companion. My spider sense went crazy—and my tact went flying out the window.

"Mrs. Banoub, I hope you take this with the exact amount of respect that's intended, but perhaps it would be best if you pulled your supercilious nose out of your blue-blooded ass long enough to notice a few things. One: That 'Murphy mongrel' is here to help protect the wedding guests. Even bitchy ones like you."

Her face went red and she started sputtering, but I continued on ruthlessly.

"Two: Harper is a beautiful woman, inside and out, and your grandson is a lucky SOB to have convinced her to marry into his tight-assed, self-absorbed family."

Her face changed from red to a most interesting shade of purple, and her mouth opened and closed wordlessly. Which, I was willing to bet, *had* to be a first.

"And three: This *obtuse child* has more important things to do than stand around listening to you blow hot air. So if you'll be so kind as to excuse me . . ."

My gods, the pleasure it gave me to watch her rendered speechless before I stalked out into the hallway was *priceless. Damn, guess that's one less reference to put on Sierra's résumé.* My lips twitched with amusement, but I tried to focus on the task at hand. Tracking down Scott and Trinity to make sure everything was all right. I activated the headset and learned they were just checking in with each team of mercs scattered around the hotel and surrounding areas.

Rather than following them to our makeshift control room, I told them to get a move on since the rehearsal was starting soon, and I retraced my steps toward the ceremony site.

Mac ducked out of the men's room across the hall and seemed surprised to see me. I grinned and stopped to adjust his tux's crooked bow tie. "Nice addition there, Mac."

He blinked before responding. "Addition, *querida*?"

I rolled my eyes. "Very funny, little bro, but stop with the act." I gestured to the fading yellow and purple marks on his face. "The bruises are a nice touch, but unnecessary. Everyone here's already seen you *sans* bruises, so you can lose them for now. Hurry, though, the rehearsal's about to start."

He nodded when I motioned toward the restroom door. "Of course, I'll just do that, then." His fingers brushed mine briefly as I gave the tie one last tug. I gave a smile and hurried back into the room to oversee the last few minutes until show time.

Rashida waylaid me before I got very far, and I winced, expecting her to lay into me for how I'd spoken to her mother. Instead, she told me in a very low voice that it was about *time* one of the *help*—her words, not mine—stood up to the termagant—again, her words. Before I could formulate a coherent response, she hurried to the front of the room and her place with the groom's family. Sitting, of course, right next to the "termagant." Leaving me to wander bemusedly toward Harper and her bevy of bridesmaids, plus Mac. I mean *Victor.*

My gaze moved from him to Harper, and then snapped back to my brother in his three-piece suit and midnight blue tie. *Not* a bow tie, and most certainly *not* a tux. What the *hell* was going on? I frowned and thought back over the past few minutes and the hallway encounter with Mac. How shocked he'd been to run into me. The way he'd called me *querida*. No, not Mac after all. Victor. The *real* Victor.

My pulse galloped out of control as horror battled

adrenaline. Harper caught my expression of panic and broke away from the others, followed closely by Mac. "Riss, what's wrong. You look like—well—like you've seen a ghost."

"No," I choked out, feeling sudden color flood my cheeks. "Not a ghost—a dead man walking."

THEY WATCHED ME WHIRL AND SCRAMBLE TO the hotel hallway with surprised expressions. Voices broke out behind me, but I didn't care. Only one thought pounded though my brain, inspiring another panicked burst of speed. *It's not Meritton after all. Victor left the hospital, and he knows about Scott. Knows I'm a Fury. Oh gods, no. Don't let me be too late!*

But I was, oh gods, but I was. I came across an unconscious Trinity sprawled just down the hall from our control room. She moaned when I bent and shook her gently, but she didn't come to. Knowing what I'd find, I checked her neck anyway and, sure enough, found the telltale pinprick proving she'd been drugged. Only she was *mortal*, which meant the drug intended to knock out arcanes could affect her worse than Cats—or better. I just had no way of knowing.

Still, she was breathing steadily, so that was *something*. But my mind finally turned to the realization I hadn't wanted to give form to: If Trinity lay out here, alone, that could mean only one thing. Scott had been taken—by Victor. The killer.

The time for playing Ms. Nice Hound had come to an ugly end. I pulled partial Fury form around me like a well-worn jacket, leaving off the wings and—for now—the Amphisbaena. Then, channeling Rage-fueled strength, I gently scooped Trinity into my arms and hustled to the nearby control room. I *might* have accidentally ripped the door from its hinges rather than wait for it to be answered, but the man I loved had been abducted by a vicious killer. Cut me a little slack.

Voices shouted until they recognized me and saw Trinity's unmoving form in my arms. Kale and Mahina rushed into action, clearing the room's only sofa so I could set her down carefully. Cass gave me a wide-eyed look from in front of the bank of video screens he'd been observing—all showing scenes from inside the ceremony site and right outside it in the hallway. *Not* outside this room, where Trinity and Scott had been attacked. The guilty realization washing over his face nearly did me in, but I choked back useless emotion by embracing pure, unadulterated Rage. This bastard would *not* get away with this. He'd already stolen so much from me. I would *not* let him steal Scott, too.

I lost precious moments giving my team a quick rundown and issuing commands for them to pass on to Mac, Ellie, and the other Shadowhounds, but it *had* to be done.

"Get Kiara in here to tend to Trinity stat. And whatever you do, say *nothing* to the members of Alabastros. That bastard hired them so I do *not* trust them one little bit."

I was heartbeats from racing after Scott alone—stupid, but hey, arcanes go a little batshit insane when their mates are in dire peril. And as much as it sometimes scared me to admit, that's exactly what Scott was to me: my mate. Unresolved issues and all.

Fortunately, though, the gods saved me from myself. "R-Riss?"

"Oh, gods, Trin?"

I hurried back across the room and crouched next to her. She was struggling to sit up, confusion on her face warring with determination. Kale and Mahina hovered nearby like mother hens, but I wouldn't let them come between us. Not until I assured myself she was okay. And she was. Either Vic had hit her with a lower dose than usual, or his drugs *did* have a lesser effect on mortals.

"I'm sorry, Riss, I tried to stop him b-but he took Scott out first and he was just so—so strong. And I thought he was Mac at first. So stupid."

My heart broke a little. "Not stupid at all, Trin. He fooled me, too. *I* should have known—but no. No time for that now. Did he say anything?"

She shook her head to clear it, but at first I thought she was shaking it *no* and my spirits plummeted even lower until she spoke again. "He said—to tell you he knows, *querida*, and that . . ." She gave a shuddering breath and motioned me closer as if she physically couldn't speak loudly. When I had my ear next to her mouth, she whispered so only I could hear. "He wants you to come alone or he'll kill Scott. Said he'd leave directions with the spider—I assume *my* Spyder— and you have an hour from now."

My mouth dropped open. Luckily the others couldn't see. I moved to whisper into her ear, "Thank you for trusting me to do this alone."

She gave me a fierce look. "I trust you to kick the *shit* out of that jackass, all right, but I'm no idiot. You get a ten-minute head start and then we're coming after you." She rained on my smug parade by one simple whispered, "GPS."

So they'd be breathing down my neck not long after I went breathing down Vic's. Still, she was giving me a precious gift. The chance to save Scott. And a chance was all I needed.

I FELT A LITTLE GUILTY FOR SNEAKING OUT amid the chaos of Kiara showing up to check on Trinity, but Vic left me little choice. The clock was ticking, had started ticking when Trinity delivered Vic's message and we'd called for Kiara over the headset. No doubt he'd listened in on Scott's receiver and started the countdown. I checked the timer on my cell as I raced to the parking garage. T-minus 56 minutes and counting; 55 by the time I made it to the floor where she'd parked the Spyder. Nothing could have looked more beautiful in that moment than the electric-blue sports car waiting for me—except Scott himself.

Trinity would have winced to find her door unlocked, but I flung it open and hopped inside, expecting to find a note waiting from Vic the Slick and finding none. Panic flared until I remembered Trinity's last word to me and glanced at the GPS panel. Sure enough, the screen was on and directions had been preset into the machine. The keys had also been conveniently left in the ignition for me. *What would we have done if some jackass stole the car before I got to it?* I waved that worry aside, buckled my seat belt, and revved the engine. Time to channel my inner Scott and pray I could drive fast enough to get the slightest edge on his captor.

CHAPTER TWENTY-TWO

I OFTEN MOCKED SCOTT AND TRINITY FOR their fancy sports cars, but I had cause to be grateful for the sleek machine that responded to my every demand for higher speeds and tighter turns. My thoughts bounced from worrying what Scott was enduring to brainstorming—and discarding—a dozen different plans of attack. Of course, not knowing exactly where the GPS coordinates were leading me made that harder. Did Vic have a safe house of his own he used for torturing and murdering? Was he worried (rightfully so) that I would kill him outright if I could and heading somewhere public in the hopes that would somehow keep him safer? Would he offer up Scott in exchange for taking me hostage instead, or had he killed him alrea—

No! Don't think like that. He's not *going to give up the only bargaining chip he has.*

That thought turned my mind to another consideration.

What exactly was Vic hoping to bargain *for*? He had to know I couldn't just let him go, not after everything he'd done. Not even if I wanted to—which I damned well didn't. Did he just want revenge for his being "duped" into falling for someone who didn't exist? If so, why had he called me *querida* both to my face and via Trinity? Surely he couldn't *possibly* think there was still hope for us as a couple. That was absolutely insane.

Oh right, so was he.

My skin tingled as I crossed over the magical barrier separating the mundane world from the arcane Underbelly. After a few more silent moments, I glanced back to the GPS and slammed down on the brake pedal. The green dot marking my position on the map nearly matched up completely with the blinking red dot I'd been tracking for the past twenty minutes. My gaze flew up and caught sight of an oversized abandoned warehouse looming just a block ahead. Well, abandoned-*looking*. I knew there were at least two people inside for sure.

Once free of the vehicle's confining space, I shifted from partial Fury form to full, relishing the feel of the night wind teasing my wing feathers and smiling at the dual sense of pleasure radiating from Nemesis and Nike. This *was* what I'd been born for. To take flight and hunt down those who used magic to hurt others, who thought that being born with arcane genes made them somehow above the law and able to do whatever they wanted. They thought wrong. *No one* was above the law, not even the gods themselves, and my job—my calling—was to prove just that point.

I summoned magic and launched myself into the air. My wings snapped back loudly before beating furiously until magic and physics reached an agreement and my body shot upward. Seconds later I hovered over the warehouse, enhanced Fury vision poring over the building as I pondered the optimal point of entry. One thing caught my attention: a large, dark-colored van parked at the rear of the building next to Scott's flashy Ferrari. The van looked familiar but at first, I couldn't place it. *The second vehicle you saw in Victor's garage!* Aha, well, that explained how he transported the drugged-up Cats from one place to another.

I turned my attention back to finding the best place to enter the warehouse. *There. A broken window on the second floor. He'll expect you to come through one of the floor entrances or the rooftop door.* And I *so* hated to do the expected.

My hand had just settled on the windowsill when muffled voices reached my ears. I stiffened, straining to hear where in the warehouse they were coming from. Sounded like they were on a lower floor, which meant I could swing myself over the windowsill and land on the dirt-covered concrete floor without too much worry. I crept down the empty hallway, eyes searching the dimness for a door or flight of stairs to check. I began to think I would have to circle back and try another entrance when the hallway ended abruptly at the head of a steep metal staircase spiraling downward. The staircase looked like it would squeal the instant I stepped on it so I hesitated. But then muffled voices became loud groans and the sound of flesh hitting flesh and instinct kicked in. I tried to think *thin* as I eased onto the staircase, which did let out a creak, but much quieter than I'd anticipated. Then again, the beating and groans had picked up in volume, masking what little noise I made. Once I realized that, I all but flew down the stairs.

I kept my eyes and ears cracked open, looking and listening for signs that Vic *had* hired new thugs to replace the old, but so far, so good. Of course, no sooner did that thought strike me than groans morphed into wordless shouts of pain, and my adrenaline surged. I darted through the darkness and neared a doorway that had to be where the noise came from. I counted to three inwardly and prepared to kick the door open. Gods, what was he *doing* to make Scott scream like that? Warhounds could take pain even better than Furies did and—

Wait, that's not Scott's voice. I tried to pull back, but my boot connected with the door before I could. *Crack!* The door swung open and eerie black-and-white light spilled over me, coming from a row of surveillance monitors set into the tiny room's far wall. Each screen revealed the same sinister image: a Cat being systematically tortured by a blurry image clothed all in blood-drenched black.

My gag reflex kicked into gear but I choked it down. *It's a Cat, it's not Scott, it's a Cat, it's not Scott.* I mentally chanted the words as if they were a charm that could protect him, protect us both, and prepared to back out of the room without disturbing anything. My initial instinct had been to shut off the graphic video, but that might alert Vic to the fact I was already here, ruining the one and only advantage at my disposal. So, much as it made my blood boil, I turned my back on the sadistic recording and closed the door behind me.

Once the door closed and the screams faded somewhat, I realized I'd been hearing two beatings in tandem: the brutal one behind me, and a slower, more systematic beating in another part of the warehouse. The low, choked sounds made by the victim were hard to hear, but I could just make them out by channeling a tendril of Rage and amping up my hearing. My heart sank when I recognized the voice as Scott's. He wouldn't give Vic the satisfaction of screaming or begging—not *my* Hound— but his low volume also made it harder for me to track him. Foot by agonizingly slow foot I explored the cavernous space, growing increasingly more chilled until finally, *finally*, I knew I'd reached my goal. A huge door stood in front of me, with the words *Cauti n: Fre zer Conta nment* etched out in peeling

paint. Scott's voice gave another low grunt of pain and
Rage stirred. *Enough of this!*

Enough indeed. I channeled Rage into every inch of my
body, gasping softly at the combined pleasure and pain
while Nemesis and Nike hissed in counterpoint, hoping
that by riding the edge of Rage, I could resist any attempts
Vic made to drug me. Or at least, resist long enough to do
what needed doing. Rage boiled through my flesh and
blood, burning hot enough I feared losing control entirely.

The cool, tempting bliss of Stacia's *Calm* beckoned, but
I fought back the urge to embrace it. I'd nearly given in to
her plan for me to use the *Calm* but had found the strength
to resist its siren call. The *Calm* was a metaphysical state
Stacia claimed only the strongest and most self-assured
Furies could reach, and had been her trick to switching
back and forth from Fury state to Harpy, and back again—
without murdering her Amphisbaena the way all Turned
Furies, all save her, did. It could also help me control enough
Rage to counteract *any* drug Vic could use against me, if I
just . . . No!

Focus, Riss!

Scott gave yet another groan, which helped me ground
myself in reality, grab hold of the freezer unit's heavy iron
bar of a knob, and force it open. I half jumped, half flew
through the doorway, flesh prickling with instant goose
bumps as the temperature cooled by several dozen degrees,
and came upon a scene straight from some twisted horror
movie.

Scott dangled from spell-worked silver chains suspended
from the ceiling, clothes already shredded and blood dripping from several cuts and open wounds. A large metal
cart—the kind you would find in a hospital's surgical ward—
gleamed in harsh overhead lighting, as did the surgical
tools resting along its trays. Several of *those* glittered more

dully than others because dark red flecks covered them. Blood. The blood of dead, innocent men.

The blood of *my* living, equally innocent man concerned me far more. Vic had made use of his abbreviated head start, judging by Scott's condition, though my heart lifted when I realized nothing major had been broken or injured. All of Scott's wounds seemed to be superficial. *Thank the gods!* My attention was captured by a second metal tray on the other side of Scott, this one filled with ceramic pots bearing all sorts of plants and flowers. Including one that bore big, beautiful red roses that looked all too familiar. Next to it I saw another plant I knew all too well: the hybrid catnip used in each of the murders. I catalogued all of this in a heartbeat before zeroing my gaze in on my target: Victor Esteban, clad in the getup Meritton had earlier described, including the gloves slitted to display vicious claws and the amber yellow eyes of a Hound. That threw me for a loop since I'd seen him with the typical slanted Cat's eyes before, but then I realized his trick. *Contact lenses. No wonder Meritton thought his attacker might have been a Hound. Bet he originally wanted to frame Penn for all this.*

Vic became aware of my presence in the same moment and spun, the wicked-looking whip with jagged barbs on its end fluttering as he did so. A smile equal parts charming and terrifying spreading across his face. "Ah, *querida*, I should have known you'd be punctual. *Overly* punctual. I thought I had at least another half hour before your arrival."

"You thought wrong, apparently. And don't call me that."

"Oh, but you *are* my dear one, no matter the face you wear. It's what's inside you that I cherish above all others."

I stepped forward slowly, cautiously, wanting to close as much distance between us as possible without setting him off. "I bet you say that to *all* the girls. Like Meredith—and poor Sylvia."

His sunny smile dampened somewhat. "Poor Sylvia liked it rough, I'm afraid, too rough even for my tastes." That went way past the point of irony, considering the torture implements spread all around him. "I warned her what would happen if she mixed mortal narcotics with my little wonders."

"So you're claiming you *didn't* kill her?" I inched forward another few feet, which didn't seem to bother him. Yet.

He twirled the ends of his barbed whip almost playfully. "The drugs killed her, not I, although . . ."

"Although what?"

"I *did* make sure her death wish was granted. The poor girl had been rather suicidal when I found her, you see, and lived only for the pleasures—and pain—she found in my arms and with my wonders. It seemed only fair to make sure she found the peace she sought for so long."

"So you *did* poison her with the catnip, same as you did Harper's lovers."

"*Ex*-lovers," he corrected lightly. "And *poison* seems such a strong word. I prefer to think of it as awakening them to their new lives."

Like I'd been in any doubt about his being stark, raving mad before. "Whatever pretty label you dress it up with, Vic, the Commonwealth of Massachusetts considers it murder in the first degree, as does the Sisterhood. Punishable, as you well know, by death. A death I would be happy to grant you so *you* can find the peace you seek."

My body tensed as I prepared to leap forward and make good my promise, but rather than look alarmed, he simply went right on smiling, standing there all calm and mockingly handsome, as if he didn't have cause to be alarmed. Which, perhaps, he didn't.

I changed my mind last minute and leaped toward Scott rather than Vic. Scott, oddly enough, shook his head wildly and made noises of protest, his eyes bulging out but his mouth staying firmly closed. Which was even more bizarre, all things considered. He should have been yelling at me—whether to hurry the hell up, or as was more likely, to save myself and leave him behind (as if I would)—and the fact he wasn't disturbed me. It was only when I landed on the ground a foot away from him that the reason for his being struck mute jumped out at me. His mouth had been duct taped.

HE MAY NOT HAVE BEEN ABLE TO *SPEAK*, BUT his eyes spoke volumes: *Do it!* So I prepared to do just that, filtering more and more Rage through my serpents and then turning to pounce on my prey only to see a blur flashing from where Vic had stood toward me. My mind had trouble processing what was going on, that's how freaking *fast* he moved. Faster than a Hound, faster than a Fury, hell, faster than a *Harpy* could have managed—and I'd found out just how fast those crazy bitches could fly months ago. One moment he was there, and the next he was *behind* me, pinning my arms in an ironclad grip and pressing my body to his.

"*Querida, querida*, you really are a vision standing there in divine indignation, prepared to strike down the wicked with the force of the gods' vengeance. Perhaps, however, you should listen to my proposal before you start striking and smiting—unless you *want* your former lover there to continue dying horribly."

My body froze in its attempts to break from his grasp, and I had a bitch of a time calming down the serpents wrapped around my lower arms. The girls wanted nothing more than to bite a hundred holes in his flesh and flood him full of venom. "W-what do you mean?"

Scott redoubled his struggles, succeeding only in bloodying his wrists and causing himself more pain.

"Why, you didn't think I'd lure you here without some

insurance for your goodwill, did you? Even now one of my most toxic wonders—made from the same catnip used on the others—courses through his veins, poisoning him from the inside out, and only one thing can save him. My antidote."

Scott's body went slack and his tortured gaze met mine. I saw the truth of Vic's words written there, something Scott hadn't wanted me to see. Stupid mutt. Like I'd just *leave* him here. Like I'd leave *anyone* here.

"What—What do you want?"

"Besides you in my bed, my love?"

"*Don't* call me that, you son of a bitch."

"Now, now, language, *querida*." His voice became uncharacteristically steely. "Behave yourself and I won't make your ex-lover suffer more than he has to."

The way he kept referring to Scott as my "former" and "ex"-lover made me nervous. "I—I'm sorry."

"That's my girl." His words so mirrored what Scott had called me recently that tears pricked my eyes. "What I initially wanted from you was your delectable half-Hound heritage in order to discover how my wonders would affect you. Falling in love with you was just a welcome bonus, *querida*. Of course, the other night when I realized you'd been misleading me every bit as much as I had you, my plans had to change. Once I realized *which* Fury you had to be, it became clear what the gods intended. Your ex-lover will make an excellent substitute for *Sierra* and ensure your best behavior both in my bed and in the lab."

"How—How do you think you're going to get away with this? With the murders?"

I shuddered when he leaned forward—in my natural form, we were very nearly the same height—and nuzzled my hair. "It's very simple, my love. Murphy here will die unless I administer a dose of antidote to him every twelve hours, starting with the first in, oh, the next half hour or so.

I have another dose, a very special one, prepared for *you*. One that will make you see things more . . . clearly . . . so you can help me."

"Help you what?"

"Finish setting up Meritton to take the fall for the murders, of course. Now that I'm done with my experiments on Cats and, in particular, Cat corpses, I don't need him as a partner anymore. Sadly, you will be unable to locate your former lover after you take out the psychotic killer in his lair. Where, conveniently, there will be plenty of forensic evidence tying Meritton to the murders and Murphy's abduction."

I couldn't hold back the words that burst from my lips. "You're crazy, Victor. Your drugs have—"

"My *wonders* have given me the type of clarity and strength most people can only dream of possessing. They'll give you the same, *querida*. Soon, you'll see how perfect we are together." He reached his free hand into a pocket and then withdrew a syringe. One he intended to plunge into my neck, no doubt.

Jesus, Mary, and Joseph, as my sister-in-law would say. *How* did I always end up with unbalanced stalker types wanting to use me for their own purposes? First Stacia and now Victor. Had I taken a bath in Supernatural Obsession or something?

Think, Riss, think! You have to assume he did *poison Scott, and Scott* docs *need his antidote to survive. You* can't *let him dose you, or you* will *go right along with his plans. So what can you do to stop him?* My mind scrambled for a solution that would both defeat Victor while letting both Scott and me survive, but kept coming up empty. I had no clue what poison Victor had used or where he kept the antidote. My gaze darted to the tray of plants and flowers next to Scott, and my pulse picked up speed. *Or did I?* Surely it wasn't coincidence that Victor stored both catnip and roses next to each other. I remembered each time I had inhaled the scent of those roses when under the effects of Victor's drugs—my mind had become momentarily clearer and my body had felt better. Stronger. *That* has *to be it!* Victor had told me which plant was his most valuable *wonder* without even realizing it . . .

But did I dare risk Scott's life on what was little more than an educated guess? What if I rolled the dice, took Victor out, and was wrong? Could I live with that? But could I live with the alternative? Becoming a drug-addicted slave to Victor's will, with Scott a tortured hostage to ensure my cooperation in his schemes? I looked at Scott and saw that his gaze had followed mine to the tray of plants—and he'd guessed what I was thinking. His eyes widened suggestively, and he nodded, saying *Do it!* once more without words.

Better one or both of us die free than as his slaves!

That realization freed me from indecision, and I burst into action, unfurling my wings and knocking Victor—and his "wonder drug"—halfway across the room. Rage and wings gave me the speed to leap upon him before he fully recovered; luck and wits helped me grab the syringe he still clutched in his hand, flip it around, and plunge it into the prominent vein pulsing in his neck. He screamed out, "No!" as I did so, and he managed to get a hand free and onto the syringe handle but it was too late: I'd already pumped the entire contents into his bloodstream.

"You stupid bitch!" He pulled the syringe out and then stabbed me with it—in the heart rather than the neck. On the plus side, no more drugs to send me to La-La Land the way they already were him. On the downside, it hurt like *frigging hell*. My hand jerked toward the handle to pull it out, but Nemesis thrust her body between my fingers and the needle while Nike leaped from my arm to Vic's writhing body to make sure he was no longer a threat. Seconds later, his body went still. What he had planned to knock me out with must have packed quite a punch.

I turned my attention back to Nemesis. "Hey, let go, you stupid sneak—snake." My words came out slurry and disjointed, revealing that, okay, I hadn't quite pumped him full of the syringe's *entire* contents. "It hurts!"

Scott made some loud but unintelligible sounds to get my attention. I glanced at him and he shook his head emphatically. Okay, so both he and Nemesis thought yanking the needle out of my heart was a bad thing. I wrinkled my brow as my thoughts grew more sluggish—though nowhere near as cloudy as they'd been the last time Vic drugged me—and decided that maybe they were right. It might be best to let my backup remove the needle from my heart, although none of *that* seemed to be—

Cue the cavalry's arrival, in the form of a now-alert Trinity, the rest of our team, and several of Scott's Shadowhounds, including one particularly beautiful Kiara, loaded down with her bag of magical healing goodness. She zeroed in on her brother right away—not that I could blame her; of the two of us, he definitely *looked* to be in worse shape. And really, even with the syringe sticking out from my heart, he was. Kale, Mahina, and Cass busied themselves handcuffing Vic, *after* Nike unwound herself from his legs and slithered up mine. Trinity's mouth widened when she saw the in-no-way-tiny syringe handle jutting out from my chest. She urged me to sit down, but I refused, staggering as I tried to take a step toward the medical cart.

"Marissa!" she barked out, the fact she'd used my full name showing her exasperation as she grabbed on to an arm—the one left conveniently empty since Nemesis had only made it up to my waist so far—to steady me. "*What* are you doing?"

I pointed toward the medical cart, or at least I tried. It

looked more like a wobbly hand wave than anything. "P-p-poisssson," I finally managed to slur out.

Kiara's head snapped from Scott's direction to mine. She'd already taken initial stock of his wounds and been trying, after ripping off the duct tape, to get him to speak to her. I saw then that his body had gone slack and his eyes squeezed shut. *Gods damn it, he needs that antidote!*

"Trin, s-sorrrrry."

"For what?" she asked with a frown, then grunted when I slammed a heel down onto her toes and ran forward—as best I could—once she reflexively let go.

Kiara deduced at least part of what I'd said and hurried over to help me. "What poison?" she asked. "I have a huge supply of antidotes in my bag, and even one that will counteract just about ninety percent of all magical poisons along with the proper spellword."

I shook my head. "No. N-need s-special p-plant."

Her eyes widened and she picked up speed, hurrying me toward the medical cart filled with life-saving—and ending—plants. "Which one?" I managed to point a shaking hand toward the bloodred roses, and she plucked one from a stem. "This one? Are you sure?"

I hesitated. *Am I?* Scott's life depended on it. Images of the way the roses had cleared my mind more than once in the past flashed through my mind and sure, sudden clarity flooded inside me. *Yes, yes, I am.* I nodded.

"Thank you!" She plucked a few more roses, grabbed a vial from her bag, and began crushing the petals into the bright green potion inside. "This is the cure-all I mentioned. Mixing the poison's antidote with it will make it effective against *ninety-one percent* of all magical poisons along with the proper spellword."

Her attempt at humor didn't fool me. She was no more 100 percent sure it would work than I had been, but it was the best chance we had to save him. "Gods, this would work so much better if I could get it directly into his blood-stream rather than having him drink it . . ."

"Oh hell," I said with a sigh. "This is going to hurt."

I grabbed the handle before Nemesis or innate self-preservation could stop me and yanked the syringe out. My knee nearly buckled at the pain, but I managed to hand the needle to a shocked Kiara. "Do it!" I ordered before giving in to agony and collapsing.

Nemesis and Nike channeled the magic I thrust toward them and set to work repairing enough damage to keep my ticker ticking until Kiara could turn her attention from Scott to me. My breath began coming in short, labored pants, but I forced myself to hold on to consciousness so I could watch Kiara fill the syringe from her vial and plunge it into the same vein I'd used on Vic. We both watched as the slightly duller green potion flowed from glass container into Scott's blood and held our breaths, both (I'm sure) praying like crazy it would work.

And thank all the gods and goddesses, after several tense moments, it did. Scott's breathing—which had grown way more labored than my own—became steadier and his skin not so pale. He mumbled something we couldn't make out, but that made it sound no less sweet. I'd guessed right. The roses had been the catnip's antidote, and Scott was going to make it. He was going to be all right.

Just knowing that gave me the peace of mind to slump down on the concrete and conserve my strength while the girls did what *they* did best—amp up my superhuman abilities—while all three of us waited our turn patiently. Or at least what, for me, *passed* as patient.

EARLY THE NEXT EVENING, THE BLUSHING bride walked down the aisle in all her glory and exchanged vows with her handsome Hound of a groom. Halfway through the ceremony—as expected—five of her family members, three of his, and no fewer than ten rabid wedding crashers stood up and shouted reasons why "this man and woman should *not* wed in holy matrimony" when the priest asked that age-old question.

My lips twitched as I glanced at the man standing across from me. "Well, guess we shouldn't disappoint them."

The priest's microphone clearly carried my voice throughout the jam-packed room, sending protestors and nonprotestors alike into shocked silence. The tall, dark, and dashing groom grinned at me. "Suppose the jig's up, then?"

I nodded, and, simultaneously, we both shifted back to our natural forms. Me to blond-haired, blue-eyed mortal form, and him into Mac. No way either of us had been going to let this charade get to the "I now pronounce you man and wife" part. Favors for friends only took you so far. Kissing my baby brother the way I would Scott? Ew!

Speaking of Scott, he catcalled from the wheelchair *we'd* insisted on when *he'd* insisted he wouldn't miss this for the world, still-haywire body or no. Commotion broke out in the room as everyone who wasn't in on the fun realized the bride and groom were not, in fact, the bride and groom. No, those two had taken up my offer to provide a diversion and done the smartest thing I'd seen them do in the past month: caught an earlier flight to Hawaii, where, by now, they'd exchanged vows on the beach with the officiate, gods, and two borrowed tourists as witnesses.

I commandeered the microphone and got everyone to shut up for thirty whole seconds. "I'm pleased to inform you that the bride and groom have eloped to Hawaii, where they can wed in peace and love rather than bitterness and chaos. Since Mrs. Neema Banoub has already footed the bill for this shindig, however, everyone's welcome to head to the reception, and party like there's no tomorrow!" The

Anubian priest—who had *not* been in on the bait and switch—took the microphone back with a bemused expression. He tried to demand an explanation, but by then I'd already skipped down the steps and plopped myself atop Scott's weak but functioning legs. My gorgeous, living, *breathing* Warhound wrapped his arms around me and shook his head.

"You loved every second of that."

I made a gesture with my fingers. "Maybe just a *little* bit." He looked surprised by my sudden, passionate kiss, but I'd been holding back my relief and elation that we'd both made it through the previous night's events for more than eighteen hours. I poured every ounce of my emotions into the kiss, willing him to *feel* how much I loved him, how much I needed him. Later, there'd be time for words. Time to come fully clean on the things I'd been concealing from him—and vice versa—but for now emotions were more than enough.

Now that we'd conquered the green-eyed monster stalking us, and he was safely locked behind magical prison bars. Well, one of them. The other green-eyed monsters waiting for me in the Palladium I'd have to deal with tomorrow morning. Not to mention put in motion the steps that would allow me to take on Cori as my apprentice Fury. Right now, though, Scott and I had a party to get to. Together.

Hell hath nothing worse than a Fury scorned . . .

KASEY MACKENZIE

RED HOT FURY

A SHADES OF FURY NOVEL

As a Fury, Marissa Holloway belongs to an arcane race that has avenged wrongdoing since time immemorial. As Boston's Chief Magical Investigator for the past five years, she's doing what she was born to do: solving supernatural crimes.

It's far from business as usual when the body of a sister Fury washes up in Boston Harbor. But when Riss reports that the corpse's identity has been magically altered, she's immediately—and inexplicably—suspended from her job. Then a human assassin makes an attempt on her life, and Riss realizes that someone is trying to stir up strife between mortals and arcanes.

When a Fury gets mad, she gets even, and Riss is determined to uncover the truth. Without the support of the mortal police department, she turns to the one man she can trust to watch her back: shape-shifting Warhound Scott Murphy. But since Scott is also Riss's ex, she'll have to keep a short leash on more than just the supernatural rage that feeds her power as they try to solve a murder—and stop a war . . .

"Sets a new standard for urban fantasy."
—Chloe Neill, author of *Hard Bitten*

penguin.com